3/23

"I loved how joyful, how t——
Her Consideration was. T———
loud, smile big, and swoon———
adore Nina and her friends, fall in love with ———,
and want to live in their world forever." —Jasmine Guillory,
New York Times bestselling author of *Drunk on Love*

"With vibrant prose, a setting that is both upscale glam
and homey comfort, and a thrumming, pounding, romantic
heart, *For Her Consideration* is pure romance magic."
—Christina Lauren, *New York Times* bestselling
author of *The Unhoneymooners*

"*For Your Consideration* is so many things I want in
a book: funny, sexy, and super queer. Spending time
in Nina and Ari's world was a joy. Amy Spalding has
written a warm celebration of Los Angeles, chosen
family, and learning how to love and be loved."
—Cameron Esposito, bestselling author of *Save Yourself*

"A fiercely funny, super sexy story about believing in
your dreams, finding your chosen family, and letting
yourself be loved. After reading *For Her Consideration*,
I'm in love with both Los Angeles and Ari Fox. Amy
Spalding has such a gift for snappy dialogue and loving,
quirky friend groups, and I'll read everything she writes."
—Kerry Winfrey, author of *Just Another Love Song*

"*For Her Consideration* is a heartening, dishy, celebratory
novel that features true-to-life queer characters—the exact
kind of book I've longed to see flourish on bookstore and
library shelves. It is an absolute delight to read and a
worthy addition to the modern romantic-comedy genre."
—Camille Perri, author of *When Katie Met Cassidy*

"For Her Consideration is the perfect kind of romance—
it sucks you in, makes you swoon, and leaves you
utterly satisfied AND wanting more. Amy Spalding
has created an authentic Hollywood love story between
two wonderfully relatable women both striving to
find themselves while also falling for each other."
—Kate Spencer, author of *In a New York Minute*

"For Her Consideration is incredibly funny, queer, sweet,
and sexy. Anyone with a toxic ex or a serious celebrity crush
will be able to relate! It's about learning to trust yourself
and the people in your life, and it's guaranteed to leave you
smiling and wanting to hug your chosen family very hard."
—Celia Laskey, author of *So Happy for You* and
Under the Rainbow

"For Her Consideration by Amy Spalding is a charming
romantic comedy with two winning heroines. I especially
enjoyed the strong family bonds, including a truly delightful
group of friends. My heart ached at the emotional moments
and I giggled aloud at all the funny parts. I loved watching Ari
and Nina learn to trust themselves and each other and follow
their dreams. Cute and heartfelt, *For Her Consideration* is a
highly recommended read." —Erica Ridley, *New York Times*
bestselling author of *The Perks of Loving a Wallflower*

"Flirty and fun, with romance and laughs on every page,
For Her Consideration is a rom-com that truly embodies the
term. I loved every moment of this book, from Nina and Ari's
love match, to their found families, to the Los Angeles-local
backdrop. Spalding's singular sense of humor and lovable
characters make for a perfect escape. I tore through this with a
smile on my face!" —Sarah Skilton, author of *Fame Adjacent*

FOR HER CONSIDERATION

AMY SPALDING

KENSINGTON
PUBLISHING CORP.

www.kensingtonbooks.com

KENSINGTON BOOKS are published by
Kensington Publishing Corp.
119 West 40th Street
New York, NY 10018

Special book excerpts or customized printings can also be created to fit specific needs. For details, write or phone the office of the Kensington Sales Manager: Kensington Publishing Corp., 119 West 40th Street, New York, NY 10018. Attn. Sales Department. Phone: 1-800-221-2647.

The K with book logo Reg US Pat. & TM Off.

ISBN: 978-1-4967-3952-0 (ebook)

ISBN: 978-1-4967-3951-3

First Kensington Trade Paperback Printing: March 2023

10 9 8 7 6 5 4 3 2 1

Printed in the United States of America

To every single member of my chosen family

Prologue

Oh, holy hell, this was just my luck.

Waze had told me to cut through Griffith Park, past the zoo and the Autry Museum, but I knew what a mess those intersections could be. Everyone ignored that right-lane-must-turn sign, instead jamming into the center lane at the last possible second. And even though this was as predictable as another sunny day in Los Angeles, it made me furious. Some would, in fact, say *overly* furious.

Taylor, absolutely, was one of the some who would say *overly furious.*

It turned out that Taylor would say a lot of things. Today, though, we'd put that behind us. Today I'd beat LA traffic and win back the girl.

Since it was possible that I couldn't trust my own instincts, I'd decided to put my faith in Waze instead. The app, just like Taylor, must have known something I didn't. So I'd turned away from my well-trodden path down the 5 Freeway, and sailed through that often-terrible initial intersection like a breeze. But then I came around the bend and saw that my own instincts *had* been right after all, because this fake-out of a so-called shortcut wasn't just jammed. It was, for all intents and purposes, at a standstill. Taylor had asked to meet at six, and my car's dashboard read 5:54. Instead of the red glow of tail-lights ahead of me for endless miles ahead, all I could see was Taylor's email flashing even redder and brighter in my mind. Taylor's list, particularly one item halfway through.

#6. Time/Promptness. Anyone who knows you would agree that your time management is extremely poor. Barring some kind of condition that renders you literally unable to process time, this is yet another example in the array of ways you center only yourself and deem other people (and their schedules) unimportant.

While there were many items on the twelve-point list that felt off base, a few felt uncomfortably close to something real. Obviously, I had flaws. Didn't we all? If I was honest, Taylor had them too, though I didn't love looking for them. Things were so good when our flaws weren't the focus.

Number Six, though, wasn't something I could argue. LA's relationship with lateness was as entrenched in its lore as its traffic, sunshine, and a penchant for yoga and crystals. But Taylor came from Connecticut, and there were no stereotypes about Connecticut and punctuality, as far as I knew.

All I had to do, I was positive, was show up at Messhall on time tonight, and the rest would fall away. The other eleven points couldn't be true if I was there, if I was on time, if I was already waiting when Taylor walked in.

I cranked up my stereo and swerved around the line of cars inching their way forward to turn onto the freeway. Why, it struck me, was I really so worried? It was a sunny day, I was driving through this lush and green park, and if I broke the laws of traffic only *a little* I'd be just in time for the love of my life. We'd be fine. We'd adopt a dog next month and we'd get engaged next year and we'd argue a little the year after that whether the wedding should be back in Connecticut or here where we'd met but it'd be in good spirit only. Our happily-ever-after was only a few turns away from—

CRUNCH.

I felt it as I heard it, the soft clip of something against the back passenger side of my Honda, and I turned just in time to see the cyclist go over.

"Fuck!"

I pulled off onto the shoulder, carefully, and jumped out of my car. Another cyclist had stopped to help the man—the man I'd hit—and he was nearly back on his feet. This didn't immediately assuage my terror, considering I'd watched every season of *Grey's Anatomy*—some more than once—and it was standard practice for a person to go about their normal business and then collapse into a pile of medical goo thanks to mysterious internal injuries. I might have just given this man mysterious internal injuries that could only be diagnosed at a teaching hospital staffed by extremely hot residents and interns.

"I'm so sorry." I watched the man's face for any impending signs of . . . disintegration? But he seemed sturdy, wearing a helmet and gloves plus a lightweight jacket and stretchy pants, none of which looked the worse for wear. "Are you all right?"

The other cyclist glared at me and stepped between us to check on the felled cyclist. You'd think a potential medical emergency *that I'd caused* would hold my attention, but item Number Six flashed into my head again, and I dove back into my car to retrieve my phone.

I'm so sorry I texted, **but I was involved in a minor accident and I might be a few minutes late. I'll message again when I'm on my way. Sorry again, T. I can't wait to see you.**

The other cyclist seemed satisfied with my victim's state of being, so we exchanged insurance information, agreed that there was no need to involve the police, and were on our respective ways. It was already six past the hour, but I felt no guilt in texting Taylor an update that I was back on the road, and smiled when she responded. **Oh good! Glad you're OK.**

Taylor and I had met three years ago, at a big, crowded party on our mutual friends Phoebe and Bianca's patio. Taylor had just gotten to LA a couple weeks before, and she felt so *new*. She wasn't anyone's ex, she didn't have a regular bar or a favorite coffee shop yet, and she hadn't even started her job. When she asked me out, it all went fast. It might have been a stereotype for queer women, but inside of our love felt nothing like a cliché. We put up with the U-Haul jokes from our friends— yes, two months in they were already no longer *my* friends but *our* friends—because our happiness was too big to see around. Suddenly I was viewing my whole life through it.

She was standing at the bar when I walked into the restaurant. It still gave me more than a tiny thrill when we met somewhere, that the tall dark-haired woman with East Coast vibes who cut an intimidating figure not just in a suit but even a flowing dress was *mine*. Tonight she was in a tailored blazer over a silky green top and dark jeans, a look she'd worn dozens of times.

I nodded toward the bar when the hostess asked if I had a reservation, though I did assume that Taylor had made one, six sharp. This was Taylor's plan and I was here to follow. I was here to do whatever it took to get her out of Phoebe and Bianca's guest room and back into our bed. A dog next month, engaged by Valentine's Day, next summer in Connecticut with her whole family.

"Nina," Taylor said by way of a greeting. She paused, but then lifted her arms to embrace me. I sank into it, completely. Her hair still smelled like oranges and jasmine, and my chin still fit right over her shoulder the way we used to fall asleep, as if even while practically unconscious we couldn't tear ourselves apart. I tried to remember the last time we'd fallen asleep like that, but quickly dismissed the jangly panic the question inspired in me. The so-called honeymoon phase wore off for all couples eventually. Taylor and I would be fine.

"So you're OK?" she asked. "How's your car?"

Somehow, I'd completely forgotten about the accident and the man whose insides hopefully weren't goo by now. "I'm fine, my car is fine, and the guy is fine."

Taylor turned just slightly to pick up her drink from the bar. We'd only been apart for a couple weeks, but still I was relieved to see it was a Rittenhouse old-fashioned, her usual. Between that and her outfit, I was thrilled to see nothing had changed.

She turned back to me after taking a sip, her green eyes wide with what I could tell was concern. Would it be too much to fall back into her arms again? "What guy? The guy who hit you?"

I grimaced. "Not exactly."

As I relayed the events of this evening, Taylor's eyes narrowed. I hated everything about this look and how often, I realized, it had flashed across her face this year. Somehow I'd fucked up again, without even knowing it.

"So, let me get this straight." Taylor set down her drink and tucked her hair behind her ears. I'd seen her make the same gesture when on speakerphone for work; it was her *getting down to business* stance. "You were—I presume—running late, and instead of having been thoughtful enough to leave on time, you thought you could get around this by, what, plowing through a bike lane?"

"It's not technically a bike lane, it's a shoulder, and I do it all the time. I was stressed out about—well, anyway, I didn't check my side mirrors and—"

"Of course you didn't." She practically spit the words out. "Because that would have acknowledged that other people exist, and when have you ever done that?"

"Taylor, I'm sorry, and you're right that I'm bad with time. But it's not because I don't care. There's no one I care about more than you—"

"I don't know why I bothered with this." She waved to the bartender to, presumably, close out her tab. Shit.

"For some reason I thought—" She cut herself off with a shake of her head. "Well, it doesn't matter what I thought. I'll schedule a moving truck for my things, and let you know when I'll be by."

"Taylor." I reached for her wrist, my fingertips grazing her cool skin. "I don't understand what happened. I love you and we can get through this. I went through your list, and, OK, I might not agree with everything, but I can work on myself."

She pulled away from me and scribbled her signature on her credit card receipt. "It doesn't matter what you work on, I've realized, it's just how you are. I don't even blame you. It's how you're built or made or however one looks at it."

"The time thing is—"

"It's not just the time thing. It's *everything*, Nina. You're so self-focused you can't see around it. Just being near you eats at me. My anxiety has shot through the roof since you got here."

"I'm sorry, Taylor, really. But if we could just—"

"I'll text when I've scheduled the movers."

"You're just . . . ending this?" My chin quivered as I asked. People were clueing in to the fact that there was a potential breakup in progress at the bar, which helped nothing at all. I'd never been the type to want an audience, much less for the worst moment of my life. "Please. We can get counseling. I'll do whatever I have to do. What we have is—"

"It's what we *had*, Nina. It hasn't been working for a while. And it's over."

I ran through everything in my head, whatever was left I could do to extinguish this fire about to burn down my entire future. I considered all those line items. Most of them weren't about Taylor and me, but me in general. Maybe if I let her know how much time I'd spent thinking about us, how things hadn't really been as bad as they seemed, she'd remember what we'd had. What we still had right now.

"We could try to start over," I said. "Or get back to normal, when things were good. Things were so good, weren't they?"

"I could never," she said, her eyes not meeting mine. "Having you in my life is actively making it worse."

This was falling apart in my hands. I wondered if it was time to switch gears.

"I took your list so seriously, Taylor." The truth was that as much as I'd wanted to dismiss it outright, I hadn't. Even if I didn't understand most of her complaints, I wanted to fix them anyway. I wanted to fix myself, and I wanted to fix *us*. Maybe if she knew that, it would be enough for now.

"When some of it implied I hadn't been there for my friends or supported them through—well, I touched base with people," I told her, because it had been a secondary heartbreak. Taylor was my world, sure, but so were my friends. The possibility that I'd hurt any of them was one of the worst things I could imagine.

Other than getting dumped in a crowded overpriced restaurant.

"I made sure that wasn't what they thought of me or how I'd been," I continued. "That my presence wasn't . . . you know, increasing their stress levels or anything, I guess. And, luckily, it wasn't. You're the only one who thought that, so maybe—"

Taylor looked right at me. I had never known that a look could feel so final. "For now, sure. Maybe they just don't know you well enough yet."

Chapter 1
Three Years Later

Nina, let me know when I can schedule you for a call with Joyce this afternoon. Minor issue with a client, no rush but Joyce would like to speak before EOD.

I glared at the email from Max, a twerpy little Hollywood bro who nonetheless treated me like I was beneath him in every sense. My industry belief system held assistants in a high, treasured place. Everyone knew they were paid badly while keeping the whole machine going, but, unfortunately, the one I'd been dealing with lately was an exception. If I could press a button and the only thing that would happen would be that Max got flung into the Pacific Ocean, I'd press it at least once daily.

Even so, I hit *reply* and hammered out a short but polite response letting Max know I was available all afternoon. Truly, when wasn't I? Joyce was cc'd, but even if she hadn't been, I'd have been polite to Max anyway. In general it was bad karma to treat assistants like shit, even if they specifically deserved it.

I didn't hear back for hours, which was a relief because I

had a larger list of emails to send out than usual. I'd only ever worked in this industry, so I didn't know if others were the same way, all ebbs and flows with seemingly little in between, but that was Hollywood for you. Last week I'd had so little work that I'd read a literary novel the internet had been buzzing about and listened to two true crime podcasts from beginning to end. Mere days later and suddenly a thousand meetings, Instagram Lives, and dinners out had to be scheduled.

I wasn't actually the one doing the scheduling; that was up to people like Max and the assistants on the other end of the equation. My job was the sort that most people outside of the entertainment industry didn't even know about—hell, plenty of people within it weren't aware, either. Celebrities often needed to connect with people after meetings and meals, or to coordinate appearances on social media, and even though they were apparently far too busy to take care of this themselves, that was the impression they needed to give. Enter someone like me, who ran email accounts for Joyce's roster of talent agency clients. I could thank a producer for a great night out at n/naka as if I were actually the actor who'd eaten kaiseki while discussing his ideal transition from indie hits to comic book blockbusters. I could make a writer feel special that an actress was going to feature her book on an Instagram Live chat but please-don't-mention-the-film-option-we-hadn't-announced-to-the-trades-yet.

It didn't matter that I'd never actually eaten there myself; Yelp and The Infatuation were incredibly helpful. And had I ever heard of the writer or even skimmed her book? Of course not. Thanks, Goodreads! The specifics didn't seem to matter as much as a certain . . . flair. And that was something I knew I was good at; I could watch two interviews on YouTube, comb through social media, and within the hour spit out an email you'd swear came from the celebrity themselves.

Obviously this wasn't why I came to Los Angeles. People

didn't move to LA with dreams of low-level talent agency jobs in their heads, but this was where I'd landed, and the truth was that it suited me better than I would have guessed. Back when I'd gotten hired, I'd assumed this would be a brief novelty item on my résumé, but it had been three years and I had no plans of moving on. Dipping in and out of personas and personalities was still entertaining, and I knew that Joyce trusted me to a level that made both of our lives easier.

While I was emailing as a "cool mom" celebrity to an up-and-coming designer about potentially partnering for a line of athleisure, Max was back with a call-in number for a meeting with Joyce set for only five minutes from now. It was probably her decision, but it was more fun to blame Max, her newest assistant, who I imagined getting the information forty minutes ago and just bothering to hit *send* now. Maybe in time we'd connect, but for now, Max was just an irritating name in my inbox that made my job more annoying than necessary.

Calls usually meant a new client—a *big* new client, that is. If you were an actor who was nowhere within sight of becoming a household name, Joyce wasn't setting aside time to discuss you with me. In those cases I got a three- or four-sentence email, and it was up to me to spend time researching. Sometimes those actors' fame grew—after all, Dan Torres was one of those emails, a conversation Joyce and I never had, and last month he played a feature role in the biggest film of the year so far—but in general, it was what it was. A lot of people came to Los Angeles to act, a small and fortunate percentage got signed with an agency, and an even smaller percentage of those ended up *stars*.

Many of Joyce's colleagues, I knew, were positioned at one end or another of this. It wasn't unusual for an agent to have a bustling list of clients on their ways up, or a smaller but jaw-droppingly A-list roster of huge stars. Agents became known for getting you there, or for being the intimidating type whose clients were all already offer-only (and, shit, what offers those were). Joyce, though, was everything. She could usher an actor through their first audition with kindness, and she could advocate for someone at the very top. Dan Torres, I was sure, wasn't thinking about replacing her now that he was a household name. People tended to stick with Joyce forever, which obviously benefited me. There was almost always an email to write. My paychecks kept coming.

I dialed in on time for the meeting, though as usual, Joyce was a few minutes late.

"How are you?" she asked in her abrupt tone. Welcome packs should be provided to people new to Hollywood, and one of the pieces of advice offered therein should be to never actually answer this question with more than one word. No one had time for your personal anecdotes. This industry did not run on endless conversation. We were here to get shit done quickly.

"Good," I said. It's what I always said. "New client?"

"I'm afraid not. Ari Fox reached out earlier today with some complaints about her communications coming out of Exemplar."

Panic flashed through me, hot and pulsing. Despite the names involved with my job, it had never particularly been high pressure. Sometimes I had to have particularly sensitive or high-profile emails reviewed a few times before sending, but it had been years since I'd had a complaint. Back then I'd been so new I'd expected guidance and correction here and there, but now I'd been doing this for so long. To some degree, I thought I was past calls like this.

Plus it was *Ari Fox*. I tried not to play favorites—after all, I wrote as every single actor Joyce represented, and I took that list seriously—but there was only one out, queer woman on that list. There was only one indie darling who'd also written guest columns for *Autostraddle* and booked a recurring role on the new *L Word*. Whenever I sent an email as Ari, I got a little thrill that we were in this together.

Sure, she was a gorgeous actor booking the kind of roles that wouldn't have even existed a few decades ago, and I was, uh, nothing more than average in the looks department, setting up lunch appointments with production companies and Instagram Lives with designer dogwear brands while pretending to be someone else. We still felt linked, as far as I was concerned.

So for anyone to be unhappy with my work, how on earth could it be Ari Fox?

"Oh," is all I said, though. I'd learned to bite down my words, and not unleash the torrent of questions, excuses, and concerns flooding my brain. "I'm really sorry to hear that. Is there something I can do, or—"

"Glad you asked. Ari would like to meet with you in person, so Max will get something on the books for you two later this week. I assume your schedule permits, even coming from the Inland Empire or wherever it is you call home?"

"Santa Clarita isn't the Inland Empire," I reminded her for potentially the hundredth time. "We're still in LA County up here, thank you very much."

Joyce laughed in a brusque bark. "Well, sure, technically speaking."

"I'll be available," I said. "Whenever Ari is."

"Great, expect to hear from Max soon."

Despite dealing practically directly with talent, my job had always been fairly low stakes, all things considered. Between myself, Joyce, and whoever was in the assistant position, we took care of the kinds of details people with money, fame, and influence were lucky to skip out on. Agents, managers, accountants, and the rest of us made a celebrity's life the kind where they never needed to think about paying a bill, setting their own appointments, or even receiving mail. And so my emails were probably never exactly *perfect*, but they did a job the client didn't actually want to think about.

Not Ari Fox, though, it hit me as I clicked off the call with Joyce. Ari Fox cared about the emails "she" sent out. Ari cared about all of this, the stuff that didn't matter to others, and I was the one who'd let her down.

My job had seemed like a safe bet, considering the limited contact and the—let's face it—joy a lot of people felt in getting email from a celebrity. Even jaded industry professionals loved seeing those names land in their inboxes. I could feel the excitement in their prompt replies, even when I caught a whiff of pragmatism that they knew they were probably talking to someone's person and not the actual someone. Out of nowhere, though, this safety seemed to take a hit.

Max emailed me with the meeting time, three o'clock the next afternoon, and I immediately typed it into my schedule. It was technically a request to see if I was free, but I'd met talent less than a handful of times before, and I knew to agree without even checking my calendar. Plus Joyce was well aware that I rarely left my little condo, tucked into the northern outer suburbs of Los Angeles. I'd be there.

I decided to leave for the meeting the next afternoon with ninety minutes to reach the Exemplar office. Much of my Tuesday night was spent checking every single traffic site and app to figure out how long it would take me to get from my place to Beverly Hills. Waze and I, after all, had not always seen eye to eye in the past. A three p.m. meeting sounded far out from rush hour traffic to anyone who hadn't been to Los Angeles, sure, but time had a fluid sense here. Sometimes the freeway was miraculously open, and even once you were dumped out onto surface streets, green lights beckoned your way. At others, the 405 Freeway might be jammed so far back you'd sit at a standstill on another freeway you were only taking to get to it in the first place—and it would be eleven a.m., a time no one would ever confuse with rush hour.

It was funny I still had these thoughts, I knew. When was the last time I'd actually set foot in LA proper? Months, maybe years? I'd moved there for college and then stuck around, and so I'd been part of the city for over ten years before I headed up north. LA didn't feel like mine anymore, but I guessed I still felt like the city's, as if it was a stubborn ex who wasn't quite ready to relinquish its hold on me.

It had taken me even longer than ninety minutes to get ready for this meeting, and I wasn't even sure I'd nailed it. I'd been working from home for so long that it had been quite a while since I'd had to dress up for anything beyond running out to CVS or my weekly lunch with Lorna. Mine had turned into a caftan lifestyle, and while I could pretend the gauzy draped fabrics combined with my who-even-remembers-the-last-time-I-saw-my-stylist flowy hair was because of some sort of throwback to—oh, I don't know, the Laurel Canyon days of yore?—in truth I'd gotten too comfortable. Pants and haircuts were for successful leave-the-house types, not Nina Rice.

Luckily, it was Southern California, where it was nearly always seasonally appropriate for a maxidress, which was sort of like if a caftan was allowed to leave the house. It was still flowing, but perfectly acceptable for an industry meeting. I mean, I assumed. Again, it had been a while. I probably could have used at least a trim to fully execute some of my dead ends, but I took the time to blow out my brown hair until it was hanging in waves, and rubbed some styling oil into the ends in lieu of trimming them myself. What would Ari think of me? I knew I didn't always read as queer, what with the long hair and the fact that I'd long ago taken out my septum piercing. Would she know we had that in common, that I respected the hell out of her and her career? I decided to cut my nails even shorter—though it had been a while since I'd been in anyone's pants, figuratively or literally—and wore my silver Birkenstocks instead of the daintier sandals I'd started to step into. I knew it didn't matter if I was wearing a dress and had what an old friend had once deemed *princess hair*; I was queer. I loved and had sex with women. Or, at least, I had once. In another life.

In my car—my aunt Lorna's old Honda that still ran like a

charm, though an aging charm—I cranked up the music podcast I caught every week (when did I start listening to podcasts about music instead of . . . just, music?)—to keep all of that out of my head, especially once I crossed into the city's limits and passed places that had meant something, once. Dates, nights out, my first internship at a shiny tall-for-LA building right off of Wilshire. Again, another long-ago life, hardly mine anymore.

I was ten minutes early, but since parking at Exemplar involved security as tight as a body-con dress—Did people still wear body-con dresses? I'd really been away from LA for a while—I felt as if I was right on time. My name was on the list with the parking lot security officer, and as a valet drove my car away from me—probably to park it between a couple of Teslas, if that was what trendy Hollywood people still drove—an attendant called in to reception so that I'd be greeted in the lobby. I was technically a freelance employee, hence the whole spectacle.

I'd only been to this office a few scattered times over the past years, and so I'd never gotten completely used to the lobby of Exemplar Talent Agency. It took up almost the entire first floor of the building. (The rest of the floor was a coffee shop strictly for Exemplar employees and clients, which had both cold brew and kombucha on tap and a no-public-allowed rule in place.) If someone confused this space with an Apple store, they wouldn't be so far off-track. Bright white dominated the room, from the wide sleek walls to the curved sofas set at odd angles from one another atop a textured white rug. How did they keep all this white fabric so spotless?

"Nina Rice?" A girl at least five years younger than me, wearing a modern white dress, extremely tailored with countless little pleats and insets, and tall leather booties, beamed at me as I entered the lobby through the huge glass door. Her dark hair was blown out to glossy perfection, and suddenly mine seemed far less princess-like by comparison. My outfit no longer seemed to scream *cool and queer* but *loose and lazy*.

"Joyce will be down in a few minutes for you," this clearly superior young woman said. "Can I get you a water in the meantime? Sparkling or flat?"

"Oh, I'm OK, thanks, I'd probably just spill it down the front of my dress," I said, and immediately wished I could take back the second half of that. It had been way too long since I'd interacted with other people in person who weren't at least eighty years old; I should have done some sort of warm-up first. Coffee not bought through a drive-thru. A dress from a real store and not the back of my closet. Dinner out, me and a waiter.

"Oh," the girl said, frowning a little for, I suppose, my benefit. She returned her attention to her giant iMac, so I got out my phone to spend some time on the daily crossword. My current streak was at 859 days, and I was determined not to break it. Everything had changed for me a few years ago, and so my goals subsequently became smaller. There was something about not missing my daily crossword solve that made me feel like I hadn't given up completely.

"Nina!" Joyce arrived into the lobby from the massive staircase that descended into the room from a huge circle of open air and mystery above. It barely looked real, more *Star Trek* than architecture. That was Hollywood for you.

"Hi," I said, my words to a minimum on purpose. We hugged, because there was no meeting in this industry that managed to start without a round of hugs. Joyce wasn't much older than me, especially considering how accomplished she already was, but unlike myself managed to express her own style as if she was supposed to be here. Her black hair was styled into a huge topknot that gave her at least four extra inches of height, which was already helped by her tall heels—and her floral jumpsuit popped next to her dark brown skin. The first time

I'd met Joyce, I remembered feeling relieved that she wasn't a standard Hollywood size zero, even though of course she was gorgeous and stylish far beyond what I'd ever manage.

"Hi to you," Joyce said with a dazzling smile that actually reached her dark brown eyes. "You look great. How long's it been? Since the Christmas party? Oh, wait, you didn't show up to the Christmas party last year. The year before? The day I hired you? No, that was by phone."

"I guess it's been a while," I said noncommittally, ducking my head to avert my gaze from Joyce's eye contact. One didn't keep her roster of talent happy without a certain level of directness.

"Ari's already here, in the café," Joyce continued, casually, as if Ari wasn't a rising star and as if my poor performance hadn't landed us in this situation in the first place. "Let's grab her and then head up to the conference room near my office. Sound good?"

"Sounds great." I followed Joyce through the lobby and into the café that shared its bright white, space-age vibe. But before I could even take that in, I spotted her sitting at the counter, not looking at her phone, though it was out. Ari Fox looked right at me.

Chapter 2
The Talent

Ari Fox stood up from the counter and made her way over to Joyce and me.

This was one of the first times I'd officially met any talent I was part of "handling," and that included colliding with Melanie Larkin at the Exemplar holiday party a few years ago when we were both reaching for free glasses of rosé. (She'd merely said *pardon* and then glided away, but I still heard her throaty *pardon* in my ear whenever she popped up on a premium cable prestige drama.)

Ari was smaller than I expected. This was a celebrity cliché, but it was said often for a reason, that reason being accuracy, a frequent occurrence in the dealings with the rich and famous. At least the filmed and fairly well-known.

"Joyce." Ari smiled widely at Joyce before pulling her into a hug. It didn't read like an industry hug. Ari's arms wrapped around tightly, and Joyce seemed in danger of toppling for just a moment. It made me like Ari—like her *more*, of course, because she'd already become my favorite, by virtue of who she was. A queer woman living out and proud in an industry that could be less supportive than it often gave itself credit for, who also gave real hugs? Letting her down —of all people!—felt terrible. I thought I'd set up enough safety guards to avoid making the kinds of mistakes I used to. My life was supposed to be *letting down*-free.

Joyce stepped back from the hug and smiled at me. Her eyes held a hint of giddiness, and I wondered if my boss, who was married to a man, felt at least a little jolted by Ari's energy. How could one not?

"Ari," she said, still smiling, "I'd love for you to meet Nina Rice, who's been with me for years as one of my communication experts. Nina, Ari Fox."

Ari leaned toward me with her hand out, and I felt myself being pulled into the handshake. In this world of hugs, it felt professional and respectful. And, obviously, it gave me this fleeting moment where my hand was wrapped inside Ari Fox's. My job wasn't for the type of person who regularly swooned over celebrities, but Ari was a bit of an exception for me.

"It's nice to meet you, Nina Rice," she said in her trademark husky voice. It was trademark to me, at least. While her fame level was still on the rise, she'd already garnered a voice-over contract with a credit card company. Frequently during commercial breaks I'd hear her advise us to *spend wisely*. It was, honestly, stunning to hear my name in that voice. *Spend wisely, Nina Rice*, I thought, not that this made any sense outside of my own head. Between the job stress and the hot woman holding my hand and the fact that I was out of my house and all the way down here in Beverly Hills, my brain was not exactly functioning at its highest capacity.

"It's nice to meet you," I said, finally, unable to hold Ari's gaze. It was as direct as Joyce's in its own way.

Ari Fox was only in her midtwenties, but her first role had been the buzzy kind that catapulted her into a career playing hot queer girls and women. After being cast on the high school drama *Brother's Keeper* as Gillian, the tough field-hockey-playing jock who sweet blonde Serena fell for, Ari started popping up everywhere. GIFs of Serena and Gillian kissing against gym lockers became regular parts of conversation between people in the LGBTQ+ community, especially on Twitter when commenting about anything sexy or romantic. If swooning or lusting was involved, it was only a matter of time before that GIF set showed up.

She wasn't around only in GIFs, though. Ari played a few other roles much like Gillian, showing up to usher a series regular into a sexuality journey, the previously untold lands of bi- and pansexuality, etc., and then being written off unceremoniously. (A writer at *Vulture* wondered in an article if any other actor had played so many high school students who transferred mid-semester.) Ari had been in her early twenties and still playing teenagers, and then suddenly she was playing actual adult roles, practically overnight. (She still ended up ushering in a lot of previously-believed-to-be-straight characters into queer identity, though.)

Ari wasn't an A-list celebrity, and probably not even a B-list one, but she was on the radar. At the start of this year, she'd received early rave reviews for a supporting role in *Treading Water*, a film that premiered at Sundance. It was immediately picked up in a bidding war by A24 Films, which was set to release the movie at peak for-your-consideration time later in the year. The internet was on top of this star turn, and I devoured feature articles about her whenever I saw one posted. (*Vulture*'s headline: "Ari, the Fox.")

I could lie and say that I'd followed Ari's career closely because she was a client and I took my job very seriously. While I did actually take my job seriously, as silly as it could be sometimes—*Don't forget to email from Tess's account to tell Shelby Feinstein you loved the homemade dog treats she sent to Rosie the Pug*—I was a full-fledged Ari Fox fangirl. Fan-woman? I was thirty-two years old, after all, five years older than Ari. But I'd never seen a career like hers before. She hadn't come out, she hadn't avoided the topic, she just *was*. Ari Fox was a breath of fresh air, someone who felt brand-new.

And, of course, if it didn't go without saying, she was gorgeous. Was *gorgeous* the right word? Ari was *sexy*. Even now, her posture at the counter, all hips at certain angles and forearms resting exactly so on the counter with her chin cocked in our direction. Her caramel-brown hair was shaggy over half her face, dipping down over one gray-blue eye, while the other side was trimmed short. I'd always wondered how one got a haircut like that; it seemed so specific as to defy instruction. Her body, which I'd absolutely thought about, was different in person than I'd surveyed on-screen. Again, a cliché, but I liked the differences. She was slim but not gym-lean, a person who took up space, and she didn't fit the Exemplar aesthetic any more than I did, though I could tell her plain black T-shirt and jeans were far pricier than anything currently on my body.

"Nina, anything?" Joyce asked, with a nod to the café register.

"Hmm?" I asked, having lost complete track of what was being discussed, outside of my potential impending job loss. That was correct, wasn't it? It was a bit strange, sure, to have a hot celebrity summoned for one's firing, but I realized it had to be what was on the afternoon's agenda. I was about to be let go while a gorgeous woman who'd broken ground for better representation watched.

"Their cold brew's great," Ari said.

"Oh, I can't have cold brew, it makes me feel like I'm on meth," I said. "Not that I've ever been on meth."

Ari grinned, instead of backing away from the meth babbling of a so-called communications expert. "Hey, this is a judgment-free zone."

Joyce was getting tea for herself, so I allowed myself a chai.

I wouldn't be any safer with it than I would have been a water in the lobby, but I knew for a fact that the upstairs meeting and conference rooms featured dark, patterned sofas and rugs, nothing like that terrifyingly bright white situation on the first floor. And Hollywood could be very much like middle school, where the smartest thing to do in any situation was blend in by doing whatever the rest of the group was up to. If beverages were being consumed, I would consume a beverage.

Ari and I followed Joyce up that massive staircase to the second floor. It was a coveted level, I knew, an upgrade from her old spot on the fourth floor. The move happened a few years ago when longtime client Tess Gardner made her way into the Pantheon Cinematic Universe. I knew these bits and pieces of Joyce's career trajectory because when things were good and her time wasn't crunched, Joyce could be chatty. And Joyce's last assistant, Reginald, *loved* me. His emails were full of exclamation points, and we often got way off-track discussing episodes of *Top Chef* or the *Real Housewives* or whatever was currently in-season on Bravo. But of course Reginald was so good at his job that he'd been promoted to the title of Junior Agent up on the fourth floor, and was too busy these days with his own clients for our TV recaps.

Joyce walked us to one of the meeting rooms, and the two of us hovered to let Ari choose her seat first. Since she took the long navy-blue sofa, Joyce perched nearby in a gray mid-century modern armchair, and I tried to sit gracefully in the overstuffed-style loveseat. (I was not particularly successful.)

"So, if I may, Ari wanted to meet with us today to talk about her communications coming out of Exemplar," Joyce said, her tone as smooth and polished as a politician's. "Ari, did you want to share your concerns with Nina?"

"Yeah, thanks," Ari said. "And, look, I know I'm probably overthinking things. Two of my friends told me I was being quote-unquote *difficult*."

Joyce laughed. "Did you tell them that's your brand?"

Ari joined in. Her laughter came out in short little bursts, so silly for someone so . . . suave? Put-together? . . . *hot?* "Joyce, they're aware!" She swept her hair back behind her ear. I noticed her ear wasn't traditionally pierced, but a tiny platinum hoop glinted from one of those trendy mid-ear spots. "It's bad enough everything's coming from an AOL address, but you said that's protocol—"

"Yes, our IT team has their reasoning," Joyce said with a wave of her hand. She always managed to interrupt in a way that didn't read as rude.

"Anyway, I know you're normally emailing people I'm not having a ton of contact with otherwise," Ari said, "but in the last month it's come up a couple of times that someone got my email and 'it just didn't sound like you.'"

Shit. That was literally all I was supposed to do. Make and follow up on appointments accurately, and sound enough like the talent to never arouse any suspicions.

"I'm so sorry," I said, without any of Joyce's polished finish. "I feel really terrible about it."

"Yes," Joyce said with a slight side-eye in my direction. I should have let her lead, and we both knew it. "We take communications very seriously, and I'm glad you reached out. I have some ideas in mind for how we can make you more comfortable with the messages coming out of Exemplar, or if you'd rather—"

"Oh, god, no." Ari held up her hand. "Nina, I'm sure you're doing a great job. This is on me. Like Joyce said, I'm difficult, and I'm specific. It's not your fault you didn't nail it. No one would nail it. If I had things my way, I'd just do this all myself, but I know that I don't have time and that there's things that should get handled through your office because of how meetings have to be scheduled. Completely get it."

"Ah, you hardly sound difficult at all," Joyce teased, and

now Ari was laughing again. "How can we fix this for you? You've certainly got a busy year coming up."

Ari fixed her gaze right on me. "Would it be cool if we just grabbed a drink or something? We can chat, I could probably show you some actual emails I've sent, if that's not the nerdiest thing you've ever heard, and we can go from there?"

Joyce turned from Ari to me. There was no gauging what she thought by her perfectly neutral expression. "That works for you, doesn't it, Nina?"

"Of course," I said, because why wouldn't it? I'd walked in here expecting to be fired, and instead I was *getting drinks with a hot celebrity?* What even was my life?

Ari gestured to me. "Give me your phone and I'll text myself from it, so we have each other's numbers."

I did so, though it seemed that I was hallucinating instead of actually living this moment. Ari handed it back to me a moment later with a grin, like we were co-conspirators instead of—I mean, what exactly were we, anyway?

"You should be fairly warned that Nina lives somewhere beyond the edge of the world," Joyce said with a laugh. Practically a cackle. "West Covina or something. Palm Springs but not good?"

"I'm just up in the suburbs," I said, the least cool correction someone could make in Los Angeles. "I can get down here easily."

"You're here right now, after all." Ari grinned. "Thanks for understanding, both of you. It's appreciated."

Joyce and Ari made some scattered small talk about, since I guess we were almost on the topic, Palm Springs. Part of me wanted to soak up Ari's presence, watch how she sat and moved when she was in this setting. But today was a reminder that I wasn't a fan of Ari Fox, I was *an employee*, and ogling someone's forearms was not in my job description. And then the meeting was over, anyway, and while I expected Joyce to detain me once she hugged Ari goodbye—for a lecture, for a big sigh of relief, for drinks prep—she merely hugged me goodbye as well and said that we'd talk soon.

"We should say goodbye to Max before we head out," Ari said. "If you're heading out. I don't know what else you're up to."

I wrinkled my nose without meaning to. Ugh, Max. I'd avoided him so far. His emails were more than enough. But if Ari could manage politeness, surely I could, too.

"What?" she asked me, as I realized I hadn't gotten away with letting my feelings slip out. Joyce would not have approved of my behavior.

"It's nothing," I said. "We should definitely say bye to Max before we go."

There I was, casually using *we* to indicate myself and this extremely hot actor. Again, what was my life?

Ari directed me with a nod, and I followed her to the space-age set of cubicles near Joyce's office. Luckily, there were no B-school bros to be found.

"Hey there," Ari said in a warm tone to a tiny girl sitting in one of the cubicles.

"Ari," she squeaked out like if a whistle became a person. "Hi."

"Nina, you know Max, right?"

I stared at the girl. She was wearing a brightly patterned button-down, and her short haircut was even more complicated than Ari's. I didn't want to stereotype, but I was positive that Max Van Doren wasn't a B-school bro but instead an adorable queer girl.

"We've never met in person," she said in her tiny voice. "Even though I email you like every five minutes. It's nice to finally meet you, Nina."

"You too." I shook her equally tiny hand and hoped I'd kept the shock out of my voice. When had I decided Max was a douchebag? Was it the hardcore WASP name? The abrupt emails? How had we, even though Max hadn't worked for Joyce for that long, never actually been on the phone together in this phone-heavy industry? Should I have, at some point, opened my mind up to another possible Max? Well—obviously, I should have.

"How's the girlfriend?" Ari asked, then flicked her eyes in my direction. "Last time I was here, Max had quite a bouquet on her desk."

"Oh, nice," I said.

"We broke up," Max said in her little voice, and Ari and I exchanged an *oh shit* look.

"Oh, man, I'm sorry," Ari said.

"That sucks," I said, unhelpfully.

Max just watched us for a bit, then nodded. "Yep."

"Well, it was nice to meet you," I said. "Put a face to the name and all of that."

She nodded again. Ari and I exchanged another look before saying goodbye and getting the hell out of there. The elevator doors were safely closed before both of us collapsed into laughter.

"Her poor little face," Ari said. "She's too pure for this world."

"Her hand felt like a bird," I said. "Like, a really small bird."

Ari grinned, leaning against the elevator wall. "You hold a lot of birds?"

It was crazy that anything this woman said could sound like flirting. Even bird-holding.

"Well, you know what they say," I stammered. "A bird in the hand is worth two in the—"

The elevator doors, miraculously, opened. We, blessedly silently, walked out, and passed through the lobby to the valet stand. But then Ari nudged me with her elbow, with a grin on her face I could only describe as *wicked*.

"I *do* know what they say."

Chapter 3

One Thousand Questions

Luckily, Ari's BMW zoomed up first, so she was long gone before my Honda clanged its way to me. I thanked and tipped the valet and headed out into traffic. The idea of sitting on a freeway for two hours with my bird-in-the-hand comment lodged in my brain was nothing less than awful, so I decided to grab a coffee and catch up on my virtual library ebook pile instead. Mid-City was tough, though; parking was already at a minimum all day long, but particularly as rush hour proper drew near, and rows of metered spots turned into driving lanes until after seven p.m. I drove from Starbucks to indie coffee-shop to the next Starbucks and so on, and before long I was close enough to my old neighborhood that I felt what I referred to as *the tingles.*

Before Taylor—before Taylor broke up with me, specifically—this phenomenon was so rare it didn't need a name. But then I was alone and—worse than alone: I was cursed. Unlike movies about curses, though, I had accepted my fate. I had been the one to take initiative and exile myself from the figurative kingdom. (I guess queer icon Elsa from *Frozen* did this too, but I was lucky not to have a plucky, headstrong sister and enchanted snowman at my heels.)

Sometimes, though, the kingdom came up. As an avid television viewer, it was tough to miss the spots on the Eastside of LA as locations. Fictional novelists got their writing done at Swork, where Taylor and I had grabbed coffees whenever we were on our way to the Pasadena Rose Bowl Flea Market. Fictional couples met the parents at Alcove Café, where we'd had so many brunches with our crew of friends. Fictional queer people longed, loved, and lusted at the Semi-Tropic, where— well, you get the drift. My old life was hard to escape. And when it intruded, I felt it all over. *The tingles.* It was like when I woke up in the middle of the night realizing my arm had fallen asleep, except that it was all over.

It was only four thirty, though, and Taylor never left her office before six. She hadn't then, at least, and I couldn't imagine that changing. So I kept going. I passed personal landmarks. It was another lifetime, but driving up Hillhurst Avenue made it seem less far away. Even so, when a parking spot was open in front of the overly fancy Starbucks, I swung the Honda in. I paid the meter. I walked inside.

I wasn't sure what I was expecting. Overly fancy or not, it was just a Starbucks. I bypassed their special menu and ordered a chai. (In a non-surprise, I'd been too nervous to drink my Exemplar chai even on dark gray furniture, and had discarded it in the trash can near sweet little Max's cubicle.) A cozy chair was open, so once I claimed my chai I settled in. Before I opened my e-reader app, though, I couldn't help but check my contacts for Ari's info. There was nothing under Fox, though, so I scrolled back up to the As to discover that Ari had entered her name as Ari and the fox emoji. Holy hell, she was cute. I closed out of the app as quickly as possible because with my luck I'd accidentally call her.

"Nina?"

I looked up so quickly that a wave of vertigo washed over me. It was far worse than the tingles.

"It *is* you, I knew it!"

I should have trusted my gut, should have trusted the tingles, should have gotten far outside of Los Angeles proper before indulging in another chai.

"There was a rumor going around for a bit that you were *dead*, but I never took it too seriously." Phoebe Reyes, part of my other life, stood right in front of me. As if no time had passed at all.

"Hi," was all I could manage to say, and from the look on Phoebe's face, she knew it was bullshit too.

"Hi to you too." She gestured to the man sitting in the nearest chair. "Sir, I hate to be a bother, but I'd love to catch up with my friend here. Would you mind giving up your chair? There's another good one right there."

The man scurried away, and I couldn't help but laugh. Phoebe hadn't changed at all. And why would she? Phoebe was a powerhouse. She'd worked for years promoting blockbuster films for three major studios before forming her own consulting firm, Big Marketing Energy. I hadn't talked to Phoebe in years—I'd hardly talked to anyone in years, after all—but Big Marketing Energy's name came up occasionally when I was reading the industry trades. The mentions always made me smile; if *Deadline Hollywood* was discussing Phoebe's company, I knew that she must be continuing to succeed.

"You look great," she said, settling in across from me, and I scoffed. "What? You do! We don't have to play some modesty bullshit game, do we?"

"I just don't feel like I look that great," I said, "but maybe that's because I spent too much time in Beverly Hills today."

"Ah, that'll do it. *Neen*." Her voice softened, as she looked right at me through her trademark thick-framed glasses. Back in the day they were black, but her current pair was a deep midnight blue. Instead of obscuring her expression, they seemed to highlight it, and I found myself unable to look away from my old friend.

Phoebe was gorgeous to me in such an incredibly professional way. Today she wore a suit made of dark floral fabric over a bright white T-shirt, and no socks under her shiny black loafers. Her nearly black hair was flecked with silver, but still styled into a very no-nonsense, Rachel-Maddow-on-the-weekend look. Phoebe was ten years older than me, but possessed a coolness that I'd never managed. A gold band glinted on her left hand, and I realized I was relieved that Phoebe and Bianca were still together. I might be alone forever—correction, I *was* alone forever, but I was a special situation. I wanted more happiness for everyone else. They deserved it, especially Phoebe and Bianca.

"It's been a while," was all I could manage to eke out, finally.

"It sure has. There really *was* a rumor you'd died, but I never believed it."

I shrugged, because in a way, I had. How did that old pop song go? The old Nina couldn't come to the phone, because she was dead.

"So you're still working for Joyce over at Exemplar?" Phoebe asked. "I'm assuming that because you look nice, and the only two things I do in Beverly Hills are take meetings at agencies and get my teeth cleaned. You don't look particularly dental."

"Yeah, I'm still working for Joyce." I shrugged, because I assumed to a person like Phoebe that keeping the same low-level job for more than three years was not just unheard of, but a failure. I usually liked the gig, and, anyway, it suited my life in a way something bigger and more prestigious wouldn't.

"Are you seeing anyone?" she asked, then casually took a sip of her iced drink. As if it were a casual sip kind of topic.

"Well, obviously, *no*." Why didn't she know better?

"What's the *obviously*?" Phoebe sipped more of her drink.

"Did you join a nunnery? Is that where you've been? Are nuns allowed to work for talent agents? It seems at cross-purposes, no pun intended."

I sighed. Seriously, why hadn't I trusted the tingles? "I should get going."

"No, no, don't." Phoebe leaned over and touched my arm. "I've missed you so fucking much, Nina."

I'd missed Phoebe too. In some ways, it didn't feel so long ago that we texted almost every day. She was truly too busy to chat as often as I could, but it was the kind of friendship where we prioritized each other. So considering what and how everything had gone down with Taylor, Phoebe was one of the people I'd worried most about protecting.

"It's . . . it's a long story," was what I ended up saying.

"I've got nowhere to be," she said. "We could run across the street and grab happy hour sushi. Bianca's got one of her exercise empowerment dance class whatevers tonight anyway. Keep me company."

"Maybe some other time."

Phoebe narrowed her eyes at me. "Are you busy? If not, we're getting sushi. It's on me, and I'll hear no arguments."

I wanted to tell her, right then and there, that I had it on good authority that I was only going to eventually make things worse, but this was *Phoebe*. Phoebe might have been a part of my before, but here she was in my now, and the truth was I didn't want to turn down that sushi invite.

"Fine," I said, trying not to grin, which was tougher when Phoebe did. "Oh, calm down, I'm not that exciting."

"My friend who disappeared without a trace? I'd say you are."

After finishing our drinks, we crossed Hillhurst and grabbed a table at the sushi restaurant in the supermarket parking lot. I didn't even know how many spicy tuna rolls I'd eaten here with Phoebe over the years, just that I was glad I'd be doing it again tonight.

Did that make me selfish? Maybe so, but my friend was hard to resist. And today had been so weird, what was one more weird thing?

"So nothing's new with me," Phoebe said, preemptively, once we'd put in our order. "Bianca's great, I'm great, the business is great. We're trying to adopt but who knows if that phone call's ever going to come."

"That's amazing," I said. "Nothing's new with me either."

"Oh, please, you're not getting away with that after disappearing for years. I'll be asking a thousand questions, and you're on the hook for all of them."

I frowned at her as our waiter brought our giant bottle of Asahi beer to split. But by the time we clinked glasses, I felt my annoyance already ebbing.

"So where are you living?" Phoebe asked.

"Question number one," I said. "I'm keeping track. You only get one thousand."

She threw her head back in laughter. "Great, I'll make them all count."

"I took over Lorna's condo when she—"

"Oh, god." Phoebe clasped both hands to her chest. "Not Lorna."

I shook my head. "No, Lorna's fine. Her arthritis made the steps tricky, and all her friends moved into the same retirement community, so she's in heaven. Er, not *literal* heaven. Again, she's fine and alive. I'll be seeing her tomorrow, because we get lunch every Thursday."

"Ah, thank god," Phoebe said. Back in the day, my friends saw plenty of Lorna. Before she slowed down so much, she drove her convertible down at least once a month, and she'd insist on taking the usual brunch crew out to wherever was the hottest reservation at the time.

"But isn't that condo way the fuck up in . . . I don't know. Wherever the Six Flags is? Further?"

"Question number two," I said. "And it's just an exit further than Six Flags. It's quiet, which is good for me."

"Hmmm. Are there women up there?"

"Question number three." I took another sip of beer. "Nope, no women at all. Every other gender, but no women."

"Oh, fuck you, Neen, you know what I mean! Queer women! People to have sex with and fall in love with, who don't have to drive all the way up from LA. Not that you aren't worth it, I suppose. I'm lucky Bianca and I lived a few blocks away when we started dating—to be honest, you know how much I hate driving."

"Well, Lyft needs someone to keep them in business," I said.

"You're avoiding the question."

"It's irrelevant," I said, and luckily the waiter returned with our bowl of edamame and miso soups. It wasn't as if I didn't trust Phoebe, but Phoebe was a mutual friend. She could have literally met Taylor for drinks last night. An unread text from Taylor could be sitting on her phone right now. I'd spent more time than I could calculate picturing the conversations Taylor had with our mutuals. I didn't have to imagine much to hear them in my head, outlining everything bad about me.

But I also had to admit that Phoebe was, firmly, anti-bullshit. And there was nothing here to indicate she was only here to squirrel away Nina tidbits for Taylor later.

"Bad breakup," I said with a shrug. It was true, or true enough.

"Oh, Neen." Phoebe leaned in a little, her eyebrows drawing together in concern. "It sucks, I know. But you're—"

"Don't," I said. "Please."

"Don't what?"

"Question number four. And don't give me a positive list of attributes. I've got a longer one ready to go." Twelve points, never forgotten, rounding out with my general toxicity. Why did I want to chance poisoning others? "Do we have to do this? You got me out, isn't that enough?"

"Fair point." Phoebe seemed to focus all her attention on her miso soup, so I did the same, letting the savory broth linger on my tongue.

"So, an in-person with Joyce? Anything exciting?"

I glanced around, and luckily the other few tables at the restaurant didn't seem young, cool, or queer enough to be interested in this conversation. "Believe it or not, I just met with Ari Fox."

"Ooh, do tell. Is she hotter in person?"

"Unfortunately, yes," I said. "Apparently, my emails don't sound enough like her, so she wants to solve the issue by getting a drink with me so I can get to know her."

Out of my mouth, I heard how bizarre it sounded. Why did Ari Fox care, anyway? Weren't there bigger things going on in her life?

Phoebe smirked. "This sounds like the setup to the torrid affair you're about to have with her."

"Stop. I highly doubt that even the drinks are going to happen. She'll feel heard now, and she'll stop worrying about it."

"It's so true. I can't believe how many problems end up going away because you listen to a person openly for a few minutes. I guess it's just that rare in this industry."

As I watched Phoebe talk, I realized that tears were forming in my eyes. I did my best to blink them away but of course that only drew more attention to them, and Phoebe saw *everything*.

"Everything OK?"

I laughed and let my tears fall. What was the point in this charade? "Can I be honest? I missed you a lot."

Phoebe reached across the table and squeezed my hand, and it was exactly then that I thought, fuck it, we were friends again.

Taylor was hardly my first breakup. Back when I still dated guys—well, boys; it was high school after all—they all dumped me. Jon and Vince and Brad and Antony. I'd never minded, which was one reason it wasn't that much of a shock when I got to college and made out with a girl at the freshman mixer I attended the first night. When that girl, Kimberly, dumped me a few months later, it wasn't nothing. I felt a whole lot.

I'd gotten good at it. I knew when I needed to dance it out, or shove a bunch of ice cream into my mouth, or make out with a stranger I'd forget by morning. (Let's be real, as a queer woman, sometimes I ended up dating those strangers for not insignificant portions of time too.)

So in some ways, I should have been ready for Taylor. Relationships ended, and it was often not my choice. But, of course, Taylor had been a first in so many ways. The first woman I lived with, the first woman I spent holidays with, the first woman I realistically saw the rest of my life with. Taylor was everything, and not the way a heady college romance was everything, Taylor was a joint checking account and a cable bill in both of our names and every invitation written out to Taylor Alderidge & Nina Rice.

When it ended, I hadn't even known who I was anymore. Half of a cable bill and the holidays with my family, alone? Lorna had hinted at handing the condo over to Taylor and me, so that it would be in good hands once she moved into Oaken Troves, but Taylor had hated the thought, even with the enticement of free rent. Unlike me, Taylor couldn't work from home, and it was tough to argue the math with her. Waze told us that there were evenings it could have taken her two hours to drive up to the suburbs. What good was free rent if our time together vanished, and if none of our friends wanted to come up to grab drinks with us anymore? Our apartment in Silver Lake was central to the world we lived in then, and while it wasn't cheap, we'd nabbed it at the right time. It was our home, and when there wasn't an *our* anymore, I'd known exactly where to go.

When I'd first arrived in Lorna's condo, I'd imagined that within a few months I'd figure out my next step. I had some money set aside, and thanks to paying no rent for the foreseeable future, I'd soon have even more. But Taylor's email and words from our way-too-public breakup got in, and deeply at that. They'd seeped into me, poured into any gaps left open, so by then I'd become changed by her and by the way she'd ended everything.

I'd tried to imagine moving back to Silver Lake, or any neighborhood nearby, but as this newly changed person. How could I keep shopping at the Whole Foods knowing that I'd usually run into Chloe, or CJ and their latest girlfriend? Was I supposed to grab a drink out with a book while Phoebe and Bianca were at the next table? If I had to give them—it—everything up, why stick around to watch their lives without me? If I'd been such a cause of anxiety and unhappiness—or worse, a ticking bomb of those things set to go off at any moment—I didn't want to watch my old world blossom without me in it.

Plus there was an annoying thing about adulthood, which was that time started to pass like it was invisible. When Taylor broke up with me, I'd been in my twenties—sure, my late twenties, but it felt like everything big was in front of me, still to come. Now I was thirty-two and I was pretty sure I'd missed all my chances. The big stuff was all in the rearview mirror, getting further and further away.

Chapter 4
Thursdays with Lorna

Late the next morning, I paused "my" email in response to an Instagram influencer and headed over to Oaken Troves. It was less than twenty minutes outside of town—if Santa Clarita could be considered a town—and tucked away from the strip malls and shopping centers and industrial parks that defined the area. Los Angeles might have been only thirty miles south, but in a lot of ways it was another world. I missed it, when I let myself.

Luckily, that was rare.

The retirement community was arranged into cottages on one half, and more dorm-style living on the other, and of course my aunt had secured one of the biggest cottages here. This was not a place that sad elderly types went to be forgotten; Oaken Troves was *a scene*. It wasn't even noon yet, and on the patio a large crowd of senior citizens was crowded around a table playing some board game I'd never seen before, arguing and cheering as a bald man moved his game piece.

And, of course, the person yelling the loudest was my aunt Lorna. That is, until she saw me, and then the game was abruptly abandoned.

"Nina Louise! Let me get a look at you."

Lorna was actually my father's aunt, my late grandmother's youngest sister. Grandma had died when I was only ten, and as I'd wept at her funeral, Lorna had swept me up in her arms and promised me she'd take care of everything Grandma had. Even as a little kid, I'd found this highly unlikely. I was living in Missouri, an hour outside of St. Louis, and Lorna lived somewhere magical—California.

But Lorna hadn't been lying. Cards began showing up once a week, all stamped in California. Some were postcards, boasting of attractions I'd never gone to: the Hollywood Walk of Fame, the Central Library, Dodger Stadium. Other times, they were greeting cards, brightly colored and just for fun. My immediate family hadn't particularly been *just for fun* types; if I got a greeting card, it was my birthday, and that was about it. Lorna clearly *was* a *just for fun* type, and the cards never stopped, even when I left Missouri and began college at USC. By then, Lorna had retreated from busy Los Angeles and was ensconced in her Santa Clarita condo. We had brunch once a month—honestly, I learned about brunch as a lifestyle from Lorna—and the cards came every week anyway.

"I look the same as I did last week," I said, but I still allowed her to hold my face in her hands and examine me.

"Are you using that skin cream I heard about from Choon Hee's granddaughter? Apparently it's very big in Korea, the Koreans seem to have the market cornered on skin care these days. They have this whole ten-step routine."

"I'm fine," I said, though I couldn't say I loved my skin being frowned over by someone in her eighties. "I barely leave my—your house anyway."

"As if that's some kind of defense! Come on, apparently there's gazpacho on the menu today. Chef Carlos promised me it would be very authentic, none of this whitewashed bullshit they try to sneak past us oldies."

"Sounds good," I said, even though in general I preferred

my soups hot. After Grandma died, Lorna started flying back on my birthday each year, and she'd always find the coolest place to celebrate. Thanks to her I had real Italian food on The Hill, Vietnamese on South Grand, tacos on Cherokee Street. Any one of those dinners on its own hadn't made me move to Los Angeles, but I was sure that the cumulative effect was a powerful one. In short, I owed what felt like my entire life to her. I could put up with some cold soup.

Lorna led me to her usual table at the outdoor cafeteria. "Couldn't do this in Missouri, could we?" she liked to ask frequently, and I smiled that for her too it was still like we were getting away with something.

"How are you feeling?" I asked, like I did every week, like I felt like I should for anyone upwards of eighty.

"I wish my legs felt better, but other than that I'm doing great," she said. "My friend Nat—you know Nat, of course—she gave me one of those so-called 'special' brownies that she got from her grandson—he's a DJ, very successful according to her—and, Nina, one minute I was watching *Jeopardy!* like usual, the next there was banging on my door because I'd slept through dinner, and you know what they think here when you do that, D-E-A-D."

"Lorna!" I laughed so hard I had to dab at my eyes with my napkin. "You have to ease into edibles. You can't just start off with the whole thing."

"Nat didn't bother to tell me that. What reasonable person would think a brownie would be more than one serving? Brownies are meant to be devoured in full."

"I'm with you there," I said, even though Lorna had always been a tiny, birdlike woman, even in photos from her youth, and I'd been in plus-sizes since college. Lorna had been the first to defend me when my parents had advised me against, for example, loading my plate up too high during our annual Christmas buffet, but it was still one of those subjects I tried not to get into too often with family. Even Lorna.

"I can probably find you some less potent edibles if you want to try again," I said, though my days of knowing where the cool marijuana dispensaries were located were far behind me. One nice thing about my closest friend being in her eighties was that it made me young, relatively speaking. Now that Lorna rarely left the perimeters of Oaken Troves, I didn't actually have to know the coolest spot. I just had to know *a* spot.

"Well, it's Thursday, that means Nina is here!" Lorna's friend Nat sat down between us, as their mutual friend Choon Hee sat down across from Nat. Nat and Choon Hee almost always joined us for lunch, so I was prepared for this.

"You look tired," Choon Hee said. "Lorna, did you tell her about the ten steps?"

"I told her!"

"You told me ten minutes ago," I said. "I haven't had time to change up my routine yet. I promise I'll look into it."

"Don't you listen to them, Nina," Nat said. "You have the skin of an angel! Have you managed to find yourself a husband yet?"

"Nat, remember, she likes girls," Choon Hee admonished. "She's not looking for a husband."

"Well, then a wife! It's legal now!"

"I'm fine single." I smiled through it because this conversation repeated itself at least once a month. "Not everyone needs a wife."

They began gossiping about an Oaken Troves resident who was apparently on the prowl for a new wife ever since his Ernesta died, and I felt myself relax as their conversation swirled around me. I was never here to discuss anything serious with Lorna; for all the meals we'd spent together, we'd never gotten into anything too deep. Even after Taylor dumped me, all Lorna had asked was if I was finally ready to take over the condo. We were both happy, I thought, to make sure the other one was still alive each week and not much more.

* * *

At home, I finished up my pending emails and made myself a cup of coffee before noticing my phone was glowing with texts. I knew it was sad, but I couldn't remember the last time this was the case, other than a few months ago when I'd somehow inadvertently gotten added to a group text between four twelve-year-olds who hated their PE teacher. They thought my number belonged to a boy named Jaden, and they were *mad* about dodgeball.

Drinks/food on Saturday night, my place, no getting out of it. Love you!

I grinned at Phoebe's text, even though *obviously* I wasn't sure that I'd actually go. An invite from a friend felt like my old life, when possibility was something that didn't yet feel closed off from me.

Drinks next week? How's your sched? 😕

I nearly dropped my phone. Ari Fox, casually using emojis with me? Extremely casually making plans with me? Somehow, Phoebe's text became the easier one to tackle.

I'm positive I won't be able to get out of this, so, fine. What time, and what can I bring?

Nothing, Phoebe texted back almost immediately. **Just yourself. Bianca CAN'T WAIT to see you. Expect an off-the-chart amount of hugging, fair warning. 7pm.**

Phoebe and I texted on and off throughout the evening, and it wasn't until I was in bed for the night that I realized I'd never responded to Ari. Was it too late now? What time did hot celebrities go to bed? Surely later than me.

My schedule's pretty open. Just let me know what works for you!

Was the exclamation point too much? Maybe I should delete it. I decided I could change it out for a period but add an emoji so there was still some character to the text. In browsing them for an appropriate pick—seriously, what was an appropriate pick?—I accidentally tapped the corn on the cob emoji, and it got worse when I went to delete it *and* the exclamation point, and hit send instead. This was what I got for attempting this without my contacts in, and when I pulled on my glasses I discovered that not only had I accidentally sent the corn, but a tooth emoji as well. How did I even do this? I was turning into my mother, who sent more autocorrected texts to me than fully legible ones.

It wasn't great news.

Hopefully Ari was out doing—well, whatever young, hot, Hollywood types did these days. I was hardly an expert on that demographic, outside of their business emails, after all. But it stood to reason that she was likely out at some little-known hidden gem of a bar or a club, and by the time she glanced at her phone she'd be far too gone on whiskey or weed or whatever mind-altering substance was in this month to notice my tooth and corn.

But, oh god. Almost immediately, the typing dots started up. Ari was holding her phone right this moment, and now that my glasses were on I had to watch the three dots blink, crisply, for an agonizing amount of time. *Blink blink blink, dot dot dot.*

I closed out of my messages and pasted Phoebe and Bianca's address in Waze to figure out how much time I'd need to give myself on Saturday. I pretended—to myself, I supposed—that I was deeply interested in this drive and weekend traffic patterns. It was much easier than the truth of the corn tooth.

How's Tuesday? And maybe I'm not cool enough, what does the corn and the tooth stand for? Is this a speakeasy or some LA nonsense no one told me about yet?

I laughed, half genuine, half relief. **I'm really sorry, I wish I had this information but in actuality I didn't have my contacts in and hit those both by mistake.**

That's too bad, I was already psyched to check out the microbrews on tap at corn+tooth with you. 😎

I knew I should have quit while I was ahead, because, god, this was great. Obviously, it was for work, and there was no actual flirty rapport I'd managed to strike up with—of all people!—Ari Fox. But lying in bed in nothing but a T-shirt and my underwear, it felt nice to text someone gorgeous, and even nicer to be texted back.

It wasn't like I hadn't gotten any since Taylor dumped me. Despite what Phoebe thought about my neighborhood—and, I couldn't lie, it had gone red in more than a few elections, though thank god none of the most urgent ones—I wasn't the only queer woman around. I might have said no to relationships forever, or the other way around, but since when was that a requirement for an orgasm or four? I'd met women at bars, on apps, once at Vons while shopping for cheese. That was never the problem. Everything was fine if they never wanted to see me again, if the rules in place were understood without a word. Chanda would text me a literal late night **wyd?**, and since I'd rarely been doing much of anything at that hour, like clockwork she'd show up and we'd make light conversation for only a few minutes before we were naked in my bed. *I hate small talk*, she'd said once, afterward or in between or whatever the time was called that we spent under my covers but not fucking. *Me too*, I'd agreed, though I hadn't—I didn't. The girl who hated small talk was just such a cooler person to be than the girl who was cursed, who'd eventually destroy anyone who felt more for her than lust.

I realized I'd let the text from Ari sit too long. The past had crept in; I wasn't fun and flirty, wild with abandon and bad at small talk. I was serious and bad with time and loved all the details that made up a person's life and, as much as I wished it wasn't true, cursed with destruction after all.

Phoebe had texted me to park in the driveway on Saturday night—truly, a generous gift from a Silver Lake resident—but when I pulled in, I saw a small group of people traipsing up to the door. Sure, the driveway *had* been saved for me, but this wasn't an evening to catch up with Phoebe and Bianca. This looked like a party.

"Oh my god! You made it!" Bianca sidestepped the guests at the door and made a beeline for me, or at least my car. Like Phoebe, she barely looked as if she'd aged at all. Her dark hair cascaded over her shoulders, perfectly blown out by a professional, no doubt, and a sleeveless bright floral dress hugged her curves down to her waist and then flowed to the floor. Elegance and cleavage, truly the full package.

Bianca was younger than Phoebe, my age, my friend first, back when I was new to the city and hungry for friends and community. She'd grown up in Los Angeles, just a few miles away. Her grandparents emigrated from Mexico not long after they were married, and most of her family stayed right in the area too. When I was too broke to fly home for my first Thanksgiving away, Bianca's family had welcomed me like I was just another one of the cousins. (Even when I'd finally started making more money, I hung around LA for Thanksgiving because I had more fun at the Suarezes' than I did back in Chesterfield, Missouri.)

We used to swap clothes and date each other's exes, laughing that we were so broke we'd take leftovers however we could get them. And then one night while we were hanging out at Akbar, Phoebe bought us drinks while having eyes only for Bianca. And that was that.

"Phoebe didn't tell me it was a party," I said out my window, and when I could tell Bianca didn't hear me, I rolled down my passenger-side window as well. It took a moment because nothing in this car was new enough to roll down automatically. "Phoebe didn't tell me it was a party!"

"That sounds like her," Bianca said, though without a hint of annoyance. Phoebe and Bianca had an extremely healthy relationship. "Get out of your car, girl, I haven't seen you in so long. If you don't, I'll have CJ drag you out, and I know you don't want that. It'll be *humiliating* for you both."

"CJ's here?" I asked.

"Of course, and so is Chloe, who's two seconds away from starting a fight, as always. Come on in, if I rile her up I'll never hear the end of it from Phoebe, but that doesn't mean I won't, if pressed."

I got out of my car and stood face-to-face with Bianca. "I—she—I wouldn't—Phoebe should have—"

"Hey there, sweetie." Bianca took my face in her hands. We'd never dated, but we had a physical closeness in our friendship, or at least we used to. Hugs, hand-holding, heads on shoulders during Lyft rides home. "What's the matter? Where've you been?"

"I shouldn't be here," I said. "If Taylor—"

"Taylor?" Bianca actually looked confused for a moment. "Oh, god, I haven't thought about her in a minute. Last I heard she'd moved to Brentwood, is she still there?"

"What do you . . ." I let my question trail off and get away from me. "I assumed you were still close."

"Nina," she said. "You were my friend first. Why would I still be that close to your ex?"

I laughed while gulping air. Hopefully Bianca wouldn't realize I was *this close* to crying. I'd cried so fucking much this week, it was ridiculous. "Because . . . that's how it works sometimes! And she'd been Phoebe's friend before we—"

"Wait, Nina." Bianca had let go of my face by now, but we were still standing close. "Did you think that—"

"Holy shit, I was right, Nina's here!"

I was tackled into a hug before I could do anything about it or even notice whose arms were around me. Finally I was able to step back, and then it was too, too much. I burst out crying.

"Fuck, should I not have hugged you that hard?"

I laughed through my tears. Chloe Lee didn't seem to have changed either. She was only five foot one, wore boys' clothing from GapKids, and should have been pictured in the dictionary next to the definition of *scrappy*, or maybe in lieu of it altogether. She'd knocked a man out one night when he catcalled us in a particularly dark and creepy 7-Eleven parking lot.

"You hugged me the right amount," I said. "It's so good to see you."

"You too, you dumb idiot." She hugged me again, even tighter this time. "How've you've been?"

"I've been OK," I said, whether or not it was true. I felt exceedingly OK, right this moment, standing between Bianca and Chloe.

"Go on in, Chlo," Bianca told her. "We'll catch up with you in a second."

"All right, all right." She fluffed up the longest part of her short black hair. "Is that girl from Phoebe's office here? What's her name, Clementine?"

"You *know* her name is Clementine, and you also know she has a boyfriend, so behave yourself," Bianca said with a grin.

"So what you're saying is *yes*." Chloe smirked with a bright glint in her dark eyes before letting herself into the house. And then I was alone again with Bianca, who seemed to be putting pieces together as if I were a puzzle.

"You disappeared because you thought we picked Taylor," she said softly, gently, her fingertips on my upper arm. Her golden-brown eyes looked right at me. "Oh, Neen."

"It's not that simple." Oh, for it to be that simple!

"Tell me the rest, then."

"The rest is boring. I'm here right now. And I guess Taylor isn't—"

"I legit don't remember the last time I even *saw* Taylor," Bianca said. "And, yes, you're here now. Sounds like the world's righting itself. You know nothing good could have come out of staying with someone who willingly moved to the Westside."

I laughed, even though I never thought I could have laughed about Taylor again. "I missed you."

"That's very mutual, my friend." She grabbed my hand. "Let's go inside. Are you prepared? I'm thinking there's going to be *a lot* more aggressive hugging."

I looked at the front door and at the silhouettes of people in the big front windows. Phoebe and Bianca knew how to throw a party.

"You know what? I don't care if you're ready or not, girl." Bianca threw her head back and laughed, suddenly looking as devious as Chloe. "We missed you and we're going to be sloppy about it."

It was so easy to get sucked into Bianca's version of the story. Hell, I *loved* Bianca's version. I could walk into the party, get greeted by CJ and whoever else was there from my before life. I could sneak off with Bianca to talk about shopping or *Grey's Anatomy* or which of our friends we thought had started hooking up, like it was five years ago, or ten. I could listen to Phoebe wax philosophical about the best bourbons while exchanging eye rolls with CJ. I could get it all back, if Taylor had been the real problem.

"Maybe I should just go home," I said softly.

"You just got here! And Phoebe says you're way the hell up

in the suburbs now; you don't really want to get back into your car, do you? Come on, there's good snacks."

"Did you really just try to tempt a fat girl into your party with snacks?" I asked, before I could stop myself, and the two of us cracked up.

"Yeah, this other fat girl sure did," Bianca said. "Come on, let's drink too much and see if we can get people dancing."

"That's more your talent than mine," I said, though I felt my body loosen up. When Bianca tugged me by the arm again, I followed. I got more hugs than I thought a person could receive in a single night. Phoebe pulled me into one of her bourbon discussions and after two bourbon flights it was determined I'd be sleeping in the guest room and not making my way back up to Santa Clarita that night. In short, it felt like it used to. And if I pretended Taylor was the only problem—which I did, as I drifted off to a warm and tipsy sleep—it was the best night I'd had since I could remember.

Chapter 5
The Decision-Making Point

On Tuesday I headed down to LA for my drinks meeting with Ari. Three LA trips in the span of a week was a previously unheard of number for me, but it wasn't as if these podcasts were going to listen to themselves, even if maybe they *would* solve some cold case murders. Fingers crossed.

Ari had asked to meet at the Thirsty Crow in Silver Lake. Los Angeles was chopped into what felt like hundreds of tiny neighborhoods within its limits, but I'd loved the East-side, where Silver Lake was located, ever since I'd arrived. My friendship with Bianca had only solidified that more, since she grew up on that side of town and knew its streets and stores, its nuances and its hidden gems. Every single one of my apartments there had been within a few-mile radius, including that two-bedroom in Silver Lake that I'd shared with Taylor, once upon a time.

On one hand, I was a bit surprised Ari had asked to meet at a spot I wasn't merely familiar with, but had spent hours at over the years, throwing back their Manhattan happy hour special with friends, girlfriends, and even Lorna, back in her more mobile days. But I also wasn't *that* surprised. West Hollywood had the reputation for being the most LGBTQ+ friendly spot in Los Angeles, but one of the very first queer protests in the whole country was at a bar just down the street from this one. The Eastside was queer as hell. It was artsy, loud, multicultural, and even now I supposed I still felt at home there. I felt *something*, at least.

I was a few minutes early—after Taylor, I'd never been late for anything again—but after showing my ID and slipping into the bar, I saw Ari right up front in a booth.

"Nina!" she called. "Is this a good spot?"

"Of course," I said, as she stepped out from the booth side of the table and pulled me into a hug. Since we'd shook hands last week, I hadn't expected to be folded into Ari Fox's arms. She smelled so . . . *good*. Musky and warm, like expensive cologne but, somehow, *more*. Tonight she wore a plain white T-shirt with jeans and high-tops, classic and somehow high-end at once. I'd worn a similar outfit, but my lightweight sweater was a little faded, and while these jeans managed to be comfortable and still made my ass look good, they were also a few years old and who knew what wash denim was supposed to be nowadays?

"Thanks for coming all the way . . . down? Out?" Ari gestured to the table. "I took the liberty of grabbing you a drink. Their happy hour Manhattans are something to write home about. But if that's not good for you, I'll grab whatever is."

I was dazed from the hug and how closely we were still standing, but I managed to shake my head. "No, this is great. When I lived in LA I came here all of the time."

Ari slipped back into the booth. "Ah, the suburbs haven't been a forever thing?"

I sat down across from her like this was something I did every day. "Definitely not. I used to live—"

"Cheers," Ari said, almost like an afterthought, as she raised her glass and waited for me. I clinked mine against hers before taking a sip of the sweet, strong cocktail. The bourbon seemed to send fire straight down to my stomach, like it remembered my drunken Saturday night at Phoebe and Bianca's.

It hit me that it was a familiar sensation to look back on a booze-infused, friends-filled Saturday night. In some ways, I realized, it was like coming home.

"Sorry," Ari said, shutting the door on my thoughts for the moment. It was nearly impossible to think of anything else once you were being looked at by Ari Fox. "I interrupted you. Where did you used to live before the suburbs got their claws into you? Do the suburbs even *have* claws? I'm imagining those little protectors they put over cat claws to make them safer."

"Wow," I said, "you know . . . a lot about cat claws."

"Really, it's shocking that a queer woman knows a lot about cats?" Ari laughed. "Hardly. My longest relationship is with my cat, and it's not even a healthy one. I'm so codependent for that jerk."

I grinned. "To answer your question, I used to live just up Hyperion, sort of behind the Gelson's."

"Such a good location. You barely had to walk to buy extremely overpriced produce, man, the dream."

It hit me that I was still grinning. Was this normally how people acted around Ari Fox? My head was light, and I was almost giddy; last time I checked, even Manhattans didn't work this quickly.

"Yeah, it was good. I did buy a lot of expensive broccoli back then. Now I have to get into my car to buy broccoli . . . or do anything, really."

"Do you miss it? LA, I mean, not the expensive broccoli," Ari clarified with a smile. "I've been here so long now that sometimes all I can think about is getting the hell out. You must have so much peace and quiet up there."

"It's just different," I said. "I have neighbors on both sides of my condo, so it's hardly a cabin in the woods. But the pace is slower, which is funny to me because LA's so laid-back as it is."

"Yeah, people say it, but there's a lot of drive here too," she said. "It's not like being in Manhattan where you can practically literally *feel* the hustle, but there are still a lot of weeks where my life is nonstop meetings and interviews and auditions and parties I'm advised I should attend, all that Hollywood shit."

I nodded as if in recognition, though of course my only experience with having a life like that was in sending and answering emails for celebrities who actually did.

"Why'd you leave it?" Ari asked. "The overpriced broccoli and the Hollywood shit?"

"I moved into my aunt's condo when she—"

Ari grimaced. "I'm so sorry."

"I was going to say *moved into a retirement community where she doesn't have to deal with stairs anymore.* Why does everyone think I'm about to tell a sad death story?"

I expected her to laugh, or at least smile, but Ari leaned forward with a serious expression.

"You have to reframe it. Lead with the good part. Ask me why I moved away from the broccoli."

I felt myself laugh, but it was only because I didn't know what we were doing here—specifically, tonight at the Thirsty Crow, and simply in general—and it wasn't easy to just *sit there* and pretend it was normal to hang out with a gorgeous actor.

"No, for real, do it, Nina."

"Fine, fine. Why did you move away from the expensive broccoli?"

"My aunt moved into a retirement community, so it was a great opportunity for me to take care of her space." Ari finished with a dazzling smile. "Media training, baby."

"Maybe you're kidding, but I can see how that sounds better."

"I'm not kidding, Nina Rice." She made very direct eye contact with me. "I'm deadly serious. Unlike your aunt, who's not dead at all."

She broke, and I laughed with her for real.

"How long have you been in LA or the sort of related area?" Ari asked.

"I came out for college—USC—and just sort of stayed. What about you?" I asked, even though I'd read enough interviews with her to know the gist.

That, I realized, was one awkward thing about scenarios like this one. And as weird as this felt, they were probably happening all over Los Angeles at any given moment, famous people and the extremely not-famous people who were paid to handle their business in some way. They might look like normal human interactions, just two people grabbing a drink at a neighborhood bar, but below the surface, the meetings and drinks and coffees and kombuchas on tap were anything but.

After all, I knew that Ari had grown up in Phoenix and moved to LA around the time she landed the role on *Brother's Keeper*. I knew she'd already done press stating that her role in *Treading Water* was, so far in her career, the one she related to most. I knew that while she was incredibly open about her sexuality, she was pretty tight-lipped about her actual love life. Even so, I also knew that she'd dated Hadley Six, a DJ/mixologist (yes) last year.

The knowledge was uneven. But, then again, she was a gorgeous semi-famous person, and I was technically her employee. Nothing about tonight was balanced.

"Seven years now," she said. "I moved out for a job, and my parents said as long as I could pay my bills, I could stay, and that was all the motivation I needed."

I nodded, but I couldn't think of anything to add, and the buzzing sound of crowded bar conversation took over the silence. And yet it still felt like awkward silence.

"I'm sorry," I said, though why I thought this was less awkward than silence, I couldn't tell you. "About the emails."

"Oh, shit, Nina, don't apologize. Like, look, I need this fixed to be able to relax, but not because you're bad at your job. It's because I'm a control freak. Remember that even Joyce, the queen of playing things neutrally, called me difficult?"

"I believe that you called yourself difficult, and she agreed. That's called *keeping the client happy.*"

Ari cracked up again, her eyes crinkled shut and her mouth open wide. It was so bold and unembarrassed, not controlled at all.

"You don't seem difficult to me," I said, and as soon as it was out of my mouth, I heard how it sounded, laced with flirtation and potential. If only I could take it back, but of course conversations and accidents didn't work that way. "Or—or a control freak."

She winked. Yes, an absolutely unironic wink. "I've been on my best behavior for you. So is this your main gig? Ghostwriting emails?"

"My main and only, yeah. I responded to an Entertainment-Careers-dot-whatever job posting a million years ago, and Joyce hired me based off of a fake email for Paul Giamatti, of all people."

"Wait, is Paul Giamatti one of her clients? Is he going to show up one year at the holiday party doing his whole *Billions* thing?"

"He is, but I've never seen him. If he's there, he must blend into the background."

"Now that," she said, "I can believe. So, are you—"

"I thought we were here to talk about you," I said, even though a big rule of Joyce's was *let the talent lead.* My cheeks were flushed, and the Manhattan was definitely running the show now. "Anyway, I'm boring."

"I doubt that. And we're not here to *talk about me.*" She leaned back in the booth, her head cocked at an angle like she was looking for a fight or far away into the horizon. Since I knew it was neither, I unfortunately found it hopelessly sexy.

Ari was all rakish angles and hard looks, and maybe it was because I was so soft, but all that hardness could be a real weakness for me.

It was absolutely unprofessional to develop crushes on people I worked for, but there was still something safe in watching Ari draped back against the booth seat, thinking for just a moment how it would feel to shove the table out of the way and pull myself on top of her. I imagined how her scent would cloud my judgment further as I lowered my mouth to her neck, but wasn't that what celebrities were for? Of course they were actual people, living real though often charmed lives, but they were also the stuff of fantasy. If one politely kept those fantasies to oneself, it was all part of the deal.

It was probably not really part of the deal to be in the middle of a conversation with said celebrity while having said fantasies, to be fair. I took another sip of my icy fiery drink and tried to center my thoughts anywhere but between my legs.

"You're low," Ari said with a nod to my glass. "I'll get you another."

"I probably shouldn't," I said. "I haven't eaten anything and I've got to get back home at some point tonight."

I didn't know why I'd phrased it that way, *at some point tonight*, as if this wasn't just a meeting so that I wouldn't fuck up Ari's emails in the future, as if we would stretch out whatever this was until the morning.

But if Ari found it odd, her face didn't show it. In fact, she leaned forward and smiled. "We're in a very good location to get food. Tacos to our right, Cubanos to our left. We can't fuck this up."

"Oh, we—you don't have to. I'll be fine. I live in the suburbs, so I'm well versed in fast food drive-thrus."

"No, come on." She slid out from the booth and pulled me by the hand before I knew what was happening. The alcohol was doing its work, so everything had that fuzzy pulsating glow, even Ari Fox's hand around mine. A couple people near the door eyed us as we made our way out, and I wondered if they knew who Ari was, and wondered who was the ridiculously average woman who currently had her fingers laced through Ari's.

"Do you have a girlfriend?" I asked once we were outside, and once again immediately regretted my phrasing. "Not that—I wasn't—there were a couple people looking, and I'd hate if someone tweeted that they saw you out with me and—"

Ari turned to me and smirked, her cheekbones glinting in the LA twilight. She was all angles, a perfect math formula.

Oh god, I was tipsier than I thought.

"You think we look scandalous?"

"I—"

"I'm kidding, Nina Rice. So we're at the decision-making point of the night."

"We are?"

She gestured with her other hand, the one that wasn't still holding mine. "Cubanos this way. And on my other side . . . tacos."

"Don't make me choose," I said, in a voice that, thanks to the alcohol, sounded far more dramatic than I felt. Ari let out a peal of laughter and I joined in.

"Fine, fine, tacos it is." She tugged me down the sidewalk before letting go of my hand. "What about you? Do you have a girlfriend?"

"Oh, no," I said, walking alongside her. While I hated this topic, I was at least relieved I'd read as queer to her. "I don't date."

"Great, then next topic," she said. "Where did you grow up?"

"Again, I thought tonight was supposed to be about you," I said.

Ari glanced at me and raised her eyebrows. In this dimming

light, the planes of her face took on an ethereal quality, as if she was too much for the rest of us. More than? Something. I was still tipsy and the symmetrical faces of actors could have this effect on even the most sober amongst us.

"If it's about me, then I want to know where you're from."

"It's boring," I said. "It's the least interesting thing about me."

"Oh?" Ari grinned as she pulled open the door of Diablo for me. "What's the most interesting thing about you then?"

Shit, I'd set myself up for that. The truth was probably that all the facts about me were equally uninteresting, at least to someone like Ari. So I got into line and stared at the taco menu on the wall. It had, obviously, been years since I'd been here, but the restaurant looked the same. There was lots of brick and wood in odd dimensions, like the idea of a restaurant had been squeezed into another building. The taco and drinks menus were still written in neat penmanship on giant chalkboards, and the whole restaurant buzzed—softly, compared to the bar, but a buzz nonetheless.

"Do you want to grab a table, and I can order?" Ari asked me.

Thank god, my interesting qualities—or lack thereof—had been forgotten. "That sounds great. Though I didn't say what I wanted. Is this your controlling thing?"

A laugh burst out of Ari. "I was gonna suggest you *text me your order* once you sat down, but now you're at my mercy, Nina Rice. Your taco destiny is in my hands."

"Fuck," I said, and she laughed harder. "What happens if I text you my order now?"

"I'll order you the opposite. Them's the breaks." She laughed so abruptly she snorted. "I have no idea why I sounded so old-timey there."

"I'll find a table," I said, and I walked through the open doorway into Diablo's dining area. It was mostly full of long tables meant for groups, so I snagged the smallest one possible.

Again, I sat on the table side, leaving the booth for Ari, which I thought was common courtesy. The larger person shouldn't have to wiggle back behind a table and potentially past some judgmental stranger.

I actually liked my body, or at least I'd come to. I couldn't believe the time I'd wasted back in high school, staring into the mirror and hating what I saw. I'd wanted to be skinny like girls on TV, like popular girls at school. Back then I'd been convinced it would have unlocked something for me. It wasn't only that I'd expected the world would have welcomed me more, but something inside of me would have been unlocked too. The world had never really felt—well, how I thought it should have felt.

Nothing changed until early into my first night at USC when I'd tagged along with my roommate to a party. She'd joined up with people she already knew better than me, and I'd ended up sitting scrunched up on a lumpy futon next to a fellow freshman. Kimberly was a gorgeous Black girl with a buzzed head and dramatic eyeliner who was majoring in Film Studies. She hailed from the other side of Missouri, a coincidence we'd excitedly exclaimed about, though all we'd ended up talking about was our love/hate obsession with the TV show *True Blood*. The night had gotten later, as nights tended to do, but no matter how many people had crowded into that dorm, I'd stayed parked right there, hanging on every last word from Kimberly's lips. In fact, I hadn't been able to stop looking at her glossy pink lips, and then suddenly those lips were on mine. Later on that night, alone in my dorm room bed, I hadn't been able to sleep, so consumed I'd been by identity and what this meant. But in that moment, it hadn't been like that at all. In that moment the only thing I had cared about was kissing Kimberly back, arching my entire body away from that shitty futon and toward her, wondering how far one should go in the middle of a party being held in a very small room. Later I'd thought about the bigger picture. But when Kimberly and I had been on only our second, third, fourth kiss, the words in my head were brief and succinct. *Yes, now,* and *finally.*

Kimberly and I had decided that first base was as far as our senses of decorum would take us in public, but only a few nights after that party I'd gotten a text that her roommate was out for the night. Underneath her, in her tiny dorm bed, I'd watched her explore my body with her hands and her mouth. Noises left me that I'd never heard from my own mouth before, moans and gasps and giggles—and that was all before the first orgasm I'd had at the hands of someone who wasn't me.

I'd been all the way back in my own room early the next morning when it hit me that I'd never remembered to be embarrassed about my body the entire time. It had been like a magic trick, because just that fast I'd known I'd never be embarrassed again. How could I have hated my body, *this body,* curves, fat, cellulite, and all? How could I ever again think *this body* might not be good enough for someone else? Whatever had been locked up for me before had been thrown open.

Still, no matter what *I* thought, living in this world could be a real reminder that it wasn't always built for anyone bigger than a size XS. I could love my plus-size everything and still not want to squish into a little booth. Leave that to my celebrity . . . boss? Friend? No, god, not *friend.* Associate?

Ari slipped into the booth and I tried to put all thoughts about—well, my body and orgasms out of my head. I only partially accomplished this task.

"So have you come up with an answer?" she asked. "What's the most interesting thing about you?"

"I'm at an 862-day strcak on the *New York Times* Daily Crossword," I said. "Is that something?"

"Hell *yeah* it's something." She leaned in a little. "So you're extremely smart."

"It's like a logic thing," I said. "Once you learn how the crossword thinks, it's not that hard."

"*How the crossword thinks?*" She laughed, but a laugh so warm and open that it didn't feel at my expense. "How does the crossword think?"

"Well, OK, for example, one rule I always go by is 'when in doubt, it's a pun,'" I said, even though this was probably more detail than she actually wanted. "Like, if it *can* be a pun, it almost always *is* a pun."

Ari raised an eyebrow. "So you've outsmarted the crossword."

"No, I just pay attention to patterns."

"Sounds like you've outsmarted it eight hundred and sixty-two times, actually," she said with a grin. "As to your earlier question, no, I don't have a girlfriend. No one will send me jealous texts about the scandalous photos you think someone's captured tonight."

"I didn't say anything about scandal," I said. "But you're—you know, famous. People must say shitty untrue things about you on the internet."

"I mean, I'm a woman on the internet, obviously people say shitty untrue things about me. Yes, add in my career and my sexuality, I level up a bit. But, nah, I'm not the kind of—do we have to say *famous*?—person who has random pictures pop up on social media. Sometimes queer kids want to take pictures with me, but they're very wholesome, and they tag me and say the nicest things you can imagine."

"That sounds ideal."

"It's *ideal*," she agreed with a nod of her head. "I don't know what'll change with this movie coming out this fall, and I feel like an asshole for partially dreading it."

"Gold Derby says you're the odds-on favorite to win Best Supporting at this point in the race," I said, and she nodded glumly. "Wait, isn't that the point?"

"Sometimes I don't know what the point is," she said softly, but then her eyes lit up as a waiter approached our table. I saw the contents of his tray and audibly groaned.

"You didn't," I said, but it was too late because the mustachioed and tattooed waiter was already dropping off the drink Diablo was known for, a beer topped with a savory popsicle to turn the whole thing into a michelada.

"I couldn't resist." She grabbed her popsicle and dunked it into the beer before popping it into her mouth. I watched her lips close around it and quickly turned to my beer for a few cold, hopefully bracing, sips. *Seriously, what was this night?*

"I haven't had one of these in years," I said, though I remembered the rhythms, switching between sips of the drink and licks of the popsicle. The whole thing was more than vaguely sexual; there was no nonpornographic way I'd ever figured out to consume a popsicle in general, much less this one. It was so *wet.*

Ari locked her gray-blue eyes on mine, as we'd accidentally fallen into some sort of popsicle-consuming rhythm. We both laughed at the exact same moment, and somehow it felt safe despite all the reasons it shouldn't have been.

"Sorry I was whining about all my career success," Ari said with a raised eyebrow. "Seriously, I'm happy! It's just strange."

"You can whine," I said, as if this was going to be some long friendship where we set boundaries with one another. Whatever this meeting had become would be over soon, and as long as I didn't fuck up any emails, the most I'd see of Ari Fox would be potentially at the next Exemplar holiday party. "I mean, I feel uncomfortable when a Starbucks barista flags me as a regular and guesses my drink in advance. I can't imagine what your life is like."

Ari shrugged and dunked her popsicle into her beer. "My life is mostly really fucking good. But I'm worried that if things change, it won't be, and that it'll be my own fault."

"To be fair, I feel like that all the time, and I haven't done anything like you."

She leaned forward. "Yeah?"

"Yeah." I didn't elaborate, but we held eye contact for a bit. I think it was enough.

The waiter dropped off two taco holders packed with—

"Ten tacos?"

"I might have gone overboard. I got nervous we wouldn't have the same taste, so I just kept ordering."

I grabbed a fried chicken taco and took a bite. The suburbs had gotten slightly less uncool since I'd moved up there, but there was still nothing like a perfectly cooked hipster taco right smack-dab in Los Angeles. I didn't mean to let out food orgasm sounds, but a bit of one definitely trickled out anyway, and I could tell from Ari's smirk it did not escape her notice.

Even with the addition of the michelada, by the time I'd finished more of the tacos than I would have admitted in a court of law, I was stone-cold sober again and ready to make the drive back home. Ari insisted on walking me to my car, even though I felt safe and, more importantly, wanted to leave her with some mystery and not the irrefutable fact that I drove a sad old car.

A storefront caught my eye as we neared the Honda, and a conversation came back to me. Before I knew it, I couldn't stop myself.

"Do you know any cool weed shops?" I asked. "Not for me, my aunt got knocked out by a strong edible but she still wants to try something for pain management. Sorry, I'm explaining way too much of this, I doubt you want to hear about my aunt's arthritis."

"On the contrary, your weed-seeking aunt is now the second most interesting thing about you." Ari grinned at me and brushed her hair back from her face. "There's a place around the corner I usually go to. I'm not sure how cool it is, but I'm sure they'll have something at an appropriate aunt level."

"Thanks, I'll try to find it on my way back to the freeway. What's it called?"

"I'll navigate," she said. "Which one's your car?"

I didn't want to gesture to the Honda straight ahead, but that was outweighed by just how much I didn't want this evening to end. So I unlocked the car and held the passenger door open for Ari.

Chapter 6
A Fifth Location

Once we arrived at T.H. Oui, a security guard checked our IDs and waved us into the actual store. Pot in all forms was laid out underneath a shiny glass countertop like something endorsed by Goop. It wasn't my first time in a dispensary, but the setup was still startling. Smoking weed felt like a dirtbag thing I'd occasionally done in college, but now it was big business in a sleek Gwyneth-esque shell.

"How can I help you ladies tonight?" a salesperson asked us, and I was about to wave him away with my classic *just browsing* excuse, when Ari spoke.

"We need something really light in an edible," she said. "It's for her grandma's arthritis."

"It's my aunt," I said, even though I supposed the details didn't matter to this salesguy. Ari snorted, and I felt silly. But, then again, she didn't have to be with me at all. This was entirely her choice, and I still had no idea why.

The salesguy recommended a few different products, and before I could do anything, Ari told him we'd take everything, plus a pack of pre-rolls, and handed him her credit card.

"It's for *my* aunt," I said.

"The pre-rolls are for me."

"That's, like, one-sixth of the order."

She flicked her eyes toward me dismissively. "Whatever, I'm expensing it."

"Trust me, your accountant won't let you do that."

The salesguy laughed as he handed Ari's credit card back to her. "You two are cute. Sound like me and my girlfriend."

"Oh, we're—"

"Very flattered." Ari took the shopping bag from him—for some reason, all high-end dispensaries had extremely fancy shopping bags—before looping her arm through mine and pulling me out of the store.

"What—"

"Oh, calm down, Nina Rice, you're way too easy to fuck with." She slid the pre-rolls out and tucked them into her pocket before handing the bag to me. "I hope one of those works for your aunt."

"Me too." I felt the fun of the evening slide away, because my least favorite thing in the entire world was watching Lorna lose mobility and freedom. I knew she was happy at Oaken Troves, but things were definitely headed in *a direction*. If I could help relieve that pain even a little bit, I couldn't imagine how grateful I'd be.

"You're close to your aunt, I guess," she said as we got back into my car.

"Yeah." I was so flooded with sudden emotion that I wasn't sure I could talk about Lorna without choking up. So I left it at that. "Where are you parked?"

"I Lyfted," she said. "I'm not sure why I got back into your car, I could just get one from here."

"Oh, sure," I said, disappointment nibbling at me even though in reality the evening should have ended after the first location, and we were leaving the third. "Where do you live? Sorry—it's none of my business."

She shrugged. "Echo Park. I think I can reveal that much. I'll grab a ride home from here, unless . . ."

I waited for her to complete the sentence, but she only trailed off.

"Unless what?" I finally asked.

"I know this is extremely irresponsible to even suggest, but you could also bring me home, we can smoke one of these, and walk to the diner near my place for pie while you sober up to drive all the way back home."

A fourth location? A *fifth* location?

"Sorry," she said. "You probably need to get home. I'm just having a good time and have, literally, nothing going on."

"I don't either," I said. "I'm in."

Ari's house wasn't what I expected, but that was likely thanks to Hollywood stereotypes and not reality. It was just one of many bungalows crammed into a crowded block, earth tones and no chance of street parking, just like every other little home here.

"You can park in front of the garage," Ari directed, pointing toward the freestanding garage next to the small house. "Come on."

I followed her across the tiny lawn, which had been turned—like many in Los Angeles—into rocks and succulents only. There were so many Southern Californian droughts that it helped lessen water use here, and it made me smile to think of Ari as someone who cared about that. Socially responsible and hot? A perfect combo, really, not that it mattered. Tonight might have had the look of a date, but it was still work. Or something like it anyway.

Ari let us into the house, and I gazed around at the front room. It was big, considering the home was small, and filled with bright framed artwork and floor-to-ceiling bookshelves packed with so many titles that some shelves seemed to be double-stacked. I'd expected something—not something *spe-*

cific, exactly, but something—thanks to her career and the paying for everything. But this wasn't how millionaires lived. I guessed that Ari wasn't actually a millionaire; she was a working actor who made more than me, but, then again, who didn't.

"That's my thing on set," Ari said, following my eye line to the bookshelves.

"Reading?"

"I mean, when you say it like that, it doesn't sound very exciting." She laughed and headed out of the room. "Want a LaCroix?"

Always, so I called out an affirmative and tried not to stalk around the room like a creep—or a superfan—waiting for Ari's return. The room felt lived in—her gray sofa was clearly expensive, but I could tell which end must have been her regular spot, and the whole thing was lightly dusted with cat hair. There were books on the coffee table too, not coffee-table books, but new hardcover novels with bookmarks holding their spots.

"I always read two at a time." Ari returned with two cans of pamplemousse LaCroix and a fancy silver lighter. "It drives some of my friends nuts."

"Why?" I asked as I eagerly popped the top on my seltzer. Why anything, though? Why was I standing here with a gorgeous actor when normally at this point in my evening I'd be checking my notifications for the latest crossword to post? Why was Ari standing here with me when normally at this point in the evening I'd have to assume she'd be doing—well, anything more exciting than that?

"Why does it drive them crazy, or why do I read two books at once?" she asked.

"The first—well, both, actually," I said.

"Apparently it 'seems chaotic.' But I was a really slow reader when I was a kid," Ari said, and gestured to the sofa. "Do you want to sit down?"

I chose the spot at the opposite end of the most-worn cushion, but then Ari sat down right next to me and held up the lighter and a pre-roll.

"So I used to get nervous to start reading a book because it took me so long to read and maybe I wouldn't like it," she said, and held the joint up to her lips as she lit it. She inhaled, waited a beat, and coughed only a little before exhaling. "Pfew, it's been a while. I'm pretty sure I'm feeling it already."

"It's been a while for me too," I said, taking it from Ari and inhaling lightly. The sweet smoke filled my lungs, and I managed only a polite cough before exhaling.

"What are you talking about, you're clearly a pro." Ari laughed and popped open her can of LaCroix. "Remember when we just called these joints? Now everything's so fancy, the first time I went in one of those shops I had no idea how to order anything."

"Same here, I felt very old and stupid all at the same time, but I guess that's just being in your thirties in Los Angeles."

Ari pulled her knees up to her chest, and I noticed that she'd slipped out of her shoes at some point. Her toenails were painted shiny black. "I know that's supposed to be a thing, but I can't wait to turn thirty. It feels like I was still playing high schoolers yesterday, and it's not like I was ever going to play some ingénue it-girl anyway."

I passed the joint back to her. "Isn't that what your new movie is, though?"

"Maybe," she said, but then shook her head immediately. "No. For like ten queer people, maybe. Not in general, no one else thinks that. Hollywood still expects that girl to be femme. And straight! Not this." She gestured to herself as if she was some unwanted, indefinable object.

"You're kidding," I said, the pot unlacing my words from one another, letting them flow out instead of holding tightly back somewhere in my brain. "I mean, you're *beloved*."

Ari flashed her smile at me. "Ah, you're one of those ten queer people."

"No, I—" My cheeks felt hot and I looked away. Her laugh found me, and I was grateful it sounded open and genuinely entertained, without a trace of malice or mockery.

"I know what you mean," Ari said. "And, it's true. This year could change everything. I'm not sure I'm ready for that, or if I want it, even if it's the thing I've been going after for practically half of my life now."

"I'm glad you are," I said, "or at least that you did. What you do does mean a lot to people. More than ten people."

She watched me, a smile holding lightly on her face. I'd been embarrassed at only about a thousand moments tonight, but for some reason I wasn't now. I held her gaze and kept the moment going.

"Thank you, Nina Rice." Her smile switched, a little, and I felt like I could tell that she was up to something. "What do you say we kill these seltzers and go find some pie?"

Nothing had sounded better in a very long time.

"Wait." Phoebe set down her coffee cup and stared at me. "Tell me again."

"What part?" I asked.

"The *entire* part, you dingdong," she said, though in an affectionate tone. I couldn't believe I'd willingly let Phoebe out of my life for so long. No matter that it wasn't the responsible thing to have her back, I found it tough imagining letting go again.

Our dynamic had been like this—exempting the three years where I didn't talk to any of my friends—since Phoebe and I had met. It was, of course, always scary when your friends fell into new serious relationships. Bianca and I had weathered a lot of new girlfriends since we became friends freshman year of college, but I'd known right away that Phoebe was different.

Wife material, we'd joked, but the truth was that we hadn't been joking that much, maybe at all. I'd imagined my friendship with Bianca shifting, becoming less important to her, but then instead, Phoebe became more important in my life. I might have had the longer history with Bianca, but it could be easy to forget that; Phoebe fit so well too.

"I can tell you're thinking that some part of this story is *meaningful*," I said. "And I can also assure you *none of it is*."

"Uh-huh. I'm always heading to five different places in one night with attractive women and my wife is *completely fine with it*."

"She would have been fine with this, trust me, because it meant nothing." I said this even though there was at least one moment from last night that I couldn't stop replaying in my head. Ari and I had watched each other, sitting close, in her living room, and if it were another night or if she were another person—or, more importantly, if *I* were another person—a moment like that could have meant something.

But, of course, Ari and I were who we were, and that was that.

"Nina, seriously, this story. If anyone told it to you, you'd think—"

"I promise you, it was never like that. Please, she's famous and hot, and I'm . . . suburban at best."

"Look, I'm not here to coach your self-esteem, but you've had hot girlfriends," Phoebe said. "No matter what you think of yourself, that much has been proven already, yeah?"

"Well, *sure*, but they weren't on an Oscar nomination short list," I said.

Phoebe threw her head back and laughed. She rarely let go that much for so big of a laugh, so it was hard not to be flattered . . . even if it was kind of at my own expense.

Phoebe had invited me for coffee today, as she had a meeting in North Hollywood, and she considered that *practically half-*

way for us to meet. It wasn't, exactly, but it was close enough, a shorter time in traffic than much of the rest of Los Angeles. Plus I'd forgotten what a firm negotiator Phoebe was. It was no wonder she was so successful in business when she made me jump in my car to battle the freeway for no other reason than to grab a latte and chat.

Plus Phoebe always knew the best places; I adored this spot as soon as I parked today. This location of Groundwork Coffee had set up inside of an old train depot, and so the coffee shop was full of original antique details. Phoebe and I sat outside under old-fashioned scaffolding.

"Can we change the subject?" I asked.

"Nina, literally, I can't think of anything other than the spring wedding I'm going to plan for you and Ari Fox," Phoebe said, and I frantically looked around to make sure that no one heard her say that. "Who do you think is sitting near us, Lesbian Twitter?"

"I know you're kidding, but Lesbian Twitter is everywhere." I gestured around us. "Anyway, please, let's talk about something else. Anything else. What's new with you?"

"Literally nothing's new with me, ever, it's great. My job is stable, my wife's the best, what else is there?"

Of course, I knew that Phoebe and Bianca were waiting to adopt, but I also knew better than to bring that up. I imagined a wait like that, no matter how long, was interminable, and that if she had news she wanted to share, she'd share it.

"So . . ." Phoebe tipped her cardboard coffee cup way back to take the last sip. "When are you seeing her next?"

"Excuse me? I thought I made it clear enough that any romantic notions are all on you. In reality it was a work appointment, and hopefully now that's all taken care of, and I can write better emails."

"Nina, seriously? You think that woman took you to four locations—"

"It was actually five," I interrupted, and immediately regretted it as Phoebe's face lit up even more.

"*Five locations*," she said, in as much of a trill as my extremely professional friend had ever used. "You think this was all so you could write better emails."

"I think celebrities—or whatever she's considered—are used to having things their way. So we had the night she wanted, she'll trust me more, and that'll be that."

Phoebe opened her mouth, so I started talking faster.

"Obviously I know what a night like this could mean for someone else. But with someone who wants things a certain way, especially someone who's—" I could have listed a collection of actor stereotypes, but after spending time with Ari it didn't feel honest throwing out *rich* or *famous*. So I just stopped there.

"I will allow that . . . celebrities occupy a slightly different corner of the universe than you or I," Phoebe said, and I burst into excited giggles.

"In the entire history of our friendship," I said, "I'm not sure I've ever heard you admit to being wrong."

"In no way was that what I was doing," she said, but with a little grin that let me know that, for once, she was admitting that I might be right.

Chapter 7
The Ari Incident

Joyce sent an email the next day, while I was getting ready for my weekly lunch with Lorna.

> *To: nrice@gmail.com*
> *From: jharris@exemplar.com*
> *Subject: Ari Fox Follow-Up*
> *Message: Hi Nina,*
>
> *Hope this finds you well. Let me know when Ari reaches out, if she does indeed do so directly, so that you and I can have a quick chat before you meet with her one-on-one. You know the drill by now, of course, but it's always good to strategize before any meeting.*
>
> *She may, of course, feel heard now that she's met with both of us, and the point could be moot, or she may connect directly with me. But do drop me a line if you hear from her.*
>
> *—J*

I felt my face pulling back into a *yikes* expression as I read Joyce's email. Why hadn't I emailed Joyce to let her know we were meeting? A kneejerk *but we had an in-person meeting where we discussed this already* reaction reared up in me, but I knew the truth. If the client had been anyone but Ari Fox, I would have jotted off a quick update to Joyce. But, no. She had been the only one I had a crush on. I'd texted Ari at night, in my bed, wearing only a T-shirt and underpants.

(All right, Tess Gardner was extremely hot and I'd always gotten a certain vibe from her that it seemed unlikely an A-list star would ever cop to publicly, but A-list stars might as well be literal stars out there in the galaxy for how likely it was I'd ever interact directly with them.)

I began a potential response.

Hi Joyce!

Hope you're having a great week!

That sounded far too upbeat.

Hi Joyce,

Hope your week is going well. Ari texted me last week and we ended up chatting for a bit and it was easier to make plans directly with her. We ended up going out earlier this week, initially just for drinks but those turned into dinner and

Good lord, Nina, enough information? It was a wonder I didn't include the detail about the T-shirt and my underwear.

Hi Joyce,
The trouble is, really, that Ari is extremely attractive, and sometimes she gives me these looks that—in any

*other circumstance, truly—I would take another way. I
would have leaned over when we were sitting side-by-
side on her sofa and seen where the night would have led
us. Maybe the fifth location wouldn't have been a diner
for pie, but her bedroom.*

Obviously, no.

Hi Joyce,

*Hope your week is going well. Ari did reach out directly,
and we grabbed drinks a couple nights ago. She seems
satisfied with everything, so I'm comfortable working on
her account moving forward.*

Thanks,
Nina

I was satisfied-ish with that answer, so I hit *send* and tried
to let the matter go from my brain. In the scheme of things, it
wasn't too horribly unprofessional. Until I thought about sharing a joint on a client's couch while wondering what said client
looked like underneath her clothes. It hadn't been a particularly
professional evening, but as it was happening, I hadn't thought
too much about that aspect. In some ways I felt like I hadn't
made any choices at all; Ari had swept me along with her, and
I was along for the ride.

My phone buzzed almost right away, and I wasn't surprised
to see it was an Exemplar number.

"Hi, Nina? This is Max for Joyce. Can you hold?"

I technically understood why busy executives often had
their assistants dial for them, but there were truly not many
things more Hollywood than getting called to be put, immediately, on hold. "Of course."

The generic "cool" hold music blared for only a few seconds.

"Nina, how's your afternoon?"

Clearly, Joyce knew that I knew that she was about to reprimand me, and yet right now I was not supposed to answer *obviously pretty shitty, Joyce.* "Good."

"Well, this won't take long. I just wanted to chat about the Ari incident."

Shit, it was already categorized as an *incident*?

"I understand you two set up the meeting—the potential for the meeting, at least—with me, but I still would have appreciated being looped in. As you know, there can be so many pitfalls and concerns when dealing directly with talent, and Ari's far from my easiest client." Joyce chuckled lightly. "Honestly, relative to fame, I'd say Ari's above and beyond my most difficult client. So I would have liked to review more with you beforehand, get some talking points in mind for you, et cetera."

"I fully understand," I said.

"If she reaches out to you directly again, please let me know," she said. "I'll touch base with her soon to make sure everything's good on her end."

"Great," I said, though maybe a tad too brightly. I tried to bring it down a notch. "I'm sorry again for the misunderstanding."

"Sure," Joyce said, and I could tell her attention was already elsewhere, putting out the next fire. "We'll chat soon."

I said goodbye and clicked off my phone, feeling the finality of whatever this had been even more clearly. If there was anything that put my night with Ari into perspective, a reprimand from Joyce didn't hurt. Ari was my job, and the job was done.

Lorna was, of course, holding court when I arrived at Oaken Troves, but she quickly waved goodbye to her friends and hustled me over to the cafeteria.

"What's on the menu today?" I asked, determined to be my usual self and not show how much Joyce's call had rattled me.

"It's taco day," Lorna said brightly, then paused. "Well, there were some complaints about how messy the tacos were last time, so Chef Carlos has invented a taco casserole that's neater to eat. Have you ever heard of such a ridiculous thing?"

"I mean, we're from the Midwest, of course I've heard of just about every single casserole in existence," I said. "I actually just went out for tacos the other night, but a casserole sounds kind of enticing."

"Ooh, out! I miss those days. Let me live vicariously through you," Lorna said, as she guided me to her usual table. "Was this a date?"

"Definitely not a date," I said. "It was for work."

Lorna made a pained face. "That email thing still?"

"Yes, that *email thing* pays my bills, thank you. Anyway, an actress that my boss represents wasn't happy with my emails, so she thought if we spent time together—"

"Ooh, an actress! Is it anyone I'd know? Is it someone, you know, like you?"

"I don't think you know her, and if you're asking me if she's queer, yes, she is. If you're talking about some other way she might be like me, you'll have to give me a few more context clues."

Lorna waved her hand. "Well, of course that's what I meant, but I still feel like I'm not supposed to say that word."

"You're absolutely allowed to say it. Anyway, her name is Ari Fox, but—"

"Nina, it's so good to see you!" Nat sat down across from us, followed by Choon Hee. "Were you two talking about Ari Fox? I just read an article about her in *The Hollywood Reporter*, she's very buzzy these days."

"Why are you reading *The Hollywood Reporter*?" I asked, as servers dropped off finely diced greens for the table. Everything at a retirement community was pretty easy to eat, and to be honest, as a person who lived in fear of eating sloppily in public, I didn't mind it.

"Nina Louise, don't you know? Nat used to be one of the top publicists in the business! We all have long lives and résumés here, after all."

It shouldn't have struck me with such force, but the truth was . . . it did. Lorna had been retired by the time I moved to LA for college, and the truth was I didn't think much about her life before that. It wasn't that I didn't care; it just didn't come up all that much. We talked about the *now*, about lunches and what was new with her friends, not the *then*.

"I'm sorry," I said, making eye contact with Nat. "Do you know I work for an agent?"

"Of course, dear, Lorna talks about it all the time! We didn't need people like you back in my day, of course. Emails? Sounds exhausting! All those social medias made for teenagers that adult actors have to play nice on? I'm glad I never had to deal with that."

"It is a little exhausting," I admitted before digging into my chopped salad.

"Well, especially when you date the talent!" Lorna said, and Nat and Choon Hee's eyes grew into wide circles like cartoons. "Nina went out with Ari Fox for tacos!"

"Lorna," I snapped, and immediately felt terrible for anything less than a polite tone to my family member who'd done the absolute most for me and who was likely just starved for younger person gossip considering how long it had been since I'd gone out on what anyone of her generation would deem a date. I wasn't the best young person to live through vicariously. "It wasn't—"

Hopefully Nat didn't have any remaining industry connections, because she and Choon Hee were already practically physically buzzing with this fake news. I had to move quickly.

"I am *not* dating Ari Fox," I said, with as much strength as possible without, hopefully, sounding rude. "It was a business dinner, thank you, and not romantic in the least."

"Nina says it's not romantic." Choon Hee gestured to Nat

and Lorna with what looked like an eye roll. The crew was extra sassy today. "But look at her face! Have you ever seen her blush like that?"

"I'm not blushing! It's the spices in the—" I looked down at my chopped Caesar salad and prayed the conversation moved along. The blush was hardly because they'd struck on something real. Why would anyone on earth presume that Nina Rice, boring and average and cursed, could date someone *at all*, much less someone deemed buzzy by this incredibly picky industry?

After lunch I followed Lorna back to her cottage and presented the fancy shopping bag I'd stuffed into my purse. "If you want to try brownies again—or a couple other snacks—these are supposed to be lower dose and more easygoing."

"Nina Louise, that's very sweet of you." She peered into the bag. "I trust you a great deal more than I trust that DJ grandson of Nat's."

"I'm flattered."

We laughed, but I saw Lorna's expression shift. I hoped this wasn't about earlier; I felt shitty enough about disregarding Nat's career—that Nat would have even *had* a career—as it was.

"You know I was just teasing you earlier, don't you, sweetheart? Of course I want you to be happy, and if that means falling in love with some buzzy actress, wonderful! But what I *really* want is for you to be happy, period, whatever that means for you."

"I'm fine," I said, and her expression deepened. If only I had the words to explain everything, to let Lorna in more. We hadn't talked much about my breakup with Taylor, simply that it had happened and that it made sense for me to take over the condo at least temporarily. And for that I'd been grateful. But it didn't make it easy to talk about my love life or *my happiness* now. Between that and acknowledging that the seniors here had whole lives before I'd even been alive, I felt like I was fucking up the one relationship I thought was secure. "Lorna, I really am OK."

"Well, my dear, I'll take your word for that," she said, so kindly, and I gave her a gentle squeeze before heading back to the rest of my life.

Chapter 8
Nina, Party of Two

My first task every morning—after starting a pot of coffee—was sitting down at my computer to hop in all of Joyce's clients' email inboxes. Even though the email addresses were only used for Exemplar-specific communication, it wasn't unusual for people, now in possession of an actor's contact information, to reach out to said actor again. If I checked the accounts at least once a day, nothing important ever slipped through the cracks. (A lot of other things didn't slip through the cracks either: invitations to baby showers, requests for donations to charity marathons, and of course the more than occasional romantic or sexual proposition. I'd gotten good at knowing which emails to forward to Joyce, but obviously the funniest hookup requests went no matter what.)

Everything was as it normally was as I zipped through the list in alphabetical order, logging in and out and forwarding a message to Joyce here and there.

And then I hit the Fs. Let's be real, I hit the *Fox, Ari*.

To: arifox1@aol.com
From: afox95@gmail.com

Subject: So what happens
Message: if I email this account?

I stared at my screen for a long moment. She was just, I was positive, testing Joyce. Wasn't she? Ari was an admitted control freak, and she wanted to see how the entire process unfolded. That was all this was, and the fact that I was suddenly out of breath and warm all over was *ridiculous*. The fact that no one could see me was the only thing saving me from total humiliation at this point.

To: afox95@gmail.com
From: arifox1@aol.com
Subject: re: So what happens
Message: Hi Ari,

This is Nina, but I'll forward this along to Joyce if you have any further questions about how email communication functions in and out of Exemplar.

Best,
NR

I swigged from my coffee mug, even though I was already too hot and out of breath. It was morning, and mornings went better with coffee. Even this one. Especially this one?

I turned back to my screen to forward the email to Joyce, but a new one had already landed in my inbox. "Ari's" inbox.

To: arifox1@aol.com
From: afox95@gmail.com
Subject: re: So what happens
Message: Nina Rice, I implore you, do not forward my very stupid email to Joyce. I just wanted to say hi. (With the added novelty of emailing MYSELF.) Hi.

I grinned and attempted going back to my coffee. This time, it was too much, between my body's sudden desperation for oxygen and the heat pulsating throughout me. I spluttered the hot liquid, barely missing my computer. And thank god for that, it was my one gift from Taylor I'd kept, a state of the art (at the time) iMac with an enormous gleaming screen and enough processing power to keep up with me as I typed scripts in Final Draft, or at least that had been the plan. It was a nicer machine than I needed to keep tabs on a baker's dozen email accounts, by far. It managed to be the one thing from my old life, though, that made me feel tethered to something from long ago without, somehow, making me miss that life too much.

At this moment, though, I couldn't even parse what felt old and new. I wasn't a complete idiot, and I knew *under normal circumstances* what messages like Ari's might mean. Hers was hardly a subtle level of flirtation, but in my experience, the more overt, the less real it was. Ari probably flirted with baristas and bartenders, servers and flight attendants, and anyone else who came across her path. I wasn't special, I was just there.

And I knew that I was a novelty; one reason I didn't usually venture out to the Exemplar holiday parties was how fascinated clients found me when they learned I was the person in charge of answering their communications that flowed through Joyce. What kind of person, I was sure they wondered, could jump from action star to indie darling and then end up in Oscar-winning territory? It would be great if I were actually fascinating, but I wasn't. I was just this random boring woman. I would let them down. Keeping to myself was wisest.

To: afox95@gmail.com
From: arifox1@aol.com
Subject: re: So what happens
Message: I'm supposed to report all communication directly to Joyce. Are you asking me to disobey Joyce? I'm normally very well-behaved.

OK, fine, this was explicitly *not* keeping to myself. I was taking advantage of the flirtatiousness of Ari's whole thing and having fun. The fun meant nothing. It would be a waste not to enjoy it a little, though, wouldn't it?

To: arifox1@aol.com
From: afox95@gmail.com
Subject: re: So what happens
Message: HOW well-behaved? Do you have to tell Joyce if we hang out again? Even if we don't get high this time?

I grinned and typed without even thinking.

To: afox95@gmail.com
From: arifox1@aol.com
Subject: re: So what happens
Message: I should be telling Joyce that you're even writing to me about hanging out again. So, yes, theoretically, I do have to tell her.

It didn't matter, though, because obviously we weren't going to hang out again, and in retrospect I seriously couldn't believe I'd gotten high with Ari. I shouldn't have even been sending *these* messages, no matter that they were leading nowhere. Joyce had made it clear that Ari was tricky—potentially trickier than it felt like when I was caught up in her aura—and no matter how fun this was, no matter how much of a crush I'd had, no matter how a moment or two had felt, this was dangerous. Dealing in celebrity was a sacred business in Los Angeles, and if bosses caught even a whiff of fandom, of unprofessionalism, they'd strike quickly.

Sure, I had a free place to live, thanks to Lorna, but I still needed my job. It wasn't just the shitty paychecks, though they did keep me fed, my car gassed, the student loan people at bay, and my savings account very slowly accumulating. Of course it wasn't the life I'd planned as college came to an end and I'd figured out what kind of future I'd wanted. Twenty-two-year-old me thought by now I'd be married with a dog and a cult-favorite TV show I helmed as head writer and showrunner. But it was something—it was *my* something, and I didn't want to lose what little I had.

> *To: arifox1@aol.com*
> *From: afox95@gmail.com*
> *Subject: re: So what happens*
> *Message: Pretty sure I'm the client and therefore in charge of communications, so I say we get dinner and leave the lovely Ms. Harris none the wiser. I can come to your far-flung suburb, just tell me when/where. How's tomorrow?*

> *To: afox95@gmail.com*
> *From: arifox1@aol.com*
> *Subject: re: So what happens*
> *Message: Seriously, I should run it past Joyce.*

> *To: arifox1@aol.com*
> *From: afox95@gmail.com*
> *Subject: re: So what happens*
> *Message: Seriously, it's OK if you don't. When/where and I'll see you tomorrow, the well-behaved Nina Rice.*

It still all felt unreal, which is why I just kept going through the motions of it, by offering restaurant suggestions and agreeing to 8 p.m. Plus my rational self really could make sense of it; besides my novelty as the person behind the person, so to speak, Ari was Joyce's most difficult client for exactly this reason. Well, maybe not *exactly*, but she was an admitted control freak. A control freak couldn't like the idea of her messages automatically forwarding out of her control. She was pushing and testing boundaries, and I was wrapped up in those. Maybe I *was* a boundary.

And then, before I could respond, she was back. Pushing more boundaries?

To: arifox1@aol.com
From: afox95@gmail.com
Subject: re: So what happens
Message: I've changed my mind. If I'm coming up to the
suburbs, I want a suburban night out. Is there a Chili's
or a TGI Fridays? Shall we split a Bloomin' Onion at an
Outback Steakhouse? Tell me when/where, Nina Rice.

And that was how I ended up at a TGI Fridays on a Saturday night, waiting in the crowded lobby for Ari fucking Fox. I allowed myself spare moments, while jostled between giant families and packs of teens wildly flaunting their bad fake IDs. (Somehow, I had been both not cool enough to have had a fake ID but also to know if I had, I would have used it for a better night out than a goddamn chain restaurant.) My heart raced every time the entrance doors swung open, and I wondered what it would be like to wait here for her, for real. To know we'd kiss when she arrived, that I'd be allowed to fold myself into her arms and inhale her scent for as long as I wanted. To know the night would move elsewhere, that we'd be in my bed later. It didn't need to be real to be a nice escape for a few fleeting moments, particularly from this crowded room.

"Nina Rice."

Somehow Ari had gotten in while I was enjoying one of my moments away from the world of TGI Fridays. I'd worried I'd underdressed, in my comfiest pair of ripped jeans and a soft J.Crew V-neck, but Ari was also in jeans and a T-shirt, and bright white sneakers I suspected were unreasonably expensive and difficult to find.

"Hi," I said, and failed miserably in trying not to smile. "I put my name in but it might be a bit. I didn't realize this was such a destination on the weekend."

"We could have gotten into Bestia more easily," Ari said with a grin before pulling me into a hug. It was hard not to enjoy the feeling of her body against mine, her harder lines cutting my softer ones, the way she smelled drifting over me like a memory.

I stepped back from the hug and hoped my expression was more along the lines of *casual* than *thirsty*. "We can go, literally, anywhere else you'd like."

"No way, I drove my ass up to suburbia for potato skins and a drink larger than my head." She grinned and shoved her hands into her pockets. Even in the middle of this place, surrounded by screaming kids and sneering teens, against a backdrop of random sports and pop culture ephemera, Ari was serving straight-up model looks. "Is this your usual Saturday night spot?"

"Oh, yeah, they all know my name at the TGI Fridays," I said as a laugh burst out of me. "No, normally my Saturday night is on my couch working on the Sunday crossword."

"Oh, yeah, your streak."

"My streak. And the Sunday ones are the hardest—well, the longest, at least. I like to give myself a lot of time."

Ari was still smiling. "Yeah, man, don't put that streak in danger."

"I wasn't really thinking about the fact that it was Saturday when you—when we—" I just let myself cut myself off. "I can't believe you don't have more exciting things to do than—"

"This is the most exciting thing I've done in ages," she said. "Also, weekends are nothing when you have my job. I'll work six weeks straight and then be off for three months. I barely understand what time or day it is."

I nodded, but she grimaced. "What?"

"I'm doing the thing again where I sound like an asshole about my amazing life that a million people would trade theirs in for."

"You're not," I said. "You're not even complaining. My old friends who didn't have typical day jobs all used to say the same thing, and none of them were in the running for an Oscar."

"Oh, fuck you," she said, cracking up. "It's such a relief when I'm with you I can just—"

"Table for Nina, party of two!" the overhead system announced with a crackle, and even though I waited for Ari to finish that thought, she grabbed me by the wrist and pulled me to the host's station.

"We're Nina, party of two," she said, and I laughed as we followed the host to a table packed into a crowded room of more screaming people and ephemera.

We opened our laminated menus, though it seemed like Ari immediately abandoned hers and was examining mine, upside-down.

"Honestly," she said, "I love a chain restaurant margarita. I love how they serve it independent of any Mexican food on the menu. It's just its own perfect thing, free of context."

"Really? This?" I point at an Andy Warhol-style portrait of David Hasselhoff hanging next to us, sandwiched in between an old Kentucky license plate and a purple and gold foam finger. "To you this isn't context?"

Ari threw her head back laughing. "You're right, I misspoke."

"Did you grow up in the suburbs?" I realized it was something, despite her legions of publicity especially as of late, I didn't know about her.

"Can't you tell from my comfort in this booth?" she asked with a grin. "Yeah, it was all I knew until I came out here for the first time."

"Yeah, in college, we used to borrow my friend Bianca's

brother's car and drive down to Orange County because all
of us from the semi-middle of nowhere missed it sometimes.
It's comforting. No matter where you go, there's going to be a
rusty old license plate and a bad portrait."

"Wait, do you not like this portrait?" Ari asked. "I was
thinking about having one commissioned for my living room."

I shrieked in laughter as the server arrived for our drink order (obviously, two of the largest margaritas). As soon as the
server had walked away, though, I remembered my call with
Joyce and my determination not to let the night get away from
me like it had last time. Ari was a client, and I was a low-ranked
underling. I was here to get better at communication, and a
jumbo The Best Fridays™ Margarita probably wasn't going to
help that matter.

"How'd your aunt like her edibles?" Ari asked me, closing
her menu, and unfortunately bringing that extremely unprofessional night roaring back to life.

"We haven't talked since I gave them to her, so I'll probably
hear at our next lunch. We meet up every Thursday."

"For drug deals, I presume."

"That's it." I let out a sigh. "So, I want to make sure you're
comfortable with my emails, and if there's anything I could—"

"Oh, stop it, I couldn't give a shit about my emails," she said,
and I raised an eyebrow. "Fine, of course I give a shit about my
emails, but I had fun the other night. I thought you did too."

"I . . . I did. Of course." My heart pounded. Where was this
even going?

"Do you know how many people I can just . . ." Ari glanced
off into the distance. "I live a charmed life, and I find it really
fucking stressful sometimes. And I can tell you get that, because you see this side of it. The fake emails and the business
dinners and the producers I have to win over with my personality instead of just being good at the thing I came out here to
do. But a lot of people don't get it, or they're too jealous of what

I have to see the flipside. And then I feel like an entitled asshole, but I just don't feel like an entitled asshole around you."

At some point her gaze had shifted back to me, and we were watching each other closely, until two extra-large The Best Fridays™ Margaritas clanked down between us.

"Cheers to that," I said, and held mine aloft. (It took two hands.)

Ari did the same, clinking her glass against mine. "Cheers to that."

After dinner—if platters of boneless wings, mozzarella sticks, and loaded potato skins constituted a dinner—Ari suggested walking around the shopping plaza before getting back into our cars. The margaritas were stronger than I'd planned for, so it was the safest course of action.

And, of course, I was in no way ready to say good night to Ari yet.

"Did you come to LA to do this?" Ari asked.

"Walk around outdoor malls? I guess I didn't *not* come to LA to do that."

She snickered and elbowed me. "To work at an agency, manage communications, get into the guts of the industry."

"Not exactly," I said, and left it at that, as a sweet and buttery aroma swept over me. "Oh my god, do you smell that?"

"Mall pretzels," Ari said immediately. "Split one with me?"

I agreed and followed her over, the scent leading us like crime dogs on the trail of a serious drug haul.

"Really," she said, once we were in line. "Why'd you move to LA? It's fine if it's embarrassing. What's more embarrassing than wanting to be an actor?"

"It's not embarrassing if you're successful," I pointed out.

"You got me there, Nina Rice." She smiled. "Do I seem like I'd make fun of you?"

"Well, a little," I said, which cracked her up. We stood close because the surrounding tweens and teens were so loud it was hard to hear otherwise, and Ari ended up getting jostled right into me. She grabbed my shoulders to catch herself, and if I was another person I would have taken a chance and kissed her right then. OK, if I was another person *and* not the only individual over thirty in a line for mall pretzels.

"Oh my god," said a voice behind us, and we both turned to see a little pack of queer suburban teens nestled into the pretzel line. I didn't like to stereotype, of course, especially given how many I went against myself, but they were just a bit more brightly adorned than their surroundings, and *two* of them were wearing Haley Kiyoko T-shirts. And, obviously, their eyes were all highly trained right at Ari.

"Hey, y'all," Ari said with a little smile and an acknowledging head nod. They sort of collapsed into a human pile of giggles and shrieks, and I felt my heart warm. What would it have been like to be a queer teen and get that head nod from an out actor?

"You made their night," I said softly. "Probably their whole year, honestly."

"Nah, probably just their night." But she grinned, and let them call her over for some selfies while I held our place in line. It was hard to keep myself from staring back, but I did overhear her casual tone with them, how one kid kept wanting to retake the photo and she just let them without a note of impatience. I could have full-on swooned when she rejoined me in line, but luckily we were next up at the cash register and it was easy to let myself get distracted.

We split a cinnamon-sugar soft pretzel and found a spot to sit, side by side, to eat. We were almost finished before I spoke.

"It's as embarrassing, I know, as wanting to be an actor, but I moved out here to write," I admitted.

"That's rad. Screenplays?"

"TV, actually. I loved TV, but—" I cut myself off because, seriously, who cared. The dream was dead and I'd survived.

Ari licked her fingertips, while I did my best not to gape. "But what?"

I shrugged. "But, you know, TV doesn't always love me back? Especially then. There weren't any fat queer girls on TV. There weren't any queer people at all who seemed like the people in my actual life."

"Oh, really? Because I thought *The L Word* was practically a documentary," Ari said with a smirk.

"No disrespect implied to the holy text," I said, and we both laughed. "I just wanted to write about people like me, people like my community. I thought it could be *important* or whatever."

"It could be," she said.

"Could have been," I corrected. "I do this now instead. And sometimes I still get to write for people like you so . . . it still feels important."

She watched me silently.

"For the queer community, I mean." I shoved the rest of my half of the pretzel into my mouth and jumped up. "It was a dumb dream, I know. Everyone comes to LA thinking they'll transform the industry into something better."

"And sometimes people do." Ari was still sitting and still watching me. "It isn't a dumb dream. I'd kill to be in something like that, even now. Maybe especially now."

"Hopefully someone will write it," I said, wishing I hadn't brought it up, much less to Ari fucking Fox. She was doing this for real, and I was yet another failed Hollywood story, the biggest cliché in the world. It was beyond embarrassing.

"Yeah," Ari said. "Hopefully someone will."

I gestured toward the parking lot. "I should . . ."

"I'll walk you." She stood up and followed as I walked back through the shopping center toward my car. Her BMW ended up being parked directly across from my Honda, and we marveled at the coincidence like it was something far more exciting. I didn't really know why I felt a sadness creeping in at my edges. Was it the night ending so much earlier than last time, my embarrassing past out there on display, or the ever-present fact that Ari Fox was exactly the kind of girl I would have fallen for, once upon a time? And this little experiment where she got comfortable with me and I got better at my job must have been drawing to a close. Hadn't we both learned enough to get by?

"Next time is your turn again," Ari said as she opened the door to her car. "I'll see you on my turf."

"Oh—OK," I said, as a mixture of emotions swirled in me. Confusion, relief, anxiety, but I realized one surpassed the others, and I smiled. I was happy.

"But not for a while," she called. "I'm up in Vancouver shooting a feature for a couple of weeks. How about I get us into Bestia when I'm back?"

"The TGI Fridays of Downtown Los Angeles?" I feigned astonishment, and Ari cracked up. "It's a deal. Have fun in Vancouver."

"Have fun here, Nina Rice."

Chapter 9
Back to Brunch

On Sunday I drove down to LA again, this time to meet the old crew for brunch. Phoebe's invitations were all but impossible to get out of, less *will you join us* than *you will join us*, and I guessed I liked that it didn't leave me with much of a choice. Was it a good idea to reinsert myself into my old friends' lives? The sliver of a chance that Taylor was right about me—and Taylor tended to be right more often than a sliver—meant I should have continued to steer clear. I didn't want to make anyone feel anxious, didn't want anyone's life to become worse due to me. I'd done the responsible thing in retreating.

But if Phoebe made that tough for me, the truth was that I didn't mind it. And so, no matter what fate I was tempting, I walked into the cozy Café Birdie, shaded from the bright sunlight outside. It would have been a bigger moment, but since I'd taken my pledge to never run late again, I was absolutely the first one there for the weekly Sunday brunch. No one waved me over and celebrated my return. But then, just when it had started feeling anticlimactic, CJ walked in and wrapped me into a tight hug.

"Phoebe said she invited you, but I didn't want to get my hopes up too much," they said with a huge grin. Their light brown hair was still cropped short, but with sleeker lines now. I had a feeling CJ had finally started going to a barber instead of using their own electric razor.

"You look great," CJ continued. "It's good to see you in the daylight when I'm not already two flights into Phoebe's bourbon."

"Seriously," I said, though I'd meant to hedge myself in some way. The party had been one thing; I'd walked into a warm place, but a buzzed place. I'd given myself permission to get swept into it, but in some ways it was also the safest reconnection I could have forged with my friends. Brunch was more sober—at least it always started out that way—and there was less I could hide without the noise, the multiple rooms, the flights of bourbon. Parties were parties, but brunch was commitment.

"This is my girlfriend, Sofia," CJ introduced. Sofia was as tall as CJ—i.e., taller than me—with thick black hair that was somewhere between a mohawk and a pompadour, groomed perfectly into place, dressed in an orange, white, and blue striped T-shirt over army-green pants and worn-in Docs, the best combination of '90s and current style. Next to CJ in their bright floral button-down and vintage jeans, it was a great complementary couple vibe. "Sof, my friend Nina."

I bit back a smile at how warm I felt hearing the phrase *my friend Nina.*

"Hey, Nina," Sofia said, shaking my hand. "Sofia Hernández, she/her pronouns. It's good to meet you."

"Nina, same pronouns, and nice to meet you too." It *was* nice to meet her, but I wondered if things were like they were three years ago, where I wanted to become instant friends with every single one of CJ's girlfriends, only for them to disappear after a few brunch appearances. CJ was legendary, especially as the crew stood back then, with Phoebe and Bianca, and myself and Taylor together for years. Chloe rarely subjected anyone to us until it got serious, so the only rotating chair had been the one next to CJ.

"Neen!" Phoebe walked in, with Bianca right behind, and they squished me into a tight hug. I was torn between wishing no one was treating my appearance here as out of the ordinary and feeling so, so grateful I'd been missed and now welcomed back.

By the time Phoebe, always the one in charge, made her way to the host stand to check in on our reservation, Chloe banged on the window from outside with her Pomeranian mix, Fernando, in her arms. It came back to me that I'd drunkenly asked the other week at Phoebe and Bianca's party if Fernando was still alive, and it was a relief to see his fluffy little ears. They were two of a kind; tiny and adorable and feisty. We'd had a strict policy to brunch mainly at restaurants with outdoor seating so Fernando could be included, and the truth was that I was relieved that so much was the same, including his presence. Phoebe and Bianca, CJ and the girlfriend of the month, Chloe and Fernando, and now, again, me.

It really was just like before, once we were settled on the sunny patio, at a long table against a brick half-wall. Bianca took way too long to decide what to order, and Phoebe got a little passive-aggressive about it. Everyone had questions about what Sofia did (art, but teaching art to pay the bills), so she was clearly as new to them as to me. Chloe apologized plenty to the waitstaff as Fernando barked whenever one of them startled him, which was literally anytime one of them walked by. And I drank too many bloody marys and laughed too loudly at everyone else's stories. We were a mix of bright patterns and flowing fabrics, approaching middle age but not quite there yet. My chosen family for so many years before, and maybe, miraculously, again.

And if Taylor were beside me, it could have been three years ago. And as that dawned on me, something else did too. I didn't miss her very much. Maybe at all.

I'd spent years picturing this table. The mental image hadn't been the only thing keeping me from my friends, but it was a huge portion of that equation. Phoebe, Bianca, Chloe, Fernando, CJ, the girlfriend of the week, Taylor, and whoever Taylor had fallen for after me. But it turned out that I hadn't been discarded, not really, because back beside these people it was easy to feel like I'd never been gone.

"So, what's next for you?" Phoebe asked me. We were sitting next to each other, so she was quiet enough that, thankfully, no one else paid her question any attention.

"Nothing's going on with Ari," I said, despite memories of last night fresh in my head, the feel of her fingertips pressing into my upper arms in that momentary stumble, the restraint I exercised in not wrapping my arms around her and pulling her against me. Phoebe wasn't getting that story out of me. Not surrounded by my friends and a cool artist, all sloppy on morning cocktails, at least.

"That's not what I meant, but we'll put a pin in it for now and circle back," she said, and I coughed on my bloody mary at her corporate-speak in such a setting. "Oh, fuck you, Neen."

"You sound like such a professional," I said, but a slur grabbed at the edges of my words, and Bianca, who hadn't even been paying attention to us, laughed.

"I meant your job," Phoebe continued, serious lines drawn across her forehead again. "What's next after this communications gig?"

I felt Bianca trying not to watch us in a manner that suggested they'd already had this conversation. The back of my neck prickled with the knowledge my friends might have welcomed me back with literally open arms, but they didn't think I was doing OK. They didn't think that Nina now was enough.

And, considering my lack of ambition was an item on Taylor's list, this felt like something of a warning.

"I don't know what you mean, *after*," I said, trying to keep my words clear. Drunk and badly employed could be a sad combination. "I like what I do. Friday I gave a local cupcake shop a heads-up that Lindsay Covington would be featuring them on their Instagram and to get ready for a big day. It—"

Yeah, I cut myself off, Nina interrupting Nina again. When I'd written as sitcom darling Lindsay and felt the joy from the cupcake-store owner, it seemed big. I helped forge this human connection, and a small business would benefit. But out of my mouth now, it was small and unimportant. I was hardly living up to the potential of my degree and my start here. Maybe I didn't have ambition and it was something else I couldn't ignore.

"You're a really talented writer, Nina," Phoebe said softly. "That's all."

"So fucking talented," Bianca said at approximately double the volume of a normal person, and everyone laughed, including me. It was clear that Phoebe was going to let the serious moment go, and I felt myself exhale. Maybe, just maybe, it didn't have to mean anything more.

After we'd eaten and split the bill, Chloe, Fernando, and I headed down Figueroa Street so we could walk off our morning cocktail buzz before getting back into our cars. (Well, Chloe and I did, Fernando was sober.) It was a crowded part of town, restaurants next to bowling alleys next to vegan muffin bakeries next to ice cream parlors, nothing like the crowded parts of my town where familiar chains sat comfortable distances apart.

"Phoebe means well," Chloe said, and it hit me that maybe our conversation hadn't been as private as I'd hoped.

"No, I know."

"I'm sure she thinks I'm wasting my potential too," she said with a laugh. Chloe had worked as a dog groomer since we'd met, though she had an undergrad in business from NYU. "I wouldn't take it personally."

"She didn't call you out on it in public," I pointed out. Also, I thought, as far as I knew, none of Chloe's ex-girlfriends had ever written about this in a multipart list against her.

"Please, Nina, no one calls me out on anything," Chloe said, which was impossible to argue. "Phoebe and Bianca are like our parents sometimes, though, they've achieved more than all of us, own a house, sometimes feed us dinner, and also probably disapprove of how we're living."

I realized I'd felt specially pinpointed as a target of Phoebe's disapproval, that it meant something vital—and potentially catastrophic—given Taylor's list, but maybe it was simpler than that. Still, once we'd sobered up with the help of a couple of vegan muffins and I was back home, I clicked around on my computer to find a folder I'd practically hidden from myself. If I managed to never be late again post-Taylor, why couldn't I also attempt a little more ambition?

Luckily—or maybe unluckily, who knew—it was still there. A whole folder labeled SCRIPTS with a half-dozen subfolders, including my untitled TV pilot episode about an Eastside crew not unlike my own. I very nearly clicked to open the file, but my chest started pounding, and I had to catch my breath. OK, a panic attack about a document might have been an overreaction, but I was clearly not ready to open it yet. So I tried again the next morning, and the morning after that. It became part of my morning routine: coffee, my email, the talent's email inboxes, and an attempt to open that file.

Finally, on Thursday morning, my phone buzzed while I was deliberating opening it, yet again, and I was just startled enough to somehow press down on the mouse, and, there it was. *Untitled Queer Friends Show*, by Nina Rice.

Luckily, my inbox chimed, and so I tabbed away from the script and kept myself busy thanking producers for dinners,

FOR HER CONSIDERATION / 101

gift baskets, and custom dog harnesses. (Tess Gardner's pug had her own Instagram, so between the Pantheon Cinematic Universe and @rosietherescuepug's popularity—actually, we were required to call it *pup*-ularity—I knew a lot about the world of high-end dog accessories.) Since it was Thursday, my schedule was tighter, and I was just about ready to jump into the shower when my inbox chimed again.

To: nrice@gmail.com
From: jharris@exemplar.com
Subject: Ari Fox Follow-Up
Message: Hi Nina,

Ari had dinner last night with some potential producers for an upcoming project, and we should send them a thank-you. Max will get you the restaurant details, and then do me a favor and send your best attempt (with Max cc'd, please). This is our first major communication since the incident, and I'd like to double-check it myself before it goes out.

—J

It was the kind of email I sent practically every day, but I thought about each and every word, erasing each one probably an average of three times. Finally, I deleted the whole thing and imagined myself sitting across from Ari in a booth at TGI Fridays. That wasn't the correct vibe for the hottest rising star in indie film right now, but somehow I felt her—her words, at least.

I took a quick shower while waiting for Max to send the restaurant details, though it was risky to drop in anything too specific—I obviously had no idea what anyone had ordered or eaten—but sometimes it provided just a touch more personalization. Once I was out and my hair was going from wet to damp in a towel-turban, I swung by my computer to see if Max had followed up. She had, and Joyce had emailed again too.

"Your assistant's the one who just sent me the fucking Yelp link," I muttered, but Joyce wasn't checking in on timing.

To: nrice@gmail.com
From: jharris@exemplar.com
Subject: re: Ari Fox Follow-Up
Message: FYI, Ari brought along someone named Gina. You don't need to mention her specifically, I don't think, but might want to use "we" instead of "I" where appropriate.

"Who the *fuck* is Gina?" And why was I talking to myself? Sure, Ari didn't have a girlfriend when I asked the other week, but I hadn't had a girlfriend in over three years and I'd still had plenty of sex in the meantime. I'd still pined over women. Unfortunately, it seemed pretty apparent I was pining over one right now or I wouldn't feel so desperate to know who Gina was and how attractive she was and how much better she probably was at giving people orgasms, I'd presume. Her name made up half of *vagina*, after all, did that give her an edge? Not that all women, of course, had vaginas, but if Gina had a head start with those who did—

My phone alarm blared, and I scrambled to turn it off and then realized I would need to put on clothes and mascara before I'd allow myself outside, and also my inner monologue sounded bananas. By the time I was in my car and thinking of any famous queer Ginas, I was running ten minutes late. Lorna, Choon Hee, and Nat had already staked out their lunch table by the time I arrived, so I slipped into the open chair while they gossiped about something inappropriate they suspected was happening between one of the villagers and the oldest yoga instructor. Maybe it was because I'd taken such a long break from my friends, but for the first time I realized how similar Lorna's group's hangouts were to mine, and it was a nice distraction from thinking about how good the mysterious Gina must be in bed and how probably she wasn't afraid to open any documents on her computer. She probably didn't even have a computer, computers were for nerds who were afraid of documents.

"Everything all right, Nina Louise?" Lorna asked, once we'd finished lunch and were strolling back to her cottage. "You seem a little blue today, my dear."

"Just work stuff," I said, trying to sound casual though anyone could have heard the weird shaking quality to my words. "It's just been more . . . well, there are more eyes on me right now. I'm sure it'll pass and get back to normal soon."

Lorna nodded, propping her sunglasses atop her head as she let us into her cottage. She'd decorated it much like the condo, mid-century modern pieces with just enough bright colors that it was cheerful but not overly zany. I'd barely touched a thing in the condo, besides adding a vintage desk that Lorna helped me find on Craigslist. (Lorna didn't know how to browse Craigslist on her own, but she'd definitely had strong opinions when I opened up tabs upon tabs of vintage options.)

"What?" I asked, even though I didn't know why I was pushing it with one of my very favorite people. No, that was a lie, it was all Gina, and *obviously* my new inability to pretend for even a moment that I had no interest in Ari. It was hardly like I felt territorial when Chloe or CJ started dating someone new. No, this was not platonic, and while I guess I'd known that, now I *knew that*.

"I know you have fun with your email job, pretending to be famous people—"

"That's not exactly—never mind, go on."

"But didn't you move here to do something with TV, or, I don't know, what do you all watch now, Hula Hoop?"

"It's Hulu," I corrected with a smile.

"Well, you get my point, don't you?"

"Sure, I do." I didn't like this course of conversation, but it *was* better than admitting I was stressing out about some mysterious but definitely beautiful woman named Gina. "Have you been conspiring with Phoebe or something? Why the sudden interest in my lost potential?"

"I never said *lost potential*, Nina Louise. How is Phoebe? And Bianca? And that little friend of yours who was always punching people?"

"Chloe, and she only punched *one person*," I said with a laugh. "Everyone's good. I saw them Sunday for brunch. CJ of course has a new girlfriend."

"CJ has more girlfriends than I've had years on this planet," Lorna said, and I burst into laughter. "You know that I just want you to be happy, don't you?"

"I do know. So how did those brownies and other snacks work out?" I asked, eager to move the subject along.

"You were right, much more my style. Nice and soothing. I wouldn't turn down another bag of those, that's for sure. A little time off from my arthritis, but no one's going to think I've shuffled off my mortal coil just yet."

"Sounds like the perfect balance, and, yes, I'll find you more." I leaned in to give her a hug. Lorna had never slowed down her beauty routine, and so she always smelled of fresh powder and Chanel No. 5. They'd probably always be the two scents that comforted me the most, since that day at my grandmother's funeral, and I tried to let that calm me now. I felt humiliated, even if no one knew, to be struck by a crush. Weren't we supposed to be over that by a certain point in life? Should one be pulling out their first gray hairs and swooning for someone unattainable at the same time?

I said goodbye to Lorna, with a promise to hit up T.H. Oui again soon, and headed back home to my inbox. But a large box on my doorstep caught my eye as I navigated my Honda into the garage next to Lorna's vintage Mustang. I walked straight out of the garage to the front door and pulled the package inside. It had a random return address that I didn't recognize, and while I knew I should have immediately checked my email and made sure Joyce had approved my message, I grabbed a pair of scissors and carefully cut open the box.

A laugh burst out of me when the package's contents were revealed. It was a Warhol-style portrait of Hasselhoff, just like the one that had hung across from Ari and me at TGI Fridays. Ari, even if someone named Gina was giving her multiple incredible orgasms *right now*, had sent me *a gift*. Ari was thinking of me from Vancouver.

I texted her right away, even though I'd never initiated contact before. **Thank you so much for my beautiful artwork. Did you . . . have this commissioned? Is that even possible in a few days' time? (I don't know how art works.)**

I, obviously, didn't know Ari's shooting schedule, but I hardly expected to hear back from her right away. So I set up the portrait on my desk, though I wasn't sure if I'd be as productive with a color-blocked David Hasselhoff watching me work. It felt like more than Hasselhoff, though, of course; it felt like a little piece of whatever this thing was with Ari was right there, tangible, proof I hadn't made any of it up. Even if she wasn't ever going to fall for me, even if I technically worked for her, even if right now at this moment I was the last thing on her mind, this much couldn't be taken away.

I can't believe it already came! You're very welcome, Nina Rice. I hope the Hoff blesses you with creative energy and inspiration.

I grinned and snapped a photo to send to her. **Yes, inspiring me already. You didn't answer my question, though. Did you seriously commission this?**

No, this was scavenged from a New Jersey TGI Fridays that went out of business and ended up on eBay. I hope that's

not a bad omen for your future creative pursuits. I still had all those loaded potato skins in my system when I had that sent to you, so I wasn't thinking with an entirely clear head.

I could never see David Hasselhoff as anything but positive energy from here on out, I texted, and turned to my computer to finally get back to work. It was a bit anticlimactic, though, because Joyce had approved the email without any commentary, and so I was back to my normal routine, especially since Ari hadn't texted back and I had no new distractions. I took a chance, even if maybe she was trying to concentrate on Gina—or her job, of course. She was up there for a reason. Plus jealousy wasn't a good look on anyone, especially myself. I had no claim to Ari, and considering I was in no way an actual option for her, I should have been happy. Ari deserved all she wanted in life.

How's Vancouver? I texted. I couldn't bear waiting to see if dots appeared to show she was typing, so I turned back to my computer.

There were no new emails in any of my inboxes, and suddenly I realized that opening my script right now might be less scary than waiting on a response from Ari with my newly realized feelings swirling in my gut. Brightly colored David Hasselhoff looked right at me, and while I knew I was imagining it, I couldn't deny that his expression was encouraging. I tabbed back to my script and started to read.

Chapter 10
Some Inspiration

My life had turned into a new routine, past and present. Thanks to my friends, I was in LA proper multiple times a week. Of course, I was up in the outer ring of suburbia the rest of the time, but I felt more tethered to the city than I had just a few weeks ago. I was back on the group text. Back weighing in on brunch location decisions before the fact. Back gossiping about celebrities and reality TV and politics. Back saying very nice things at CJ's prompting about their girlfriend, while knowing Sofia's days were numbered.

Of course, deep down, I knew it wasn't as simple as a warm return to the fray, like the last three years hadn't happened at all. Like Taylor's list had never been sent to me. Like Taylor hadn't told me exactly who I was. Didn't girlfriends see more of you, at least the ones who were so entrenched in your life? If Taylor and I had paid bills together and spent every night together and talked about the future like it was one shared thing between us, of course she'd known me better, deep down, the nasty crevices and hidden shadows that stayed unseen by others.

And so, of course, it could still happen, at any given moment. These people that I loved so much—plus the extra girlfriend I wouldn't get too attached to and the dog—could be struck down by anxiety and despair and whatever other sinister possibilities lurked because I was in their lives. But I pushed down those fears and worked on being the best Nina possible. If the old Nina was dead, this simulation would scavenge all the good parts and try to let the old go. Just like the Hoff portrait that now watched over me.

Ari was back from Vancouver, but I didn't want to pester her. Maybe she had just started a relationship, maybe she had features or TV to film here, maybe she just needed to unwind after her shoot. Regardless, I didn't think she needed my interference in her life right now, even though the truth was that I missed her. Well, *missed* wasn't exactly accurate; I missed the possibility that a text from her could arrive and I'd be swept into her plans like magic. I missed the five locations and the mall pretzel and the way her laugh rang out without a trace of self-consciousness. And, yeah, I missed her scent, the way she pulled me into her arms for hugs, the energy that occasionally hummed between us as if it hadn't been informed it was pulling together a rising star and an industry lowling.

We hadn't *not* texted while she was away, but all I could think about was the possibility she could be with someone else, as well as my undeniable crush that made me feel like a lovelorn and thirsty teen. Nothing had actually shifted, I knew, but also it felt like everything had. So I made myself respond more slowly, less eagerly, and got ready—despite that previous Bestia offer—for Ari to disappear from my life except as an email inbox I spent every day inside.

I knew that the little chill that ran through me whenever I thought about her too much was sadness, but I also wasn't *that* sad, I told myself often. One day, probably not too long from now, Ari would be a huge star, and at parties I'd dig out the story about that month when we were sort of friends. People would beg to see the Hasselhoff portrait. It'd become part of my lore. I'd be fine.

I was headed back from a lunch with Lorna when I heard my phone buzz, and I—ignoring California traffic law—grabbed it from my bag at the next stoplight. I'd set my group text to mute so, for example, the seventy-nine messages that came in when the new Kristen Stewart trailer dropped didn't drain my phone battery while I ran out for a chai. So since I knew it wasn't the whole group, I told myself that my urgency was because it might be Phoebe with an important message. It had nothing to do with the name and emoji that appeared on my phone sometimes, nope, not at all.

What are you doing tonight? If anything, cancel it. I have a surprise for you.

I stared at my phone's lock screen, my pulse racing, my panic letting up, my relief bounding. Then the phone buzzed in my hand and I almost screamed.

Be at my place at 6:30. You can park in my driveway.

BEEP. The car behind me held its horn down for, in my opinion, an overdramatic amount of time, but to be fair the light was green and I'd gone into some kind of fugue state. I sped back to the condo and sat down at my desk, and, under the supportive gaze of Warhol Hasselhoff, composed a reply.

I'm free tonight. Can you remind me of your address?

Calm, cool, a bit removed. I was proud of myself.

By 6:25, though, as I pulled my Honda into Ari's driveway, I was anything but. Anxious, sweaty, and overly eager for any details of what this evening was about—and, of course, to lay eyes on Ari.

It hit me as I walked to her door that maybe I was meeting Gina tonight. Or some other woman. Was that the surprise? That would be a terrible one, though, right? *Surprise! I'm happily coupled, and this is how I'm telling you.* No, that wouldn't make sense. Oh, holy hell, this thing had made me stupid.

Ari swung open the door and grinned at me. "Hey there."

"Hi."

She was wearing a black jumpsuit, the top unbuttoned revealing her collarbone and her smooth skin halfway to her waist. Ari was so slim that she didn't have cleavage, but it was undeniable how much of her body was visible in this outfit and also how desperate I was to see more. The shift had fully happened and I wasn't getting this genie back into the bottle. Did that metaphor even make sense? Obviously I was merely trying to distract myself from thoughts of naked Ari Fox, who was sort of my friend, sort of my boss, and absolutely inappropriate in either case to picture this way.

"It's good to see you, Nina Rice," she said huskily before pulling me into a hug. I inhaled her scent and let myself linger there for more than a moment. Why did this too feel like coming home?

"How was Vancouver?" I asked.

"I'm getting us a Lyft, hang on." She got out her phone and tapped silently for a few moments. "Great, Karl with a K will be here in two minutes. Vancouver was good. I was so relieved to get away from the city for a second—you're in the suburbs, you get it—but it's literally nicknamed Hollywood North, so it was less of an escape than I wanted."

"Well, also you were there to shoot a feature," I said, without thinking much, but Ari cracked up.

"Yeah, fair. The shoot was fun, though, and I think it's going to turn out really well, and Deborah Huang—she's directing it—said she wanted to talk to me about a bigger role in something she's filming next year. It could have been, whatever, you know how the industry works. A bullshit conversation. Or it could be a good connection to get to do something interesting in the future. So how've you been? How's Joyce?"

"Oh, fine," I said, my heart beating a reminder in my chest. "She's been keeping an eye on my—on *your* emails. I hope everything's been OK."

"I could give a shit about my emails," she said. "OK, obviously that isn't true, or we wouldn't even know each other, but I'm sure you're nailing it now. Karl just turned off of Sunset so we should head outside."

"Am I dressed OK?" I asked, as Ari had given me absolutely no indication where we were going, and her jumpsuit was nicer than her outfit had been for our mall outing. I was in my nicest maxidress, royal blue with gold stripes and a plunging neckline, an old gift from Bianca, who'd always said I could stand to be a little less covered up. Unlike Ari, a little plunge showed a whole lot for me, so I'd also brought a cardigan in case it wasn't the sort of situation where my boobs should be so much on display. I already regretted the whole thing; I worried I looked desperate. Did the outfit even make sense? Slutty plus librarian? But as we got into the white Prius, Ari flashed her smile at me and my nerves stopped zapping around cold jagged anxiety and switched to something warmer.

"You look great, Nina Rice," she said. "You're dressed perfectly."

I leaned forward to look at the driver's—at Karl's—GPS, but Ari saw what I was doing and pulled me back. Her hand stayed on my forearm.

"No cheating," she said with a raised eyebrow, but then burst into laughter. "So how's your day going?"

I started to answer before realizing she was talking to Karl, who was an older white guy probably in his fifties.

"I just started my day," he said. "You girls are my first pickup of the night. Big date night?"

Ari grinned at me and winked. "Huge."

"Well, your boyfriends are sure lucky," Karl said, and Ari squeezed my arm tightly. We shook with laughter but, miraculously, didn't make a peep. Tears pricked my eyes and I blinked rapidly to keep them from spilling over my cheeks. Karl meant so well, probably had never watched *Brother's Keeper*, and wouldn't know that was a pretty gay jumpsuit Ari was wearing.

"That's really kind of you, thank you," Ari finally said, while I had to keep my face down and my gaze on my own feet. Well, I tried to focus on my feet but my cleavage was distracting, no matter that Ari said I was attired *perfectly*. I'd just wanted to look *nice* and it had been so long since I'd tried for *nice* in any other setting but professional. I felt exposed, in more ways than one.

When I looked up, ready to get through the rest of this mysterious drive without laughing, Ari and Karl were wrapped up in a conversation about where to get the best pastrami in town (Ari swore by Langer's while Karl was a Canter's man), and I was content to sit here inches away from Ari with the world flying by. As Karl drove further into Downtown Los Angeles, I had a sneaking suspicion where we were headed, but I let Ari keep her secret. Sometimes it was the kindest thing you could hold for someone.

I let down my façade once Karl pulled up in front of Bestia, and Ari elbowed me. "This isn't your surprise, this is just the first stop of the night. Karl, thanks so much, I hope you have only the best passengers tonight."

"They won't be as fun as you girls," he said as we unbuckled our seat belts and opened the doors. "You remind your boyfriends how lucky they are!"

"We sure will," Ari called as we got out of the car and slammed the doors.

"You're tipping him well, right?" I asked her.

"Don't worry about poor heteronormative Karl. Five stars, big tip." She grabbed me by the arm and pulled me toward the door. Bestia was a tough reservation, always booked up months in advance. I knew this not from my previous life in LA, but thanks to my job where a meal here often elicited an extra level of excitement from whomever the talent was dining with.

But Bestia, as alluring as its modern Italian menu had always sounded, had no extra allure tonight. I'd been just as happy at TGI Fridays, because I was there with Ari. Tonight there were no rusty license plates or multicolored portraits of any *Baywatch* stars, though. Bestia was deep in Downtown Los Angeles, only a block from the LA River, in an old loft space converted into a restaurant that managed to be both bright and shaded, new and classic all at once. We were seated at a cozy booth in the middle of the dining area, under simple chandeliers that lit up the walls of brick and tile, as well as Ari's perfect bone structure and glowing creamy skin. She could have been a model, here, under this lighting. Under any lighting, really, but tonight's illuminated her as if she was practically otherworldly.

We both stayed quiet as we were given menus and served water. The truth was that I didn't know what—if anything—had changed while Ari had been gone. I really only had so much access into her life. Would I have felt something slip if not for the Gina mention? I didn't know, because by now one feeling was impossible to extricate from all the others.

"Ms. Fox?"

We both looked up, and then laughed because it was hardly my name. Ari nudged me under the table, which just made me laugh harder.

A blonde woman wearing a chef's apron over a button-down and cuffed jeans smiled at us, but really mainly at Ari.

"We're big fans here, and we wanted to know if we could

treat you and your guest to a custom chef's tasting menu tonight."

This was absolutely the coolest thing that had ever happened to me in a restaurant. Honestly, ever, in any setting.

"Thank you, truly," Ari said, and I felt a *but* coming. Oh, no, my heart was already set on that tasting menu. "That sounds incredible, but I can't let you treat us. It's really important to me to support local restaurants. Not that you guys need my help, but it still matters to me."

The woman beamed, fidgeting with her apron straps. I was pleased to see Ari had this effect on everyone. "Of course. Well, let me take these menus off your hands, and we'll handle it from here. Any allergies or dietary restrictions?"

We shook our heads, and that was that. The woman—Beth, we learned—was back soon with wine, and then almost immediately with an elaborate charcuterie tray. Ari and I both went for the prosciutto first, which meant we were laughing again as we twirled the salty, thinly-cut meat into our mouths. Of course, I let out a little sound of pleasure, which normally combined with my boobs and my feelings-slash-*feelings* swirling around in my heart as well as between my legs, would have embarrassed me beyond recognition. But Ari's eyes closed in pleasure too; the food and the wine and the special care extended to us was *so good*. How could we *not* feel washed over with bliss?

"I can't believe how amazing this is," Ari said. "It's just a piece of meat."

"Thank you," I said. "I've heard about this place for so long, and this is . . . already incredible, thanks to you. Does this kind of thing happen all the time?"

"Practically never. One time a teen lesbian gave me free toppings at Cold Stone Creamery, but I still had to pay for the cone. That's the only example coming to mind."

"That's pretty good, though," I said, which made her laugh.

It felt so warm to make Ari Fox laugh again. No—not Ari Fox, the semi-famous rising star. *Ari*, the person sitting across from me. Making her laugh felt better than—well, maybe not the places my mind wanted to drift, a land of mutual and simultaneous orgasms. But it still felt great.

"How've you been?" she asked, and I detected a note of concern in the quirk of her eyebrows.

"Fine . . . why? Did Joyce say something?"

Ari smiled as she smeared pâté on a crostini. "Joyce and I discuss you much less than you seem to think. No, you just seemed a little quiet while I was up north. I worried I annoyed you with my suburban demands. I'm sure you have plenty going on without me wresting control of your evenings."

I couldn't help but laugh. "You gave me like four hours' notice tonight, and I still don't even know what we're doing after this."

"Well, *fine*," she said, but she laughed too. "This is my only setting, Nina Rice. I'm in charge or that's it. I know it can be a lot, and so I thought maybe you needed a break."

"I thought maybe *you* needed a break," I admitted, and reached for a few olives to munch on as I thought what to say next. "I mean, I'm a lot too. And this is a big year for you, you've got important industry stuff to—"

"No," she said sharply. "Shit, sorry, that came out—anyway. I'm still me, and I know you haven't known me long, but no matter how fucked up my calendar gets due to this Oscar that many people are intent on me winning next year, I'm just me. I like mall pretzels and I like spending time with the people I like spending time with."

After too many courses to even keep track of, Ari checked her watch and announced that it was time for our next destination. I felt physically full with gnocchi, spaghetti, Wagyu steak, and the Pink Lady apple crisp we'd finished with, and could have stayed in that cozy booth across from Ari for the rest of my life—or the night, at least. But after thanking Beth as many times as we could, we were on our way, out into the night and into the next Lyft. The wine and the meal had cast a sated fuzzy radiance on the evening, and I fell into the back seat of the night's second Prius with practically the feeling of afterglow, hours spent in pleasure with Ari. Again, no, it was hardly on par with the places my mind wandered, but I decided not to talk myself out of the buzz that pulsed within me. For tonight, I could enjoy my crush—Was there a more mature word than *crush*, something to make me feel my age and not like a tween at a BTS concert?—and savor the flashes of fantasy. That was the magic of tonight.

This time, we were driven only a short distance, to the Theatre at Ace Hotel on Broadway. The marquee read VARIETY PRESENTS: WOMEN IN TELEVISION.

"I got an invite to this," Ari said, and thanked our driver while pulling me out of the car on her side. "Normally I blow off industry events, and I feel like 'women in' anything these days is pretty outdated—I'd rather hear from marginalized people of all genders. But I thought maybe it would give you some inspiration for your writing."

Her hand was still clasped around my wrist, and so we were standing close as I thought about Ari planning this evening specifically for me. Did it matter that we weren't destined for each other? It was the most anyone had done for me in a long time.

"Shit," she said, with a flash behind her gray-blue eyes. "Is *this* too much? Should I have—"

"No," I said. "This is really nice. Thank you, Ari."

We, of course, had seats up front, roped off just for us. I already knew that Ari didn't like to use her fame for favors, and so to be here in a prominent place in a seat reserved for her brought on a new flush of gratitude and wonder. Wonder? Shit, I was *hopeless*.

The panel was made up of producers, showrunners, writers, and a couple executives, and while Ari was right that it didn't seem like enough to limit speakers to only one marginalized gender, at least the panel featured women of color, including at least one network development lead who definitely read as queer to me. It was a huge step in the right direction compared to the talks I'd attended a decade ago.

After I'd graduated with my degree in screenwriting, I'd gone to as many industry events as I could find. I'd scribbled pieces of advice and words of wisdom in Moleskine notepads and mingled whenever there was an opportunity. I'd learned about the different paths into TV, from fellowships to assistant gigs and seemingly endless other possibilities. I'd heard what people wanted, in scripts, in interviews, in actual writers' rooms, and dedicated a huge portion of my life to figuring out how I could fit into that world. I, no question about it, had ambition.

Suddenly, those nights didn't feel so long ago or of another life entirely. And as the panel discussed what they'd overcome and what they still wanted to achieve, I realized that I felt a sense of belonging in this room. Obviously I still had a long way to go—that untitled script was in no way ready for another set of eyes on it yet—but Ari hadn't been wrong. As I thought of changes I'd make, jokes I'd add, a romance I'd build up to differently, it hit me. I was *inspired*.

Afterward, I expected to file out with the rest of the audience, but Ari pulled me by the arm yet again. I'd sobered up entirely by now, but the buzzy feeling was apparently independent of the bottle and a half of wine we'd consumed.

Ari nodded at a security guard, and suddenly we were on the other side of the heavy doors next to the stage. Most of the panel was walking away, but a couple weren't, and they waved at us as if we'd been expected.

"Ari, I'm so glad you could make it," said the network development exec. She was a Black woman probably only a few years older than me, with wide waves of glossy black hair, wearing a multicolored wrap dress in jeweled tones with metallic sandals. "I've heard so much about you from Jenn."

"This is my friend Nina," Ari introduced, while I wondered who Jenn was. Gina, now Jenn, so many other women in Ari's life. I guess in mine too, of course, to be technical. This was not a side of me I loved. "She's an up-and-coming TV writer."

"I wouldn't say that," I stammered as the woman shook my hand.

"Peyton Butler," she introduced. "Are you staffed on a show right now?"

"Not at all, I work in communications for a talent agency," I said, for once happy to gloss up the truth a bit. "I have a pilot in progress, that's it. Ari's exaggerating—"

"Oh, yes," Peyton said with a wide smile. "I've heard all about Ari from Jenn."

"Jenn's not to be trusted," Ari said. "She's known me too long, too many secrets." She looked to me. "Jenn was a writer on the first show I did here, so she's seen me all the way through. And therefore knows far too much."

"Jenn's like that," Peyton said, still smiling. Hollywood was full of smiles hiding fangs, poison, and all sorts of hidden weapons, but I felt almost immediately that that wasn't Peyton Butler, just like it wasn't Ari Fox either.

Peyton introduced us to the woman to her right, who was a writer on a streaming TV drama I hadn't yet watched but had heard good things about in the trades. It seemed like we were all still hopped up on the crowd's enthusiasm, and while at Exemplar I was good to know my place and keep my mouth shut as much as possible, backstage felt different.

"Thank you for everything you said up there," I said to them, with a fluttering in my chest like I was getting away with something. Yes, I was Nina Rice, master of nothing besides emails disguised as someone else's, but feeding off of the energy in this room I didn't feel so far away from everyone. Maybe one day I could figure my own way in. "As someone who's still starting out—or whatever the step is before starting out, even, it just meant a lot to hear about inclusion and diversity and new voices."

"I'd love to read your script," Peyton said, and I felt my cheeks redden. "I understand it's not ready yet, but I'm here when it is." She opened her clutch and took out a business card that she handed right to me. "It was great meeting you both. Ari, Jenn says she's doing a holiday party again this year, so maybe we'll both finally be there the same year."

"Yeah, we'll see what Jenn's up to by the time December rolls around," Ari said with a smile. "But it was great to finally meet you."

"Nina, I mean it, get in touch when that script's ready," Peyton said, and I promised her that I would. Even though I was so far from being ready for that, it meant a lot to suddenly feel like the next step was possible.

We shook the panelists' hands again and were guided out the stage door with them. They had cars waiting, so suddenly it was just Ari and me again.

"Thank you," I told her. "That was . . . really perfect."

"It was no problem," Ari said. "I know I complain about this whole industry, but there really are people out there who want to help each other. Jenn was happy to make sure her friend waited for us. The other week up in Vancouver I took my co-star out to meet these producers since she's been wanting to get behind the camera instead and I thought they might be a good connection."

I realized that had probably been the mysterious Gina, and therefore no one to worry about. Ari was so giving with her time, with her connections, so of course one day—maybe soon—there *would* be someone to worry about. Not that I should have worried, it was none of my business. I was still glad that right now felt safe again though.

"It's really kind of you," I said, and she smiled softly. I volunteered to get the next Lyft since Ari had been so generous, but she stopped me with a look.

"We *could* do that," she said. "Or we could walk over to Spring Street and get ice cream on top of miniature waffles. If more dessert doesn't sound insane."

"I mean, it sounds a little insane but in a way I relate to. Plus we're walking. I'll be starving by the time we get there."

"*Exactly.* You get me, Nina Rice."

I glanced at her, and she held my gaze for this moment, behind the theatre, near the buzz and thrum of downtown but a few steps back from it. What would happen, I wondered, if I did it? I could imagine the whole thing so clearly that I could actually feel it. My fingertips on her jawline, her hands holding my waist, my breasts against hers as we leaned in at the same time, our mouths hungry and ready.

But seeing and feeling something so sharply it ached didn't make it reality. And so what actually happened was that I followed Ari down the block and over to a dessert shop where I fed my hunger for her with a waffle sundae.

It wasn't, of course, the same. But I couldn't deny it was a very good way to end a very good night.

Chapter 11
Nina Rice, Version 3

The week after Ari got back from Vancouver, Bianca begged me to join her in an exercise dance class at a gym not too far from her house that was supposedly fat-friendly and a lot of fun. She actually said *fat-friendly* and not just *body positive*, so obviously I was intrigued, but I'd just gotten to the point where I could do regular brunches with my friends again. I'd been far too removed from society—actual cool Eastside Los Angeles society—to dance in public without the assistance of alcohol, but I did offer to meet her for coffee or whatever was appropriate post-dance class afterward.

I told myself that it wasn't a big step, but I knew that it was. Back in college it was rare for Bianca and me to go even twenty-four hours without hanging out or at least studying quietly in the same place. She was the closest thing to family I had in LA, next to Lorna, and of course she was the one I'd missed the most during the last three years. Being back in her life was definitely what I'd wanted, deep down, when I ignored Taylor's words. Even if she'd been right about me, maybe it was OK to tread back a little now, hold space for my old life. If I went slowly, I couldn't destroy anyone else with anxiety. I couldn't make anyone's life worse. I could stay right here at the edge of things.

And I literally felt at the edge of things when I walked up to the café Bianca suggested we meet at. Spokes Bicycle Café was by the LA River in Frogtown, under freeways and train tracks, but still lush and green and hidden. The café's seating was a mismatched rambling collection of outdoor tables and chairs, and even though I was early, I spotted Bianca right in the middle of things. She was wearing hot pink workout gear and looking glowing and blissed out after exercise, which was not typically the post-workout vibe I exuded. Bianca was an event photographer, which meant her schedule was usually all hers and she could make time for workout classes and coffees, whereas, in order to be here, I'd set all my Exemplar-related notifications to *push* so I didn't miss anything.

"Hey, Nina." She gestured to the collection of beverages in front of her. "I took the liberty of getting you a chai, but you won't hurt my feelings if you're not in a chai mood today."

"You know that I'm always in a chai mood." I pulled the steaming mug toward me. "I'm really dull that way."

"You're not dull, you're steady." She gestured to the three beverages in front of her. "Me, I'd love to be steadier. I get so panicky once I sit down that a smoothie won't sound good and only cold brew will do. You know how I am."

I grinned and took a sip of my spiced beverage. "Thanks for asking me to meet."

"Thanks for driving all the way down."

I shrugged. "It's not so bad this time of day, and I'll be able to get home before it fully gets terrible again. I don't mind."

"Is it nice up there? I assume it must be or you wouldn't be hauling your ass back and forth all the time."

"I don't haul my ass all that often, thank you," I said, and we both laughed. "I guess. It made sense when I had to leave my—our—my place, and . . ."

"Yeah," Bianca said after a few moments of silence. "Of course. And it's Lorna's place, right, so I'm sure it's very cute."

"Well, it's a condo, on the outside it looks like every other unit there, but, yes. She decorated it perfectly, and I get to reap the benefits of that."

"How is Lorna?" Bianca asked, switching from her cold brew to a frothy pink beverage. "I was just talking the other night about the time she whisked me and you away from studying for finals to get that fancy meal out somewhere? It was like you had a real-life fairy godmother and I—well, talk about reaping the benefits!"

"Lorna's good. I worry about her arthritis because she seems so fine otherwise, like in the kind of shape I'd be thrilled to be in, in my eighties, but if her movement is more limited or her pain's worse or she becomes a 'falling risk'"—I do air quotes—"she could be moved to the other side of Oaken Troves, which isn't like a nursing home—though I think that's lurking somewhere back there too—but more assisted care. I know she wants to avoid that for as long as possible."

I noticed my breath coming more difficultly, and I blinked back tears. "I guess I'm wanting to avoid that for as long as possible too. Lorna's all I have."

Bianca reached across the table and squeezed my hand. "Lorna's amazing, but she's hardly all you have, girl. Speaking of, are you and Ari Fox fucking yet?"

I burst into shocked laughter, and Bianca sighed—defeatedly? All the nearest tables were empty, but I still looked around to make sure no one had heard her.

"I guess that's a no. I'm disappointed, Nina."

"I wouldn't hold your breath on this topic," I said, though warm thoughts rolled through me. Phoebe might have been the most bullshit-free person I knew, but none of my friends excelled in it. For Bianca to wonder, I supposed, was nice. "Though, obviously, I'm flattered."

"She's the one who should be flattered," Bianca said, like

we were talking about a girl in a mutual class sophomore year and not an honest-to-god celebrity. "If not Ari, fine. Anyone interesting lately?"

"Nah," I said with as casual a shrug as I could manage. "I don't really date anymore. It's fine. I'm fine."

"I didn't say you weren't fine. Can't I want you to be happy? Like as happy as possible? The cute condo and a cute woman and, I don't know, whatever else sounds good and cute?"

"Thank you, I know you mean well, but especially now that you're married and living in a perfect house with a baby—"

"There's no baby on the way at this point in time. I'd alert you if there was," Bianca said. "And, yeah, I know, I've been domesticated. But I'm still me, and you're still you, and we've always wanted the best for each other, right? I can want that even if I'm a homeowner with an accountant and a money management team—did you know those are two different things? It's ridiculous."

I laughed. "Sometimes I just worry—the last thing I'm going to do is talk shit about your wife, especially because as you know, I love your wife. But I know she thinks I'm not where I should be in life."

Bianca's gaze softened, and she tucked a spare lock of hair back into her topknot. "First of all, my wife can be exhausting. The other night I caught her lecturing the kid who cuts our lawn about his SAT scores. Secondly, we all thought we lost you. Remember? Not even because of the death rumor, but . . . not *not* because of the death rumor! So now that you're back, we want it all to be *great*, OK? You and your life and your happiness and all of that. That's it."

"OK." I felt something unclench in me. And by the time I was home later and had caught up on work, I opened my script again and started thinking about ways it could be stronger. I didn't know if it was that bit of relief I felt thanks to my conversation with Bianca, or the bigger fact that at least right now

I'd somehow pieced it all back together—or at least enough of it to fake it. My friends, my script, a life that wasn't just about getting through quietly. I knew that I wasn't a full puzzle to be reassembled, that the things that Taylor had warned about were at least one missing piece. Hopefully it was something off to the side, not an edge, something that in a certain light no one would catch being gone. There was no guarantee I wouldn't hurt people again, but maybe I could figure out a way not to for the time being. Maybe I could keep trying to be better. How long could I keep that going?

I saved my script as *version 3* and laughed when I thought maybe that was me too. Nina Rice, version 3, nontoxic for the foreseeable future. Version 4 or 5 could be a problem again, but I wasn't her yet. I'd hold tight for as long as possible.

It's your turn. I'll drive to suburbia. When/where?

Texts from Ari weren't *normal* normal; I did almost spill my coffee when the latest came in about a week after the night out at Bestia and the Women in Television panel. But also, I supposed that the texts *were* normal now. We had some sort of established friend hangout deal in place, LA and the suburbs, and it was my turn again.

I'm pretty open. Is there something suburban you are craving? The mall?

I've been taking a ton of meetings lately. Nothing but conference rooms and coffee shops. ☺ How about something outdoors?

I knew I'd regret it, but I texted CJ. **Do you know of anything fun outdoors in my area? I'm more of an expert on our many Starbucks locations.**

CJ, master of coming up with activity ideas, worked in coding, managing the back end of websites so the sites ran correctly and efficiently. This meant that their phone was rarely far from them between the hours of eight a.m. until at least seven. So I'd correctly guessed their response would come in quickly.

Is this for a date???

Aaaaand it was even the response that had given me anticipatory regret.

Obviously not. Why do you all think the only thing you can do with a hot celebrity is date them?

Well, you said "outdoors" so I assumed this wasn't about fucking. Not that I wouldn't support that sense of adventure. Don't forget to put lube in your bag.

CJ I am going to murder you.

I've got you, don't worry. Give me an hour and I'll send you a link or two.

Thank you, you're my hero today.

Happy to do my small part bringing you two together. When are you bringing her to Sunday brunch?

Seriously. I will murder you.

Luckily, Ari was up for my-slash-CJ's idea, and we met a few days later in the parking lot of the William S. Hart Museum. CJ promised there was lots of room to wander and hike outside, so hopefully it would be exactly what Ari needed.

"Hey," Ari said as she got out of her car, parked right next to mine. We were both again in jeans and T-shirts, though Ari was wearing cool sneakers and I was in hiking boots I'd borrowed from Phoebe and made me feel like I was cosplaying as lesbian Cheryl Strayed.

"Hi," I said, and smiled as Ari pulled me into a hug. No matter the size of my feelings for her, the way everything in me seemed to chime in anticipation when she came into view, I always let her take the lead there. I waited to be folded into her arms, to be put into close proximity with her body around mine for just a moment, to take advantage of the one time I could inhale her scent.

"The website said we have *a chance of* seeing buffalo from the hiking trail," Ari said as we made our way to the entrance. "But I swear to you, Nina Rice, if we don't witness any buffalo I'm demanding our money back. I am primed for buffalo."

William S. Hart was a cowboy who'd starred in 1920s films, and his ranch and estate had been turned into a museum, tucked into the hills of Santa Clarita. His mansion—which apparently was a mind-boggling twenty-two rooms—was the museum itself, while the acres around it honored, among other things, his departed dogs, and housed buffalo that had, incredibly, been a gift from Walt Disney. LA was so fucking weird sometimes. But CJ knew I hadn't wanted a boring day out for Ari, and CJ had provided. No wonder they had so many girlfriends.

We headed together up the trail. While Ari gazed around at the trees and the scrubby brown landscape below, I kept forgetting to take in my surroundings because my gaze snapped to her instead, every single time. Her hair burning golden under the sun. The light glinting off of her cheekbones and highlighting her profile. The way she tucked the wavy chunk of her hair behind her ear before folding her arms against herself when she really concentrated on something.

It wasn't fair, I thought, because there was so much I wasn't telling her. Ari claimed she talked to me because *I got it*. I saw behind the bullshit veneer of Hollywood, how fame could be a curse and a trap and not just a prize. Would Ari feel that openness with me if she caught me looking at her like this? Would she jot off casual texts to me if she knew she might have been catching me picturing her naked?

I had to say something, I realized. Maybe not now, while we were still on our way up a trail, while there was no real escape from one another. But when we were on the other side of things, down from the peak and back at our cars. *Ari, I don't think we can be friends anymore.* I wasn't about to say why, of course, because I'd gotten pretty good at protecting myself from humiliation. I could cite Joyce's close eye on my work. I'd make it sound convincing. The texts would stop, these outings that weren't dates no matter how much I now wished they were, would end. And my life would be fine, because it would be an honest life, and wasn't that the most important thing? It was part of being less toxic, I realized, exactly the kind of thing that would make me less likely to ruin people the way Taylor had predicted.

"Oh, yes!" Ari let out a little squeal that was one hundred percent off-brand for her. Fuck, it was charming. How could she get more charming? "The buffalo are out."

She pointed across the land to a grassy section where, sure enough, the buffalo actually roamed.

"Now you don't have to burn anything down," I said, and she laughed.

"I never said I was going to burn anything down. Just some light yelling." She smiled back at me and then fixed her gaze on the buffalo again. I forced myself to join her, to let this opportunity to watch Ari Fox in the wild slip away. "This was exactly what I needed, Nina Rice. How did you know?"

"I should be honest with you, I just asked my friend who knows stuff in every part of the city. I'm actually very dull."

"Not possible. But thanks to your friend, it's perfect. Every time my life starts to feel chaotic, I have to remember to just go outside. The stress seems to drain away."

"Is everything OK?" I asked.

"Everything's good," she said quickly. "It's just all starting to build, and I'm looking at my schedule for the fall and . . . you know, it's interviews and events and all this travel, and no time at all to actually act. And there'll be more media training because even though I think I'm pretty good at the whole being-Ari-Fox thing, apparently the studio has notes. They really want that Oscar."

"What about you?" I asked.

"Nina, of course I want it too! That's the worst part of all." She buried her face in her hands, and we both laughed.

"There's just never been someone like you before," I said.

"Right? You'll be the first out queer Best Supporting Actress. It's groundbreaking. *You're* groundbreaking."

"You're very sweet," she said, looking back to the buffalo. "It's a lot of pressure. The studio, the community, Joyce, my manager, my publicist, all the people who get or need something from me. I don't want to let anyone down but I also want to do it my way. I'm the only expert on Ari Fox in this business and I wish people saw that."

"I think people see it," I said. "There's just a lot of fear in Hollywood, so everyone tries to do everything the exact right way. My whole job is just appropriately emailing people so they feel appreciated and heard and so people's schedules stay organized in this manner that lends a personal touch. If we weren't all so worried about making the exact right impression, everyone could agree that people like you are way too busy to manage all these logistics and *of course* there's a person like me who has to handle it. Though obviously if we could be transparent about that, I wouldn't have a job at all, and it would just be Max and Joyce handling everything."

"Oh, no, Nina, that's not true," Ari said. "Poor little Max could not handle that additional level of work. Her delicate heart couldn't hold all those client emotions in."

I laughed so loudly I worried I'd create a buffalo stampede. Was that a thing? Luckily they seemed indifferent to us. "Fair point. I guess it's good for Max that Hollywood has so much bullshit."

"It's good for me too," Ari said with a grin. "Bullshit or not, I wouldn't be up here on this trail if I didn't have an email person."

I smiled back at her, hating how good this part felt. In another world, I knew that we could have been friends. Too bad my stupid heart and other body parts had to fall for her. I was right; the only thing that made sense was to quit while I was ahead.

Chapter 12
Emergency Contact

We lingered as we made our way up the trail. I couldn't deny that Ari was right; it felt good to be out here, away from my desk with my phone tucked away into my pocket. If this was about to end, I was all for this slow last afternoon.

Ari got out her phone to take a picture of the view—"Even though I've been trying to live in the moment more"—and so I did the same. I'd set my notifications to *push* as always, but somehow hadn't felt the buzzing of three missed calls and two voicemails.

"Is everything OK?" Ari asked, as I was apparently making panicked faces at my phone.

"I'm sure it's fine, Joyce is probably courting a new client—*shit*." The missed calls weren't from an Exemplar office number. They were from Henry Mayo Hospital.

"Nina, what's going on?" Ari asked, as I tapped the first voicemail and held my phone to my ear as best as I could with trembling hands.

"Hello, Nina, this is Camila Flores from Oaken Troves—"

"Fuck!" I shouted, bursting into tears. No good news ever

came from an employee of your aunt's retirement center calling from the nearest hospital.

Ari grabbed my hand but stayed quiet.

"—*and you're listed as the emergency contact for Lorna Rice. Unfortunately, Lorna stumbled today and broke her foot. We're waiting right now to make sure that it's nothing more serious. Everything's being handled, but Lorna wanted to make sure you knew what was going on. I'll give you a call when there's more news.*"

"Oh my god," I said, still crying. "If you call from a hospital you should be legally required to start the message with *this person is not dead.*"

"No shit," Ari said, her hand still clutching mine. "Your aunt?"

I nodded, as my heart kept hammering away. "I have to listen to the other message but I think she's OK."

Ari let go of my hand to rub little circles on my back. "Of course."

"*Hi Nina, Camila again. Everything else looks good with Lorna—I'm sure it's not news to you that your aunt's a tough one—and since it's just a few hairline fractures, it shouldn't take long to finish up here. I'll wait with her and bring her home, but feel free to call me on my cell if you want to talk with me or with Lorna, I'm at 818—*"

I yelped. "I have to write a phone number down."

"Doesn't your voicemail do that transcription thing?" Ari asked, and I realized of course she was right. I just had to tap on Camila's number, which would have been a small task if not for the massive amount of adrenaline flooding my system.

I'd never met Camila before, but she was patient and cheerful. As soon as she confirmed that Lorna was fine, would only need a walking cast, and would be released within the hour, I asked her to pass the phone to Lorna.

"Nina Louise, they made such a fuss about a little trip-and-fall!"

"Lorna," I said, and burst into tears again. "I'm so glad you're OK."

"Well, of course I'm OK! I'm as healthy as a horse, that's what the attractive doctor here just told me."

He must have been in the room, because I heard laughter in the background. Here I was, convinced my favorite person had died while she'd been hitting on doctors.

"Lorna, I am buying you a cell phone and you can't stop me," I said, and she laughed.

"Oh, Nina Louise, I hate those dreadful things, but if it'll make you feel better, I'll go with my friends to one of those fancy tech stores and get my own. How's that sound?"

I felt like I was ten again, buried in her arms at Grandma's funeral. "It sounds good. Can I come and get you? Would you like me to bring you back to your place?"

"I'd love nothing more. I'll hand you back to Camila and she'll tell you how to find me."

Camila gave me all the information I needed, and as I said goodbye I realized I was almost breathing normally again. Almost.

"So she's OK?" Ari asked, and I nodded.

"Hairline fractures in her foot, and she's hitting on the doctor, so I guess she's not dying today."

Ari crushed me into a tight hug. "I'm so relieved, Nina. I know how much she means to you."

"I'm sorry I have to cut this short, but—"

"No, Nina, come on. I stood in the sunshine, I saw wildlife, I'm great. Let's get back to your car."

Humiliatingly, I started crying again as we walked back. The relief I felt at the good news hadn't communicated with my body yet, and there was nothing I could do to fight off the waves of panic and emotion that continued smacking at me. Ari kept her arm around me, all the way down the trail, all the way to my car. I was supposed to be breaking up this friendship—or whatever it was—but the timing was hardly appropriate.

"Hand me your keys," Ari said once we stood between her BMW and my Accord.

"What? Why?"

"You're in no shape to drive, Nina Rice," she said kindly.

I knew she was right. "I'll call a Lyft. Maybe Karl's up here today."

"While I'd love a Karl reunion, no. I'm taking you there myself. No arguing."

I silently got into the passenger seat and watched as Ari started up my ancient clangy car. The cults podcast I was in the middle of blasted out of the stereo, and I hit the power button as quickly as I could.

"Nina Rice," Ari said, "do you mean to tell me we could have been talking about cults this whole time and you never brought them up?"

I sniffled into a questionable old tissue I found in the glovebox. "Excuse me, Ari, you never brought up cults either. Why am I the one at fault?"

Ari drove to the hospital with the help of my navigation, and thanks to Camila's clearheaded instructions, we located the appropriate parking section right away. I texted Camila as we walked up, and she met us right at the entrance. She was around my age with her hair styled into a fade, dressed in a very professional button-down and navy slacks. The three of us did an LGBTQ-family acknowledging nod at each other, and then laughed, and it helped distract me from the hospital smell. There was nothing good associated with that heady hit of disinfectant and stress sweat.

"Your aunt's fine," she said, "though I'm sure you're not surprised. Lorna is a tough one."

"She's tough, but . . . I mean, she's old. I'm scared all the time."

She patted my arm. "I know, I know. I deal with the absolute worst of this sometimes, and so I know what families go through. Heck, I know what my own family's gone through. But Lorna's a solid one. I'm sure you've got some time left together."

Her eyes flicked over to Ari, and I was positive she was thinking about those field-hockey-to-kissing scenes in *Brother's Keeper.*

"This is my— This is Ari," I introduced, and they shook hands. "Ari, you can go, if you don't mind grabbing a Lyft back to the park."

Ari nodded at my hands, which were, unbeknownst to me, wringing one another and still shaking. "I think I should probably drive you and your injured aunt back, yeah?"

"That sounds wise," Camila said. "Come on, I'll take you to Lorna."

We followed her to an elevator and then down a long corridor. Lorna was in a big room of patients, sitting up on an examination table with a walking boot on her right foot. She looked small in this big room, but otherwise she looked like herself, especially once she saw me and smiled.

"I'm so glad you're OK," I said and gave her the gentlest hug I could manage.

"Well, me too, Nina Louise." She pulled back from me and patted my cheek. "Thank you for coming. Camila's wonderful—married, alas, or I would have set you two up ages ago—but there's nothing like family."

"You're right about that," I said. "The family thing, that is, not the—anyway . . ."

I heard laughter behind me from Ari and Camila. Great. Where was my queer solidarity?

"And who's this?" Lorna asked.

"Hi, Ms. Rice, I'm Ari." Ari walked up next to me and held out her hand to shake Lorna's. "It's great to finally meet you. Nina's told me so much."

"Oh, Ari *Fox*," Lorna said, and I felt my whole face burning hot. How had I gone from worrying that Lorna was dead to wishing I was? "It's wonderful to finally meet you too, and none of this Ms. Rice stuff, it's Lorna. I hear you're about to win an Oscar!"

"Did you hear that from Nina?" Ari asked with a note of—delight?—in her voice.

"Oh, no, you know Nina, so withholding. My friend Nat reads all those industry papers, she knows everything about the whole business."

Ari shoved her hands in her pockets and grinned. "Ah, yeah, that makes much more sense."

Lorna's doctor had already cleared her to go, so Ari, Camila, and I walked out to the parking lot together with the orderly who gently wheeled Lorna alongside of us. We thanked Camila and said goodbye before I sat down in the back seat of the Honda so Lorna and her cast could be helped into the front. I navigated again, and Ari kept the ride miraculously bump-free all the way to Oaken Troves.

"You can take a Lyft back now, if you want," I told Ari once she pulled into a parking spot.

"Nina, I'm fine. I'll keep myself amused for as long as you need. Lorna, it was so nice to meet you. I hope your foot heals at lightning speed."

"Me too, my dear," Lorna said. "It was lovely meeting you as well. You know, Nina joins me each Thursday for lunch, and if you're free I'd love for you to join us next time. Nat would flip her lid!"

"I'd be honored to join you for lunch," Ari said, as my face burned even hotter than at the hospital. Again, how had I feared for Lorna's life such a short time ago, when now it felt like—well, it wasn't that I wanted to murder her, not exactly. "I'm sure Nina can give me all the details."

"Nina's great at the details," Lorna said, as I exited the car and helped her up. I had so many things to say, mainly, *you shouldn't have done that*, but I truly was just so fucking grateful she was here and alive and barely hurt at all. How could I not be grateful for every single thing about her, even the annoying ones?

The day had, unsurprisingly, taken a lot out of Lorna, so I made sure she had everything she needed and hugged her goodbye. I knew the staff here could assist with anything that might come up later, but it was still hard to walk out the front door of her cottage and leave her alone, though of course she insisted. My emotions were stuck again on a time delay, and while I did my best to hold it back, by the time I got back into my car, I was crying again.

Ari leaned over the console and wrapped her arms around me. "Shhh. She's fine. You're fine. We're all fine."

I let my breathing return to normal before settling back in my seat. "Thank you. Seriously, I can't even— Ari. I couldn't have managed all of this without you today."

"Yeah, you could have," she said. "But I'm glad I was here too."

"And, obviously, you don't have to go to lunch with us on Thursday. Lorna will understand that you—"

"What are you talking about? Of *course* I'm going to lunch with you and Lorna and Nat and whoever else. Tell me when to be here on Thursday."

Understandably, I didn't tell a soul about Thursday. The group chat had turned to talk of nothing except for a weekend in Palm Springs that Phoebe wanted to plan for our whole crew, and so it was easy not to mention it. There were too many Airbnb links for anyone to send GIFs of Ari and ask if she had Foxed me yet. My friends were powerful, high-achieving people within their fields (Chloe might jest at her non-use of her degree, but she made a tidy sum grooming the dogs of trendy and rich Eastsiders) and yet had all regressed to middle school tactics when it came to Ari.

I hated it and loved it simultaneously.

Normally I tried to look a little nicer for my lunches with Lorna, I told myself, as I flipped through the entire contents of my closet and wished I'd had more notice. It wasn't exactly as if I didn't have enough options; the thing about Southern California weather being so consistent for much of the year meant that most of my wardrobe worked, well, most of the time. It was that I'd gotten lazy, and I wasn't sure about all my clothes I'd bought at least three years ago, back when I'd gone out in public all of the time.

I selected a fitted knit dress, soft material in a muted blue. The last time I'd worn it had been a night out with Taylor, right before the end, right before she left our bed for Phoebe and Bianca's guest room. For the last years, the dress had felt like it held too many memories, and no amount of Febreze would banish the scent of heartbreak. But I supposed time faded everything, including metaphorical bad smells, eventually. The dress was casual but clung to my curves, and the color brought out my eyes.

"Fuck," I said to my reflection. "What am I doing?"

Seriously, though, I'd been minutes away from ending my friendship with Ari. It had been the right thing to do. If Lorna hadn't fallen, if the day had unfolded differently, Ari would have already been gone from my life. So what did it matter how my ass looked in this dress? (Great, to be clear.) Ari and I were friends, nothing more. Not even friends! We were business associates, sort of, who'd leaned on each other when the other was the one who'd understood.

My ass, great or not, did not factor in.

I beat Ari to Oaken Troves, and waited in my car finishing a podcast episode about an old-time murder when it dawned on me that perhaps Ari felt the same way. Not about the illicit thoughts, but the fact that whatever we had wasn't sustainable.

I checked my phone to make sure she hadn't already mes-saged that she wasn't coming, but when I looked back up from my quiet phone screen, her BMW pulled right in next to me.

"You made it," I said, getting out of my car as she did. She was in her bright white T-shirt over black pants, always just so much exactly *her*. Not me and my assorted closet full of the past. Ari seemed to know exactly who she was, every single day.

"I made a promise to Lorna, of *course* I made it." She held a small bouquet of brightly colored wildflowers in one hand, so when she hugged me, it was a fragrance overload, floral and Ari, all at once. "How're you doing?"

"Fine—good, yeah. Better. Sorry, I still sound jumbled and crazy."

"Barely," she said. "And it's understandable. Come on, take me to my lunch date."

I smiled and guided her through the entrance and toward the dining patio.

"This is *nice*," she said, and I tried to take in the sun-dappled setting through her eyes. "I used to think I'd want to retire to a house in the middle of nowhere with just some cats and a guard dog to keep me company, but maybe senior citizen suburbia would suit me too."

"Oh yeah, I should discuss it with my friends that we all end up here," I said. "Also, I don't want to oversell it, but the food is better than average."

Ari cracked up. "Better than average, a killer blurb."

"I mean, I like it, but I'm very Midwestern and prone to love casseroles and things cut into very small bites. I understand that's not everyone's jam."

Lorna's table came into view, and her eyes lit up as she waved us over.

"Don't get up," I told her, as we reached the table.

"Nina Louise, it's called a walking cast, I'm very capable of standing when I need to." Lorna slowly rose to her feet and hugged me. "You look beautiful. Are you doing the ten steps Choon Hee told me about?"

I had, in fact, ordered about a dozen skin care products late one night instead of obsessing over Ari or my script, my regular late-night activities these days. It wasn't clear if my skin was any better off, but I did like the ritual of it. I'd given myself so little over the past years, afraid that Taylor was right about my centering myself too often, but some extra time with my face seemed acceptable.

"Ari came," I said, perhaps unnecessarily, and Lorna gave me a look as if she was thinking exactly that.

"Of course she did! She promised me she'd be here, and I expected nothing else. Hello, my dear."

Ari presented the bouquet to Lorna, who buried her nose in them right away.

"They're beautiful. You didn't have to, but I'm certainly glad that you did. Sit down, girls. Nat and Choon Hee will be here soon. Big day, Chef Carlos made his special gourmet potpies."

"Oh, I love those," I said practically involuntarily.

"Nina says the food here is really good," Ari said as she dropped into an open chair. I took the one between her and Lorna.

"It's quite excellent, all things considered," Lorna said. "I don't know how much Nina's told you about me, but I promise you that I didn't always get all my meals from an institution like this one! I had many years going to all the sorts of places you girls like."

"How long were you in LA?" Ari asked. "Were you born here?"

"Good heavens, no, but that's a flattering thought! I moved to Los Angeles when I was in my early twenties, more than a few decades ago. It was thrilling, so much bigger and so many more people than my hometown."

"That was St. Louis?" Ari asked. "Like Nina?"

"Just like Nina. And just like Nina, I wanted out," Lorna said. "What about you, Ari? Where are you from?"

"Phoenix, ma'am, just outside in the suburbs."

"Oh, Phoenix is lovely. And may I ask how old you are?"

"Absolutely. I'm twenty-seven."

"Oh," Lorna said, sounding delighted. "That's a great age."

Ari grinned. "I'm glad you think so because I can't do anything about it."

Nat and Choon Hee arrived at the table, their eyes wide as they sat down and surveyed Ari. To be fair, they saw the same people every single day. Even without Nat's industry knowledge and Ari's Oscar fate, a new person would likely be cause for excitement.

Lorna made introductions, and Ari got up to shake their hands. They raved about Ari's haircut ("So modern!") and outfit ("My grandson who's a DJ would love those sneakers!"), and I tried to flash her a look of—I didn't even know. Apology? Agreement? Solidarity? It didn't matter, though, because she was so engaged in their conversation that she was focused purely on them.

Once the potpies were served, our table settled into an easy silence while we ate. The pies were as full of comfort-food bliss and nostalgia as I'd remembered, and I reminded myself that this was a good day.

Ari finished as I did and winked at me. "Five stars, better than average."

Fuck you, I mouthed, and she feigned indignation.

"Ari, it's so nice Nina brought you today," Nat said. "I keep reading all about you on the internet, and I couldn't believe it when Lorna said Nina knew you! You must be so excited about your big movie."

Ari flashed a grin, one I hadn't seen her use with me. I knew it was her public-facing smile. "It's a great opportunity for me, and I'm excited to share it with everyone when the film comes out later this year. The rest is all bonus."

"Nina, it must be so exciting to have a famous girlfriend," Choon Hee said, and I opened my mouth to correct her. "Your last girlfriend did something very boring, yes? Some job with accounting."

"Financial consulting," I said, and realized I'd made the wrong correction.

"Oh, Taylor," Lorna said with a downturned mouth. "She did have a way of making it sound boring, though, didn't she?"

I could feel Ari staring at me, and the truth was that I didn't know what to address first. And then luckily the waiter arrived with tall sundae glasses of banana pudding and whipped cream, so I shoveled that into my mouth and hoped every single topic had been forgotten. Nat was asking Ari a bunch of publicity-specific questions, and Lorna and Choon Hee had questions for me about my skincare routine, and by the time lunch was over and we were walking Lorna slowly back to her cottage, I pretended no one could possibly remember anything from before dessert appeared. We were living in a post-pudding world now.

"It was very nice to see you again, Ari," Lorna said. "I know it's a long drive up from your home, but anytime you'd like to join us, you're very welcome."

"I'll hopefully be able to take you up on that offer soon," Ari said, giving her a hug goodbye. I did the same, made Lorna promise me she really was going to get a cell phone in the immediate future, and headed out.

"Hey," Ari said, her tone colder than I was used to. "Do you think we could talk?"

"Oh, um, sure. I'm sorry about my aunt's friends, they—"

She waved me off. "Is there a nearby coffee shop that's good?"

"I mean, I think Starbucks is good," I said, and luckily she laughed.

"Great, how about I drive? I'll bring you back to your car later."

Heart pounding, I agreed to that and sat down in the passenger seat of her car. So far we'd only been in mine and a couple Lyfts, and so for a moment I was caught off-guard by the shiny interior, the polished leather, the way Ari's scent hung in the air.

"Nina," she said.

"I'm sorry, I didn't tell them that you were my—"

"Nina," she said, again, with a sharper tone. "Who's Taylor?"

I shrugged. Suddenly this didn't feel like a big deal. Unless—it wasn't possible that Ari knew Taylor, was it?

"My ex," I said. "You don't know Taylor, do you? Taylor Alderidge?"

"No, I don't know the most WASPy fucking name I've ever heard," she said, and we both laughed despite the tension in the car, thick as Ari's presence. "You have an ex."

"I mean, I have lots. Taylor's just the . . . you know. The serious one. The one I thought I was going to marry. Which sounds crazy now, I know, but—"

"I thought you said that you didn't date," Ari said, her words precise and almost clipped.

"I mean, I don't. After Taylor and I broke up—"

She exhaled so loudly I stopped talking.

"What?"

"When you said that, it sounded so . . . case closed," Ari said. "All things settled. I just assumed you were ace or aromantic or something of that nature, and I let it go, nothing worse than someone pushing back against your orientation, trust me, I grew up a lesbian in the Phoenix suburbs."

"Wh-why does it matter?" I asked.

"Because, Nina, I didn't think that you were an option," she said, and my breath caught in my throat, my heart shook my entire body, the hairs on the back of my neck stood up. "I've been living this whole time I've known you like you weren't an option."

I didn't think I could breathe enough air into my body to answer. I stayed silent, watching her.

"Nina Rice," she said, and I felt my whole body turn toward her in this warm leather seat, a flower to the sun. "Tell me you're an option."

I could have said anything. That I was toxic, that I destroyed things, that the love of my life had warned me away from everyone. But I was exhausted with all of that. If I could have Sunday brunch, if I could have my script in progress, couldn't I have this too?

"Of course I'm an option," I said, and neither of us moved, and then I didn't know if I should keep watching Ari, so I looked away, and she laughed, and holy hell, I'd forgotten how awkward this part could be. But then, suddenly, it wasn't.

Ari leaned over the console, her chin cocked at just the right angle, her lips parted. I knew that Ari, the woman who sent me *be here tonight* texts was waiting for me, and that it was possible that everything I'd wanted was about to happen. The emotions washing over me were endless, joy and nerves and incredulity. But with my eyes on her lips, the pink of her tongue waiting, pressed up against her teeth, one emotion overtook the others. I sat up and twisted my body so that my mouth found hers.

I'd imagined it, of course, but it hadn't been like this, Ari's lips urgent against mine, her tongue pressing for entrance almost as soon as the kiss began. I took her face in my hands as we continued kissing, gulping each other down like no amount would leave us satisfied. Her hands found my waist and pulled me toward her, and I stroked my fingers through her hair while our mouths overlapped again, again, and again.

The console was in the worst possible location, of course, and I found myself practically kneeling over it to find all the angles I needed. For Ari sucking my lower lip into her mouth. For my teeth nibbling at her jawline. For her mouth trailing down my neck while a low moan escaped my lips.

Ari's hands, still this whole time, had suddenly slid down to cup my ass, and it was too much, this console and this distance between us. I climbed over, as she slid the seat back, and I lowered myself on top of Ari Fox, exactly as I'd imagined it.

Actually—not *exactly* as I'd imagined it.

"Ari," I said, as I tried to catch my breath. Her hands found my ass again, but under my dress now, her fingertips skimming under the bottom edge of my underwear. "We're—"

"Yeah?" she asked, shifting back so I was all but lying on top of her. Our bodies connected at so many places my brain was practically short-circuiting logging the points of contact. Our breasts together, her denim-clad legs rough between my bare thighs, my neck a hot throb against the hard jut of her chin, my fingers clutching her shoulders while hers squeezed my bare ass under my underwear.

"Ari, we're in the parking lot of a retirement community," I finally managed to say in one breath, and she laughed so hard I was momentarily shoved back from the force. "Not here."

"No," she said. "I can't risk my standing with Lorna and the gang."

I tried to find a graceful way to get back to the other side of the car, and instead tumbled ass-over-feet, slamming against the passenger-side window. Ari did in no way disguise her laughter at this move, but it didn't hurt. I wondered if anything could ever hurt again, as long as my body stayed on fire just like this.

"Let me take you out," she said.

"To the Starbucks?" I asked, and she laughed.

"For real. Tonight? Tell me your favorite food. Tell me your favorite place. I'll take you anywhere you want to go, Nina Rice."

"I'm good with anything," I said, "if I'm with you."

"Oh, *fuck*," she said, and let out a ragged groan. "I don't know how to wait until tonight for you."

I didn't either. After all this time feeling so certain this could never happen, how on earth were a few hours without Ari suddenly the most impossible thing I could imagine?

Chapter 13
Two Options

After the heat of the moment had ended, once I was at my desk and my pulse had returned to normal, it was easy to believe that it hadn't happened. If I'd completely lost my grip on reality, I was sure this was where it would have started, an imagined make-out session with Ari Fox in the parking lot of a senior citizen retirement village.

There were tangible bits of proof, though, from the way my dress was stretched out below the waist to the red streaks at the base of my neck where Ari's eager mouth had gotten a little rough. I'd been marked for all the world to see.

Two options, Ari had texted, and I laughed because I didn't care and told her the first restaurant was fine without clicking through to the Yelp link. I loved that she wanted me to be happy, even though the truth was that I loved how she'd never checked before, that Ari Fox had shoved herself into my life with force and without question.

I got ready powered by that, the marks and the texts. The night ahead flashed in my head, the desire practically stabbing through me that would finally be satisfied. What a simultaneously absurd and glorious thought.

I rubbed one of my new lotions into my skin from head to toe, resurrected an old impractical bra and panties set, blew my hair out into soft waves. There was a dress I'd come across earlier in my frantic dig through my closet, shimmery and swingy, exactly what I'd wanted for New Year's Eve four years ago when I'd clicked around my usual shopping sites. When it had arrived, though, it had barely skimmed the tops of my knees. I loved my body, sure, but I doubted that enough other people did for the dress to be worn in public. A fat girl with good self-esteem was still a fat girl in a society of exacting standards. Especially in Los Angeles.

Tonight, though, I grabbed the dress and pulled it on over my head. My bedroom light danced off of it in muted glimmers, and the fabric gracefully draped itself around each of my curves. There was no denying that if it were actually the perfect dress, it would have been about an inch and a half longer, but I wasn't counting down to the New Year tonight. I was counting down to this dress being taken off, and it seemed more than appropriate for the next few hours.

The drive to Ari's was both long and fast once it stretched out before me. Earlier today it'd seemed impossibly far away, but now that I was on my way I wondered what, exactly, I was doing. Could I, Nina Rice, of exile and solitude and suburbia, drive myself to the home of one of Hollywood's fastest-rising stars to—

I mean, it sounded ridiculous, even without sex.

But, of course, it had been ridiculous this whole time, hadn't it? Who was I to sit in Exemplar's modern offices, and who was I to exchange texts with someone like Ari Fox? The ridiculousness was so far behind me at this point. It was awfully late to be taking stock of the improbability of the situation now.

I'd given up on all of this, though, hadn't I? Maybe I'd allow that I'd gone too far, pushed too many people away. But if I were to get back into the game, was this the wisest move?

FOR HER CONSIDERATION / 149

Dating the highest-profile woman I'd ever known? Shouldn't I have warmed up with some no-pressure app dates with women who didn't intimidate me?

It was public, too. Not, of course, *public* public. Ari kept a low profile and no one out there in the world gave a shit about me. But other people were involved. Lorna, my friends, Lorna's friends. They already were so determined to see something happening that if it actually *happened*, where would that leave any of us? Could I weather that scrutiny after years of avoiding it completely?

Driving to LA this time of day, even during the tail end of rush hour, was against traffic, and so Waze kept slicing off minutes, and I turned my car down Ari's quiet street ten minutes before I'd planned. There was nothing I could do to silence the massive pro/con list my brain had become, so I simply pulled into her driveway and texted.

Waze lied and I'm here early. If it's way too soon, I'll just wait in my car.

The front door opened, and Ari stepped out. She was dressed in a jumpsuit again, this time more casual, navy like a mechanic's work suit, and her feet were bare. She gestured to roll down my window, which I had to do manually given the car's age.

"Get in here, Nina Rice. I've got ideas for how to spend the next ten minutes."

It would have been sexier if I didn't have to roll up the goddamn antique window, but then I did and got to watch Ari's eyes take me in once I stepped out of the car. There was no worry left in my head; even my dress seemed the right length now.

"Hey," she said as I made my way to her.

"You look nice," I said, and touched her collar. The material was sturdy but soft. Just like her.

"You," she said, bringing her mouth close to me, her breath warm on my ear, "look really fucking hot."

I leaned toward her but she laughed and pulled me into the house. "Didn't we learn our lesson about being in public earlier?"

"I've forgotten everything useful already," I said, and wondered if it would be awkward again, ramping back up to this new way of being. But then Ari's arms pulled me close and her mouth was on mine and there was clearly no warm-up necessary. I dragged my fingers through her hair again, keeping her close, keeping our lips on one another's. Once her hands roamed to the small of my back, I let mine explore too, while marveling that Ari Fox seemed as eager to learn my contours as I was for hers. Her hold was tight, fingers pressing into my back to secure me in place, while I was busy skimming her collarbone with my fingertips, clasping her bare shoulders and biceps snug underneath her jumpsuit.

She didn't feel like I'd imagined because imaginations could be generic, swapping in old sense memories and daydreams for what it didn't yet know.

But now I knew.

Ari walked me back against the door, as we'd barely gotten inside. We kissed more, a tangle of lips, teeth, tongue, while our bodies learned to fit together. Her knee nudged me insistently, and I slid my legs open so that hers fit between mine, the fabric of her jumpsuit soft between my thighs. By now, there was no way to tell Ari's breathing from mine, with our mouths barely able to pull apart from one another and our bodies panting rhythmically together. I wanted more, but this desperate climbing ache was like nothing I could remember, and instead of satisfying its end, I wondered how high we could take it.

Ari took hold of one of my thighs from behind and shifted it to hug at her hip, and this difference in angles drew a moan from deep within me. She sucked at my neck and collarbone as we grinded together, while I clutched at her, anywhere I could reach, feeling her hard angles and gentle slopes through the fabric, learning the topography of her body.

"Nina Rice," Ari murmured. "We have a decision ahead of us. Two more options."

I tried to answer, but she'd grasped one of my breasts and was rubbing tiny circles with her thumb over my nipple.

"I could call a Lyft right now," she said, as I let out more sounds that were nothing like words. "Or I could take you into my bedroom instead."

The countdown was already over. I took hold of the hem of my dress and pulled it up and off over my head. It was so much easier than talking.

It should have, I knew, been a vulnerable moment. The entire time I'd known her, Ari had seemed off-limits in so many ways. Even now, even here, I could have dwelled on her Hollywood life. She'd dated younger, tinier, cooler DJs. She'd been with women who, undoubtedly, spent time at the gym, four figures on haircuts, emerging shiny from waxing salons. In Los Angeles those things weren't another world, they were right up next to you and there was no way not to notice them and how they set you apart.

But there was nothing about tonight that had set me apart. I'd forgotten to care about any of that, about the size of my thighs or the curve of my stomach. I liked all those things, after all, and drenched in Ari's gaze, I wouldn't have swapped my body for anyone else's.

"Thank god." Ari laced her fingers through mine and led me down the hallway. I expected to pick up where we'd left off, but she stood a couple feet from me with her hands on my waist like a middle school slow dance.

"You're so fucking beautiful," she said. "Do you know how long I've wanted to see you like this?"

"I—" I tried to go for sexy, but honesty tumbled out instead. "Honestly, no. I had no idea."

"Well," she said, drawing me closer, her breath hot on my

neck, "I thought you were beautiful the moment we met. But then, that dress the other week, Jesus Christ."

"What dress?" I asked, though I knew, especially when her soft hands cupped my breasts, lifting them out of my bra cups. "Oh god, I was so worried it was unprofessional to wear that."

"Nina, your tits in that dress were all I could think about for days."

"What about yours?" I asked, impatiently pulling at her jumpsuit's collar as she fully unfastened my bra and tossed it aside. "Why are you still dressed?"

She winked and slowly unbuttoned, letting the fabric drop to the floor. She was braless, wearing only boy-cut briefs underneath, and I was desperate to let none of her soft skin go untouched. We fell back onto her bed, our hands and mouths on exploratory journeys, though the truth was that every mission was a success. It was as if we were simply trying every possible way to make the other shiver or moan. It was map-making and science, a mission I'd never expected to depart on alongside Ari Fox.

But here we were, all over the bed, finding new angles and new locations. And then, at a certain point, practically as if we'd agreed on the precise time, we settled into something soft and slow. Ari was on top of me, my legs hooked around her hips, our mouths on one another's, our bodies moving in a rhythm we'd found together. Our evening had started in a frantic rush but we'd slowed the pace, stretched this part out to a lingering rise. Time became something we were outside of; I had no idea the minutes or hours that had passed in this room. The entire universe had collapsed into Ari's skin on my skin and Ari's mouth on my mouth.

Every so often we'd pause kissing just long enough to look at each other, as if we both needed to make sure this was real. This, truly, was the part I could hardly handle, not Ari's lips on me but the thought that she'd had similar designs on me practically this whole time. I'd tear myself away from her gaze and find her mouth again, drinking her in to believe.

This slow, steady dreaminess was enough, a state of want and also *not yet*, and then it wasn't. The throbbing between my legs was no longer something I could—or wanted—to ignore, no matter this surreal situation I found myself in. I felt delirious from want. There was nothing I could think of but the release she could give me.

"Ari," I murmured, and apparently it was all I needed to say. She rose to her knees and reached out to tug my underwear down my legs and off completely. It could have been another vulnerable moment, between my desperation and all the awkward maneuvering we had to do, but I only felt safe.

"What do you want, Nina Rice?" she asked, her voice huskier than usual as her eyes tracked over me, perhaps considering possibilities.

"Why did you pick now to ask what I want?" I said with a laugh. "You spent all that time telling me when and where to be. I thought you liked being in charge."

Ari grinned, leaning forward and positioning one of my thighs up against her hip again, a higher angle now. I let out a soft whimper, as I ached for release. I throbbed for *her*. "Do you want me to be in charge right now?"

I nodded, and my hips rocked up to take her as Ari's fingers eased into me. She was slow and gentle at first, as we found this new rhythm. Ari kept eye contact as she fucked me, which meant she finally got to watch me watching her. What a goddamn time to start.

Together we pushed it deeper, faster, a little rougher, something else we were finding mutually. I felt freer than I could remember, writhing against Ari with nothing held back, telling her *yes* and *more* and *harder*. I nearly kept saying *you know me* because she did, she wasn't a random woman picked up in a cheese department or from an app's *just casual* search results.

But also, now *she knew me*, how I felt and how I sounded and how I moved under her. How I'd begged for this. I'd sworn I'd never be in this position again—literally or figuratively—with someone who wasn't all but a stranger, but there was no part of *right now* that I would have changed, no morsel of knowledge I wanted to lock up.

Even though I'd barely felt it build, it had been of course climbing the whole time. The explosion of light from deep within seemed to detonate without warning, though, and I arched into Ari with a sharp cry of pleasure and surprise. And then we were silent, as silent as any two people could be who were gasping for air as if emerging from a deep ocean. Our breath was heavy, ragged, triumphant.

"Holy shit," I murmured, and she laughed. "Ari."

"Nina Rice," she said, and we giggled like the only two in the world let in on a secret. I guessed that we were. "We really should have done that a lot sooner."

I couldn't agree more. I'd been so afraid of falling for someone, of someone falling for me. But now that I was lying here next to her, I only felt drunk, giddy, ravished. I wanted to know more of her too, her secrets and the sides of her I hadn't yet seen. My desire might have been satisfied, but I still longed.

"What about you?" I asked Ari.

She kissed me softly before sliding over to lie against my side. Her eyes remained locked on me, as if even without mystery I was to be marveled. "What about me?"

I slipped my fingertips beneath the waistband of her underwear, feeling her soft skin turn to goose bumps at my touch. "What do *you* want, Ari? Honestly, I hope it's for me to go down on you. But I'm flexible."

Her laugh came out in a slow rumble. "In sheer coincidence, Nina Rice, that's exactly what I want too."

We kissed, messy but still urgent, as my fingers dipped lower, toward Ari's warm, wet heat. I was sated, sure, but still hungry, now for Ari's release. Just *thinking* about making Ari come was such a rush that I felt close to it again myself. My nerve endings still felt electric everywhere, and as Ari grinded against my hand, it was easy enough to imagine we'd invented a new form of power, right here together in this bed.

Ari dipped her head down to suck one of my nipples into her mouth, but I gently pushed her away—after a few blissful moments, I was only human of course.

"I need to know what you taste like," I told her, and blushed, even though my fingers were circling her clit as I said it. I'd never been a big talker in bed, but right now I couldn't hold back what I wanted. Right now I couldn't tell any of it apart, what to say and what not to say. It didn't make any sense not to let it all out.

"Oh, god, you're so hot," Ari murmured, and I took it as permission to work down her black briefs. Her hips rose in anticipation, but I slowly parted her legs, keeping my hands cupped against the backs of her knees. Ari groaned as I took my time kissing the tender skin inside of one of her thighs, then the other, and though I reveled in her eagerness for me, I couldn't wait, either.

I lowered my face to her, and Ari moaned as my lips brushed her. Her hands found their way into my hair as I took in her scent, her taste. Every one of my senses knew Ari now. I started gently, but Ari was already so hot, so wet, so *ready*. Days ago I couldn't have imagined this, Ari Fox desperate for the climax only I could give her. Feeling powerful and grateful and awestruck by this day we'd had, I pushed past my gentle rhythm until her breath hitched and her hips bucked. I looked up to watch the waves of pleasure wash over her. It should have felt unreal, but now that we were on the other side of this, brought here by each other, it had never made so much sense to me.

I slept over at Ari's, though it was less sleeping and more making up for lost time. It wasn't only sex, though of course there was plenty of sex. There was cuddling and kissing gently and fifteen minutes of silence so I didn't mess up my crossword streak and laughing about the absurdity of it all. It was, simply, everything I hadn't thought possible, and now it had all happened.

In the daylight I yet again feared something could shift. We ended up waking at about the same time when the sunlight swept sharp lines into the room through the blinds. It only took exchanging smiles to feel something deep inside of me settle.

Plus, of course, then we ended up staying in bed for another undefinable amount of time and then sharing a shower. By the time we were clean and fresh, the night seemed worlds away.

"I have to go home," I told Ari as I tugged my dress back into place and pondered where exactly she had tossed my underwear last night. "Waze says if I head out now, I'll be at my desk in time."

"Can't you just work here?" Ari was wearing a badly tied robe, which seemed to me a very shameless attempt to keep me here longer. "Don't you just need email?"

"Ari, I have to log in to over a dozen accounts a few times a day. Doing it on my phone is—no. I need my computer."

"Fine, fine," she said with a grin. "When are you coming back? Shit, I have a drinks thing tonight. Tomorrow?"

"Tomorrow's good," I said. "Though I have brunch on Sunday morning, so I'll be fleeing early again."

"You're like Cinderella," she said.

"Cinderella had to be home by *midnight*," I said, and leaned in to kiss her. Of course I didn't want to leave either, but I had a feeling I'd already broken a lot of work rules last night and this morning. I could at least be at my desk at nine sharp.

"Nina Rice," she murmured, her hand on my waist to keep me right there. "I'm bad at this part."

"You're good at every part," I said, and she grinned.

"No, not that. This part. Where I don't say the right thing and you leave here and it's . . . Anyway. I like you a lot."

"I like you a lot too," I said, and we kissed again.

"Tomorrow?" Ari asked, and I nodded. "Wear that dress."

"This dress?" I asked, and she laughed and let go of me.

"No! The one from the other week. The one that rendered me helpless."

"Unlike this one which left you a model of decorum," I said, and we laughed together. "Hey, Ari. For what it's worth, I think you're pretty good at this part too."

Chapter 14
New Plans

At home I felt like the picture of responsibility as I logged in to the first email account at five minutes until nine. I couldn't even imagine how little sleep I'd gotten total, but between this morning's events and a venti coffee I'd grabbed from a Starbucks drive-thru on my way back, I wasn't sure I'd ever felt so awake. I'd even traded my dress for a proper outfit of an actually supportive bra, underwear that didn't match but had great coverage, and a T-shirt dress that flattered nothing on my body except its comfort. Nina Rice, a complete professional who certainly hadn't spent the evening, night, and morning fucking the talent, except of course that she had.

A text from an unknown number flashed on my screen, and fearing—what, exactly? If Joyce had, somehow, found out, hers wouldn't be an unknown number. And then who else was there to fear? This was *good*, I reminded myself. Wasn't I trying to get away from the last three years? I didn't have to keep waiting for the other shoe to drop.

It seems extremely rude, but Nat says not to start a text with "Dear Nina" or sign this like a letter or I'll seem as old

as I actually am. This is of course Lorna on my brand-new cell phone! I bought the nicest one in the Apple store and Choon Hee is getting me on something-gram later today. Please respond or whatever you young people call it so I know I did this correctly.

I grinned and started typing back right away. Of course you go from no phone to a better iPhone than me! Thank you for complying with my demands. I'll worry less if it's easier for us to get in touch with each other. (Nat is right, you don't have to sign your texts, etc.)

You don't have to worry so much, my dear, but it's very sweet. PS (are we allowed to say "PS" in a text or is that a dead giveaway that I'm ancient?) there were some juicy rumors last night at dinner that Gloria T. saw two girls necking in the parking lot! Would you know anything about that? ☺

How the hell had Lorna used the ancient term *necking* in the same text she'd added an emoji to?

PPS (again, if we are allowed to use such signifiers on these phone messages) Choon Hee is helping me add smiles and such. She says it adds personality!

Choon Hee is training you well. As for the rest, I plead the fifth.

☺ Oh is that what you young folks call it nowadays!

I laughed and turned back to my computer, where an email from Max had just landed in my inbox. Now that I'd stopped reading them in a frat boy's lazy drawl, they were much less offensive. Plus, truly, I had nothing to worry about on the Ari front, no reason to tie my stomach up in knots. Joyce seemed to know everyone and everything that went on in Hollywood, but that hardly could include who her clients secretly hooked up with. She was good, but no one was *that* good.

Nina, let me know when I can schedule you for a call with Joyce this morning. Big client, Joyce needs you prepared.

I replied with my open schedule and, while waiting to hear back, opened a few other tabs. If I was going to start going out on a regular basis, maybe I should own more things purchased within the last—well, within the now. If life were more like movies, it would be perfect timing for a shopping montage, but when you wore plus sizes, there were never enough cute stores in one place to manage that. There was a lot online, though, more than I'd had to choose from pre-suburbs and pre-breakup and pre-new life.

As I added outfits to my virtual shopping carts, I assured myself I hadn't gone off the deep end, that Sunday brunches alone required a better variety of looks than I was currently capable of, and my friends seemed determined to see me as much as possible these days. Not that I minded. Not that the thought of outfitting myself for a four-day weekend in Palm Springs sounded so terrible, especially considering it gave me the excuse to buy an overpriced but delightfully floppy sun hat.

Max was already back in my inbox with a call-in number, so I paused and dialed in. Joyce, of course, was seven minutes late, but I didn't mind because I'd gone back to shopping for hats and daydreaming of desert heat and tiki drinks.

"Nina, how are you?" she asked.

"Very good," I replied, one more word than I usually allowed myself. "How can I help?"

"I'm glad you asked. Strictly confidentially, of course—"

Every single thing we did at Exemplar was strictly confidential, of course.

"—I have a meeting set up tomorrow with Gregory Hart, and word on the street is he's been unhappy with his representation at A.T.G. He's, obviously, a frontrunner for next year's Best Actor races, so if this happens, it'll happen quickly and I need you ready to hit the ground running."

"Of course," I said, opening a new tab on top of all of the shopping in progress. Gregory Hart was in his fifties, the kind of actor who turned in awards-caliber performances consistently but had somehow never snagged one of the big trophies. He'd been a character actor, never a heartthrob or typical leading man, and I knew that those types of careers really benefited from an award or two. His lack might be why the rumor mill was churning and why Joyce was suddenly in contention.

"It would make for a big year for us," Joyce said. "A *great* year for us, if I'm being honest, and so if I sign Greg, and Ari remains at the forefront of her awards race conversations as well, there will be a lot of eyes on us. Not the agency, our team specifically, and I don't want to create any room for error."

"Of course not," I said quickly, my heart thumping at the mention of Ari's name. "If there's been any issue with my communication—"

"Not at all, Nina, we both know that the Ari incident was mainly about her comfort level—or I suppose her lack thereof with the whole process. I'd like to keep her happy but she's not easy. I know you're doing your best with her, all things considered."

A moment from last night flashed into my head, Ari's head thrown back and her mouth open, my face buried between her legs, and it occurred to me that I absolutely was doing my best, every single thing considered.

"You'll get official word on Greg once—well, once it's official," Joyce said. "Until then, get ready to go. I think he may be a challenge too."

"I like a challenge," I said, though I wasn't sure that was

true. Bosses loved people who anticipated being tested, but I liked that my job didn't surprise me too often. The requests were all different, but they generally boiled down to the same few categories: appointments/dinners/drinks, promotion especially via social media, and thank-you notes. I was good at those categories.

"It's good to hear." Joyce paused, but I could hear in her silence that she wasn't finished talking. "Nina, have you thought much about what the next step is for you?"

Why did everyone suddenly care about my steps? "Wh-what do you mean?"

"I think you've shown real skill for handling, shall we say, challenging clients. Are you interested in transitioning to a junior agent role? Obviously, not until next year, when we're through this awards season. I'd be happy to mentor you through the process."

"Oh, I—" Honestly, I couldn't believe it. Me, an agent? With Joyce's mentorship? "I'd never really thought about it."

"I think you'd be good," Joyce said. "If it's what you want. If it's not what you want, it's too tough a path to tread to make it worth it. But, really, Nina, it's something to consider, all right?"

"I . . . I will," I said, and I meant it, script revision or not. Had anyone ever placed such faith in me? Not professionally, nothing like this. "Thanks, Joyce. No matter what sounds right, it really means a lot."

"Why don't we grab lunch next week? It's been a while. You can get down here from Fresno?"

"Really, it's just like the Valley's Valley," I said. "It's practically right on top of North Hollywood."

"Nina, do you think I ever drive as far up as *North Hollywood*?" she asked, and we both laughed. "I'll have Max shoot over a couple dates, let her know what works."

We said goodbye and I abandoned my shopping to ponder

what it would mean. Literally, I'd never dreamed of having a job like Joyce's, but it was hardly due to lack of respect. Joyce was one of the smartest, most driven people I knew, and if she thought I'd be good at something, there was no way I could just let that go. No, I hadn't moved to LA for a job like hers, but there was no guarantee I'd ever get the job I actually wanted. If I became someone like Joyce instead, I wouldn't seem like I was floundering anymore. I would have new ambitions. Phoebe and I could talk industry strategy. Lorna could tell her friends that I'd leveled up. My future would be laid out right in front of me, junior agent to agent to . . . retirement? It was a clearer path than writing, that was for sure.

My phone buzzed, and I grabbed for it.

Nat signed me up for Facebook and I discovered that all of my ex-boyfriends are dead!

I arrived right on time at Ari's on Saturday night. None of my orders had even shipped yet, but the good news was I didn't need to be Nina, made over, tonight. Ari had requested the slutty maxidress, and it was happy to come out again (as, clearly, were my boobs).

"Hey." Ari opened her door almost as soon as I rang the doorbell. She was dressed in a dark gray blazer over a white button-down, open halfway to her waist, and perfectly fitted jeans. "Let's go."

"Are we in a hurry?"

"Nina Rice," she said with a sigh in her voice. "If we set foot in my house together, especially while you're wearing that dress, we're going to forget dinner again."

I grabbed her by her shoulders and pulled her close, her hip-bones jutting against the curve of my hips. "That doesn't sound so bad to me."

"We have all night," she said, though her lips found mine for a long kiss. "I want to take you out. I want to do all the date shit with you."

It was amazing, even more amazing maybe than the night we'd shared together. Falling into bed with someone was easy, or at least it had been for me, but so many fears I could have had about—well, whatever Ari and I were doing, were allayed by the simple act of being driven by her to Hippo. It was a bustling restaurant over in Highland Park practically hidden behind a coffee shop and a pizza place. Once inside their door, though, it opened up into a room with high ceilings and modern touches like the bold orange print on the back wall. Phoebe and Bianca had raved about it recently, but the point wasn't the location but the fact that we were out together. Ari wanted to make sure we had time to talk, and her eyes kept drinking me in as if I was something to behold. I felt *treasured*.

"Lorna got her first iPhone," I said, while we were browsing our menus.

"Oh, I know. She followed me on Instagram."

"I'm sorry, she's—"

"What do you mean?" Ari nudged my foot with hers under the table. "Lorna's amazing. I can't wait to see what she posts."

"Yeah, I've avoided social media outside of my job, but that might be enough for me to sign up."

"Is Lorna your only family?" she asked.

"No, I have parents and an older brother back in Missouri, and they're fine, just . . . they don't get me. I don't even think it's a queer thing, they're just all analytical people who got reliable well-paying jobs and don't understand why anyone would have taken the risk to go off to Los Angeles to attend an expensive school and attempt a career that more people fail at than succeed."

Ari snorted. "Tell me about it, mine definitely think the same about me. Even now. They're proud, sure, but my dad still pushes me to get a degree 'in your spare time.'"

"Trust me, mine would say the same thing, and send a list of jobs that don't fluctuate with the market. Believe it or not, TV writer is not on that list."

"Lorna's different." She said it, didn't ask it.

"Yeah. She just wants me to be happy. I have to keep telling myself she's immortal or I'll completely fall apart. I seriously can't imagine not having her in my life. What about your family? I mean, besides your dad and his degree pushiness?"

"No siblings besides my parents' very spoiled cockapoos, Apple and Sauce."

"Wait," I interrupted, "Sauce?"

"Unfortunately, yes, you heard correctly." Ari laughed. "Sauce is the nice one, though. Apple has peed on my suitcase at least four times. I think he's homophobic."

"How can you tell, does he bark when *Ellen* comes on?"

She cracked up. "Yeah, exactly. That might be about the toxic workplace issues though. Anyway, they have a lot of advice for me—my parents, that is, not Apple or Sauce—and it all seems so rooted in . . . I don't know. I'm well aware that if I'd gone a different direction with my career, I might be more successful. My parents begged me to cut my hair before I flew out for my first audition. I don't know if you remember, but I had like this fashion mullet back then—"

"Oh, trust me, I remember."

"My mom thought I was doomed before I started with that haircut." She shrugged. "And then I wasn't. But it doesn't stop the suggestions, and it makes me feel like they'd love me to be in the closet. Not in my personal life, just so that people at their golf club don't think of them as Jake and Kelly with the lesbian daughter."

"The *famous* lesbian daughter, though," I said. "Don't you get points for that?"

"You'd think." Ari reached across the table and threaded her fingers through mine. I pulled my hand back. "Everything OK?"

"I'm sure that it's not allowed by Joyce if we—"

"Fuck Joyce," she said, a corner of her mouth tugging upward. "I'll fire Joyce tonight if it makes you happy."

We both laughed, as Ari's hand found mine again.

"Not really, I hate Hollywood sometimes but—contrary to my parents' opinion—I'm not an idiot. But people don't actually pay attention to me, Nina, not in normal life."

I glanced around and saw that she was right. There were no frantic looks away, no phones secretly pointed in our direction. Ari blended in, and so we were safe.

A server stopped by for our drink order, and the truth was that neither of us had absorbed a single word on the menu. Ari fixed her smile—her real smile—on the server.

"Any recommendations? I think waiting for us to decide would be a bad idea, if you ever want to turn this table over tonight."

He laughed and pointed out his favorite cocktails and non-alcoholic beverages on the menu. We chose from that and sent him on his way, with a warning he'd need to do the same for our food.

"I had an . . . interesting conversation with Joyce today, actually," I said, though I hadn't planned to bring it up. "She asked if I'd want to become a junior agent after awards season and that she'd mentor me."

Ari frowned. "How'd she take it when you shot her down?"

"I . . . I didn't. I'm still thinking about it."

"What's there to think about?" she asked. "You're not here to agent, you're here to write."

"Well, plans can change," I said. "My parents aren't wrong that becoming a TV writer isn't much likelier than winning the lottery."

"Fuck that," Ari said, as the server dropped off our drinks.

"I'll give you two a moment," he said, and hurried off.

"Sorry, it's just that you're *not* playing the lottery. You're a funny, interesting, brilliant woman who has things she wants to say, who's already in Hollywood—well, close enough—and is building connections. Any writers' room would be lucky to have you."

"I think you might be biased," I said, though I wished I could somehow capture *funny, interesting, brilliant* and save them tangibly somehow.

"I already adjusted for bias. I didn't say any network would be lucky to give you an automatic series order, did I?" She leaned back against her side of the booth and folded her arms across her chest. "I'd just hate to see you give up the dream now."

"I'm not giving up anything," I said, and tried not to think about the possibility that Ari didn't think I was ambitious enough. "I just didn't tell her no. I'm willing to keep my mind open to the fact that life doesn't always go the way you plan, and that it's not always bad when that happens."

She didn't look moved by this, so I nudged her foot this time. "I didn't plan for you to go this way, after all."

"Unfair using that against me," she said, but she beamed as the waiter arrived to ostensibly take our order but of course we all but forced him to tell us what to get. All I'd thought about my entire drive down was Ari's bedroom, but now that we were seated in the Saturday night noise of this beautiful restaurant, I was in no hurry to get back there. I loved Ari's face in the glowing light, I loved getting a little buzzy on cocktails and sobering up as plates of food kept arriving. Our server apologized for perhaps over-suggesting, but we could only laugh because we'd brought it upon ourselves.

Afterward we decided to walk down the block to grab another drink, and I had a moment where I marveled that Ari's arm was around my waist. A few days ago, I never would have believed it. Would I ever? Would it last long enough to get used to it? Did I ever want to get used to it, or could I live in a world where it was always a bit like magic?

"I'll grab us drinks at the bar," Ari told me when we pushed into the crowded building. "You trust me?"

"Mostly," I said, and she kissed me before heading over. It seemed so long ago that I'd loved seeing Taylor from afar, but as I grabbed a table and waited, it rushed back to me a little, because I liked this too. I liked Ari's easy grin and how I saw her charm work its wonders on the bartender. She wasn't Taylor, and I hadn't earned the right to be proud of her yet, but I felt way more than nothing.

"Hey there," she said, arriving back with two nearly over-flowing tumblers. "I told the bartender I needed to impress a girl on our first date so he mixed up something special for us."

"You don't need to impress me," I said, though I smiled ridiculously hard as we clinked our glasses together. "You know that I think you're kind of amazing, right? The way you're so out, and that you don't compromise your identity for the industry . . . I'm inspired by you, Ari."

She shrugged, ducking her head. "I can't imagine doing it any other way."

"I *know*, that's the point, that's what makes you so—"

I cut myself off as she looked back up and right into my eyes.

"What does it make me?" she asked, and I felt myself blushing. "No, I'm not trying to put you on the spot. I want to know what you were going to say."

"I think you're incredible. And you don't have to act like it's not a big deal. Imagine if when we were little there'd been someone with your haircut who won an Oscar."

Ari's face was flushed, and I realized she was blushing too. "Let's not get ahead of ourselves."

I tipped back another drink of the gin-heavy blackberry cocktail. "You're really bad at compliments, aren't you?"

"No," she said quickly, which made me laugh. "I told you I was bad at this part."

"What are you talking about? You just took me to an amazing dinner. You had a hipster bartender with a ridiculous mustache handcraft a drink just for me *and it's delicious.* You're great at this part. Just not compliments."

She took a big swig from her glass. "Girls think they know me, is the thing. Since I'm so public and I . . . I don't know. I stand for something. And then we go out and I'm just an idiot who's good at picking restaurants. I'm not larger than life. I'm not that GIF set. I'm just this person."

"I like this person," I said.

"I didn't mean *you,* Nina Rice." She rested her elbows on the table and leaned forward. "Why do you think I'm so fucking nervous? You've only seen me as I actually am. There's no hiding."

"Well, good," I said, because I didn't want to tread carefully with Ari anymore. Two days ago I'd dived off the deep end and I wasn't paddling back to shore. "I like you. *And* your GIF set."

"I like you too." She finished off her drink in a gulp. "I'm ready when you are."

"Oh, is everything OK or—"

"Wait, was I too subtle?" She leaned in, practically climbing across the table, until her lips touched my ear. "I wish I was already inside of you."

I downed my drink too. "Believe it or not, you might have been too subtle."

We waved to the bartender as we left, who saluted us with a sly grin. I didn't mind that he knew where we were headed.

Back at Ari's, though, we moved more slowly than last time. She hung up her blazer neatly before setting the coffeemaker for the morning with carefully measured scoops of artisan dark roast. I took the time to walk around, poking into her bookshelves, examining the art framed down her hallway and into her bedroom that—for spending many hours in—I'd barely noticed. It felt crisp and clean, pale gray walls with a sleek dark wooden bed with a black and gray striped duvet, as if Ikea had a more mature cousin. The color in the room came from the artwork on the walls, everything from bold photography to modern splashy abstract paintings.

I heard Ari walk in behind me, but I didn't turn.

"What are you thinking about?" She walked right up behind me and slipped her arms around my waist. I settled back against her, loving the way we fit together.

"I like all of your art. Not just each piece, but the effect together is . . . joyful, somehow? Seeing all these different things together. Is that weird to say?"

"No, that's how I feel too. One of the first things that happened when I got my first paycheck for *Brother's Keeper* was that I was at this little coffee shop with a friend, and they had these gorgeous paintings on display. I started talking to my friend about how I wished I could support local artists and have something that beautiful in my apartment, and then I realized I could." She pointed to a colorful abstract piece, different shapes overlapping on top of a bold blue background. "So now whenever I see something, I just let myself buy it."

"That explains the Hasselhoff," I said, and she practically collapsed into me laughing, her breath warm on the back of my neck.

"Don't you dare mock the Hoff," Ari told me once she'd regained her composure.

"Never," I said with my hand up like a pledge. She caught me around the waist again and kissed me as we realigned to face one another. I worked at unbuttoning her shirt as our eager mouths overlapped, frantic as if the quiet moments had never happened, fast and desperate to fulfill this need again. I dipped my head to taste her collarbone, pulled her open shirt aside to let my mouth continue roaming to her breasts as she murmured appreciative sounds.

Ari eventually guided me back so that we were kissing

again, deeper and with a knowledge of each other we hadn't had at this point on Thursday. I unbuttoned and unzipped her jeans, asking the question with a gentle caress on her bare hipbone, and she groaned an affirmative into my ear before I slipped my hand into her briefs and stroked her, slowly to start, as her hips grinded against me. Last time, Ari had made certain I'd come first. Tonight after the dinner and the custom drink and her vulnerability—even though I liked that she was a little in charge in this room—I'd made a decision. Ari Fox came first tonight.

Chapter 15
Brunch Interrogation

Even though I'd prided myself on punctuality ever since my breakup with Taylor, it was a miracle I'd even managed to park at All Day Baby, a three-minute drive from Ari's house, by 11:00 a.m. the next morning. I'd packed fresh clothes with me, but I didn't feel fresh. I was wrung out and used, a map of places notated by Ari's hands, Ari's lips, Ari's mouth. A shower and a fresh pair of underwear couldn't undo that. Not, of course, that I'd want to.

Even so, brunch was only to be missed for emergencies, and I was hardly about to explain to my friends that this might qualify as one. Dragging myself out of Ari's bed and into the shower, alone, could have been categorized as a catastrophe. Luckily there was an unspoken truth that I might go right back, after brunch, to see what else we could discover. I was hooked.

Chloe shouted to me from a table in the back when I walked in, and I made my way to my friends. Before I'd even sat down, though—

"Holy *shit*, Nina, have a good night?" CJ bellowed at me. (Yes, bellowed, I stand behind that description.)

"What?" I asked in my most innocent tone, smoothing down my hair. I should have definitely spent more time on my hair.

"You could *not* look more fucked," Chloe said.

"That's ridiculous," I said, though it obviously *wasn't* and I didn't know what I was hiding or why. This thing just felt so safe and protected now. Only Ari and me—and I guess a bunch of senior citizens up in Santa Clarita.

"I barely know you," said Sofia, who had outlasted almost every previous CJ girlfriend by this point. "But even I sense that you're lying."

"Was it on the trail at Hart Park?" CJ asked, which made Bianca shriek.

"CJ, what are you even talking about, and what do you know?"

"Give me some credit, I don't have sex *on trails*," I said, and then it was like I'd somehow said everything, and my friends made such intense noises of surprise and validation that our approaching server changed her mind and headed away from us.

"Now I'll never get a bloody mary," I groused, though not sincerely. Why did it feel so good to get shit from your friends? From my friends, at least. They were the absolute best at it.

"So you finally got Foxed," said CJ, who was clearly leading whatever was happening this morning.

"Nina, tell us everything." Chloe leaned forward with her chin in her hands like a child waiting on an ice cream sundae. "I mean *everything*."

"I will not," I said, and tried to shoot apologetic looks across the room at the server so that I could have a brunch cocktail in my hand as soon as possible. I was sleep-deprived and hungover from lust, and while Ari's hipster coffee had done its best, dealing with my friends in this state required an additional layer of assistance.

"Is it just sex?" Bianca asked, right as the server arrived with a menu for me.

"Could I please get a bloody mary?" I asked. "And also I'm very sorry about my friends. Some of them are over forty and should really know better."

Phoebe and CJ practically gasped, while the server looked pained on her journey away from our table yet again.

"We are tipping at least thirty percent," I said.

"Yeah, yeah," Bianca said. "Answer my question."

"No," I said, biting the inside of my cheeks to keep from smiling. I couldn't believe this was an answer I was giving, a place Nina Rice found herself. "It's not."

The reaction sounds rang out again, and every other table shot us murderous glares. And I was still embarrassed and didn't know how much I could bear to say, but I loved this obnoxious and embarrassing table of people so much. And I knew that the shrieks and dirty jokes meant that, just maybe, they loved me too.

I snuck into the bathroom as brunch was dying down to text Ari, because despite my lack of sleep and two bloody marys, my plate full of eggs and carbs had sobered me up. It no longer made sense to me that Ari Fox, who I'd spent about fourteen hours with, would want me back for more. Would it keep swinging that way in my head? After all, I reminded myself, she wasn't Ari Fox, Rising Star, not with me. She was just Ari. And she supposedly liked me because I knew that.

Still, holy hell, it was a bit too good to be true. Ari, her accomplishments, her raw sexiness, and then me. Nina Rice, cursed, normal, still hadn't done anything about her split ends.

Yes, come back. Want to do something outside? Reservoir walk?

I texted back a quick agreement before heading out to say goodbye to my friends as we went our separate ways for the week, though not really. The group text went on practically every hour of every day, with only a brief time off for sleeping, and it made LA feel a lot closer when I was up in Santa Clarita. Though I guess spending two of the last three nights in LA made it feel a lot closer too.

Ari was dressed in one of her standard expensive basics outfits, and she nodded at my—well, my everything. Obviously I was still waiting on my wardrobe upgrade—though I'd gotten some *just shipped!* emails—so I was in a lazy Sunday maxi over my Birkenstocks, not that Birkenstocks ever needed an upgrade, they were an iconic queer footwear classic.

"Are you good to walk in those?" Ari asked. "Where are your big outdoorsperson boots?"

"Those were my friend's, and we should probably discuss now that I'm not very outdoorsy. My feet will be fine in those. Dusty, maybe, but fine."

Ari pulled me close and squeezed my ass. "Don't get in my bed later with those dusty feet."

"Oh damn, too bad your bed's the only place in your house to fuck," I said, and it felt dirty, *I* felt dirty. I hadn't been like this with Taylor; the two of us had an upstanding respectable relationship where we had plenty of sex but we didn't talk about it a lot. We'd figured out early on what we liked, and so we stuck with it, and in retrospect I knew that it sounded boring, but it hadn't been. It was good—great, even—and we were happy. I'd had plenty of orgasms. I'd thought about our wedding and future children, Taylor's ascent to the top of her firm, and my plans to land in a dog-friendly writers' room so that our rescue dogs were rarely home alone.

Now I was older and planless and I talked about *fucking*. And the truth was that maybe this version of Nina Rice was just as *me* as that other one with the plans and the polite sex. Maybe I could still get rescue dogs, though. Actually, that reminded me of something.

"Ari, don't you have a cat?"

She ushered me out the front door, setting the alarm and checking the locks on her way out. "Yeah?"

"Why haven't I seen it?"

"Nina Rice, are you accusing me of *inventing* a cat?"

"It just seems weird I've never seen it," I said with a laugh as we walked to the garage and got into her car.

"I don't want you to take offense, but Steve has never liked one of my girlfriends." She made a face. "Not that—I know that we're still—not—"

"Hey." I tried to touch her arm without inhibiting her driving ability. "I knew what you meant. Mainly I'm concerned you have a cat named Steve."

"He came with that name," she said. "Who was I to change it? Haven't you seen *Cats* the musical?"

"Uh, no," I said, and she let out a sound like I'd just confessed I'd never tried pizza. "Ari, I thought maybe we were compatible, but now I'm worried."

"You are not alone there, babe," she said, and we both felt that *babe* and then chose to let it stand. By Silver Lake Reservoir, Ari found a nearby parking spot, and we began to make our way around. It was a fairly wide path that circled the titular basin reservoirs plus dog parks and a rec center. Even as someone who didn't gravitate to the outdoors without the push of a girl I was trying to impress, I'd walked this path plenty. It was only a couple of miles long and a mix of city and idyllically green park, as green as this side of town got, anyway. There was plenty of shade and only a couple of steep inclines.

"Has *anyone* met Steve?" I asked, and Ari laughed.

"My friend Cade fed him the entire two weeks I was in Vancouver, and knew he was alive because the food kept disappearing, but they didn't see him once."

"So . . . that's a no?"

Ari laughed. "That's a no. But I promise that he exists. Who else would have been eating the food?"

"I don't know, rats?"

"Nina Rice, did you just compare my beautiful feline son with *rats*?"

"Feline son?"

We couldn't stop laughing. The two miles were up before I knew it and Ari took me to Starbucks for chais before we went back to her place and got creative since I did indeed have dusty feet.

I kept thinking that I didn't know what I was doing, because this was a world I'd said I didn't occupy anymore. But the truth was that I knew exactly what I was doing, I made the choice to be here with Ari instead of fleeing. There was no panicked drive back to the suburbs; there was no wall I put up to keep this to small talk and casual fun.

I never saw Steve. We ordered in vegan Thai from Bulan, a mainstay of my old life, but it felt new out of takeout cartons at Ari's dining room table. Instead of watching a movie, as planned, we kept pulling up funny videos on YouTube and passing our phones back and forth. She called out suggestions over my shoulder as I did the daily crossword. That night I slept with my head nestled next to Ari's shoulder and when I woke up early on Monday morning, we were still there, right in the same place.

Max emailed me on Monday with options for my lunch with Joyce, and I picked Wednesday over Friday because it was closer and it gave me an excuse to be back in LA sooner. I wanted the option of casually texting Ari, and I went ahead and threw an extra dress and pair of underwear into my purse just in case I didn't go home afterward. By the time I was in my car in a new dress and some uncomfortable but lacy underpants, I was very determined that I wouldn't go home afterward.

I was early to AOC, as I suspected, because the industry did not run on time and of course for the last three years I did. I ran early. The paradoxically elegantly rustic restaurant didn't *not* intimidate me as I loitered near the entrance (sitting down without Joyce felt like too much of a power move I was in no position to make), but the floral dress that had magically arrived just hours ago via the glory of online shopping looked fresh and practically stylish, and Bianca had coached me via FaceTime into replicating an updo that was chic, made me look taller, and—bonus—hid my split ends. Why hadn't I taken care of my stupid split ends? The truth was that the only hair stylist I knew up near me was the guy who cut Lorna's hair and was almost as old as she was. He was still sharp with scissors but told me so many stories about his youth that I ended up being out of reach from work for long stretches of time, as he didn't keep evening or weekend hours.

I sighed and got out my phone to text Bianca. **Fine, I give in, give me your hair guy's name.**

Oh my god, girl, I'm so excited. What are you going to get done??

Literally nothing, just a trim, but if I can do it in less than an hour without any stories about World War II I'll be thrilled.

Nina, I have A LOT of follow-up questions, but I'll email you the salon link! And can we get dinner soon, just us? I promise I won't ONLY ask you about Ari.

Dinner sounds great, but can I be extremely pathetic and tell you that I'm going to see when I'm hanging out next with Ari before I make plans with you? I promise there are no Uhauls yet but I'm something like addicted right now.

No explanations needed, especially to me, the girl who moved in with her now-wife after a month. Do you remem-

ber how we'd only gone out TWICE when I made her take me to my worst cousin's baby's baptism? I have no room to judge.

"Hey there, Nina, sorry I'm late."

I looked up from my phone and smiled as Joyce walked in. "No problem, I'm always early, I know it's an LA taboo."

She burst into laughter. "You've got that right. Where were you raised? Somewhere exceedingly proper?"

"Missouri, absolutely not."

"You look great," she told me, surveying my outfit. This new red and pale yellow floral dress had more structure than the dresses I'd been getting by in for the last while, but only by a little. The front dipped low but far less dangerously so than Ari's requested dress, and the fabric hung gracefully, somehow, down to my feet. I'd traded in my usual Birkenstocks for, of course, just a newer pair, but in a different shade, metallic rose-gold. It was now perhaps the nicest outfit I had, though of course Joyce still put me to shame in a bright green structured dress that nipped in at the waist, with sky-high snakeskin heels, plus a gold single-chain statement necklace. She looked like the boss she was.

"Thanks," I said. "I went shopping for the first time in—I shouldn't tell you how long."

"You're so responsible. It's all I do in my downtime, my husband has to keep his things in the guest closet."

I loved that Joyce read my laziness as responsibility, but given that she was in charge of my employment, I wasn't about to correct her.

The host led us to a table tucked against a wall, behind the enormous indoor tree. AOC was the kind of restaurant my friends and I would definitely frequent if it were on our side of town, the same which could not be said for many spots west of La Cienega Boulevard. It was a different world over here, crisper and a bit more formal. The Eastside could feel messier, more willing to find room for someone like me, fat and queer and—normally—bad at knowing what was *in* at the moment. This spot, though, didn't feel so rigid, and our smiling server put me at ease immediately.

Not that I was ever completely relaxed around Joyce.

"I'm really glad you were open to this," Joyce said, once we'd selected an array of small plates to order. "You've really proven yourself with Ari; I know she's tough."

I mumbled some noncommittal nothings and then hid behind a big gulp of water.

"Would that be the kind of specialty that might work for you?" Joyce asked, and chuckled. "Not difficult clients who could stand to trust the process a little more if you ask me, but—well, I think there could be a real need for someone who has an insight to LGBTQ talent and the extra challenges they face in Hollywood. It's not that I'd want to limit you, but it could be a nice corner to start from."

There were a lot of things I could have reacted to, from Joyce's shade thrown at Ari to a question about the career I didn't know I even wanted. But, holy hell, that last thing, she was right. There *was* a need for people like Ari to have more understanding from the people who worked with them.

"I agree," I found myself saying. "Yeah, I could maybe see myself doing something like that."

"Fantastic. We'll be done with the post-awards season by April, so should we tentatively plan on transitioning you then?"

"I . . ." I gulped more water to buy myself time. "Sorry, it's just—well, there's a lot to consider. Could I keep thinking about it?"

Joyce watched me with her dark brown eyes. There was no looking away once you were in her view. "What's holding you up?"

"Well, this—I don't know how to say this, but—"

"This isn't what you came to Los Angeles to do?" she asked, and let out a brusque peal of laughter. "Join the club! I doubt anyone moves to LA to be an agent, except maybe for a stretch in the early 2000s for a certain brand of terrible man who watched *Entourage* one too many times. No, for most of us, it's just where the cards landed. And I'm lucky they did, that's for sure."

There was definitely a feeling in the Hollywood-and-surrounding air that opportunities weren't to be turned down. Even ones you didn't want. You don't take this job or appreciate it enough? There were another hundred people in your place who'd kill for it. Who were you to want something else instead?

Who was *I*?

"Good news," Joyce said, and I exhaled as I felt the conversation moving on to calmer waters. "Gregory is a go."

"Congratulations," I said. "I've already been researching, and I'll do even more now that he's official."

She smiled her dazzling smile. "Please tell me what your research consists of."

Our food began arriving as I explained my tour of social media, clips from talk shows, press junkets, always in search of the most candid and real-seeming moments. Joyce actually had a few suggestions, not just Gregory Hart–specific ones, and I logged them for later. Then, somehow the subject of podcasts came up, and it turned out we had similar tastes in true crime, and we shared our theories on a long-running murder whodunit. The truth was that I liked and respected Joyce, and if she believed in me, it meant a lot, far beyond simply taking this new career opportunity just because it was more of a guarantee than my initial dream. Dreams, I knew, were notorious for changing.

Chapter 16
Girlfriends

After lunch wrapped up and I said goodbye to Joyce (she'd valeted like, well, a boss, while I'd found street parking a few blocks away, i.e., free and no need to force a valet at a classy restaurant to motor the Honda to a safe spot), I dropped as casual a text as possible to Ari, and was thrilled that I'd barely hit *send* when I saw her three dots. **Yes, all I have to do today is read a script, I'm home. Come over.**

She answered the door in a ripped blue muscle shirt over black joggers, and her eyes widened as she took me in. "Fuck, babe, you look gorgeous."

I very much liked being *babe*, maybe even more than *gorgeous*. We pulled into each other's arms, something closer and slower than a hug.

"Thanks," I said, still wrapped up in her embrace. "I feel like I have to look nice on that side of town."

"You always look nice," she said, "but this is next-level. Can I take you out tonight? You shouldn't waste this on me alone."

"You alone are not a waste." It was obviously a line, and from her raised eyebrow she knew it, but even cheesy lines did the job sometimes. We kissed, our bodies still pressed up against one another. "Seriously, there's no pressure to take me out."

"Too bad, I'm already making plans in my head," she said. "How was Joyce?"

"Great, she just landed—" I paused. "I'm not sure it's public yet."

"No problem."

"You'd sooner die than run to *Deadline* with the story, so I know that doesn't it matter if I tell my g—"

We both froze, and then laughed because when your bodies were perfectly aligned, you couldn't hide a reaction like that.

Ari took a step back from me. The distance felt massive. "We could . . . talk about that."

"Oh, sure, we absolutely can," I said, hating my use of *my*, loving her use of *babe*, wondering where that landed us. Considering that I'd planned never to be in this position again, I felt more awkward than usual wading into this discussion.

"As you know, I'm bad at this—"

"As *you* know, I think that's bullshit—"

"*Anyway.*" Ari grinned as she raked her hand through her hair. "I like you a lot, Nina Rice. I know we didn't get our shit together until last week, but I've liked you since we met when you said something about doing meth."

"I did *not* say anything about doing meth!" I said and then remembered my inane chatter about cold brew. "Of course you'd remember that."

"I haven't officially asked someone to be my girlfriend since tenth grade," she said. "It always just . . . happened. So I'm not exactly sure how to do it."

"I . . . think you just did it," I said, and closed the distance between us again. "Obviously, yes. It's fast but also it's not, and also I guess that I don't care. It's fun making rushed decisions."

We both laughed because somehow in our sex-addled brains,

rushed decisions sounded like a euphemism, and we made out for a while, right there right inside her door again, like horny teenagers who wondered just how much they could get away with in a few minutes with their clothes on. Finally I extricated myself because I couldn't remember when I'd last checked my work email, and Ari had a potential script she was supposed to be reading for consideration. In LA it was always so easy to forget workdays weren't weekends, with the sunshine and freelancers dripped everywhere. Santa Clarita had made me more responsible, and I didn't want to let that go, girlfriend or not.

Holy hell, though, I had a *girlfriend*. That seemed almost worth the risk of irresponsibility. It was all irresponsible, wasn't it? I'd never expected to be in this role again, much less like this, but here I was. Nina, version whatever. Maybe I should have put up more of a fight, claimed I needed to think longer on it or that it was the wrong time to be starting a relationship. All the things I'd gotten used to saying when the winds shifted even a little during something easy, something casual. Instead, the first woman who'd come out and asked had gotten an immediate *yes* from me.

It was hardly like Ari was just a random asker though. In all my years away from—well, everything, I'd never counted on someone like her.

Ari read her script while I checked emails and researched Gregory Hart, and every so often a glass of water or a fresh cup of coffee would appear next to me, like magic. I couldn't remember the last time someone had taken care of me, and while I wasn't sure I deserved it, the thoughtfulness Ari showed warmed something far deep within, something I'd assumed might be cold and locked up forever. I wanted more afternoons like this. I wanted to be taken care of.

"Question," Ari said, glancing up from her script. "Would it be easier if I talked to Joyce? If the client's always right—"

"Just so you know, we don't say that about clients," I said, and she laughed.

"I'm devastated. Still, there's technically more power on my side, yeah? She'll have to find a way to be OK with the two of us."

"I . . . I don't think we need to hurry to tell Joyce," I said.

"Yeah?" Ari watched me for a moment. "Is this about the job?"

I shrugged. "I guess it's not *not* about the job. It's also about the job I have, right now, that keeps me fed and the student loan people off my back."

"Of course," Ari said quickly. "I'm sorry. It's just—"

"I'm still working on my script," I said. "I'm just considering other things."

"I hate playing things by ear," Ari said, smiling and scowling at the same time. It was, of course, very charming. "But I will."

Once the sun began to dip down, Ari let me know she was making dinner reservations, and disappeared into her bedroom to change. I'd, of course, found no fault with her casual home clothes, but then she reappeared in cropped black pants with a matching blazer over a very low V-neck tee that showed what felt like miles of smooth glowing skin.

"Holy *hell*," I muttered, and she grinned.

"Had to up my game tonight," she said. "You couldn't be seen out with someone in soft pants."

"You call them *soft pants*?" I asked. "Aren't they just . . . sweatpants?"

"But they're soft," she said, which was somehow a valid argument and yet still the funniest thing I'd heard all day. We decided to order a Lyft so we could start with cocktails on empty stomachs and not task ourselves with a long night to sober up later, and Ari gasped as she held her phone.

"Karl! We've got Karl again!"

I squealed in disbelief, but sure enough, Karl's Prius hummed up, and we leapt into the car. It hit me that he probably drove dozens of people every day and wouldn't find this special, but his grin took over his whole face.

"Ari F.! And her beautiful friend! Another big date night for you girls?" he asked, zipping down the back way to, presumably, avoid the snarls of traffic on Sunset.

"It is a big night," Ari confirmed. "Karl, my beautiful friend here is actually my beautiful date."

A spike of panic jolted through me, because Karl was nice but he was an older guy. Who knew how he thought about women like us? Straight people spoke of *coming out* like it was this big, dramatic one-time thing every queer person did, but the truth was that there were a hundred ways you might have to come out every single day, like with this random old man Lyft driver.

But Karl's grin cracked open into a warm laugh. "Good for you two! What'd'you need with some lousy good-for-nothing guys. These young ones, today, hopeless. You're better off."

Ari smiled right at me. "We sure are."

Bianca and I met for dinner the next Monday, a perfect quiet evening to snag a table and sit there all night if we wanted, and I realized as I walked into Fred 62 that it was exactly what I wanted. I saw her plenty at brunch, and we texted a fair amount, but I didn't remember the last time we'd gone out to catch up, except that it had been before Taylor and I broke up. It had been another life.

The diner, a mix of old red vinyl booths and hipster artwork, was open twenty-four hours, and Bianca and I had probably seen every single one of those hours over the course of our friendship, ordering from their special late-night hangover menu back in our freshly post-college days and meeting up before and after dates, breakups, and a myriad of other girl incidents. It was overpriced for diner food but cheap for a place that would let us set up camp for hours, Diet Coke refills coming without any passive-aggressive comments to leave. It had seen us through a lot.

"Oh, shit," Bianca greeted me as she walked in. Other diners looked around to see what she was reacting to, and then immediately grew disinterested and looked away. The boring truth of the matter was that I'd snagged an appointment this late afternoon at a salon just down Vermont Avenue. I'd selected *long haircut* from the list of available gender-neutral options, but once I arrived, Bianca's—and now my, I guessed—stylist Julian announced that the appointment after me had canceled and didn't I maybe want to do color while I was there? The change was subtle, a slight warmth to my brown hair that hadn't been there before, some subtle highlights that made me seem like I went outside more than I did. Not a completely new Nina, just a little turned up.

I stood up to hug her. "He basically made me do it."

"No offense, girl, but you needed it," Bianca said with a wicked cackle. "I'm kidding! A little. You look amazing, and you smell like a salon, so good."

"Well, I bought every single thing he put into my hair, so hopefully I'll smell this good for the foreseeable future."

Bianca sat down with a smirky grin. "Sounds like new girlfriend behavior."

"I know what it sounds like," I said. "It's also just . . . I barely left my—Lorna's condo for three years. My clothes were mostly stretchy things, and my split ends were threatening to overtake the rest of my hair."

"Also when you have a new girlfriend it's fun to look cute for her as often as possible," Bianca said from behind her menu.

"Well . . . sure," I said, as if of course that hadn't been a motivating factor. It was hardly just that I had a new girlfriend; I had a new girlfriend with the wardrobe of a teen heartthrob centerfold in the alternate universe where soft butches were who all the teens were talking about. Ari still got her hair cut at the cozy queer neighborhood barber, she'd told me, but her skin was partially that luminescent because there was a whole dermatology team in Larchmont Village seeing to it. She mainly shopped—or used to, at least—for her own clothes, but designers, especially queer ones, loved her—or loved what she stood for, at least, and how their clothes hung on her lean angular frame—and so boxes apparently just *showed up*, at Exemplar, at her manager's office, at her publicist's. Ari actually spent less money on clothes than I did, because the clothes found her. (She had admitted to having paid for those sneakers, though, and wouldn't tell me for how much.)

Bianca looked over her menu at me. "If I order the fried mac-and-cheese balls, you'll share them with me, right?"

"I'm offended you have to ask."

She laughed, but it faded quickly.

"What?"

A waitress showed up to get our drink order, and Bianca requested the mac-and-cheese balls as well. I was torn between wanting to encourage the waitress to hang around longer with unnecessary questions and immediately running her off to see what had turned Bianca's mood sour.

"I'll grab your drinks and be back in a few," the waitress told us, and then it was just us.

"What?" I asked again, though I wasn't sure I wanted to know. These glorious weeks where life wasn't just back to normal, it was possibly *getting better*, had perhaps stretched things too thin. Of course it could snap now, soon, at any given moment. Taylor had warned me, and I'd stopped listening.

"You left me," Bianca said. "I know your breakup was— honestly, I don't actually know, because you didn't tell me. You were just . . . gone."

The waitress set down our giant Diet Cokes and glanced at our faces. "I'll give you girls another minute."

"Bianca," I said once the waitress had walked off. "I'm . . . I'm sorry. I don't even know how to explain it—"

"We've been through *so many breakups*, Neen. So many collective girls have broken our hearts."

"Sometimes the same girls," I said, hoping to break the tension, change the subject, make it all stop. Bianca smiled and rolled her eyes toward the ceiling as if seeing something appear from her memory.

"Goddamn Jenny Chao," she said, and I laughed so hard I snorted air into my Diet Coke and it splashed in Bianca's direction. "Ew, get your nose beverage away from me."

The waitress showed up again with a cloth to wipe up the Diet Coke and her pad out for our order. Nothing had gotten fixed and yet I still felt it, pieces fitting back into place. I'd managed not to fully destroy someone for at least another night.

"I wish I had a better way to explain it," I said, even though a part of me ached to walk Bianca through the entire thing. She was right that we'd lived through so many breakups together. We'd heard it all: fights, misunderstandings, getting cheated on, getting ghosted. But Taylor's summation of me was different. Worse, she'd given a warning that there was more to come, and when I dwelt too much on what that could mean, what the *maybe they just don't know you well enough yet* could hold, all I wanted to do was retreat, and not just from Bianca. The safest thing to do was quit the brunches, break up with Ari, turn down Joyce's job offer, *and* give up on my script. But all of that sounded terrible. How long could I outrun fate? Maybe not forever, but . . . a while?

"You could try," Bianca said, her words soft. We'd never had a full-on fight, because we just didn't seem to clash that way. I already felt whatever this was fizzling out, thank god. "You know I'm here for you, right? There wasn't anything I'd done or—"

"No, *no*," I said. "I'm sorry if any of it seemed that way."

"OK," she said. "You can make it up to me by telling me *everything* about Ari. When did it start? Officially?"

I filled her in, the whole entire story, because of course I'd left plenty out last time we'd talked. The fried mac-and-cheese balls arrived, and I dipped the chewy cheesy bites into ranch dressing like the trashy Midwesterner I was at my core while Bianca made faux grossed-out faces but urged me to keep talking. Before, my growing feelings for Ari had been embarrassing, proof that I'd lost track of reality somehow, except that I'd been wrong about that. And so now it didn't seem so bad to let my friend in on the whole thing, or at least a PG-13-rated version. Everything but Taylor's warning and the possibility that I was toying with Ari's happiness, at least. If I said it aloud, listed all the flaws that Taylor saw in me even when others couldn't, I wasn't sure Bianca would see me the same way, and right now the thought of giving up even one piece of my life was unfathomable.

"So . . ." Bianca paused as the waitress dropped off the tuna melt and big salad we'd decided to split. It was a perfect diner meal. "Do you think it's serious? Or are you just having fun? By the way, despite my marital status, I completely advocate for fun, if that's what you want. No judgment here."

"I . . . I don't know. I'm trying to take it one day at a time for now," I said. "Not that I haven't thought about it."

"*It*?" Bianca asked, not one to let me get away with vagueness. I was lucky to have skated by earlier in this conversation. "Marriage, babies, the TV show you write that she stars in?"

"Sometimes I really hate how well you know me," I said. "Because yes. But I also think that this is crazy and we barely know each other and we're on very different life paths and she's like this . . ."

"She's famous and gorgeous, but you're also great, sweetie. You're kind and talented and beautiful. She's lucky. Don't pull this stuff again."

"Again?" I asked.

"Don't you remember when you and—she-who-will-not-be-named started dating? Oh, you didn't make enough money, your hair wasn't sleek enough, your car was embarrassing—"

"My car *is* embarrassing!"

"That's the only thing I'll allow you," Bianca said. "You were good enough for Taylor—too good, it turns out—and you're more than good enough for Ari too."

I almost burst into tears thinking of the whole story. But it was hard to stay down around Bianca, so I got through the moment and then it was her turn to fill me in on everything new with her. Before long we were laughing about college girlfriends and bad twenties jobs and the three years apart from her felt melted away.

On my walk to my car, I thought about texting Ari, but the truth was that the way I felt after hours with my oldest and dearest friend had set off something in me. I was eager to sit down at my computer and tweak a scene early on in my script when two friends navigated some family drama together. I'd wanted to make clear the difference between family of origin and chosen family, but it had never quite clicked. Tonight, though, I thought of Bianca and her seemingly limitless well of love for me. I thought of the three years melted away. I thought of fried foods and big salads. The characters weren't based on us, but I pulled those feelings into it anyway, and I wrote, deleted, and wrote some more. I stayed up way too late and nearly missed my crossword streak, but once I was mostly awake the next morning, I reread my words and felt something glow between the screen and me. I'd figured out the scene.

I'd figure out the rest of it too, I realized.

Ari asked if I'd head to her place on Thursday after my lunch with Lorna for, ostensibly, the whole weekend, and I agreed without being too specific. It was easier to blame Ari's frequent lapses of consideration for my job as part of the new relationship haze than dwell on her feelings about my career. And I could easily wake up early on Friday, slip away for several hours, and return once I knew Joyce and Max were done with my inbox for the day.

She greeted me at her door, like usual, casual in a T-shirt and jeans and bare feet. I pulled myself against her as her arms wrapped around the small of my back, our dimensions now memorized. My bags were still in my hand as her tongue pushed eagerly into my mouth, and I let them drop with a satisfying *thud*. I loved this part, heating up but not yet at a boil. My fingertips worked down Ari's back, feeling the jut of her shoulder blades, the muscles underneath, the softness to her sides, especially when I slipped my hands underneath her shirt. Here, for some reason, she felt vulnerable, gentle and unprotected, and just for me.

A fleeting thought sprang to mind, and I did my best to set it far aside. But it was hard not to think about the fact that Ari felt safe with me, while there was potentially this countdown going, until she looked at me the way Taylor had. Until she knew everything on that list, because she thought it too.

"Hey, you good?" Ari rested her hand against my face and pressed her thumb into my cheek, just a little, as her fingers cupped the back of my head. She'd held me like this before, of course, when our mouths were on one another's, but right now was different. Ari was ready for whatever she thought this was, bad moods and hard talks and shitty days. But there was no way she'd be ready for *this* so I tucked it down.

"I'm good," I said.

"Maybe we'll eventually learn to greet each other politely," she said with a big grin. "You've made me *messy*, Nina Rice."

"Oh, it's all my fault?"

She kissed my cheek and then held her hand up as she dashed out of the room. "I'll be right back. I have a surprise for you."

I moved my bags to a less obstructive part of the room and watched as Ari walked back in with a large box, wrapped in bright blue paper.

"Is there . . . an occasion?" I asked as she presented it to me.

"Just open it," she said. "And the occasion is that I like you."

I put the box down on the coffee table to unwrap, and took a step back when I realized what it contained. "Ari, this is—"

"Don't say that it's too much, remember I'm really overpaid for what I do."

I slid the paper completely off and stared at the Apple logo. "I have a computer at home."

I remembered Taylor presenting me with my current computer on our first Christmas together. I'd been using a hand-me-down from Bianca and the computer fan would spin so loudly that I couldn't use it and listen to music at the same time. Taylor hated it and I didn't blame her. The computer had been the first step; suddenly we were keeping things at each other's places and inevitably before long we'd found our apartment together. Taylor had loved joking that the old laptop had been the only thing keeping us apart.

"You said you have some unmovable desktop beast at home," Ari said. "Now you can work wherever you want."

I laughed, though it *was* too much. "Like here?"

"Well, *yeah*, sure, here. And aren't you going to Palm Springs at some point before long with your crew?"

"I don't have to work from Palm Springs," I said. "I already cleared it with Joyce to take a couple days off."

"But you could *write* from Palm Springs," she said. "I heard that in Southern California, these babies practically write the scripts for you. Think of how much you'll get done now."

"Thank you," I said, though I wasn't sure I'd open it. I wasn't sure I liked everything it might mean.

Ari and I took a walk through the residential streets around her house, and I convinced her that instead of going out we should stay in with delivery food and a new episode of *Grey's Anatomy*, which she'd somehow never seen. There was no way to catch her up on eighteen seasons so I did my best to explain things while we were curled on her sofa together. I was in the middle of telling her about the time a surgical resident had sex with a ghost when Ari laughed so hard she actually started crying.

"OK, it wasn't technically a ghost, she had a tumor—"

Ari wiped her eyes on her sleeve. "Wait, but this is your *favorite show*?"

"Oh, what's your favorite show, something dour with anti-heroes?" I asked.

"No! I barely watch TV, really—"

I gasped, and I wasn't really exaggerating.

"I mean, I watch everything gay," she said. "And—"

"Ari, this show is *super gay!*"

"—any shows where people do talents, I find those calming. Give me a bunch of kids singing or old dads doing amateur magic, perfect. And of course I'll watch *your* show, Nina Rice."

"Don't get ahead of yourself." I eyed the laptop, still in its box on the floor next to the table. "I might not become a writer, you know. I might just be a junior agent who's able to pay down her debt."

"Is this because I said I don't watch TV?" She started laughing again, and I wanted to believe that she understood. Hopefully junior agent Nina would be OK for Ari, too. "Tell me the thing about the ghost-fucking again, please. Spare me no detail."

"Well," I said, "it all started with a tumor. Actually, no, we should go back a few seasons . . ."

What ended up happening was that, after a certain point, we turned off regular TV and opened up Netflix to start the series from the beginning instead. Ari quieted down and leaned against me while we watched together, only occasionally interrupting to share feelings about Sandra Oh, all positive. At some point during the episode I'd made a decision, but, still, it wasn't until the next morning that I got up before Ari and opened that box. The shiny silver computer practically winked at me, and before long Ari was in the kitchen pouring coffee and I was answering Joyce's emails like I'd always worked from Ari's living room floor.

"So you're here all weekend now," Ari said, sitting down next to me with her coffee and her phone.

"I guess I'm here all weekend now," I said. "But I do have to work today."

"I'll be completely quiet," she said, and turned to her phone while I tabbed through "my" email accounts. "Wow, did you see the Gregory Hart news is out?"

I took a sip of coffee. I couldn't deny Ari's snobby hipster roast was very, very good. "What Gregory Hart news?"

"That he signed with Joyce," she said. I started to speak and she held up her hand. "You were constantly googling him in your spare time, every time you had your phone out. It was the only explanation that made any sense."

"Maybe I sleep with all of Joyce's clients and I'm getting ready."

Ari let out a shocked laugh. "Shit, where do you find the time? I'm pretty demanding. Also I have a lot of questions about Paul Giamatti."

"I signed an NDA," I said, which just made her laugh harder. "Ari, seriously, I don't know if I acted grateful, and I still think it's way too much, but thank you."

"I just wanted to make your life easier," she said. "And if the bonus for me is that you're around a little more, great."

"I shouldn't have mentioned my student loans or—"

Ari waved her hands at me. "No. I didn't do this because of money. I did this to try to be nice to you. I don't have ulterior motives; I'm too obvious for that."

My computer dinged, and I snorted an ugly surprised laugh. "Joyce needs me to send a thank-you email for Paul Giamatti, actually."

Ari collapsed onto the floor in laughter while I did my best to get back to work. There was a lot I still had to figure out, because the truth was that I didn't really know if my future would be compatible with my present. It wasn't that Ari might not ever understand if I didn't pursue writing, though of course I knew that was possible. I knew, obviously, that the laptop was probably mostly well-intentioned, but might not be here if I'd already decided to become an agent.

And of course, jokes about NDAs aside, I *was* supposed to be a professional, and yet I was sleeping with one of my boss's clients. And so even if Ari could accept me in this new role, could I pursue it while seeing where we were headed? If I allowed myself thoughts about dogs, weddings, and babies again, how could I ignore the fact that at some point, Joyce would have to find out about us?

Chapter 17
Judgment Awaits

"And another thing—"

Ari laughed and squeezed my hand as we walked up to Brite Spot. It was so close to Ari's that we'd walked, and with each step my panic set in more. I didn't know when the appropriate time to bring your new girlfriend to brunch was—after all, I was no CJ—but once Phoebe and Bianca had started pushing, I'd stood no chance.

"I'm sorry," I said. "I'm just worried that they'll be a lot, and you'll hate them, and then they'll think—"

"Nina Rice, you're very cute when you're nervous," she said. "Annoying, but cute."

"Fuck you," I said, and we both laughed. I kept waiting for the newness to wear off, but over a month in and it was still like this. I felt drunk all the time, drunk on sex and cute texts and walks in the sunshine and Netflix and takeout on Ari's sofa. Also occasionally literally drunk, as Ari was taking an online bartending course in her spare time before her next gig started, just for fun. Ari didn't know there was a hot bartender in my script, so it made for fun research for me.

"Hey," CJ said as they walked up with Sofia.

"Hi," I said, hugging CJ and then Sofia. Incredibly, she was still around. I was getting attached to her, despite that I knew she could disappear at any moment. "This is Ari. Ari, this is CJ and Sofia."

"Hey," CJ said, shaking Ari's hand. "CJ, my pronouns are they/them."

"Ari, she/her," Ari said, and then turned to Sofia to introduce herself. By that point, Phoebe and Bianca had arrived, and with them came another round of introductions. My heart was still going a mile a minute, but by the time Chloe and Fernando arrived, I realized it was possible that my friends wouldn't try to embarrass me and that Ari would see how amazing they all were. The group was good with new girlfriends, weren't they? It was just a lot scarier when said new girlfriend was mine.

Fernando scurried forward and started sniffing Ari before letting out a series of angry barks. He weighed something like seven pounds so it wasn't exactly threatening, but I still threw myself in between them, which made everyone laugh except Fernando.

"He must smell Steve on me," Ari said, and then at everyone's raised eyebrows, "my cat."

"How the hell can he smell him on you when I've never even seen him?" I asked, which made everyone laugh harder and start shouting questions at us. Phoebe handled getting us seated at the large outdoor table she'd reserved, and I felt my nerves settle as the seven of us, plus Fernando, who had settled into a low growl, sat down together.

"Wait," Ari said, and the entire table turned to stare at her. Oh, god, what was happening? "No, sorry, that was overdramatic. Sofia, are you an artist? I think I went to one of your shows the other year and tried to buy a painting."

"I am an artist," Sofia said with a smile. "Was it the group show in Hollywood the other year? I only had so much space, and they were bought up so quickly."

"That was it. I mean, congrats on such a successful show, but I was really disappointed, I'd already started picturing a certain painting in my living room."

"Ari has an amazing collection," I said. "Not too amazing, of course, if it's missing one of Sofia's paintings. Amazing minus Sofia."

"I'm putting together another show right now," Sofia said. "And now you have a connection and can probably reserve something ahead of time, if you'd like."

"I'd *love*," Ari said, and I saw how CJ and Sofia were already won over. "Is it flash portraits again, or something different?"

"It's a mix, but, yes, there are flash portraits again and . . ." Sofia glanced around the table. "If you didn't know, a lot of the work I do is an ongoing series of portraits I paint from memory, from life. And I've painted all of you."

"Just our faces?" Chloe asked. "You're not doing some Georgia O'Keeffe imagining kind of thing, right?"

Everyone laughed, but it was clear we were all thinking it, at least a little.

"Just your faces, yes," Sofia said.

"Are we going to be on display at the show?" Bianca asked. "And can we call dibs? Can I buy the Phoebe?"

"This part is depressing," Chloe said. "Who's going to buy the Chloe?"

"I'll handle it for Fernando," I said, who barked as our waiter walked up. "See, he's into it."

Bianca leaned forward in Chloe's direction. "Chlo, do you want to be set up?"

"Ooh, yes, especially—"

"It's not the girl from Phoebe's office," Bianca said, as the rest of us attempted to put in our drink orders. Ari's hand was casually on my thigh, and I wrapped my hand around her wrist.

"I'm glad you're here," I said softly.

"Me too," she said with a grin. "Now I have a shortcut to getting that Nina portrait."

"Do *not* buy the Nina portrait," I said, though I already wondered what it looked like and where it would be hung in Ari's home. We were too new for portraits, though, weren't we? Besides the Hoff, of course. The Hoff transcended relationship timelines.

"Is everyone set for Palm Springs?" Phoebe asked once our drinks had arrived and Fernando had calmed down again. "Chloe's riding with us, CJ and Sofia are taking one car, Nina . . . are you carpooling with one of us or just heading out from wherever the fuck you live?"

"Wait, is Ari coming?" asked Bianca, who was married to the trip's organizer and *fully aware that Ari was not coming*. I shot her a look, but she merely raised her eyebrows innocently.

"I'm sure Ari's busy," I said. "And there's no room, if Chloe and I are sharing."

"No," Phoebe said, "remember I switched our reservation for the four-bedroom house because the hot tub was bigger? There's room if Ari wants to come."

"Yeah, I'd love to come," Ari said, and I wondered if she— *and everyone else*—should have checked in with me first. I loved my new relationship but it was just that, *new*, and I didn't know if this was a risk to take yet. One brunch with my friends had felt like a big enough step, but the first trip that all of us had taken together in years? And now it was Ari's and my first trip too? It was fun when Ari was *in charge*, but Ari was not actually in charge of me, of us.

Everyone continued talking about the trip, but Ari noticed that I'd stopped joining in, and nudged her elbow into my side.

"You good?" she asked, and I nodded. "Wait, did I—"

"It's fine," I said softly.

She frowned slightly but returned to the conversation at hand. And I let myself ease up, because I loved everyone here—well, I loved my friends and I liked Sofia a lot and I—I *something*'d Ari. What was the word for the rush of feelings I had so newly inside of this relationship?

After brunch wrapped up, we headed back to Ari's. Somehow this whole time she hadn't been to my place, but I couldn't blame her because it was exceptionally inconvenient and also because I hadn't invited her yet. Obviously I'd had sex in the condo, but not with anyone I hoped to build something with. And wasn't my great-aunt's condo the least sexy place I could take Ari? It felt like proof of my failings, the old Nina coming back to haunt me.

"I know," Ari said as soon as we were safely away from my friends. "I should have checked in with you before agreeing to the trip. Bianca was just so—I don't know, do people ever say no to her?"

I found myself laughing. Holy hell, I was relieved. "No! Her and Phoebe team up and it's impossible."

"Also it sounded so good," Ari said. "The hot tub, the weekend away." She shot me a sly look, an eyebrow cocked. "Fucking you quietly while your friends are in the next room."

"I'm not the noisy one," I said, already picturing it all: the hot tub, the tiki drinks, fancy unfamiliar sheets twisted in my hands as Ari hovered above me.

"Are you serious?" Ari let out a scoffing noise. "You're so much louder than me."

I found myself walking faster. "Should we practice for Palm Springs?"

"Oh, you're *on*," she said, matching my pace and leading me to her home. We were barely through the door when Ari pushed me back on her sofa with one hand while working my dress up and my underwear down with her other. A moan slipped out of me in anticipation, and we both laughed, her breath dusting my thighs, the curve of my stomach.

"You lost already, Nina Rice," Ari said, holding my gaze as her lips found me. I clutched my hand over my mouth, opening up to her as her tongue explored. It was somehow funny and hot, fully-clothed and dirty. We maintained eye contact because without sound there was less I could tell her, but the truth was that she didn't need my input. An orgasm burst through me quickly, and I tugged at Ari's hair with my spare hand for something, anything, to do other than let out sound.

"Do you still think that I lost?" I asked Ari, as she kissed the tender inside of my thigh. It was incredibly difficult in that moment to feel like a loser, with this woman kneeling before me while my body shook with aftershocks from pleasure.

"I guess we'll have to find out," Ari said, climbing up so that we were face-to-face again. I kissed her deeply, tasting myself in the kiss, wondering how I could ever doubt this—*us*—for even a moment. We switched places, and though we wordlessly watched one another, I knew that I was still telling a story with my lips and tongue. *Let this last*, and *let's not destroy any of this*, and *I never want to be old Nina again*. And then Ari's hips bucked into me as she let out an audible *fuck*, and the moment was over. We laughed until we cried, and I declared myself the winner.

I'd never felt so much like a winner in a long time.

Of course I knew that I couldn't outrun my fatal possibilities forever, but I wondered just how far I could get. When, hours later, I was drifting off to sleep with my head on Ari's shoulder, I wondered if I really could save my destruction until the last possible minute. I could manage to hold Taylor's truth and make room for this future at the same time, couldn't I?

* * *

Lorna invited Ari, via a text to me and an Instagram DM to her, to our Thursday lunch, and Ari texted me before responding.

See, I can check with you before I agree to things. Can I say yes to Lorna or is this a bad week? And does this mean I finally see your condo?

I stared at my phone for a bit and turned back to my computer without responding. I liked that Lorna and Ari wanted to see each other, actually, but my home made me nervous, or at least the thought of Ari in it. I'd been living on top of things for so long, not within them, and even though I'd managed to push past that lately, it was hard to avoid here.

But I didn't like saying no to Lorna, and I guess I didn't like saying no to Ari either. So I let them both know we were on, and I abandoned a low-priority email about Rosie the Rescue Pug's Chewy.com influencer campaign to walk through each room in search of—I didn't even know. Mostly, Lorna's condo was still Lorna's condo, a living shrine to her bold and sophisticated taste and the life she'd built for herself. I had a desk with two computers and a portrait of David Hasselhoff, all gifted by girlfriends, a closet full of, mainly, stretchy clothes built to work from home in, or dresses to go out in three years ago, and a vanity full of skincare products. That was it, the summation of my life, and would Ari be able to see a future with someone who had so little present?

Still, I threw open the door late Thursday morning when she texted that she'd parked across the street, and beamed as she strode up with a messenger bag strapped across her chest like the hottest delivery person I'd ever seen.

"Nina Rice," she said as she got closer, "this is some suburban fucking shit."

"I *told* you," I said, though I pulled myself into her arms once she was close enough. Let the suburbs watch two women kiss with enough force to start a fire. "I want you to promise that you won't think less of me, but I know it doesn't work that way."

"What are you talking about?" she asked, stepping inside. "This place is gorgeous. Everything's vintage?"

"Well, yeah, it's all Lorna's," I said. "I get no credit."

She gazed around the entranceway, and I led her into the living room, through the kitchen, and into the spare bedroom I'd turned into an office. Her face lit up when she saw the Hoff, and then she stared at my computer screen.

"Don't," I said, leaning past her and command-tabbing to another screen because, *fuck*.

"It's your script," she said, her voice the same tone as when we were headed to a favorite restaurant or about to watch that week's episode of whoever had the most talent. "Can I—"

"Absolutely not, it's still rough and I'm revising so much," I said.

"I completely get it, I won't treat it like a final script," she said. "I'd just love to read what you've been up to."

"I just said no, Ari."

"Yeah, but I just want you to know that I understand, I'm not expecting a finished product. If that's what's holding you back."

"We should get to lunch," I said, pulling her out of the room. "Nina, I'm—"

"I need to go at my own pace," I said. "I'm not even sure I'm finishing this, OK? I know you want me to be a writer and—"

"I never said I wanted you to be a writer, I just don't want you giving up on yourself because it's hard or—"

"It's not because it's hard!" Was that what she thought of me, that I couldn't handle hard work? It was too close to Taylor's words about my lack of ambition. "I *like* the hard work. No, it's because it's risky and I have another opportunity that's more solid. If hard work guaranteed something, I'd be so ready. But sometimes it doesn't mean anything at all. Not everyone's life falls into place like yours."

I heard her inhale sharply, and I realized that *this was it*. The countdown was on.

"Ari, I'm sorry—"

"Nope, I'm being an asshole." She sighed loudly. "Can we hit reset or something?"

"How . . . far back?" I asked, my heart pounding.

"To like five minutes ago when I got here," she said, and I practically burst into tears I was so relieved. "Nina, Jesus Christ, what did you think I meant?"

I shook my head. "I don't know. I don't want to fuck this up."

"*Neither do I*. Come on, Lorna messaged me that tamale pie is on the menu today, and it's all I've been thinking of the entire drive up."

I led her to the garage, and she whistled when she saw the Mustang.

"Shit, this baby's *gorgeous*," she said.

"Wait, are you a car nerd?" I asked.

"Was that not clear?" She walked over and ran her hand over the hood. "*This* is Lorna's old car? Who the hell's old car are you driving?"

"Lorna didn't think a convertible was a responsible everyday car, even in Southern California, so the Honda was that. By the time I graduated college, she was driving less so she pared down to the Mustang and gave me the Honda. It's hard for her to drive now, so she relies on her friends and the center's shuttle, and this stays perfect in storage."

"Oh, but she's so wild and pretty," Ari said, tracing her hand down the side of the car, just like she'd done often to my naked body. "She doesn't want to be locked up in this cage, do you, girl?"

"Ari, are you . . . flirting with my aunt's car?"

She winked at me. "She made the first move."

I was afraid, for some reason, that Ari would bring up the Mustang to Lorna once we were at Oaken Troves, but luckily between Lorna and her friends, it would have been difficult for Ari to start her own conversation anyway. The Mustang just seemed to be reminiscent of something, Lorna's old life, Lorna's youth, and it felt cruel mentioning it. Even, thanks to Lorna and her crew, with the topic off the table, I felt an uneasiness pressing on my chest, muting the afternoon. It hadn't been a fight, not exactly, but the same thing kept coming back in the same way, and I couldn't imagine being on the other side of it. I wouldn't magically have a writing job by next year that made my future more guaranteed, but if this relationship held, would the agency job even be viable? And would Ari still want me if I had neither?

"Just a reminder," I said as Ari and I walked Lorna to her cottage after lunch. The tamale pie had dampened my anxiety for the moment, as good comfort food did, and I was happy to be hand-in-hand with my girlfriend in the bright sunshine next to my favorite relative. "I'm going to Palm Springs with my friends next weekend, and we're heading out Thursday morning, so I'll miss lunch. If you want, I can—"

"Oh, who cares about lunch! Palm Springs, what fun. I used to think I'd retire there, but then Choon Hee leased her cottage here, and that was that."

"How long have you three been friends?" Ari asked.

"Since I was your age, my dear," Lorna said, as we reached her cottage. "So I know a thing or two about weekends in Palm Springs, though I guess none of you will fight over any attractive waiters."

"Lorna, I have so many questions for next time," Ari said.

"I look forward to that," Lorna said, hugging Ari. It stunned me how happy I felt—despite everything—that these two people seemed to genuinely like each other so much. "Nina Louise, I'll be out of the cast the next time you see me."

"That's right! Do you have a big night out planned with Nat and Choon Hee?"

"I think we'll keep it low-key, but you'll hear all about it in two weeks. Have fun in Palm Springs, and tell all your friends I said hi. Who's CJ dating these days?"

"Oh," I said, "I didn't tell you. It's still Sofia, the artist."

"That's wonderful," Lorna said. "See, everyone can find new ways of being. Don't forget that, my dear."

I glanced at Ari and smiled. "Don't worry, I know."

Chapter 18
Into the Desert

The next Thursday, Ari and I set off for Palm Springs from her place. I'd spent the night there so we could leave early, and Ari asked if it could be her place instead of mine so Steve wouldn't be alone for as many nights.

I'd still never seen Steve.

We left with thermoses of Ari's hipster coffee but she swung through Starbucks so I could have a chai for the road, and I felt so full of gratefulness walking back to the BMW with my sun hat on, a drink in my hand, and my gorgeous girlfriend behind the wheel. My work emails were paused until Tuesday, and barring some kind of celebrity emergency, that meant I was completely free.

"Ooh," I said, settling back into the passenger side, "there's a new episode of—"

"No," Ari said. "We're on vacation, we're listening to music. Not cults or murder."

"Fine," I said, as she switched on a playlist from her phone. "I know it's too late to do anything about it, but is it weird we're taking our first trip with all of my friends?"

"Now that you mention it, maybe?" Ari grinned over at me

before backing out of the parking spot and pulling onto Sunset. "I'm kidding. Your friends are great, I love Palm Springs, it's going to be a blast. You're overthinking things."

"Maybe you underthink things."

She laughed. "You'd be the first person in history to accuse me of that."

I sipped my drink as she navigated to the freeway. We were still in the last dregs of rush hour traffic, but time didn't matter to me. Sure, Palm Springs had a pool and hot tub awaiting us, but I was already sharing space with one of my favorite people. Why would I be in a hurry?

"I got an offer on that script that came in the other week," Ari said. "My whole team seems happy with it, so I think it's happening."

"That's amazing," I said. "So you're taking it?"

"Yeah, I think I'm taking it. It films in Georgia, though, so I'll be mostly gone for two months." Ari was wearing sunglasses but I was pretty sure she glanced over at me and then back to the road ahead. "You could . . . come with me for part of it. If you want. You said normally your Joyce gig doesn't require you to be in LA, and I know you'd hate not seeing Lorna for—anyway, I'm not saying for the whole time. Maybe a couple weeks, a couple of times?"

"Yeah, maybe," I said, realizing this could be my life in the future. Following Ari to locations, working while she worked, nights together in hotel rooms and Airbnbs. Finding time together no matter what. I'd tried not to jump to what was next for us, but sometimes the possibilities were so clear. Right now I could imagine it all.

"No pressure," Ari said. "I'll just miss you."

"No pressure felt," I said. "If Lorna's out of the cast and Joyce stuff seems calm, it should work out. And it might be nice to get out of town to have fewer distractions while I'm working on my script."

Ari sat up straighter. "How's it coming? How're you feeling about it?"

Was it terrible that I immediately regretted bringing it up? It wasn't that I wasn't grateful; Ari clearly wanted all my dreams to come true. She was just so . . . *eager* about it.

"It's fine," I said.

"When can I read it?" she asked. "You know that I've read things in a million stages of development, right? Outlines, shitty first drafts, I've seen a lot. I'm not expecting it to be perfect."

I hadn't been like this before, actually. I used to share my work with my close friends, and Taylor used to read everything. She'd caught typos I missed, printing out scripts and circling errors in red pen like a sexy teacher. And Taylor wasn't even creative, she'd been interested in numbers since she was a kid. Why was I so scared of showing my work to Ari? Sure, she'd read a million scripts by professionals, but I knew that she was right. She understood the process.

And the truth was that—while I knew I needed to do a lot of revising before a professional had eyes on my work—I *was* proud. I could feel the script getting objectively better each week. The jokes were funnier, the emotional moments more resonant, and I'd eventually find a way to tie everything together at the end that made more sense. If Ari didn't want to read it as the kind of professional I feared but *as my girlfriend* I wondered if it was time to let her in. Maybe she seemed pushy because I wasn't flexible on this. Maybe I needed to be pushed.

"OK," I said.

"Shit, did you just say *OK*, Nina Rice?" Ari reached over with her right hand to squeeze my knee through the fabric of my maxidress. "Let's pull over, I'll read it on my phone right now."

"Oh, shut up." I pretended to shove her away. "I already regret this."

"I'll show my appreciation," Ari said. "Don't worry."

I knew it was an innuendo, but the truth was I always felt appreciated by Ari. The extra stop to get my chai, the saline solution and case that appeared in her bathroom after she found out I'd been sleeping in my contacts at her place, the quiet ten to fifteen minutes she gave me every evening we spent together so that I could complete the daily crossword. I had a million worries about our relationship—well, mainly that I was a self-destructive time bomb of a woman, but that covered a lot of ground—but Ari's appreciation and care of me never factored in.

Traffic cleared once we were out of LA proper, and Waze said we'd be there by noon. I texted Bianca, who replied that Phoebe had demanded they head out at 8:00 a.m., but the good news was that they were already there, the house was perfect, and Phoebe was having lunch delivered so that we wouldn't have to leave the poolside until happy hour that night.

"I love vacation," I said. "You get to go from being like a semi-productive member of society to someone who's too lazy to drive somewhere for food and it's *encouraged*."

Ari laughed. "You're the one who has food delivered every time something you like is on TV."

"Only when I'm with you; normally I'll just eat tuna salad out of a bowl or something," I admitted. "I've been trying to shield you from how gross I am."

"Oh no, now I know why you get so excited about the Oaken Troves menu," she said. "Though to be honest I've thought of that tamale pie more than once."

"See?" I asked, though she wasn't far off from the truth. When I'd fallen for Taylor with the high-powered job and long work hours, I'd briefly imagined myself as a supportive stay-at-home wife and mom, but I'd ended up spending more time writing than learning how to cook. Once I was alone and thinking that aloneness was permanent, it seemed even less vital to learn. "Wait, can *you* cook?"

"Oh, absolutely not," Ari said, and we laughed together. "I think I'm getting really good at drinks, though."

"Oh, yeah, I should warn you that there's a hot bartender in my script, but she's been there since I started it like four years ago," I said.

"You're so cute when you're nervous," Ari said.

"I'm gonna seem real cute for a while then," I muttered, which made her laugh though obviously I wasn't entirely joking. It seemed so crazy I'd agreed to let her see the script, but at the same time, there was no reason to wait. And because I didn't trust that I wouldn't work myself into a panic over it later, I got out my phone and forwarded the latest version of the file to Ari's email address.

The LA landscape faded into desert before too long, almost no traces that we were just outside of the second-biggest city in the country. And then, an oasis just a few miles off the freeway, Palm Springs. It was full of hotels and museums, restaurants and bars, a full-on tourist destination that ran at about a hundred times slower than the pace of notoriously laid-back Los Angeles. I loved it because it wasn't too far away but it felt like another world, and because while there were undoubtedly very fancy ways to do Palm Springs, there were a lot of affordable ones too, and so it felt like it was for all of us.

We were somehow the last two to arrive—when had my friends all turned into such morning people?—and heard conversation and pool sounds as we got out of Ari's BMW, which she'd pulled in behind Phoebe's Audi. It was a huge midcentury modern house, and I watched as Ari's eyes took it in as we carried our bags to the front door.

"Phoebe did well," she said.

"Yeah, she always does, it's a little irritating," I said, and we laughed as I rang the doorbell. Bianca, wearing a flowing coverup over a hot pink two-piece, flung open the door and pulled me into a hug. She already smelled like sunblock and White Claw.

"I'm so glad you're here this year," she said. "Hi, Ari, I'm so glad you could make it. Not that I gave you a lot of choice."

Ari flipped her sunglasses up on top of her head and grinned. "I was gonna say."

They hugged and I wondered just how many ways my heart could fill, seeing this easy camaraderie between my oldest friend and the woman I was falling for. Bianca led us to our room for the long weekend, and while I'd planned on unpacking, Chloe started banging on our window from outside while yelling *POOL!* so we changed into our suits and joined my friends.

The whole crew greeted us noisily, and I almost burst into tears thinking about our time apart, the years that now felt like a silly waste. Or were they? Would I have appreciated these amazing people without the time away, or without the knowledge that they'd immediately reembrace me like nothing had even happened?

Palm Springs was a true desert, not like the coastal combo of LA, and the sun glowed hot. The hot tub would have to wait until dark; for now we joined the group in the pool. There was a swim-up bar at one end, and Ari volunteered her newfound bartending skills, eliciting excited affirmative responses from the rest of the group.

"You know what this means," Bianca said, swimming up next to me. "Phoebe will *not* be able to handle someone being better than her at something, she is definitely finding out about this online bartending class and signing up within the hour."

We looked to Phoebe, who was studying Ari with a focused intensity, and cracked up. Everyone was just *so themselves* this afternoon: Chloe doing cannonballs into the deep end, CJ and Sofia having a loud conversation about local museums, Phoebe and Ari competing to be the most useful, and Bianca and me gossiping about our significant others and our families and anyone else who came to mind.

The whole group stayed in or around the pool all afternoon, until Bianca announced that she and Phoebe had planned out our evening, and that we should be ready for a night out starting at five for happy hour. Even so, we lost track of time and I barely had time to blow out my chlorine-scented hair into something resembling presentable. Ari pulled on her nicest jumpsuit, so I slipped into a newer floral dress, and I studied us together in the mirror.

"What?" she asked, making eye contact with my reflection.

"I just like seeing us together," I said, feeling sun-drunk and also maybe a little drunk-drunk. My feelings had nowhere to go but out.

"Me too," Ari said, a smile spreading across her face. "I'm really glad I'm here."

We joined everyone in the living room while Phoebe calculated the logistics of how many Lyfts were required. I didn't care about the details because regardless I'd be crowded into a car with some of my very favorite people, and real life seemed far away. Not that real life was too hard these days.

The first stop was a tiki bar on the main strip, and of course Phoebe had a large outdoor table reserved for us. It took forever for everyone to decide on the first round, especially because apparently only Ari and I liked to hand all control over to the waiter's recommendations. By the time our drinks arrived, the evening had started to cool down and we felt talked-out and content to look into the mountains quietly.

"I know that we have a lot of night left," Phoebe said, breaking the silence, and the whole table turned to her the way I imagined conference rooms full of important industry execs did, though tonight Phoebe had gone full-on resort wear in a floral short-sleeved button-down over matching formal-length shorts, with gold prescription aviators instead of her regular glasses. "But I wanted to talk to all of you our first night here."

Bianca reached over and squeezed Phoebe's hand, and Phoebe paused for a moment to smile at her. After five years of marriage they still seemed deliriously in love, and I couldn't help wondering if that was possible for me. I couldn't help but let myself want it.

"This trip is always so important to us, but it's extra so this year, because—if we're lucky—this actually might be the last trip we take for a while."

"Oh my god!" Chloe shouted. "Phoebe, are you dying?"

"She said *if they're lucky*," CJ said, which made all of us burst into laughter. Except Phoebe and Bianca, whose expressions were somewhere between *mildly irritated* and *why are we friends with these people again?*

"We're in strong consideration right now, the adoption agency says," Bianca said with a nervous smile. I grabbed her hand from across the table and squeezed, hard. "It's not a done deal, but it's a really good maybe."

"The agency says that letters from our families and community could go a long way into the decision to place with us," Phoebe said, adjusting her glasses and then her collar, and I realized my badass friend was *nervous*. "And so we wanted to ask you—well, the three of you who've known us for so long—if you could do something like that, it would mean a lot."

"Of course," I said quickly.

"Obviously," Chloe said.

"What they said," CJ said. "I'm honored you asked us."

"I'll email you the deadline and some guidelines," Phoebe said. "Thank you so much, all of you."

"It means a lot to think that—fingers crossed—if we have a baby they'll have this big family to welcome them," Bianca said, and all of a sudden she was crying, and then Phoebe's glasses were off and she was rubbing her eyes with a napkin, and it spread around to the entire table, even Sofia and Ari.

"What about us?" Sofia exchanged a look with Ari. "I'd be happy to help too."

"Yeah," Ari said. "I haven't known you for very long, but it's pretty easy to see the family y'all have built here. If it would help, I'd love to write a letter too."

"You're all too much," Phoebe said, continuing to cry, and now the rest of us had cycled out of it and couldn't laugh enough at our toughest friend falling apart like this. "Yeah, yeah, enjoy it while you can, assholes."

After a couple of drinks, we took a walk to Birba for our dinner reservations. Their patio was lush and green, and I felt like I was in paradise, since my version of paradise looked like this and had an extensive Italian menu.

"I'll be right back," Ari murmured to me, and I nodded, watching her slip away.

"You two are so cute it's disgusting," Chloe said, and I laughed.

"I know, it's terrible. I didn't even know I could be this gross."

"No, you and Taylor were pretty gross," Bianca said. "This is better."

"I hope you're right," I said. "I haven't been proven not to fuck up relationships."

"Well, none of us have been *proven*," Bianca said. "You just somehow manage not to do it. That's it. People always want our secret, and we're just like . . . we like each other a lot."

"Yeah, I might not like anyone that much," Chloe said with a sigh. "But that's OK. Ever since I got my own place the other year, the thought of sharing it with anyone, even someone stupid cute, sounds bad."

"I mean, Fernando's a lot," I said, which made everyone laugh.

"Have you seriously never seen your girlfriend's cat?" Chloe asked.

"Have you even seen a picture of it?" Bianca asked.

"Yeah, it's her lock screen photo on her phone, but it's not like I have proof it's her cat, there are a lot of cat photos on the internet." I picked up Ari's phone, next to me on the table, and tapped the screen to illuminate the photo. But she must have changed it out recently, because a photo of me at Hart Park smiled back at me instead, and Bianca and Chloe squealed loudly enough for the rest of the table to demand to know what was going on. Bianca was triumphantly holding up Ari's phone as she returned to the table.

"I . . . was trying to show them that photo you claim is Steve," I said, flushed and humiliated and a little guilty.

"That I *claim*?" Ari unlocked her phone and quickly tapped to her photos. "Again, what would be in it for me to fake having a cat?"

Ari showed off photos of a gray tabby cat, which made CJ share photos of their cat, and the table remained a blur of pet photos until our appetizers began arriving. We'd decided to do everything family-style, and as I served myself from every plate that circled the table, I thought about how right that was. This was my family.

After dessert we were back to sharing photos and memories in the cool desert air. I'd forgotten just how much the temperature could drop, but Ari's arm was around me, so I felt like I could have sat here all night, even with the hot tub beckoning. Finally, our waiter swung by, and when Phoebe asked for the check, he instead gestured at Ari.

"Ms. Fox has already taken care of your dinner. Have a great night, everyone."

I turned to her. "You didn't have to do that."

"Yeah, I know," she said with a shrug. "I'm so grateful y'all have welcomed me this weekend. This was the least I could do."

The table practically fought to thank her the loudest, though Bianca and I laughed because somehow Ari had out-Phoebe'd Phoebe, and the mildest irritation shone from behind her glasses as she added her thanks to the din.

Back at the house, everyone hurried back into their suits for the hot tub, but my phone buzzed while Ari and I were still getting ready.

Meet me on the front patio instead! Bianca had texted, so I told Ari I'd join her in a minute and made my way out the front, where Bianca sat in a purple hoodie over jeans.

"You're going to freeze," she said, eyeing my two-piece that had far too much coverage to ever call itself a bikini.

"I was already half dressed!" I said and sat down next to her on the porch swing. "What's up?"

"I wanted to tell you first about the potential baby," she said. "But then once we found out about these letters, we really wanted to ask all of you together. I'm sorry that's how you found out."

"Oh, god, no apology needed. I'm just really excited for you."

"No jinxing," she said.

"No jinxing." I leaned into her. "Can we share that hoodie?"

"Oh my god," she muttered, but slipped one arm out of it and let me squeeze in. "This is just like every party in college when you'd be cold and drunk outside, freaking out about some girl."

"I'm not freaking out," I said, and when Bianca snorted, I added, "at least right now."

"You know what I'm thinking, actually?" Bianca asked with a nod to the loud chatter coming from the back patio. "Wife material."

"Don't," I said, blushing and overwhelmed with the rush of memories from years ago, watching Phoebe and Bianca fall for each other.

"OK, girl," Bianca said, leaning her head on my shoulder. It really did feel like it could have been ten years ago, for just a moment. "No jinxing."

"No jinxing."

Chapter 19
Naked and Naked

Palm Springs was everything I'd remembered, a quiet place where my friends and I talked nonstop. Days scheduled to go from brunch to the pool to happy hour to dinner to the hot tub. Flashbacks of old trips, the time we got kicked out of a matinee of *Mamma Mia! Here We Go Again* because Chloe wouldn't stop singing along, the time CJ brought a very new girlfriend who turned out to be a vegan and blew up all of Phoebe's dinner plans, the time Bianca ran into one of her cousins and we all ended up at a family barbeque where Phoebe beat all the old men at horseshoes.

Mainly, though, it was a world that didn't seem to be any bigger than us. Of course we had jobs—well, I had a job and my friends had careers—and family, and other responsibilities. Here, though, we just had each other. And we were more than enough.

On our last night in Palm Springs, the whole crew shivered out early from the hot tub into the cold night. We'd already decided to grab breakfast on our way out of town, timed to arrive

220 / Amy Spalding

just behind rush hour traffic, and Phoebe insisted we'd all have a better time if we had full nights of sleep first.

That was fine with me, though I didn't plan on sleeping any-time soon. The weekend had been, so far, shockingly chaste. Between the hot tub, the late night chats, the big dinners, and Ari's cocktails, once I'd gotten into our cozy guest bed each night I'd been *out*. We'd snagged a quick moment on Friday when we were ostensibly in our room to change for dinner, but I craved more than a stolen moment, frantically finding release before anyone yelled down the hallway that the Lyfts had ar-rived.

"Hey," I said, wandering from our private bathroom toward the bed. I'd thrown a gauzy coverup over my least comfort-able bra and underwear, and then decided to forgo them all together. As I caught my near-naked reflection in the mirror, standing before Ari, I wondered who I'd become, and if I could manage to stay her forever.

"Hang on," Ari said, her eyes on her phone and not me. I awkwardly tried to find new ways to stand patiently while avoiding my reflection in the floor-to-ceiling mirror across from the bed. This was not a look I'd planned to wear for this long while waiting. This was a look that required interaction.

"Ari," I said, and her eyes flicked up toward me. "Hey."

"Fuck," she said, and bit her lip. "Get up here, Nina Rice."

I climbed onto the bed, straddling her bare legs. She'd changed into boxer briefs and the T-shirt she referred to as her *sleep shirt*, and I arched toward her to feel the soft material against my bare skin.

"We'll have to be quiet," I murmured, seeing myself in the mirror and marveling that this *seducer* was me, Nina Rice, awkward and average and cursed. The woman in the mirror draped in sheer black fabric and nothing else looked nothing of the sort.

"Nina," she said, and held up her phone. I, truly, had no

idea what was going on, but I didn't love that both of her hands weren't already on me. "I just finished reading your script."

"Oh," I said, rolling off of her and jumping to my feet. I couldn't believe the most vulnerable moment I'd had in maybe years was happening while I was *literally naked*. "I didn't think you were actually going to read it on your phone, I—"

"Nina," she said, sitting up taller. "It's *amazing*."

"You don't have to—"

"No, obviously I know you're still working on it and it's not a final product, but I love it. The characters are all so real, and it feels like—I mean, it feels like this weekend. It feels like going out with my friends. It's the thing you wanted to do."

"Thank you," I said, though my heart was still racing.

"The moment where Xan and Emilia talk about their families," she continued, "holy shit, I almost started crying."

"That was my favorite part to write so far," I confessed.

"Seriously, every single character's great. I might like the hot bartender best, though," she said with a grin. "It'd be fun to play the hot bartender, actually."

"Yeah, I hadn't, like, *not* thought about that," I admitted.

"OK, I have a lot more to say," Ari said, tugging her sleep shirt off over her head. "But we have a two-hour car ride together tomorrow for talking and I think you had a better idea how to spend tonight."

Still shaking just a little, I climbed back onto Ari, though we remained just like that for another long moment. She'd seen so much of me already, of course, because sex could be intimate and revealing, another language to learn together. I'd had plenty of sex in the last few years, but with Ari it was different. We discovered new things about each other, as basic as what got each other off and as complicated as letting our guards down over time. Still, as much as we'd explored, I'd never felt so exposed before. With my script fresh in Ari's head, I'd never had so little left to hide.

"What are you waiting for, Nina Rice?" Ari asked huskily.

"I thought you were in charge," I said, my words predictably having their desired effect, as Ari sharply inhaled before pushing me over onto my back. She dipped her head to kiss my neck, my collarbone, spare stretches of skin, teasing me with no apparent rush to any assumed destinations. I turned my head to moan impatiently into the mattress, and Ari chuckled, the rumble vibrating warmly through my skin.

"Something else you had in mind?" she asked. "I thought I was in charge."

"You could be in charge faster," I said.

"I promise," she said, sliding down to nibble at the inside of one of my thighs—*finally*—but then sliding right back up. *Goddammit.* "The destination will be worth the journey. Trust me as your—fuck, navigator? Chauffeur? You're the writer."

"Ari, please don't make me think of metaphors right now."

We were on the road back to LA by eleven, full of carbs and low on sleep. We'd grabbed the largest coffees from Koffi on our way out to the freeway, and Ari spun the dial up so her vacation playlist buzzed through our ears.

"I'm so glad you came," I said, over the noise, once my coffee cup was empty and my brain felt a bit less foggy.

"I'm glad you came too," she said, the corner of her mouth twisting up into a smirk. She reached her right hand toward me and I caught it in mine. "I'm glad you came *so many times.*"

"Stop, I'm having a nice moment," I said, though, holy hell, those had been nice moments too. I was still a little pleasantly sore. "It was so good having you there."

"Yeah, it was good having you—"

"*Ari,*" I said, and she cracked up. Silliness wasn't necessarily something I'd ever looked for in a relationship, but, damn, it was cute on her.

"Your friends are like you." She let go of me just long enough to turn down the music. "I got to be . . . just me all weekend. Do you know how much that means?"

"They're the best people," I said.

"They really are. I'm . . . I feel lucky to be included. Thank you."

"Thank *you*," I said, leaning down to press my lips to her thumb. "I feel really lucky too."

"Tell me how y'all met," she said. "Now that I know everyone."

"Well, Bianca and I went to college together," I said. "We had a class together and then both showed up at the LGBTQ+ campus group for the first time the same night, and we just . . . we became instant friends."

"Were you ever together?"

"No, we're just . . ."

"Exactly the same type so it'd be weird?" Ari asked, and I laughed.

"Maybe. We do have a lot of the same ex-girlfriends. Phoebe hit on Bianca when we were out one night, and it was also like an instant thing. And then Phoebe was my instant friend too, she's just so *great*. I never had that weird moment where I wondered how their relationship would affect Bianca and me. CJ and Phoebe used to work at the same studio so they knew each other through that. And Chloe and Bianca dated for like two weeks right after college and then stayed friends."

"That seems wise," Ari said. "Chloe and Bianca together sounds . . . chaotic."

"Yeah, it's funny, I guess it was, but I barely remember it now," I said. "Maybe this is what it's like getting old."

Ari snorted. "You're like four years older than I am."

"Five," I corrected. "They're big years. Being in your thirties feels a lot different."

"Everyone tells me I'll give less fucks then," Ari said. "Which seems unlikely. And if I'm not giving fucks, who will?"

I laughed. "Yep, just you, the only person holding this universe together."

"Nina Rice." She looked at me for just a moment. "I'm really falling for you."

It was, I knew, a half step. It was the appropriate leveling up before *love* was appropriate to confess. I was taking steps toward love, after I'd told myself I couldn't have this again. I *shouldn't* have this again. But here I was, just *having it.* Having her.

"I'm really falling for you too," I said, though I felt a bit like a movie cop saying it was his last day before retirement, jinxing himself right into a terrible crime to solve.

"Whew," she said, and I laughed, probably too much, just relieved to be on the lighter side of a big moment, feeling less like a movie cop and more like myself.

"How long until Georgia?" I asked.

"Two weeks. Have you thought about it?"

"I want to talk to Lorna, and check in at work to make sure I don't have any in-person meetings coming up but . . . yeah. If that's all good, I want to come for at least part of it."

She squeezed my hand tightly. "I'm so glad."

My phone buzzed, and I checked my messages. "Lorna's out of the cast!"

"Did she send a photo?" Ari asked.

"Well, she did, but it's just of her face, which doesn't look any different." I tapped out a reply. **Congrats! We're on our way back and it'll be so good to see you Thursday. What's on the menu?**

"So do you have a busy week lined up?" Ari asked. "Lots of Joyce duties?"

"I managed not to give in to curiosity and even look at my work email," I said. "Right now I'm blissfully ignorant and pretending nothing's waiting for me."

"I can't comprehend living that way, but good for you," Ari

said. "*I guess.* Let me know once you do, though. I thought maybe we could set up a dinner with my friend Jenn and our mutual friend Peyton, who you've met, and—"

"Ari," I interrupted, "no."

"I haven't even said anything yet," Ari said, with more than a note of frustration in her tone. "It would be great to get, as Joyce would say, some face time with her, and remind her of how fun and interesting and brilliant you are—"

I cut her off with a loud sigh. "I'm going to give you credit and say you're sleep-deprived and suffering from vacation brain or something."

"Nina, what are you talking about? You have a great script that's close to being ready, and there's no reason to sit on it when—"

"When *what*?" I demanded. "My girlfriend has connections so I should rush the process and do everything before I'm comfortable with it?"

"She's your connection too," Ari said, both hands on the wheel now. "She told you to reach out—"

"She told me to reach out when I was ready. But I'm not ready! The script could be better, and just because you like it doesn't mean something has to happen with it right now. I never would have let you read it if I thought you'd act like this." I sighed, as realization hit me. "Actually, I knew you'd act like this but I pretended I didn't because I wanted to share it with you, like I would have shared it with someone else."

"Oh, I'm the issue, cool," Ari said. "Not you and your inability to believe in yourself."

I glanced down at Waze. We still had an hour and a half before reaching Ari's.

"Do you want to just get off at the next exit?" I asked.

"Why, is there a Starbucks?" Ari asked, and I ignored but didn't miss how her tone had softened.

"Probably but—maybe I can just grab a Lyft back."

"I know what you're thinking," she said, her hand back, our fingers entwined again, "but Karl doesn't drive out this far, remember? He likes staying on the Eastside."

I wanted to stay mad but she did pull off to get me a chai as well as, unbelievably, a venti Frappuccino for herself. ("Nina Rice, I need the sugar.") I snapped a photo of her, eyes shut in a sugar high, gleefully sucking down the Frappuccino while we sat in the parking lot, and switched out my generic lock screen for the photo.

"No," she said when she caught me doing it. "That's a terrible picture."

"You look so cute," I said, holding my phone away from her. "Also it's blackmail for anytime you get too high-and-mighty about your hipster beans."

"Nina Rice, don't you dare," she said, but she laughed and kissed me. I licked the whipped cream off her sugar-sweet lips. "Don't get a Lyft. I'll be nicer than a Lyft."

"Promise?"

She kissed me again. "I swear on this desert Starbucks."

Of course I didn't want a Lyft. I just didn't want to feel this way, trapped with my fears and my countdown clock, a movie cop jinxing himself. After a weekend that couldn't have felt more perfect, still marked on my body from Ari's mouth and teeth, I couldn't ignore that we now felt creepingly close to the edge. My disastrous possibilities lurked not deep within, but right beneath the surface. If only I could have been the Nina that Ari wanted me to be, ready for meetings and maybe full of more ambition, but I was just me. Vacation Nina was already gone. I thought about Taylor's face that last night, as the other patrons at the bar tried not to gape, and wondered just how far off Ari's frustration had been from that moment. Right now, even with the chai and Ari's promise, it couldn't have felt closer.

Chapter 20
Meanwhile in Hollywood

My week flew by once I was home from Palm Springs. There had been a lot of non-urgent communication needs while I was away, which meant that Max had compiled all of them into the longest email I'd ever received from Exemplar. I'd literally only been out for two business days, which made me realize how much I did on a daily basis without thinking much of it. There was a lot to handle when it was laid out like that, all together, but—besides the Ari Incident—it was rarely a strain for me.

Joyce was right, I thought, as was Phoebe, and Lorna too. No matter what my next step would be, I needed a next step. This had stopped being a challenge, and the truth was that while sometimes I felt like all my youth was gone, I was only thirty-two. If I was lucky, I had a lot of life left. And a challenge didn't sound terrible. Scary, sure, but like a rollercoaster or a haunted house, where the safe ending felt all but guaranteed.

As always now, I packed up for the weekend and headed to Ari's. Her week had sounded busy too, a flurry of meetings before heading soon to Georgia. In fact, she texted me as I was driving down on Friday that she was out longer than planned and that I should let myself in. The key hadn't been a huge deal; Ari had tossed it to me the other week when I'd wanted to walk out to grab a chai and she'd been stuck on a call, and when I'd gotten back she'd told me it would be easier for me to keep it. So now I had this key and my own code to the security system.

"I'm here, Steve," I called as I let myself in, though he never responded. It still felt polite to acknowledge his presence before I sat in my usual spot on the floor and opened my laptop on the coffee table. Work had quieted for the weekend, so I opened the latest version of my script outline to see if I could figure out the final act. It wasn't really that simple, because any changes there in the fifth act would end up affecting the fourth, and before long I was rewriting the outline again, from the ground up. But right now, it *was* my challenge. It was nice to have one of those again.

"Hey," Ari said, walking in. "I really need to get a setup so you can work here. I feel terrible every time I see you on the floor."

"I don't mind the floor," I said, though of course the thought of Ari reorganizing her home *for me* was a nice one. "How was your meeting?"

"Don't make me talk about it." She collapsed on the sofa behind me, and I turned around to kiss her gently. "I'm fine, it was fine, they're just all the same. Everyone talks a good game and is your best friend, and then you wait to see what's real. And I'm the one who loves calling out bullshit, but I get sucked into it too, and I leave thinking I really have transformed the industry, and then nothing. So I just let them all blend together."

"Sounds wise," I said.

"I don't know about that, but thanks," Ari said. "Also I have to grab drinks tonight, don't kill me, but after that, Cade texted that a bunch of people are meeting up at the Mermaid later so I thought maybe we could go to that?"

I heard the note of vulnerability in her voice and grinned. "Ari, are you asking me to meet your friends?"

"I am indeed, Nina Rice. How's that sound? I'll buy you dinner on the way. No one's meeting until at least after ten."

It sounded, well—a lot of things, really. I actually didn't know much about Ari's crowd, because she didn't have a solid, rarely changing crew like mine, but I suspected they were all much younger and cooler than me. We ran into people sometimes around town, seemingly plucked from an editorial feature on the coolest queer people in Los Angeles, who knew Ari and who Ari introduced to me as her friends. There were books on her shelf written by people she knew, buzzy podcasts hosted by her friends and acquaintances, events written up breathlessly online that had been organized by someone in her sphere. My crew was close to middle age and thinking about babies; her crew was defining culture and starting their nights after ten p.m.

But I said yes because this was one of the next steps and because Ari did so much for me. I could consume extra caffeine to stay up late and meet cooler and younger people. If I wanted a future in Hollywood, it was time to get used to that anyway.

The bar was in Little Tokyo, which was a neighborhood in Downtown LA, so we grabbed sushi nearby beforehand, and I thought about how different it was, packed into a tiny booth in a raucous restaurant, from last week when the whole desert had been ours. Last week I'd felt as at ease as I ever did, and tonight I was using every spare moment to wonder if my new dress was cool to people under thirty or if I'd somehow slipped into Cool Aunt territory without knowing it. And without even being an aunt.

But then we got up to leave and my very hot and very cool girlfriend slipped her arm around my waist, and I decided to give myself at least the walk over to the bar off from worrying. Inside the crowded nautical-themed bar, a packed crowd glowed in the undersea lighting, and my heart pounded. But one by one, the crowd was OK, I realized. It seemed, upon casual glance at least, a very mixed crowd—hipsters, queer people, nerds, just . . . *people*—and I was definitely not the oldest person there. Though then Ari tugged me toward a crowd hanging out in the back corner, and I tried not to stare at all of their twentysomething faces, untouched by age.

"Hey, y'all," Ari greeted them, and was pulled into nearly a dozen hugs by the group. They were clearly the coolest crowd in the bar, with bright hair colors and architectural haircuts and outfits in every version of *stylish* I could have imagined. Maybe I wasn't even a *cool* aunt.

"This is Nina obviously," Ari said, and I realized the *obviously* meant something, that her friends knew about me and expected me to be there, the way my brunch crew had been so adamant about getting introduced to Ari. I was *Nina obviously*. No one's aunt at all.

There was a whirlwind of introductions, names and pronouns and relationships, and I felt the warmth in people's words, the private jokes that I didn't get, volleyed back and forth, the ease in Ari's body language. Ari left me alone to grab drinks at the bar, and I took a chance and sidled up next to Cade, who was a tall redhead dressed all in black.

"You're the one who feeds Ari's cat, right?" I asked, and they burst into laughter.

"Tell me you've seen that fucking cat," Cade said, and I shook my head. "I swear, I'd go in, refill his little cat water fountain, measure out all his fancy organic cat food, and *nothing*. You? Nothing?"

"Nothing. I've never seen him either."

"And you're there all the time, yeah?" Cade asked. "So you'd know."

"Are y'all talking about Ari's cat?" Another of Ari's friends, Laser, pushed their way over. They had blonde hair that was streaked with teal, styled into swooping waves, and was dressed in bright jewel tones. "Nina, you follow Cade's Instagram, right?"

"Oh, I'm not on social media," I said, feeling very much the oldest and most boring person there, though they actually both gave me reverent looks.

"I really admire that," Laser said. "Instagram is part of Facebook and therefore part of the downfall of humanity. But Cade runs a whole account for cat-sitting for Ari called @wheressteve and it's amazing."

"That almost makes me want to join," I said, as Ari arrived back with margaritas.

"They're no TGI Fridays recipe, but hopefully you'll still be happy," she said with a grin. "What'd I miss?"

"Just finding out that Nina hasn't seen Steve either," Cade said, which made Ari start ranting on the unlikeliness of inventing a fake cat. I could tell they'd had this faux fight a thousand times before, and instead of feeling left out, I felt warmed by the closeness here. It felt like Sunday brunch, just later and louder. I made a mental note to remember how these moments felt too, because my script had a lot of softer moments, quiet patios and dinner reservations. Smashed into a corner at a tiny bar could feel the same way.

I was home by Monday morning, because even with my new laptop, the bigger pile of work that tended to hit at the beginning of the week was just easier to handle from my desk. Of course I thought about Ari's casual words, wondered if we were in the midst of an invisible countdown to shared furniture, but sometimes I also liked coming home alone. I drank my supermarket coffee and took way too long to get showered and dressed and I felt—well, I felt different. Was I Nina version 3 or 4 now? It didn't matter; this was a good one.

There was an email when I hit Ari's inbox, and not from her, either. She still liked to find me here, sometimes, which gave my job just a little more excitement. Maybe we'd get even more used to each other, but as of now I still grinned when I saw her name pop up in my inbox, and in "her" inbox too.

Today, though, the new email was from Peyton Butler, who

I remembered from the Women in Television event we'd attended what seemed like a lifetime ago. It was rare for a contact to reach out first, but I knew that Peyton was different, sharing a mutual friend with Ari already. In fact, I was surprised Ari had given out this email address, but that probably just meant she'd wanted proof of good behavior for Joyce and the rest of her Exemplar team.

Obviously, I found that adorable.

To: arifox1@aol.com
From: pbutler@pbjamproductions.com
Subject: So good to see you!
Message: Hi Ari,

Thanks again for grabbing drinks on Friday, I know your schedule's starting to explode so I'm glad you found time and that we were able to drag Jenn out too. Hope your night out after was fun. Would definitely like to get on your schedule again once you're back from your shoot, and, yes, your girlfriend's script sounds exactly like something I'd be interested in. Can you connect us, or at least get us a digital version of the script and her contact/ rep info?

Thanks again,
PB

I stared at the email. I read it over and over. I tried to find a way where I'd made up parts of it or imagined words. But, no. There it was. I'd asked Ari not to do this, and Ari did it anyway.

It was bad enough—it was *terrible*. But there was also the fact that Joyce didn't know Ari had a girlfriend. Joyce certainly didn't know that *the girlfriend was me*. And so, the thing that I was supposed to do—i.e., forward the email to Joyce and wait for instructions—was impossible. Plus, I didn't want to. Even if we could skate over this girlfriend and her script, Joyce would want to keep the network exec happy. Joyce would be thrilled to help along a big connection for her client, get Ari on more TV screens in more homes. And if that meant sending along some shitty literally not-ready-for-prime-time script, why the hell not? What were my career dreams when Hollywood bullshit came first and foremost?

So I just started typing.

To: pbutler@pbjamproductions.com
From: arifox1@aol.com
Subject: re: So good to see you!
Message: Hi Peyton,

Thanks as well. I'll be happy to schedule a meeting once I'm back from my shoot. My team or I will reach out then.

As to my girlfriend's script, I apologize for misspeaking on Friday night. At this point the script is still under heavy revisions and is not ready to be shared.

Best,
Ari

I hit *send* and started to delete Peyton's email so I wouldn't have to look at it anymore and so I wouldn't accidentally forward it on to Joyce or Max. But I also wanted proof that this had happened, so I printed it out, a single sheet that had changed everything, before deleting.

Normally we texted and emailed, but I grabbed for my phone and dialed.

She answered right away. "Hey, babe, what's up?"

"Ari, did you go out with Peyton Butler and tell her about my script even though I told you specifically not to do that?"

There was more than a moment of silence.

"Shit, I—Nina, I can explain."

"Unless your answer is *no, she's lying via email*, I don't know what you can say."

Ari was silent again.

"I didn't just say I wasn't ready, Ari, I specifically said not to talk to Peyton about it, not to set up drinks," I said, trying to hold on to a reasonable tone but feeling my voice cracking. "I can't believe you went and did it anyway. I knew you were eager or whatever, but . . . fuck."

"No, Nina, it didn't happen like that," she said. "Unrelated to any of that, Peyton's team reached out to mine and set up a drinks meeting like we'd been planning to do for forever. And she started talking about how the network is hungry for something young and modern, and everything she said reminded me of your script. And I couldn't hold myself back, when *my girlfriend* had written just the kind of thing she wanted. It felt stupid not to say something."

"What about not saying something for like *the one hour duration* of your meeting and then telling me when you got back?"

"Because I already knew how that would go! You'd say you weren't comfortable yet, but, Jesus Christ, Nina. If we waited for you to get comfortable with things, we'd be waiting forever."

"What's that supposed to mean?" I asked, though I knew. How could I not know?

"The script that you've been writing for, what, four years? Us? You won't even let me tell Joyce we're together. You're not comfortable with anything, so what was I supposed to do?"

I blinked back tears. "You could listen to me. It wasn't that simple. My career and my current job are on the line."

"Let's just—anyway, fine. I'll let Peyton know you're finishing a revision and can send it before long. We'll figure out Joyce later. You can manage that, right?"

"I handled it already," I snapped.

Ari audibly inhaled. "What does that mean?"

"It means I handled it. I responded to Peyton and let her know you'd misspoke, the script isn't anywhere close to ready, and you shouldn't have mentioned it."

"Nina, what the fuck," Ari said. "You don't get to make those kind of choices for me. I thought my emails coming out of Exemplar—"

"Weren't written by your girlfriend who you just betrayed?"

She sighed loudly. "*Betrayed* is pretty dramatic for trying to help you with your career. I can't believe you sent that without asking me."

"Really?" I asked. "Do you of all people want to talk about doing things without asking right now?"

"Seriously, Nina, the only demand I've ever made in my career, as you know, is to have control over shit like this. It matters to me above just about anything. And you just decided, fuck that, you're mad so who cares."

Shit, shit, shit.

"You're right," I said quickly, as an icy feeling spread through me.

The countdown clock hadn't been to shared furniture. It had been to me, the time bomb. Ari had only asked one single thing of me, from before we were even together, and I'd fucked up. Worse, I'd been warned long ago I'd fuck up again, and I'd thought some time away in the suburbs and a respite from dating would . . . what? Fix me? Push back my worst traits into the faraway future?

I'd been so fucking stupid.

"Ari, I'm sorry."

"So where does it stand with Peyton right now?" Ari asked.

"I said you'd reconnect about everything else when you were back from your feature."

"OK," she said.

"I—I'm sorry. I'm so sorry. I should have—I shouldn't—

anyway." A loud, wet sob escaped from me. "I hope I didn't fuck things up for you too much. You can request Joyce take me off your communications. I—"

"Nina," she said. "Let's—"

"Ari, I'm sorry for everything," I said. "This has been—"

But I didn't know what to say. Because maybe these shouldn't have been the best months of my life. What right did I have now?

So I just clicked *end*.

Chapter 21
An URGENT Request

It was a lot easier this time. I was already in the condo, far away from everything. No one could check in on me when I begged out of the next Sunday brunch. No one could check in on anything.

On Thursday I drove to Oaken Troves, even though I now hated the parking lot where I'd first kissed Ari, and I hated that I knew I'd be letting down the whole table with my breakup and my general state of—well, whatever I was. I missed Ari at any given moment, missed the texts and the emails and the way she let me sleep against her shoulder. I missed the sex and I missed the dinners out and I missed when she'd casually wrap her arm around me in public and draw me close. I missed thinking about shared furniture and babies and retirement cottages in Palm Springs. I missed every single part.

Except, also, that I didn't. What was there to miss about monitoring myself for whatever ugly truths awaited? How was I ever truly myself with Ari when she didn't know Taylor's warning, didn't know that she had been spared? I'd been living a double life this year, trying not to enjoy things too much and usually failing. I'd always known it, deep down, and though hiding it had worked for a while, now the truth was out. I wasn't to be trusted. And so now I simply wouldn't trust myself, period, no hard choices to make anymore. Life, I was sure, would get easier.

"Nina Louise, hello," Lorna greeted me, and then studied me for a moment. "How are you, my dear?"

I shrugged and let her hug me.

"Is there anything you'd like to talk about?" she asked, and I shook my head. "Well, I have an idea, and it's a pretty good one, if I do say so myself."

"Oh?" I asked.

"Well, it's a boring day on the menu, chicken noodle soup and those sandwiches I'm not particularly fond of, so why don't you drive me to that little restaurant we went to for your birthday the other year and I'll treat."

"Lorna, you don't have to—"

"I want to! I didn't save up my whole life to end up eating cafeteria soup and forcing my beautiful niece to do the same. No, let's have a fun day out."

It wasn't a fun day out, of course, but I knew Lorna had saved me from a thousand questions from Choon Hee and Nat about Ari. I knew that by next Thursday, they would have been filled in and appropriately silent on the topic. And, amazingly, I felt lucky. If one had to be this way—and I clearly had to be this way—it was incredible, beautiful luck that my one exception was Lorna. I knew I wouldn't have Lorna forever, but I had Lorna right now.

"What's that coffee place you're always talking about?" Lorna asked when we were in the Honda on our way back to Oaken Troves. "I'll treat to that too."

"Starbucks?" I asked, and actually found myself laughing. "I don't think I'm always talking about it. But, yes, we can go to Starbucks. There's a good one near you."

"It's true, even with chains, there's always good ones," Lorna said.

I laughed. I really couldn't believe that I was laughing. "Very wise."

After getting my chai and her cappuccino, I was ready to take her back, but she asked to sit at one of the outdoor tables. It wasn't exactly scenic; the shopping plaza was on a major thoroughfare. But it was hard not to enjoy the sunshine and Lorna's presence even with the traffic noise and smells.

"How are your friends?" Lorna asked. "Is CJ still with that artist?"

"As far as I know," I said. "I'm . . . taking a little time away from everyone right now."

She frowned. "Are you sure there's nothing you'd like to discuss?"

"I'm positive. Except . . ." I tried to wipe my eyes under my sunglasses without looking like I was crying. I was fairly certain it wasn't successful. "Lorna, if I ever do anything to stress you out or make you worried or—well, you'll let me know, right?"

"Nina Louise," she said with a sigh. "Well, of course I would! Have you ever heard me hold in my feelings about any subject?"

I let out a laugh. "OK, fair point."

"My dear, I know you're hurting today, but hopefully that means tomorrow will be a little easier, and soon it'll all be— well, not fine, of course, life can be rough that way. But better."

I squeezed Lorna's hand. "Thank you. I really hope you're right."

But the thing was, I already knew she was right. Being alone was getting easier every day.

Work kept rolling in. Every time my inbox chimed I assumed it would be Joyce, or Max setting up a call with Joyce, but workdays crept by as if nothing had changed. I still had access to Ari's inbox, which stayed busy with meetings leading up to her departure for Georgia. I thought about those two months, and the time I was supposed to spend there with her. Already it seemed like another lifetime. Every night when I crawled into bed alone I was grateful we hadn't spent any full nights together here, that this was all just mine. It'd be just mine forever.

My second workweek after the breakup was winding to a close when I saw it. The thing I'd feared was in my inbox.

This Message Was Sent with High Importance
To: nrice@gmail.com
From: mvandoren@exemplar.com
Subject: URGENT Joyce call request
Message: Hi Nina,

Joyce needs to talk to you immediately. Call me as soon as you can and I'll patch you though.

(Sorry. Hope you're doing OK! ☺)

Thanks,
Max

"Fuck," I muttered, icy cold and hot all at once. This, like my breakup, was the other shoe I'd been waiting to drop, but it might have been even worse. If I lost my income—which I was about to, obviously—I didn't know what my next steps were. It wasn't as if Joyce was going to provide a good reference after this mess, and unfortunately this was a part of the industry that really required a good reference.

I picked up my phone with shaking hands and saw that my notifications screen was lit up more than usual. Of course, I'd muted my old group text long ago, but everyone had texted individually too, every last one of them, even Sofia. There was a lot of confusion and a lot of *I know you're not on social media but*— statements, and I didn't know where to begin with figuring out what the hell was going on. I dialed into Exemplar instead.

"Hey, Nina," Max said in a whisper, which was rough because her little voice wasn't easy to hear anyway. "Just a heads-up that Joyce is pretty upset."

"OK," I said, nodding though no one could see me. "Thanks, Max."

"For what it's worth I think you're really cute together," she said in one quick, barely understandable gulp—*What??*—and then I was holding for Joyce. Countdown to my unemployment.

"Nina, hello." Joyce sighed loudly. "I'm sure you've seen social media this afternoon."

"No, I—why is everyone asking me that?"

"The short version of the story is that some LGBTQ influencer-type retweeted a friend who posted that they saw Ari Fox out the other night and that she seemed to be *very cozy with a beautiful curvy femme.*"

Oh god, I wasn't ready for Ari to have moved on. No matter how much it was over—how much *all of it* was over for me—it was impossibly terrible. How had we been making plans for the future just the other week and now—though, *wait*. Why was Joyce mad about Ari dating someone? Joyce wouldn't know how fast and shitty this seemed.

"And there are pictures, but I'm not an idiot, Nina, or at least I didn't think I was. The second I read *beautiful curvy* I knew."

"You knew what?" I asked, increasingly confused by this conversation.

"That one of the people I trusted most in my department had been secretly sleeping with talent," Joyce snapped. "Why are you trying to get out of this now, Nina?"

"Oh, I—" I exhaled while trying not to let out any other

sounds like sobbing or relieved sighs. It didn't matter that the person was me, Ari and I were over. And it was inappropriate to be flattered that Joyce saw me as curvy and beautiful, but I was, at least a little. "I didn't realize—Joyce, I'm sorry."

"Nina, I'm not sure what to do here. We're lucky that no one here really knows your face, and that Ari's not the kind of public figure inspiring any frantic search for her girlfriend's identity. As you're aware, I'm in the middle of perhaps my most high-profile year since getting into this business, and the last thing I need is the appearance that I don't even know what's happening in my own department with my own team."

"I understand."

"And the truth is, right now, Nina, I still need you. You're the best person who's ever been in this role, and I practically get hives thinking of getting through the rest of the year and awards season without you. So I don't know what I do now."

"If it matters," I said, "Ari and I aren't—it's no longer—"

"And that's true?" Joyce asked. "I'm sorry, but you can see why that's difficult for me to believe after however many months this must have been kept from me."

"It's true," I said with more confidence now. "It's completely over. And if you don't want me on her communications—"

"Oh, god, no, Nina, what am I going to do, put Max on them? I don't think so. For now, please continue as you've been, while I sort out this situation."

"OK," I said, counting weeks and paychecks in my head. How long would it take her to sort out the situation? How much longer was I guaranteed this income?

"Actually," she said, "why don't you bcc Max on everything for the time being. If someone connects the dots between you and Ari, I'd like to show that I did something internally to guard against potential impropriety here."

"Sure," I said. "Max on everything."

"I'm pissed, Nina, if I'm being honest," she said, and by

now fat tears were rolling down my face and dripping onto my T-shirt like rain. "And I'm disappointed. You've been part of my team for years—longer than anyone in this role—and you know how important professionalism is. To me, to the talent, to the other teams handling the talent. To risk all of that for—"

Joyce stopped herself and actually started laughing. "I mean, to risk that all for love or sex or whatever you were up to, honestly, that's what people always risk it for. I mean it's always that or it's power and money, and I sure respect love and sex a lot more. But, obviously—"

"I won't again," I said, unsure of where we were in this conversation. It was more comfortable for me when she was flat-out pissed. Pissed, disappointed, and *laughing* was an unsettling combination.

"Well, luckily the rest of my roster doesn't seem as much a temptation for you," she said, still laughing. "Gregory Hart will be fine. Anyway, Nina, it's four p.m. on a Friday, why don't you call it a week and we'll get back to work on Monday morning. And I'll be in touch next week or so about—well, with any changes to your responsibilities or employment status."

"OK," I said. "Joyce, truly, I'm—I'm so sorry."

"Have a good weekend, Nina," she said.

I clicked off of the call and opened my texts, which currently numbered an improbable 333. I marked the group text as *read*, did the same to each individual chain with the brunch crew, and then saw it, buried beneath them all, the fox emoji. I slid my thumb to delete the message without even looking at it. I realized our whole text history would be deleted with it, the logistical texts like **I just parked, should I come in?** and the random thoughts like **Is it weird I love chai but I hate hot tea?** And the late night messages like **I wish you were in my bed tonight instead of your suburban abode** 🌑 🦊. Every single one of them, gone.

"Good," I muttered, the opposite of what I was thinking,

and left my phone there on my desk in search of a long hot bath that would take my mind off of everything. But in the hot sudsy water, I was just an idiot who'd fucked up her job, ruined things for a really good person, and was immersed in water on a Friday afternoon like someone who'd lost their tether to functional productive society.

I tried to give myself the weekend off from worrying, but I wasn't great at it. The writing seemed to be on the wall, so I googled career ideas and redid my résumé. I didn't really want another job like I had now, but the future where I got to go onward and upward from here was gone, and suddenly I couldn't imagine a better fit.

So I abandoned my updated résumé and open browser tabs on ZipRecruiter, and drew up my budget instead. I saved different versions, anywhere from me fired next week to hanging on through the Oscars. Seeing my life listed out in terms of the stark numbers was calming, actually. If I could hang in through March, I'd definitely be OK, especially now that I'd stopped using money on brunches and nights out. It was easy to save money when you sat home doing nothing, which was good news for me because I was great at sitting home and doing nothing.

But if Joyce decided next week that I was out, the numbers were scarier, even without a social life draining any of my income. Without a job I could probably put off the student loan people for a while, and I supposed that unemployment would cover my rent-free life, though I wasn't sure. And the last thing I wanted to do was pull Lorna into any of this. The free place to live was more than a gift; if I couldn't keep up with what remained—well, I was determined not to tell her. I was determined, no matter how right Taylor had been about me, not to spread that into Lorna's life. I wouldn't let my failings become hers. I'd figure out a way through.

* * *

By Sunday night, once the daily crossword had been completed, I couldn't hold back my sick, masochistic, unrelenting curiosity any longer. I pulled up my browser and typed into the search bar: *ari fox beautiful curvy femme.*

It was mainly on Twitter, though a few gossip and queer blogs had picked it up too. The photos had been snapped, obviously, surreptitiously, so they were dim, lit only by the Mermaid's blue-green lights, and one would have to know what to look for. I was facing Ari in all of them, my hair waving down my profile, just a glimmer of my face shown. I hardly recognized myself, this smiling radiant woman tucked into Ari's side. It felt like years had passed since I'd been her. I tried not to look at Ari's face, the way her gaze was on mine like I was someone special. She hadn't known then, of course, that she was only days away from getting hurt. She'd had no idea just how dangerous I was.

Chapter 22
Running To or From

Magically, miraculously, mercifully, I made it through an-other week without losing my job. Bcc'ing Max was not a new favorite task, but somehow I felt that Max didn't like it much either, or at least wordlessly acknowledged that this was mildly humiliating, and that did help somehow.

She'd taken to randomly emailing me memes, especially from an account called @talentagencyproblems that was run by an anonymous assistant and did nothing but skewer the spe-cifics of our industry.

Is this you?

I finally replied to Max.

Ha ha Nina I'm flattered, I'm not that funny. I just love memes! Especially weird specific ones like these and ones that are super outdated! I'm determined to find out who it is at what agency though. I'll update you if I do! Hope you're doing OK!!

We weren't becoming friends, but it was nice having a co-worker, even one from afar. It was nice sensing that someone understood that I was heartbroken and embarrassed and terrified about employment at any given moment. Sometimes I got the feeling she felt the same way, this tiny nervous person doing the kind of job no tiny nervous person was meant to. So though I had no idea how to find funny memes or even what a funny meme was to a very young person, I sent her animal GIFs and that seemed to forge something. We were in this together.

I'd also gotten extremely fast at hunting down animal GIFs that conveyed very specific agency-related emotions, which seemed, in today's changing world, like it could be a potential résumé item in the future.

As my second post-Joyce-call week drew to a close, I felt my panic dissipate even more. At this point I trusted that Max would give me a heads-up if any danger was particularly imminent, and yet Max's meme links rolled in without doom or gloom. She was my little agency barometer and, weirdly, I think we were both happy with that arrangement.

I—my new routine—dashed off a message to Max that I was stepping out for lunch with Lorna and would be back in about an hour. The truth was that in some ways I'd never felt so responsible, and I hoped that somehow Joyce noticed. It was pretty surreal how quickly I'd decided I was never letting go of this gig.

As I walked to the garage, I noticed I had a few more notifications than usual, but once I made sure that none were from Lorna, Oaken Troves, or any hospitals, I tossed my phone in my bag and headed out. It was baked ziti day over with Lorna and her gang, and they managed another full lunch plus dessert (a shockingly good tiramisu) without bringing up my dead relationship or anything in the remote area. Lorna had handled them so, so well.

"Next week, let's go out again," Lorna said to me as we walked back to her cottage without her friends. "Anywhere you'd like, as long as we end with coffee again. I want to try a flat white, apparently they're very big in Australia."

"You can't make your friends behave for another week?" I asked with a smile. "It's OK. You're nice to baby me, but I'll be fine."

"No, I'd just like to have a talk that might be easier with a little more space," Lorna said. "So let's find space somewhere delicious. Oh, I know, what about that Mexican place? I'd love a taco that's not been turned into a casserole."

I laughed and agreed to that, though I wondered what Lorna was up to, and if I should have been worried. Lorna, though polite, tended to live a pretty bullshit-free life, so I wanted to believe that if something were wrong that she would just *say it*. We were alone in her cottage right now, after all. If she was dying, why wait until we were sharing a basket of chips and salsa at a nearby Mexican restaurant? It seemed a terrible setting for that news.

Still, it was yet another unsettled thing, and as I sat back down to work once I was home, I wondered if I'd ever feel secure at Exemplar again. If I survived Oscar season, maybe. And Oscar season was about five months away! Did that mean this tangled knot of fear would tie up my stomach for *five full months*? At least whatever the Lorna situation was would reveal itself within a week. A week seemed a manageable amount of time for a tangled knot.

My inbox was blessedly free of work emails, and I reflexively started to delete an email from Phoebe to inbox-zero it completely. By now my old friends plus Sofia must have understood I wasn't showing up to brunch again, I wasn't meeting for drinks, I wouldn't be attending any art shows. But Phoebe's email was a forward, and when I noticed *adoption* in the subject line, I clicked *open* in a wild panic.

Honestly I couldn't believe how much of my life was clicking open emails in wild panics.

Hey Nina, I really hope all is well. I wanted to check that you'd sent the letter advocating for us as adoptive parents to the agency? The deadline was last week, and as of today they hadn't received yours yet. I know the USPS can be sluggish, but thought I'd touch base. Also just a reminder since I'm not sure you're getting our texts that this week's brunch is at Café Figaro. See you there.
—P

I checked my calendar, as if Phoebe and the adoption agency would have gotten the day wrong and I wouldn't. I double-checked Phoebe's initial email with the information, and then checked it against the forward sent today.

And there was no way around it. I'd completely fucked up.

It had been nearly a month since the breakup, but the truth was that I hadn't really cried. Tears kept slipping out at inopportune times, but I'd mainly held it together. This, though, there was no stopping. I wept for everyone. Ari, gone. Phoebe and Bianca's potential baby, probably adopted to someone else by now. Lorna, engineering location lunches to protect my dumb feelings. My job, on the bubble. And me, the one common denominator in all of this.

I wondered if Taylor still had the same phone number, because I longed, for some stupid reason, to text her that she was right. I was bad, after all, at every single thing she'd called out in that email. I had hurt everyone by now. I was toxic as hell and there was no way around it, no outrunning it, no Nina version whatever. Nina Rice, cursed—no. Nina Rice *was* the curse.

Still, instead of texting Taylor, I opened the Word document I'd started, the paean to Phoebe and Bianca's incredible relationship and community. It had been a joy to write, back when I was part of that community. But my words were still all true. There was no one I could think of who'd be a better set of parents than those two, and even now the words still flowed. I reread the finished letter a few times, jotted off another note to Max, and dashed off to the post office to send it overnight express delivery to the agency. I thought about letting Phoebe know I'd sent it, but she'd know soon enough, and without any annoying communication from me that might send mixed signals.

It might have been too late, and I couldn't help picturing a tiny baby carried off by people who weren't Phoebe and Bianca, but it was, I decided, a little better than nothing. And when I sat down later with my bowl of tuna salad and latest episode of *Grey's Anatomy*, I realized I was done crying for the moment. I was heartbroken and alone but somehow I was also slightly better.

Lorna's Mexican restaurant date rolled around before I knew it, and I congratulated myself for not having gone down too many weird dark tunnels with my concerns. Life had absolutely gone off the rails for me, but once Lorna suggested afternoon mojitos and we were splitting a bowl of queso fundido, I felt all those dark tunnels disappear.

"So." If there was no terminal diagnosis—no jinxing—I was impatient to know what was up, beyond Lorna's need for tacos not eaten with a fork and knife. "Why are we here? Besides the lack of casserole of course."

Lorna laughed. "Well, my dear, obviously that's the first reason, and a lunchtime cocktail is the second!"

I grinned. "I knew it."

"I've been doing a lot of thinking lately," Lorna began, "and I think it's time for me to accept my fate as a mortal being, and let go of my condo."

Wait, *what*? A dark tunnel opened up again. Or narrowed. Whatever the danger of tunnels was. In all my anxious hypothesizing the last week, this had never come up.

"Lorna, I . . . I didn't know you were thinking about that," I said, though of course she'd lived in Oaken Troves for about five years, and I knew from its website and its casual use of words like *luxury* and *premium upscale senior living* that her cottage and amenities weren't cheap. The condo was paid off so I supposed I thought she had settled on this arrangement. I *needed* this arrangement.

"Well, Nina Louise, the truth is that I've been very stubborn about many things, but mainly my age and capabilities level. I kept thinking that there'd be some magical cure or new physical therapy that would take me back to how I felt, well, even ten years ago! I thought I'd manage those stairs again, drive my beloved car—not the Honda, of course, the other one—and let my cottage at Oaken Troves go to someone older and more infirm than I. And now here I am, eighty-one years old, breaking my foot by falling over nothing. Nina Louise, darling, I'm not taking those stairs again, and I'm not driving anything anymore, much less a stick shift."

I realized I was crying, and tried to subtly wipe my eyes with my napkin.

"I'm *fine*," Lorna said forcefully. "I plan on many more good years at Oaken Troves. There's no need to cry for me. It was high time I accepted reality. My stairs-free no-Mustang reality."

"OK," I said, nodding to show I was fine, even though I was still crying. Lorna, never one to miss my bullshit, laughed.

"You're positively not, but I've had more time to sit with this than you," Lorna said, squeezing my hand. "But I don't want you worried about anything. Remember, that handsome ER doctor said that I was fit as a fiddle."

"I do trust handsome doctors," I said, though there wasn't

252 / Amy Spalding

just the issue of Lorna's mortality. "I . . . I don't want to seem . . . insensitive, but how long before you need me to move out?"

"Well, that's certainly part of this conversation," Lorna said. "I'd like to hand over some responsibilities to you, if you can deal with some realtor appointments and such. Nat apparently has a very good realtor, so we have a phone appointment scheduled for next week."

Next week. How long did it take to sell a beautiful condo in pristine condition in a safe neighborhood in a good school district? I couldn't imagine very long.

"Of course," I said. "Anything you need."

Lorna probably thought I was well-paid for my job, I realized. Yes, I'd managed to put away a little money, but I had no idea how steady my income was—though Lorna obviously had no idea that I'd fucked up at work—and Southern California housing was almost unfathomably overpriced. I had no idea how I was going to manage this, I realized with a heavy thud in my chest that didn't let up. As soon as that condo sold, there was a chance I'd be homeless. No, not *homeless*, even for me that was ridiculous. Unlike many people in my financial situation—the low-paying job, the nagging student-loan debt—I was lucky to have Lorna, who I knew would help me somehow. But I'd have to reveal so much more to her, my massive failings, and my goal had been to protect her, not make her life more complicated.

"I've thought long and hard about it, and I'd always planned to leave the condo or the money from its sale to you once I was gone," Lorna said, and I blinked away more tears at *once I was gone.* "But I'd rather, even if it's a smaller amount without any future investments and all of that boring stuff, give you the money now so that I can see you enjoy it, see the home you'd create for yourself if it was all up to you."

"Lorna," I gasped, and somehow started coughing on a chip, even though I hadn't eaten any since this conversation started. We both laughed hysterically at this, and two waiters came over to make sure I wasn't dying. They felt so bad they comped us another order of queso fundido.

"Lorna," I said, once we were digging into our second order of delicious melted cheese, "you don't have to do this. I'll figure things out."

"Did I ever tell you why I moved up here in the first place? Remember, I had that darling mid-city place for years."

"I remember the mid-city place," I said, "barely. And I think you moved here because it was quieter."

"I did," she said. "I'd had such a busy, packed, wonderful life in Los Angeles, but once I retired, it was a bit too much for me, all that hustle and bustle. And so my friends and I drove up here thanks to some tip from one of their realtors—Nat's always been connected with the best realtors—and I just fell in love with it. The peace and quiet, the little bit of extra space to breathe. I suddenly saw my life come into focus again, and that's pretty good for a retired broad like myself."

"I think it's pretty good for anyone," I said.

"You see, Nina Louise, I was running *to* something here. I love this place and I loved my condo. But it wasn't an escape. I wasn't running from anything."

"Lorna, I'm hardly—"

"You're going to take this money, once this fabulous realtor has done all her magic and made me dollars on dollars, and you're going to figure out what you want to run *to*, my dear."

"I don't want to run to *anything*," I said. "If that's the reason—"

"Well, the condo won't be sold overnight. You think about what you want, because that's what I want too." Lorna took a sip of her drink. "How's Ari?"

"We broke up, Lorna," I said, because I hadn't actually yet said the words aloud to her, just kept showing up looking pathetic and brokenhearted.

"Well, sometimes these things need a moment to breathe," Lorna said.

I shook my head. "I don't think so."

"Hmmm," Lorna said. "I certainly liked Ari a great deal. And I liked you around Ari too, I could see how happy you two made each other."

I shrugged. "I don't think that was—anyway, it doesn't matter."

"I remember when you were with Taylor," Lorna said, as if I hadn't spoken. "You never seemed that happy, and she never did either."

I had no idea what Lorna was talking about, because everything there had been so good until the end. Until I learned that I couldn't have helped myself. Until it was over.

"I could tell what Taylor thought," Lorna said. "You see it at Oaken Troves all the time, young people viewing a visit with their relatives like one of the errands to check off their chore list. Groceries, post office, say hi to Grandma. I knew that Taylor was checking me off so she could get back to the rest of your life."

"Lorna, I'm sorry if—"

"And here's the thing, Nina Louise," Lorna said, again as if I hadn't interrupted at all. "Old age, while I complain about my pain and the things I've given up, is a gift. I can't believe the things I've gotten to see, including watching you grow up into a very kind and smart woman who I love spending time with. And so when I see a young person who has no interest in that, I know that they're the one missing out. You know that I watch all of those real housewives of all those cities and keeping up with that terrible family, because Nat and Choon Hee make me, and I can state that objectively my friends and I are much more fun to hang around with than any of those reality people all you young people watch."

I laughed and chugged back the rest of my mojito, now watered down from melted ice. It was really just minty water by this point. "You're the most fun person I know, Lorna."

"Well, I don't quite think that's true, but you're very sweet," Lorna said with a smile. "And you've of course never made me feel like an errand, and it was clear to see that Ari didn't feel that way either."

It was strange to still feel a jolt of affection and pride for Ari, in having fallen for someone who lived so earnestly and wholeheartedly. No matter how it had ended, that much couldn't be changed.

"Just think about it," she said, and I was sure she did that—left *it* so vague—on purpose. Because Lorna had left me with a hell of a lot to think about.

After work that evening, I googled. I might have been a researcher, in my own way, for work, but truly I'd never researched like this before. I made a list of all the similar condos that had sold in this neighborhood over the last six months, and I came up with a rough figure for the sale of this one.

It was a lot of money, more than I'd expected. But I knew that things weren't quite that simple, so I then spent some time figuring out what realtors charged, and what Lorna could actually expect to walk away with.

The sum was still huge, as far as I was concerned. And the truth was, it was kind of nice to think about having it. I could pay off my debt from USC, and still have money to get started somewhere. The panic about work could recede a little. If it took me some time to sort out what I really wanted for myself, the money would be there, holding my hand through it.

The *somewhere*, though, was just a big blank.

Deep down, I still had a dream life. A place on the Eastside, a job in a writers' room, a couple of rescue dogs for company. Even if I kept to myself, that much sounded good. Was it selfish though? Was it OK to want that much happiness after everything that had happened?

I didn't know, but I went back to the realty sites. There were ridiculously small homes for comparatively ridiculously large

256 / *Amy Spalding*

sums, and with Lorna's money they might actually be possible. After all of this—heartbreak and fuckups—I didn't realize I still had it in me to want something. I wasn't ready to tell Lorna that I'd figured something out, because I was still figuring. But I was a lot closer to it.

My inbox chimed, and I tabbed over to make sure there wasn't some kind of late-night work emergency. It *was* Max, but it had nothing to do with work.

> *Nina, I went on the worst date ever tonight, she tried to get me to JOIN A CULT. Can you please tell me it gets better, not like the uplifting queer youth slogan it gets better, like tell me IT ACTUALLY GETS BETTER because I hate my twenties. Text me if it's easier, I'm staying at this bar and hoping the cute bartender gives me this drink for free because I don't make enough money to be paying for these fancy cocktails I keep ordering.*

I laughed and grabbed for my phone. **I think I'm proof that it doesn't actually get any better, sorry. Sometimes I kind of miss my twenties, actually, my friends and I had all sorts of disasters and they make for good stories now.**

Holy hell, I missed my friends.

Did you ever end up on an app date with someone who literally tried to get you to JOIN HER CULT, Nina?? If not I don't think you're allowed to compare!

I wasn't going to become actual friends with Max. But I liked thinking of myself as some older and just-slightly-wiser guide of some sort. A little bit I could do for someone else. Plus without my urging, Max wouldn't have spoken to the bartender, and even though she ended up chickening out from keeping the conversation going long enough to get somewhere with her, she promised she'd go back after her next paycheck to keep the rapport going. I Venmo'd her for the drinks and told her to go back sooner than that.

And that gave me an idea, and—I couldn't believe it—I got out my script, the script that had blown everything up, the script I thought I'd never be able to look at again, this poor fucking script—and I *save as*'d again. I started revising.

Chapter 23
Kinda Foreboding

To: nrice@gmail.com
From: mvandoren@exemplar.com
Subject: Joyce call request
Message: Hi Nina,

Joyce would like to speak to you this morning, if you're available. Call in before eleven if you're able.

Thanks,
Max

My phone dinged with a text almost immediately. **Sorry, that email looks kinda foreboding but I don't think anything is up!**

Then it dinged again. **Also did you read the thing on The Cut? Just in case it has something to do with Joyce's call, maybe read it before you call in.**

I texted back a thank-you to Max, plus a GIF of a sloth that seemed grateful, and shakingly typed The Cut's URL into my open browser window. Ari took up about half the screen, as she was this month's digital "cover." *Ari Fox on Her Big Year and Her Soft Heart,* alongside a close-cropped black-and-white photo of her face. While I hated dwelling on how much I'd missed her, there was no denying it as I studied her cheekbones, that wry arch of her eyebrow, her slightly parted lips.

Obviously, I clicked on the story. The journalist had interviewed her on the set of her film in Georgia, but the details weren't new to me. There was something comforting about that, that we were apart but Ari had still grown up in Phoenix, still had made a name for herself kissing girls on teen shows before growing up to kiss slightly older women on network dramas, still was everyone's odds-on Oscar favorite months before the race actually got started. The quotes made me ache, because I couldn't help but hear them in her voice, and I couldn't help but think of hanging out with her to get better at my job. I couldn't help but think that I did send better emails now.

Buried down near the end of the story I spotted it. The paragraph must have been what made Max urge me to read the article in the first place.

> Professionally, Fox is on the cusp of a new level of fame. Personally, she's notoriously kept those details to herself. I ask about her relationship status anyway, and the actor quickly states that she's single. "I just went through a breakup so I'm too brokenhearted to think about dating right now," Fox says in what I take as an earnest manner. "No matter how people tend to write about me—" I interrupt to clarify: "People like me?" Fox laughs, an unabashed giggle at odds with her cool exterior. "Yeah, Samantha, people like you! There's always this sense that I'm tough and aloof, but honestly I'm softhearted as hell. I need some time to heal. I'll be spending this cuffing season with my cat Steve."

I read those words over and over. I couldn't even figure out what I was feeling, though perhaps that was because I felt so much at once. It felt illogical to be so relieved, so happy that what we'd had was real enough to miss and be wounded from. But, holy hell, I didn't want to be the one who wounded, that was the whole point of all of this, of me staying away, of me being alone.

Also I just fucking missed her. I missed her unashamed laugh, her stupid invisible cat, her ability to charm anyone. I missed being taken care of. I missed waking up in the morning in the same spot I'd fallen asleep next to her. I missed the way she'd wrap her arm around me, our togetherness a simple fact and nothing she overthought. Not like me.

What I really wanted was to read the article another ten times and then maybe cry in the tub, but even for me that sounded too sad. Plus I had to call Joyce, so I chugged some coffee and dialed.

"Hi, Nina," Max greeted me. "I think she's available. Hold, please."

"You're so professional," I said, which made her giggle.

"I'm trying, at least. Talk to you later, OK?"

The "cool" hold music came on, and I paced.

"Hey, Nina, how are you?"

"Good," I said.

"Believe it or not, I'm taking a meeting later this week in North Hollywood," Joyce said, a smile in her voice, "and I thought you might be free for drinks once I'm done. It's been a while, and with so much going on I thought catching up in person might be useful."

"Sure," I said. "I can be free whenever you need."

"Friday around five? I'll have Max send over a location and confirm that time."

I agreed to that and said goodbye. It didn't make sense how quickly I'd stopped being afraid, but I wasn't afraid, and also maybe it made sense after all. I did trust Max's read on Joyce, and I also potentially had a pile of money with my name on it headed my way. With less fear, my job was less scary.

I had lived for months waiting for shoes to drop, and by now, the shoes had all fallen. My relationship was over, my friendships were behind me, my job was tenuous but at least my missteps were out in the open. It felt different than my original exile. I was living openly in a way that I couldn't fully define but felt in my bones. Maybe there weren't versions of Nina. Maybe there was just this one.

That sounded OK to me.

Joyce and I were scheduled to meet at the Federal on Friday evening, and while the happy hour crowd was already loud when I arrived a few minutes before five, I found a quiet booth to slip into. Max texted a warning that Joyce was running behind, so I opened up an ebook and tried to lose myself in a thriller. Max kept sending me details about her upcoming app dates, though, so it was hard figuring out who was the murderer when instead I was judging girls' profiles and giving advice. I had no right to give anyone advice! Max just seemed like the one person who had worse judgment than I did, so it felt safe. It *was* true after all that no one had ever tried to lure me into a cult.

"Hey there." Joyce made her way to the table, and I awkwardly slipped out of the booth to hug her. She was in a bright blue jumpsuit with towering wedge boots, though her hair was down in beachy waves so for once she didn't fully tower over me. "How've you been, Nina?"

"OK," I said, and she laughed.

"Great, an honest answer." She surveyed the bar. "God, it's packed in here. This is what happens when you let your twenty-something assistant choose the venue."

I laughed. "Max is great, though. She's trying her hardest." I didn't know why I felt I had the right to defend Max; the wisest and most professional thing to do here was agree with Joyce. But, fuck it. Everything was out on the table now.

"She's definitely always doing that," Joyce said, laughing more. "I'm lucky to have her, absolutely."

We sat down together and I tried to look neutral, not like a person desperate for news of her fate. And *desperate* wasn't the right word anyway. I was somewhere between *desperate* and *mildly curious.*

"So," Joyce said, once we'd put in drink orders, "I guess I'd like to have another conversation with you about your career, Nina."

"Oh," I said.

"Luckily this latest incident blew over," she said. "I've never been so happy you rarely come into the office or grace us with your presence at holiday parties. But, to be honest, it gives me a lot of pause about pushing you into a bigger role next year."

I nod. "Yeah. That's . . . more than fair."

"Ari connected with me to make sure I knew that the secrecy had been all her, not you, not that I hadn't already suspected as much," Joyce said, while my mind spun. Ari had lied for me? Even now? "Her reputation for . . . well, there's no one at Exemplar who's unaware that she's difficult. That alone would have gone a long way if people had started asking questions. But luckily, no one did."

The waiter dropped off our drinks, and we clinked our glasses together, though the mood felt anything but celebratory.

"I'm—I'm really sorry," I said once we were alone again. "It had just—I mean, I'd never expected to be in a situation like that. I had no idea how to handle it."

Joyce chuckled. "No, I can't say I prepared you for that possibility in your job training. Do I need to start working that in?"

"I don't know, *don't sleep with the talent* seems pretty basic, I was just an idiot."

Joyce laughed harder. "You said it, not me. All right, since we're in the Valley around a bunch of loud people, should we give in and split some bar food?"

"Ugh, that sounds great, I'm so glad you asked," I said, and it hit me that I was just being *my actual self* with Joyce for maybe the first time in our history working together. And of course it was partially because I'd let go a lot of fears and I needed this job less than I had a few weeks ago, but it was hard not to notice that being myself was not going poorly.

We ordered a few appetizers, switched out our cocktails for Diet Cokes the next round, and handed over our menus to the waiter. Joyce updated me on the state of her client roster, with one notable exception, which I appreciated. The food arrived before long and I appreciated that—both as something for my empty stomach *and* a distraction—as well.

"Can I ask?" Joyce dipped a tater tot into a side of aioli and I marveled that I was sharing trashy Midwestern food with one of the classiest women I knew. "Off the record. What was it like dating the infamous Ms. Fox? Did she make your life as difficult as she makes mine on a regular basis?"

"No," I said, my cheeks flushing. "She was . . . she was great."

Joyce shot me a bemused look. "Really."

"Really. Ari was . . . Anyway, I was the problem. Not her."

"I'll just say that I find that hard to imagine," Joyce said.

"She's not difficult," I said. "Or, well, maybe she is. But there's no one like her, you know? She's attempting this career there's really not a blueprint for, and I think she just wants some control over it, especially when she feels like people don't understand."

Joyce's face was expression-free, and I wondered if I'd just been a bit *too much* myself.

264 / *Amy Spalding*

"I'm biased, I'm sorry," I said quickly.

"No, it's good to hear your perspective, biased as it may be." She studied me for a long moment. "You know, Nina, the truth is that if you're still interested in this career, I wouldn't turn you away from a larger role in the future. I think you understand how people function in a way that's really key to doing this well. But as good as I think you'd be, I don't think it's what you want."

I shook my head. So much honesty today. "No. Probably not enough, at least."

"Do you mind me asking," Joyce began, and my mind darted to so many things I did not want to be asked. "What *do* you want, Nina? It's not a trick question. You can keep writing talent emails as long as you want. But what would you be doing if it was up to you?"

I took a sip of my Diet Coke to stall. Joyce's eyes were fixed on me.

"Writing," I said, finally. "For TV. It's all I've wanted since I was in college."

"Oh, I can see that," Joyce said. "I mean, you fake writing as my entire list of clients, you could be dropped into any writers' room and figure out the existing characters."

I'd never thought of that, but it actually made a lot of sense.

"Do you have scripts?" Joyce asked. "Ready to go?"

I shook my head. "I'm revising one right now. The others I wrote when I was younger and I don't think they're that good anymore. But this one . . . I don't know. It might be something. It feels special to me."

"I'd be happy to take a look when you've finished," Joyce said. "Obviously it's not my area of expertise, but someone at Exemplar might be a good fit. I'd be happy to make a connection for you when the time is right."

"Oh, you don't have to—" I caught myself because all I'd done was beg Ari to let me figure out my own path and my own connections, and here, perhaps, were my own path and connections. "Sure. I'll let you know when it's finished."

"Great. As you probably know, no one's likely going to make your pilot, but it might get you into a room so you can build a résumé and enough contacts to get something of your own made someday."

"Yeah, trust me, that's all I want," I said. "Thank you, Joyce."

"Thank *you* for being honest with me," she said. "And now I'll be honest with you. I'd like to request a dessert menu to continue our evening of gluttony or whatever this has turned into. What happens in the Valley stays in the Valley, right?"

"I mean, based on my twenties, yes," I said, and laughed along with Joyce. This wasn't some huge revelation, not really; it was safe because I was obviously leaving before long. Someone else would have my job and would parse her own communications for signs of having too much of a personality or too little professionalism. But that didn't mean I couldn't enjoy it while it was still mine.

I gave myself the night off but once I was up the next morning and fully caffeinated, I decided to spend my entire Saturday on the script. After a while, though, I felt like I was only fidgeting with it, moving small things around and trying to make slightly smarter word choices. At a certain point, I was not going to be enough to fix my own script, and maybe that point had already come. I'd turned the Hoff portrait around after the breakup, so I didn't even have his encouraging gaze.

I did have a stack of scriptwriting books, somewhere, a box untouched since moving in, so I googled instead. I was a researcher, after all, kind of. And while I'd planned on buying a few newer books for my collection, I stumbled on a Reddit thread where multiple people referenced the same pilot script revision class they'd taken in Hollywood that was, apparently, an incredible help. I took a chance and googled the class. It was through a small writing collective, and while the current session had sold out, there was a wait list for the next session that started in a couple months.

I typed in my name and email address and submitted to hold my place. Yes, it would mean strangers would read my work. Yes, it would mean I'd have to admit my goals to a whole room of people who I suspected would be younger and cooler. But it was the next step, and maybe I was ready for it. I realized that I wanted to be.

While I was googling to fix myself, my stomach growled. I tried to figure out for how many more meals I could stick with my sad tuna salad bowl before fully losing my mind, and then made another decision. If it was going to be just me, forever—and it *was* going to be just me, forever—I could at least eat real meals sometimes. No one was going to show up and rescue me from my sad piles of food.

Nina Rice would have to rescue herself.

The truth was that even searching for "how can I, a kitchen idiot, learn to cook" pulled up results that seemed beyond me, but some slick ads for a meal kit delivery service convinced me to click, and their stupid site testimonials fully suckered me in. Maybe I really did just need a script class in Hollywood and a box of organic, locally sourced ingredients to get my shit together.

No, I was absolutely not officially rescued yet, but getting the two email confirmations in my inbox made me feel like I might be closer. I might be OK.

Chapter 24

Another Two Options

My doorbell rang at 11:00 a.m. sharp on Sunday morning, startling me from my ebook. I was seriously never going to find out who this goddamn fictional murderer was.

I couldn't remember the last time the doorbell had rung, but I'd lost track of when Girl Scout Cookie season was, and I hoped it might have something to do with that. Sure, I was going to learn to cook, maybe, if all went well, but that wasn't going to allay my snacking needs.

Oh, holy hell.

I wanted to run and hide as soon as I walked up to my front door and saw the crowd assembled on the patio. But there were too many windows; I'd already been spotted.

"Open your goddamn door!" Chloe rapped frantically on the biggest window. "We can see you in there, Nina!"

I threw the door open mainly so the neighbors wouldn't complain about the loud, cursing pack of queer people in suburbia on a Sunday morning. It definitely wasn't to *let them in*, it was to stave off the HOA. But in they came anyway: Phoebe, Bianca, Chloe, and CJ.

"Nina, this is a really cool space inside." CJ surveyed the front room calmly as if they forced themselves into people's condos every single day of the week. "Outside's a nightmare, of course, but this is great."

"Lorna wouldn't have chosen to live in a nightmare," Bianca said. "I'm not surprised at all. It's *perfect*."

"What are . . . you all doing here?" I put my hands on my hips to try to look stern, but I was wearing, sans bra, a faded old sweatshirt that said *Grey Sloan Memorial Hospital*, and pajama pants printed with tiny sloths. It was a tough ensemble for stern.

"We knew you did your run-away-from-society thing again because of heartbreak," Chloe said. "And we were like, nah, fuck that shit."

"That's not what I was—"

"No, girl," Bianca said sharply. "It's exactly what you were doing. And we're not letting you. It's that simple."

"How did you even find me?" I asked, because I'd managed to never give out this address. This place was just for me.

"We're all friends with Lorna on Instagram," Phoebe said. "So I just had to ask for your address. She was happy to help."

It did feel inappropriate just how often I wanted to murder Lorna.

"We have eleven-thirty brunch reservations down the street," Phoebe said. "So you should hit the shower fast so we're not late. You know how much I hate being late."

"But I—I didn't—I'm not—"

"Shower, clothes, brunch," CJ said. "In that order. I'm going to check out all of your aunt's furniture in the meantime."

"I feel like I've made myself really clear here," I said, but they all just *stared at me*, and so I didn't know what to do besides trudge up the stairs to my bathroom for a fast shower. Somehow I managed to both pull myself into looking semi-respectable and be back downstairs by twenty-two minutes past the hour. We crowded into Phoebe's car, and she drove us to a bistro only a few stoplights away that I'd gone to a few times with Lorna before she'd moved into Oaken Troves. I sat in the back seat, squished between CJ and Chloe, wondering how the last twenty-something minutes had even happened. What I wanted—well, what I was supposed to be doing was sitting on my couch getting up the energy to pour a bowl of cereal and put together more clues about a fictional murderer. I wasn't supposed to be here at all. And looking at my friends in this suburban surrounding, it was easy to see that they weren't supposed to be here either. None of this was supposed to be happening.

Phoebe had, of course, reserved us a table outside, and I sat down between Bianca and CJ. Last time I'd reconnected with my friends, we'd had far more time away—three years and not three weeks—but it felt bigger now, for reasons I couldn't fully comprehend. It didn't make any sense that I was sitting here, that my old crew had driven practically an hour out of their way for me. Me! Stupid toxic self-centered cursed Nina Rice.

And they all looked so great too, and not just compared to unprepared me. Bianca was in a gorgeous purple dress that made her light brown skin glow. Phoebe was, amazingly, in one of her Palm Springs outfits, florals, formal shorts, new glasses. Chloe was in a brightly patterned Nooworks jumpsuit with the same broken-in Dr. Martens she'd worn since we'd met. CJ was in jeans and a green button-down, quintessential CJ.

I'd missed all of them so, so much.

"I can't believe you're all here," I murmured, and Bianca squeezed my hand. "I don't—you shouldn't have—"

"Breakups *suck*," Chloe said. "We know! You don't have to abandon us, though."

"I wasn't abandoning you, I . . ."

The crew didn't interrupt me. They just waited. But I didn't know what to say so I picked up my menu and read about all the different styles of eggs Benedict. A server stopped by, and magically everyone was ready to order, even Bianca.

"Sofia's frantic with art show stuff," CJ said, "or she'd be here. I'd be helping her if it was anyone other than one of my best friends. She sends her love."

I buried my face in my hands, because it was too much already. *One of my best friends. Love.* For me. Nina goddamn Rice.

"Hey," Bianca said, grabbing my hand again. "What's going on, sweetie? Do you want to talk about it?"

I looked around at my friends, these incredible people I was so lucky to know. They had so much they gave the world, Bianca's warmth, Phoebe's savvy, CJ's fire, Chloe's feistiness. I wanted it all, wanted my friends, wanted every Sunday just like this.

And, suddenly, I realized something. If Taylor was right, and I guessed I'd really fully accepted that Taylor was right, I didn't just have the one option. Yes, I could continue to hide, and keep the world away. I could accept that this was my last Sunday brunch ever.

Or I could tell the whole truth, for the first time in a very long time.

"No," I finally said. "I don't want to talk about it. But . . . I will."

And so I did. I told them about Taylor moving out and her twelve-point list. Actually, I knew that it was still somewhere in my Gmail so I searched for it and read the whole thing.

Nina,

  I know that you feel that I owe you an explanation, or at least the promise to schedule some kind of talk, but there's been so much on my mind for so long that it makes the most sense to send this along to you this way. I'm sorry; I know this isn't how you ideally wanted to have this conversation, but it's what works for me right now.

I've struggled so much lately in this relationship, and have held back quite a lot. My resentments have been building, and that's on me; I should have talked to you much sooner than this. That said, there's no way we can move forward, together, if we don't address all of this, so I thought I'd send you this message.

#1. Extremes. Being in a relationship with someone who expresses such overly large emotions is, frankly, exhausting. Whether or not it's getting overly furious at someone for cutting you off in traffic or extremely excited because Del Taco puts an item back on their seasonal menu, navigating your moods on top of everything else on my plate has really become too much.

#2. Centering Yourself. I constantly feel as if your only priority is yourself, which is a fairly terrible thing to have to think about one's partner.

#3. Support. I'm far from the only one who knows that your myopic focus on yourself holds you back from giving others what they need.

#4. Stress. Again, this isn't just about me; there's an overwhelming sense about you that frequently sets my anxiety on edge, and I know it happens to others as well.

#5. Priorities. We've talked so much over the years about our big life plans, but sometimes I get the feeling that you have no idea how to prioritize to actually make any of this happen. It's scary to imagine a future with someone who doesn't seem to have any idea how to get there.

#6. Time/Promptness. Anyone who knows you would agree that your time management is extremely poor. Barring some kind of condition that renders you literally unable to process time, this is yet another example in the array of ways you center only yourself and deem other people (and their schedules) unimportant.

#7. Lack of Concern. There have been times, especially in the last few months, where you've really hurt my feelings, and the truth is that it doesn't seem that you picked up on it at all. Your shock at my moving out all but confirmed this for me.

#8. Choices/Decisions. I often feel that when I leave important decisions up to you, you panic and let your instinct guide you (poorly). I'm not sure how to continue building a life with someone who reacts this way.

#9. Ambition. I'm well aware that it isn't, supposedly, polite for women to discuss their own ambitions without it being weaponized against us, but in fact the opposite is true for me. I'm concerned our levels of ambition don't align, and what this means for us further down the line. What steps are you actually taking in your life to get the things you supposedly want?

#10. Partnership. Simply, much of this boils down to the fact that I'm not sure how to maintain a solid partnership with someone who doesn't seem invested in doing the work.

#11. Trust. As you can imagine, with all of this, I've found it harder to take you at face value or trust you. This started with smaller things, but by now it's leeched through the bigger, more serious aspects of our life together, too.

#12. Toxicity. The combination effect of all of this is that it eats at me—and others, too—so that these choices and attitudes and behaviors don't only affect me, but other people in your life.

Nina, I don't think this is irrevocably broken, but it's going to take a lot of work. After you've had a chance to absorb this, if you're interested in moving forward, together, please drop me a line.

—Taylor

Our food arrived but I just kept going. The texts back and forth between us and the hope I'd salvage all of it. The part where I was thoughtless and practically killed a bicyclist. The whole conversation at the bar. The warning she'd made, right to my face, that even if I hadn't yet, I'd eventually drive everyone else away, too—the warning that had shifted everything for me.

I finally stabbed into my crab eggs Benedict, watching egg yolk drizzle across the plate onto the polenta rounds and kale hash, while waiting for my friends' determination of my fate. It was a fancy breakfast to accompany potentially being cast out forever. And now that my friends had heard it all, I couldn't imagine what they were thinking—and if they'd still be up here in the suburbs if they'd heard it sooner.

"See?" Chloe said. "I told you guys Taylor was garbage."

"She wasn't garbage," I said quickly, because that wasn't what this was, a Taylor-bashing session or a sly opening to talk shit about her. "I loved her so, so much. And she's well respected and has a great career. I mean, she was and she did. I assume that's all still true."

"She has exacting standards," Phoebe said, the only person here who'd known Taylor longer than I had. "And sometimes they didn't feel particularly fair."

"*Sometimes?*" Bianca scoffed loudly, and turned back to me. "It's a shitty thing to do to someone. To give this list and then when you try to discuss it to say anything that's not true will be eventually? That the longer people know you, the more they'll see all of it, and you can't do anything about it because it's how you're built? Of course you worried you had to hide away, Neen. But also—"

"But also, you stupid idiot, we had your back!" Chloe said. "We *still* have your back!"

"We happen to like how you're built," Phoebe said, and grinned. "Sorry, that came out like I'm hitting on you, but you know what I mean."

"You can hit on her, baby," Bianca said. "I mean, just a little, nothing serious."

"Some of that letter is, like, here's what's great about my girlfriend, but I'll be an asshole about her instead," Chloe said. "Like, having big emotions is hardly all bad. You know I lose my mind whenever the McRib comes back."

"Clearly, the two of you weren't a good fit," Phoebe said. "We all have flaws. I like to think we've all improved in the last few years, and will keep doing so, and I'm sure I'm not alone that plenty of that list sounds nothing like the Nina I know."

My friends, incredibly, nodded in agreement.

"Plus Chloe's right," Phoebe continued. "What's a bad fit for someone can be wonderful for someone else. We, obviously, think you're wonderful, Nina."

I shook my head, even though I felt that *wonderful* right in my heart, right where I needed it.

"What happened with Ari?" CJ asked gently. I loved how gentle CJ could be sometimes. "To be honest, I was pretty neutral on Taylor, other than the objective fact that she was gorgeous as hell."

"Drop. Dead. Gorgeous." Chloe waved her hand dismissively. "But dead inside."

"Anyway," CJ said, as Chloe and Bianca cracked up. "I liked Ari a lot."

"Well, yeah, me too," I said. "But I fucked it up. Just like Taylor said I would."

So I launched into that story too, in between bites of my breakfast and giant gulps of coffee. I didn't have any evidence for this part of my presentation, as I'd deleted that email and also thrown away its printout.

"This is sort of the dumbest story I've ever heard," Chloe said.

"What?" I asked. "Which part?"

"The entire thing, you dummy," she said. "Yeah, you both fucked up, big deal. Who doesn't fuck up?"

"What Ari did was pretty shitty," CJ said. "Absolutely. I'd be pissed too. But—"

"No, the thing I did was so much worse," I said. "Since I met Ari, there was only one thing she cared about. And I completely disregarded it. Don't you get it? Taylor was right that I'm self-centered, and the longer someone knows me—"

"What Ari did was *so much worse*," Bianca said, as CJ and Chloe added their affirmatives. Bianca shot a look to Phoebe. "Baby."

"Well, Nina did interfere with Ari's business correspondence," Phoebe said, which made the rest of my friends shriek with laughter.

"No," Chloe said. "You both messed up, and you both need to apologize, and that's it. No offense, Nina, but if you think you're going to do better than Ari Fox, me and my friend reality would like to have a long talk with you."

"Trust me," I said, "I'm aware. But I did mess up with Ari, is the thing. And I messed up with all of you too. Taylor wasn't wrong about me."

"How did you mess up with any of us?" CJ asked, though I detected that Bianca was frowning.

"The deadline for the adoption agency letter," I said. "If anything I did—or didn't do caused—"

"Oh my god, no," Bianca said. "The deadline was just because, well, you have to give people a deadline. But a week later wasn't a big deal. The agency called us and said you'd overnighted the letter, so dramatic, and that the administrative assistant who read it *ended up crying*."

"This is why I kept texting you to help me," CJ said. "My letter was like, *Phoebe and Bianca are good people. Give them a baby. I work with computers. Goodbye.*"

"Sorry I ignored your texts," I said to CJ, though I then realized I should direct my gaze to the whole table. "I just didn't know what to do. This whole time I've seen that conversation with Taylor as this ticking time bomb until you all felt the same way."

"You know who sent a really lovely letter?" Phoebe asked.

"Not me," CJ said, and I laughed and squeezed their hand across the table.

"Ari," Phoebe continued.

"I'm sure it was right after we got back and you sent us the info," I said. "We didn't break up for another week."

"No, it arrived right at deadline," Phoebe said. "She's a good person, Nina."

"Do we have to talk about Ari?" I asked. "Of course she's a good person."

"Good people mess up sometimes," Bianca said gently. "Including you."

I sighed and wiped my eyes. "I mess up more than that. And what if I'm destined for more?"

"You didn't mess up because Taylor foretold that you would," Bianca said. "It's not destiny. It's just being human."

"You realize that *none* of us know the future, right?" Phoebe asked without a patronizing note to her voice.

"Not even fucking Taylor!" Chloe added.

"Not even Taylor," Phoebe continued. "But you know that, don't you, deep down? This whole thing—life—is a gamble. And I happen to think it's all worth it."

Bianca grabbed my other hand. By now, our entire table was crisscrossed with everyone's hands. I didn't think the surrounding tables knew what to make of us.

"Sure," Bianca said, "you might hurt me some day. Phoebe might have a midlife crisis and leave me for a younger woman."

"Whoa." Phoebe held up her hand. "I don't love that that's your example."

"Sorry, baby. My point is that we can't predict where life will take us, and no relationships come with guarantees." She turned back from Phoebe to me. "But you're worth it to me to find out."

"To me too," Phoebe said.

"What they said," CJ agreed.

Chloe rolled her eyes. "Obviously. Taylor is trash, you are treasure."

"Taylor's not trash," I said. "She had a right to not be happy with me. I used to be really bad at time and inconsiderate about some things—"

"Yeah, and also people are allowed to break up with each other," Bianca said. "But to act like that meant you weren't good for anyone was shitty of her."

The table continued adding affirmatives.

"But, also, sweetie . . ." Bianca made very direct eye contact with me. "We're all here for you, and we don't care about the risk of loving hard. But some of this stuff is really big, and your reactions were so huge, and . . . I think some of this would be best to work out with a therapist."

"Oh, thank god you said it," CJ murmured under their breath, but we all heard them, and everyone laughed, even me, as my friends chimed in about the therapy I needed and the therapy they were all in. And I realized suddenly that I was on the other side, not across some huge expanse from the people I loved, but right next to them, hands held, truths out, risks assessed, love expressed. I'd shared the worst things someone had ever said about me, and they were still here. It hit me that it didn't even matter, to some degree, whether or not Taylor had been right about me. My friends had the whole truth, and my friends were still right here.

The mood lightened, thank god, and we ended up ordering more food because big talks apparently took a lot out of all of us. The second round arrived—more carbs-heavy this time—and Phoebe asked for a toast. Also Phoebe was making the toast, of course.

"We all missed Nina, of course, but it was also important for Bianca and I to have her here this week before we shared with y'all that Bianca and I have been chosen to adopt this baby, and it's about as definite as it'll get before she's born."

"Oh my god, *she?*" Chloe squealed. "So she's like an actual baby."

"She is indeed an actual baby," Phoebe said, "or, she's going to be in January. Which gives us hopefully enough time to turn the spare room into a nursery and learn everything there is to know about babies."

"Three months, sure, why not, babies are really easy, right?" I asked.

"We met again with the baby's biological mother last week," Bianca said. "She was really overwhelmed actually by all the letters sent on our behalf, but she couldn't stop talking about Nina's. Seriously, everyone wanted to talk about Nina and the way she described us and—and this chosen family right here at this table. Plus Sofia, of course! Plus—well, no jinxing."

"It won't be Ari," I said. "But hopefully maybe it can be someone else someday."

This seemed to annoy everyone, but they didn't know what a big deal it was for me to think that. I was proud despite their dismissals.

CJ ordered a bottle of champagne for the table, and we toasted to our friends' future daughter, and to all of us. The mood lightened yet again, and while Chloe and Bianca discussed decorating ideas for the nursery, CJ filled in Phoebe and me about Sofia's art show.

"Can I ask you something?" I was blissed out from this brunch of friendship, and brave enough to ask. "Why is it different with Sofia?"

"What do you mean?" CJ asked. "Different how?"

"Well, just that . . . you . . ."

"CJ," Chloe shouted from her side of the table, "you used to bring a different girl like every other week to brunch. And now you're helping put together an art show with this woman and using the word *we* like that's normal for you!"

"Yeah," I said with a smile. "That."

"I mean, it's not different," CJ said. "Or, I guess that it is. I just mean that I've never gone into any relationship with some goal or idea of the future. I just see how it feels, and if it feels right, I keep going. And it feels really right with Sofia. And I know she feels similarly, that neither of us are looking for marriage or kids, maybe even not monogamy, but what we're figuring out together is really great. I like that neither of us feel like we have to define it. I mean, as a nonbinary person I'm not exactly into labels, so a relationship with someone who isn't into them either feels right. It's good building something with someone else."

"CJ, I've never heard you say something *romantic* before," Chloe said.

"Well, no one's ever asked before," CJ said, which I realized was true. CJ had always just seemed so cool, much cooler than my heart-eyed dreams of a white dress, a sperm donor baby or two, forever and ever with one wife. I hadn't wanted to seem less evolved or something by comparison. But this was my *family*, and even though all five of us had different lives and different goals, we had each other's backs. We valued each other's personal outlooks.

Every single risk, I realized, was worth it.

"So how's work?" Phoebe asked me, as I finished off the table's one remaining waffle. "Have you thought about—"

"Yes, Phoebe, I've thought about next steps, and it's not being an agent," I said. "And not just because—"

"You slept with the talent?"

"Yeah, that. Actually, how would you feel about helping me figure out next step career stuff? I want to keep writing, but I need to make money in the meantime, and I think I'm done with the agency world."

"Actually, we could use someone at the office," Phoebe said. "Our marketing coordinator just put in her notice, and I don't think it would be too awkward if you worked for me. It's a good gig for a writer; you'd need to put together presentations and put decks together, but someone who's got good professional written communication skills is really going to excel in the role. And there's usually some downtime; if work's caught up and no one needs you, you'd be able to have a little time for writing or whatever you can do quietly at a computer."

"That sounds perfect," I said, even though the thought of working for my most badass friend was a little intimidating. "I can work on my résumé tonight and send it—"

"Oh, god, Neen, the job is yours if you want it," Phoebe said.

I frowned, even though it did seem like an answer to my current prayers. "Isn't this nepotism? Shouldn't you look for the best possible candidate?"

"You know, white B-school men use nepotism every day to get each other jobs," Phoebe said. "I don't feel bad about doing it myself occasionally. Also it doesn't pay great and you can't work remotely, so the commute might kill you. But if you want it, email me later and we'll work out the details."

"Actually," I said, and filled the whole table in on Lorna's plans to sell the condo. I was absolutely no closer to knowing what my next steps were, but plans sounded fun again. I mentally upgraded the space I'd find for myself; I'd need at least enough room to host dinners for my friends occasionally.

I really was pinning a lot of hopes on those meal kits. No, I realized, even if the meal kits were a failure, there was still delivery. I'd host my friends, however I could.

"You can stay in my extra room until Lorna's place is sold and you get your own," Chloe offered. "The commute to Phoebe's office would be practically walkable."

"I thought you decided you never wanted to share space with people again," CJ said, though we were clearly all thinking it. This was a table of people often all thinking the same thing at the same time.

"It's not *people*," Chloe said with a huff. "It's Nina! We won't kill each other."

"Maybe," I said, smiling. "And just temporarily. According to the realty blogs I checked out, the average timing for selling the condo should be on the fast side, it's apparently a seller's market right now."

"Oh my *god*, you sound so grown up," Bianca said.

"Just don't ask me any follow-up questions," I said, "as I'm not entirely sure what that means."

"Do you want me to explain it?" Phoebe asked.

"*No*," Bianca said immediately. "Phoebe stayed, like, BFFs with our realtor. They golf most Saturday mornings together."

"Ooh, is your realtor hot?" Chloe asked.

"It's a *man*," Phoebe said, and we all shrieked in laughter. I'd laughed more today than maybe any day on record. It all seemed so simple now, these people and me. My family forever.

Chapter 25
Further Negotiations

I texted Lorna the next morning, bright and early. **I know it's a Monday, but would you like to have coffee this afternoon? I can swing by around 3 and drive to Starbucks.**

Lorna agreed to that, so I set a reminder to leave the condo on time, and opened my inbox, plus the cycle of talent inboxes, to start my day. I wanted to be completely caught up before I sent the letter Phoebe had helped me draft yesterday.

After brunch, the crew had come back to the condo for almost the entire afternoon. It made me sad I'd never used it to host before, no friends and not even an overnight when I briefly had a girlfriend. It was a beautiful place that had been my home for over three years, and I'd never treated it like I should have. Soon it would be someone else's, so I was going to enjoy it while I could.

Bianca and CJ had helped me get started packing the few things that were mine, while Chloe snooped around and Phoebe strategized with me on how best to put in my two weeks' notice. We'd decided that less was more, and that there was nothing big that Joyce didn't already know. A simple message would be enough.

Still, though, I anticipated an email from Max, a semi-urgent call with Joyce, perhaps some disappointment that I wasn't seeing anyone through Oscar season. So I flew through each email inbox, making sure nothing was left to handle, before I set that in motion.

Ari's inbox—every day a little less painful to log in to—only had a random publicity email, and I hurried to forward it and get the hell out. But then I noticed the subject line. It was the publicist for the art gallery that was hosting Sofia's show Friday night. According to the email, it would be the *LGBTQ+ event of the night*. The entire thing was written at such a level of publicity-speak that I determined it had nothing to do with the fact that Sofia and Ari had known each other briefly, through me, and probably every celebrity lesbian's agent, manager, and/or publicist had this email in their inboxes as well.

That impersonal nature made me thrilled to, without guilt, delete the email. It was one of the most unprofessional things I'd done in this job—I mean, it was a far step down from sleeping with the talent, but I hadn't misbehaved much, so it was still within the top three or so—but I rationalized that Ari was in Georgia anyway. And I was minutes away from quitting! I deserved a little unprofessionalism.

The chain of events unfolded as I suspected it would. The email from Max, the call scheduled with Joyce, the text warning me Joyce's mood was *not great*, and a terse but ultimately understanding phone call.

And, just like that, I was two weeks away from my new life.

At Oaken Troves, Lorna was waiting near the parking lot when I pulled up, but I still got out to hug her hello. I felt like it had been ages since I'd seen her, not days. They'd been such big days.

"OK, I have a lot I'd like to discuss with you," I told her, once we were at an outside table at Starbucks with our drinks and slices of pumpkin loaf. I got out a notepad and flipped to my list—obviously written with help from Phoebe. I still didn't actually know what a seller's market was, after all.

"Nina Louise, you seem very fired up today," Lorna said.

"I've made . . . a lot of decisions since we spoke last week, actually."

"Oh," Lorna said, and held her hand to her mouth. "I'm sorry, my dear. I fear I sprung too much on you when you're still—well, I know you're hurting. I wasn't trying to make your life even tougher right now."

"No, I'm weirdly glad you did talk to me last week," I said. "There's been a lot of things that I've put off or tried not to think about, and it's time that I did. I mean, it's *past time* but I feel ready now."

I told her about my new job at Big Marketing Energy—the pay wasn't any better than my agency job, but because I wouldn't be freelance, I'd get health insurance that covered therapy, plus vacation days and sick leave, all sorts of unsexy things I wanted desperately. Lorna raised her eyebrows upon hearing I'd be rooming with Chloe, at least for the time being, but maybe I hadn't been lying after all when I'd claimed to like a challenge.

"She really hasn't punched that many people," I found myself saying.

"But that you have to clarify it at all!" Lorna chuckled. "Yes, you're right, for the time being it should be a good arrangement. And you can really walk to work?"

"Well, honestly, I probably *won't*, but, yes, I could. Though . . . speaking of driving." I closed my notepad so she couldn't see the last line item on my list. "I'd like to negotiate for something."

"Oh?" Lorna asked, and then recognition flashed in her eyes. "What's in this for me?"

"I'll handle every single aspect of the condo sale," I said. "I will make the appointments, keep the appointments, work with your realtor to get the place set up, and then I'll be at Chloe's anyway so it can be shown whenever the realtor likes. I will run every single errand you need, and bring you flat whites and cappuccinos whenever I can."

She studied me. "Do you even know how to drive a stick shift, Nina Louise?"

"Yeah, don't you remember I let that girl I was trying to impress teach me back in college?" I asked, and we both laughed at the memory.

"Of course you can have the convertible," Lorna said. "I honestly couldn't believe you hadn't asked sooner. That Honda has seen some better days! Though haven't we all!"

"The Honda was what I needed at the time," I said. "But I feel different now."

Lorna nodded. "Needs change."

"Yeah, I guess they do. Speaking of changes, I won't be able to do Thursday lunches anymore once I start my new job," I said. "Phoebe isn't huge on people working remotely, so I'm moving to Chloe's next weekend."

"Of course," Lorna said. "Don't you worry about me, I've got Nat and Choon Hee to keep me entertained."

"But maybe we can do dinner sometime, and coffee on the weekends? I thought about what you said, and even though I loved having our Thursday tradition, I hope that never made you feel like I thought of you as an errand to check off my list."

"Never," Lorna said.

"Good, because I don't feel that way. And I'm going to keep seeing you at least once a week, even after I'm at my new job. It's a promise."

"Good!" Lorna said. "And it's also fine if you can't. We have our phones now, we get to chat all of the time. Speaking of, Nina Louise, when are you getting on Instagram? You know that your friends are all on it. You're really missing out."

"I'm fine," I said.

286 / Amy Spalding

"No, I have only one demand for the convertible," Lorna said.

"Didn't we already close this deal?"

"I'm eighty-one! I'm allowed to take my time. I will sign the car over to you, but you'll sign up for Instagram and post photos of it in that beautiful LA sunshine for me to see from here. How's that sound?"

It actually sounded perfect to me. Though once I was home, signed up for Instagram, and posting my first photo of the car sitting, shiny and ready, in the garage, I thought about Ari's hand running down its side. No one would be as excited for me as she would have been, and my stomach twisted with the recognition that it meant just a little less not being able to share this with her. I hit *share* anyway.

Bianca asked me over for dinner later that week, but I'd already successfully cooked one meal from my new subscription service and was feeling puffed up about my newfound culinary skills, so I asked her over instead. I'd be out of the condo in a few days, other than realty responsibilities, but I hated that I'd never truly let it become my home. One dinner with my best friend wasn't going to fix that, but it was a good way to go out.

"Thank god you're here," I greeted her, letting her hug me even though I'd splattered olive oil all over my T-shirt. "The recipe is way more confusing than the one I did Tuesday. If you don't help me I'll never find my way out of this."

"I mean, girl, you could just *google*," Bianca said, but followed me into the kitchen and leaned over the recipe card. "Oh, no problem, we've got this. I'll walk you through."

"I knew you would." I squeezed in next to her at the counter. "Thanks for driving up. I figured I could host you for dinner here at least once."

"I'm honored! Plus now Phoebe can get home from her business dinner and play her stupid video game all night and neither of us will be annoyed at each other. She's determined to get through this whole *ultra violent* series before the baby's here, which means there is a lot of virtual gunfire in my living room lately."

"You're going to be *a mom*," I said, unable to hide the awe in my voice. "Can you believe it?"

Bianca picked up the recipe card and studied it more closely. "Tell me the first thing that confused you."

"It wants me to cut off part of an orange peel but not the white part and I cut off part of it and you can totally see white underneath and I—"

"Ignore this. Do you have a tiny grater? We'll just zest it that way." Bianca opened a drawer of cookware items I'd rarely touched and began rooting around. "Phoebe and I are both really . . . I don't have the words for it, Neen. Scared and excited and grateful and nauseated. *Aha.*" She extracted an item I did not recognize. "Try this microplane instead. Didn't your mom teach you to cook?"

"That's sexist," I said, watching in delight as the orange zest fell into a small bowl as I grated. Who even knew what zest did, but I felt like I was really accomplishing something here.

"Fine, did your dad teach you to cook? Did *anyone*?"

"No, I thought it was apparent I grew up on a lot of Hamburger Helper and Rice-a-Roni," I said. "As far as I knew, that hamburger glove made everything."

"Oh my god, you're hopeless," Bianca said. "I guess this'll be good practice for having a child."

We worked side by side, Bianca coaching me whenever I started to panic. For the most part, though, I realized that cooking could be as simple as just following the instructions in order and being as prepared as possible for what came next. That was a lot more straightforward than many things in life were.

Even though I normally ate on my couch, I set the table and

even lit a couple of old candles for us. The orange chicken had turned out amazingly—better than Panda Express, we both agreed—and Bianca promised I could FaceTime her over the weekend when I cooked my next dish. Tomorrow was Sofia's show, so we planned to all meet there and go out after.

"So obviously I wanted to see you one-on-one," Bianca said, "and I want to make really clear I don't want that to stop once the baby's here. Phoebe and I are really determined to keep up our friendships and our own lives, as much as possible at least."

"I'm not worried," I said. "Plus I'll be closer. We can do like five-minute catchups if you want. And I can babysit! I used to be great at babysitting. I'm sure I've still got it."

Bianca smiled. "Anyway, that's part of why I wanted to get together tonight. The other part is that I'm really, really angry at you, and I think you deserve to know."

I stared at her. "Bianca, I'm—whatever it is, I'm sorry."

"I know you are," she said. "But you ignored me—your best friend, your oldest friend, the—and I quote—'sister I never had.' And then *you did it again*."

"I . . . like I said. I was trying to protect all of you."

"This whole time I thought you were just too devastated after Taylor," Bianca said. "And I got it, sort of. Your life changed then, and that shit's scary. But to find out it was all this protection thing, this Nina's-cursed thing, I don't know. I can't believe you didn't trust or love me enough to tell me all of it sooner. I would have told you it was bullshit, taken you out for drinks or carbs or both, whatever you needed."

I didn't know what to say.

"This whole thing of *protection*, some idea that you suffered along without us because we were all better off . . . Did you not think I might have needed you at any point in those three years? Hell, in the last three weeks! I found out I'm going to be a mother, and I couldn't even talk to my best friend. I know that you think it was about you but—"

"But it was about you too," I said softly, as tears dripped down my face.

"Yeah," she said. "You acted like this guest star that could just drop in and out of our lives as you needed, as if our needs didn't matter at all."

"I swear, I didn't think—"

"No," Bianca said, gently, "of course you didn't. I know all of that now. But that's not how it came off then. That's not how any of it came off until *four days ago*."

I nodded frantically, channeling every bit of sincerity into that nod. "This stuff makes me nervous that Taylor was right about me being self-centered—"

"Don't," Bianca said, though her tone was still gentle. "We're all self-centered and stressful and bad partners sometimes. Yeah, you weren't the right fit for Taylor—but she wasn't the right fit for you either! I know you so well, Nina, and I know you're not going to *just let this go*, but, girl, it's past time to just let this go."

"I'm starting therapy as soon as my insurance kicks in," I said. "And I'm really trying in the meanwhile too."

"This year's felt like *a miracle*, Nina, having you back. I tried to be so careful. But I'm not being careful anymore. So there you go. I'm really mad, but I'm getting over it. And if you ever pull this shit again—"

"I won't," I said. "I know you have no reason to believe me, that things are different now, but I promise you. If people can get married and pledge their love, I can look at you right now and pledge our friendship, right?"

"Goddammit, Neen, don't make me cry," she said, blinking her eyes a few times. "I trust you. Just don't fuck it up."

"I can't promise *that*," I said. "But I promise that if I do, I won't run again."

"That's good enough. And I promise I'll stop protecting you. The old Bianca is back, so watch out."

"Oh, right," I said, laughing and wiping my eyes at the same time. "You forced me into inviting Ari to Palm Springs. You did all sorts of devious stuff. The old Bianca has been around *plenty.*"

She batted her eyes innocently. "I read the piece in The Cut."

"Do we have to talk about that?"

"Old Bianca says yes." She laughed, though her expression grew serious again. "*Nina.* She's hurting. You're hurting. What are you waiting for?"

"I'm not waiting for anything," I said. "It's over. Like everyone said, we both screwed up. I promise you that I no longer think I'm destined to be alone forever. I just need some time to be sad and get some things sorted out. Like I'm sure Ari does too."

"Tell me," she said, "really. Knowing all of this, the Taylor stuff. Were you really in it, all the way, with Ari? Or were you pulling some one-foot-out-the-door business because of your supposed curse?"

I took a sip of wine, thinking of one of the memes Max sent often. *I'm in this photo and I don't like it.* "I see what you're doing with that question so I'm not going to answer it."

"*Nina!*" She rolled her eyes. "Come on. If it was that good when—before—I mean, imagine what it could be like now. What the hell are you waiting for?"

"It's *over,*" I said. "And she's in Georgia. Isn't that enough?"

"I'm pretty sure phones work in Georgia," Bianca said.

"Can we let this go?" I asked. "You can bother me about anything else. OK?"

"We can let this go for *tonight,*" she said, reaching out to shake my hand like we were brokering a deal. "The future is another story."

Chapter 26
The Event of the Night

The thing about deciding, over three years ago, to never be late again was that the majority of my life took place in Los Angeles, a city where time had fluid interpretations. And now that I actually went out, attended events, saw my friends, it hit me that I'd become the weird one. The polite and punctual one, but the weird one indeed.

At least, I thought, the early weird bird got the good parking spot, as I slid the Mustang into a space at the end of the same downtown block that housed the art gallery. Before walking away, I took a photo, posted just for Lorna. The Mustang gleamed in the light of the sunset and the street lamps. It turned out that I might actually be pretty good at Instagram. My nine followers were lucky.

Unsurprisingly, the gallery was fairly empty when I walked in, as far as people went, but the walls were packed. Sofia's vibrant paintings took up practically every spare inch, and I was reminded of Ari's walls, Ari's collection, Ari Ari Ari, as always.

I checked my phone for the group text, just as someone

touched my back. I looked up and saw CJ already halfway across the room.

"I'm helping with some final stuff, but I'll find you later. It's so good seeing you, Nina. Sofia's gonna be thrilled you're here." They nodded to a section of the gallery that snaked around a corner. "Did you check out your portrait yet?"

"No, I just walked in."

"Let me know what you think." CJ hurried off, and I spotted the bar, which sounded like a great idea before coming face-to-face with—well, my own face? I still didn't fully understand the flash portraits, and there'd been so much going on I'd somehow forgotten my plan to google. I'd done *so much googling* lately.

The crowd was already picking up as I approached the bar, and it was exactly the crowd the publicist's email had promised, artsy, queer, and diverse. *The event of the night* hadn't felt like a huge promise—even in a city like LA there were only so many things to do—but the energy was already building as people walked in and connected. To each other, the art, the space. This was what I'd left behind, and already I was confident that I was never giving it up again.

I jumped into line at the bar and checked the group text. No one had messaged that they were running late, which meant that hopefully I wouldn't be alone much longer. The thought made me grin to myself so hard that I bit the inside of my cheek to keep from looking like a complete madwoman, smiling to herself and her phone. It was fine that strangers didn't know. *I knew.* Nina Rice had mistakenly exiled herself, but she'd returned in a classic car and a new dress and a blowout that made her hair look bathed in the motion of a wind machine. This Nina was here to stay.

I finally reached the front of the line, but the bartender held up her hand and gestured to the second line forming at the other side of the bar. I nodded, always patient with bartenders, particularly cute ones, and turned back to my phone, but then—

"A Rittenhouse old-fashioned, please."

This really *was* the queer event of the night.

I whipped my head up and over, and there she was. It might have been three years, but Taylor didn't look as if she'd changed much. Her dark hair hung straight to her shoulders, tucked neatly behind one ear, her skin was dewy and clear, even in the gallery's dim lighting, and her jumpsuit looked like something straight out of a Cate Blanchett movie.

"We have well bourbon," the hot bartender said with a sigh, and I thought of a meme Max loved sharing, *ma'am, this is an Arby's.* "That all right?"

Taylor must have said yes, because the bartender got to work.

"Nina," Taylor said, casually, as if we'd been planning on meeting. She strolled over, stood right next to me. "I thought that was you when you walked in."

"Yep, me," I said, suddenly having no idea where to put my phone or my hands. Taylor was always the sophisticated one with ease; I'd been, at best, her awkwardly adorable counterpart. Right now I only felt awkward.

The bartender was back with Taylor's drink, and I appreciated that she tipped generously, even on cheap bourbon. I asked for a glass of white, and hoped I could get through this moment quickly.

"You look great," Taylor said, as if we were old coworkers and not that we'd once planned on spending our lives together. Not at all like she'd broken my heart. Not at all like I'd been responsible for some terrible dark force in her life that pushed her to warn me away from everyone. "Life's good, I presume."

"Sure," I said, counting out my cash for the drink and the tip. "You?"

"Busy," she said, and as she took a sip of her cocktail, I saw a gold band flash on her left hand. At one point I couldn't even imagine what that would have done to me, but it inspired not much more than mild curiosity now. Who was Taylor married to? Was she perfect? Was she punctual? Was she ambitious? And then I sort of lost interest.

"Neen!" Phoebe and Bianca squeezed into the front of the line, causing some annoyed muttering behind us.

"We're just getting our friend, not butting for alcohol, don't worry," Bianca called, which made me laugh. Her arm was already around me, steering me apart from Taylor. "The crowd's restless already."

"It's filling up in here." Phoebe surveyed the room. "Hi, Taylor, good to see you."

"You too," she said. "Bianca."

Bianca barely smiled at her, which made me laugh. The bartender finished pouring my wine, and I thanked her and tried to slip away. I was protected now.

"Did I see," Taylor asked, still right next to me, "that you were dating Ari Fox?"

"I—"

"You sure did," Bianca said. "Come on, Nina, let's go see our portraits."

"Oh, sure," I said, as Bianca started pulling me away. "Bye, Taylor."

"Have a good night, Nina," she said, and I watched her walk away, just this human, one person, no longer part of my life. It was like I hadn't exhaled so fully in over three years.

"I can't believe she's here," Bianca said with a frown as we navigated to the portraits section of the show. From across the room I saw them, bold colors, wide brush strokes.

"It *is* the LGBTQ plus event of the night," I said, "per the press release at least."

"That might actually be true," Bianca said. "I heard people saying Kristen Stewart might be here."

The three of us, adult women all working in some corner of the entertainment industry, murmured excitedly like fangirls at that prospect. And then the back corner of portraits fully came into view. The paintings weren't large, just a couple feet square each, and while the colors and brush strokes made them abstract, Sofia had captured something specific about everyone. I spotted Phoebe's portrait first, the bold glasses and the intense gaze. CJ's had, somehow, their strength but also their tenderness. And then I saw me, waves of hair and a spark of something like laughter in my eyes. If this was how my friends saw me, I really was doing OK.

"Oh my god," I murmured, seeing the red dot on the card next to the painting. "Someone *bought* me?"

"Not *someone*," Bianca said. "*We* bought you! We bought all of us!"

I searched the wall until I saw Chloe, ready to fight, and Bianca, challenging and open and, of course, drop-dead gorgeous.

"We didn't buy that one." Phoebe's eyes darted to another spot on the wall. *Ari.* Eyebrows, cheekbones, that jawline. "But I'm sure none of us are surprised the one celebrity portrait was the first to go."

"Let's be real, we would buy celebrity portraits if there were any others," Bianca said, and we schemed how we'd get other queer celebrities into Sofia's life for more portraits in the future. It didn't seem like a far-out proposition. The Kristen Stewart rumors were still getting whispered around, and Chloe announced upon arrival that she'd run into a tiny brown-haired Canadian that was definitely Tegan or Sara.

"I used to be able to tell them apart," she said with a shrug. "Not anymore."

"I had no idea Sofia was such a big deal," I admitted, and was relieved my friends agreed. The *sold* dots were going up fast, even on the larger, pricier pieces, and all of us watched CJ at Sofia's side, proud and helpful and full of small talk. Sofia was part of our family now, I realized, and this fuller glimpse of CJ was ours too. How lucky was I?

How lucky were all of us?

Obviously, at some point, Chloe managed to bump into the woman at Taylor's side and report that the wife was blonde and pretty—"not as pretty as you, Nina, but, still"—and wearing an expensive-looking suit. I never got a good view of her, but it was fine. I'd never wanted Taylor to be unhappy, and I was glad that she wasn't. That door to that part of my life finally felt closed.

"Where are we headed after?" I asked, as the room got louder and the crowds packed in more tightly around us. "I feel like I might be ready to sit down somewhere quiet by now. Did you make a reservation?"

"It's not for a while, but there's a little nook around the back." Bianca pointed. "We noticed it when we first came in. Want me to come with you to get some air?"

"You OK, Nina?" Phoebe asked.

"I'm actually fine, just didn't expect to have to go through some emotional journey about my ex tonight," I said. "I could use a moment."

I worried that our new levels of honesty would make this a concerning statement, but my friends, thank god, laughed. It seemed safe to slip away for a bit, but before I could, a loud murmur rippled through the building.

"Ooh, who's here now?" Bianca asked, twisting around to see. "*Oh my god.*"

I turned to the entrance, and there she was. Ari Fox, her eyes searching the crowd, wearing a hoodie and joggers. Her soft pants.

"Ari!" Chloe screamed. The room turned to gawk at her. "Nina's right here!"

Ari's face broke into a wide grin and she strode across the

floor to us, crowds parting like magic as she advanced in her fancy sneakers. I was wordless and breathless when she reached us, nothing left inside but my pounding heartbeat.

"Thanks, Chlo," Ari said, fist-bumping Chloe, who beamed. "Nina, do you have a moment for me?"

"I—I thought you were in Georgia," I stammered.

"Girl, she's obviously not in Georgia, she's *right here*," Bianca said. "Ari, there's a little quiet spot right around the . . ."

She gestured, and Ari's gaze followed, as she nodded.

"Thanks. Nina?"

Phoebe pushed me—*physically pushed me*—toward the back of the gallery, and I followed Ari there. It wasn't completely quiet; other people had discovered it and were sitting on benches, talking quietly to one another. But compared to the main gallery floor, it was silent.

"You're not going to believe this," Ari said, her eyes wide, her expression like no time had passed between us. "Guess who just picked me up at Burbank Airport."

"*No*," I said.

"I almost *cried* when his name popped up on my phone," she said. "I got in, and he was all, *Ari F., where's your beautiful girlfriend?* And I told him I'd fucked up but I was there to win you back."

I clutched my arms tightly around myself. "What did he say?"

"He said, *I saw the way that girl looked at you, you're not going to have to try too hard.* And then he told me about the fight he had with his wife when they were still dating, and we discussed the best places for Chinese food in the Valley. As always, I came away wiser from time spent with Karl."

"Ari," I said, "you didn't fuck up. That was all me."

She laughed and shook her head. "What are you *talking* about?"

"I mean, yeah, telling Peyton about my script was—I told

you specifically not to. But I should have called you before emailing. And I shouldn't have—well, I have a tendency to run, Ari. I am *really good* at running."

"Yeah, and I'm really good at not listening to anyone else," Ari said, raking her hands through her hair. "My whole life, for better or worse, I've always tried to do exactly what I wanted, and you were the first person who wouldn't let me."

"I'm sorry—"

Ari grabbed me by the shoulders. It was at this point that I realized the quiet section of the gallery had started filling up, and people were definitely watching. I thought back to that night at the bar, three years in the past, all eyes on me as Taylor broke my heart. This couldn't have felt more different.

"I *need* someone who won't let me," Ari said, her face only inches from mine. "I've got to learn to let go of some things. There's so much I could focus on, but . . . it started to feel like a waste of energy when the only things that mattered were the parts of my job that I love, and you. The rest doesn't even come close."

"It's not you," I said, and then shook my head. "I should say that it's not *only* you. I've been holding back this whole time."

Ari gestured subtly to the crowd not-so-subtly watching us. Holy hell, I'd missed this, her expressions, the way she cocked her head, the humming sense of recognition between us. Her hands on my bare skin. "Because of who I am?"

"No, because of who *I* am." I did my best to push the tears from my voice. "I was so scared of ruining things that I held back from falling in love with you."

"Nina Rice," she said, her face drawing closer to mine, her breath on my face. "It always felt like enough to me."

"No, Ari, you have no idea," I said, and found her mouth with mine. We kissed gently, tentatively, as Ari's hands circled my waist and I cupped her face in my hands. I tasted tears in our kiss, and pulled back to make sure she knew they were happy tears. But her face glinted with wet streaks too, so I didn't waste any time talking. I pulled her closer and we kissed again, deeper, drinking in the weeks apart and the mistakes we'd made.

The crowd, hopped up on gossip and art and the cash bar, got a little rowdy with that last kiss, and I laughed and pulled away from Ari.

"This isn't going to keep your private life very private," I said, but she tugged me right back and kissed me again. "We're probably all over Lesbian Twitter already."

"Didn't I just say I have to learn to let things go?" She held my gaze, but, then again, she'd always been able to hold my gaze. "At first I really thought—well, I could find a new agent, someone who didn't know I'd been so unprofessional, I could start over again and still feel like the smartest one in the room. I was *humiliated* that Joyce knew how much I'd disregarded the exact kind of rule-following I'd expected from everyone on my team. But maybe it's good for me. It turns out I'm actually not always right."

"I probably do need a push sometimes," I said. "You weren't wrong about that. But I have to do it on my own terms. It may never be as fast as you want, but I promise I'm always getting there."

She held my face in her hands and shook her head. "I can't believe this is happening. I can't believe you're here."

"I can't believe *you're* here," I said. "What about Georgia?"

"I have the whole weekend off," she said. "And last night I was sitting in my hotel room, and—Nina, you did not warn me there was a *musical episode* of *Grey's*, and all I wanted to do was text you. I've missed you so much, but in that moment it was like there was this hole torn through my life. And since I'd just gotten the invite to this show, I knew where you'd be tonight. So as soon as I wrapped this morning, I caught the next flight out."

"You kept watching?" I asked. "You kept watching *a lot*?"

"It's all I did," she said. "I worked and I watched that show, which, of course, you were right. It got super gay."

"I told you!" I shrieked softly, delighted. "So you're hooked now?"

"I'm completely hooked," she said, her arm around my waist. "More this weekend? Your place, since Cade's cat sitting and I don't want to scare them by being here when they think I'm in Georgia."

"I think the internet will take care of letting them know your whereabouts," I said with a smile. "And, actually, I'm moving this weekend. But you can help me, right?"

"What?" Ari raised her eyebrows, those perfect arched eyebrows. "How much have I missed?"

"Honestly, a lot." I pulled her close again, kissing each eyebrow, her cheekbones, the jut of her chin. I'd missed all these pieces of her. "Want to get out of here so I can fill you in?"

She dropped her head close to my ear, her lips grazing me. "I'd like that a whole lot, Nina Rice."

I grabbed her hand and we walked into the throngs of the main gallery floor. "I know this might not sound romantic, but we were all supposed to grab dinner after, and . . . I don't know. Do you want to come before we head up to my place? I know everyone'll be really happy to see you."

"I actually do want to come," Ari said. "I missed all of them too."

We turned to find them in the crowd, and practically stumbled over someone.

"I'm so sorry!" said a very tiny and very familiar voice.

"*Max!*" I waved my arms like, *it's me.* But I saw that she already knew that. She also didn't seem very surprised to see Ari, her client-via-Joyce, who was supposed to be in Georgia. "I didn't know you were coming to this."

"My roommate's the assistant to the publicist for the gallery," she said. "So I had the whole RSVP list and saw that you were coming, Nina."

"Why didn't you just text me?" I asked. "We could have hung out here."

"Well, I saw that Ari got an invite, so I just . . ." She blushed. "Please don't tell Joyce, I know that I'm not supposed to forward anything without her permission, but I just thought maybe—"

"Wait," I said. "I deleted that invite. You have access to all the inboxes too? You have access to *Ari's* inbox?"

"Yeah, I check them all every day to make sure nothing slips through. It's way too big a responsibility to make you handle all the communications *and*, like, filtering and sorting through everything."

"Oh," Ari said, just a moment behind me with this, "so you've seen everything in my Exemplar inbox. Because we've used it for—"

Max nodded, her cheeks bright red. "Yes, there was a lot of sex stuff. I exited out of those whenever that happened, barely remember any of those specifics."

Nope, I couldn't even think about that right now. "But why did you un-delete that invitation?"

"Because—because of *this*," Max said, gesturing to us. "It seemed like you were so great together. I just thought—if Ari knew she had a chance to see you she might—I don't know. Please, please don't tell Joyce."

"Oh, come on, I live to break the rules," Ari said. "Well, I did, and I'm learning, but this is completely in my wheelhouse, Max. You're good."

"And I only have a few days left anyway," I said, loving Ari's shocked reaction to that. "So your secret's safe with me. I can't promise whoever replaces me will be so understanding though."

"There's no way she'll be the kind of person I would even

want to break rules for," Max said. "But, seriously, Nina, don't even joke about that. Do you know how scared I am of Joyce?"

We swept Max off with us, and made sure to get her in front of the hot bartender before rejoining my friends. *Our* friends. The gallery was packed by now, and we were all ready for a comparatively quieter restaurant.

"Wait," Ari said. "Shit, I never—hang on, everyone."

Ari dashed off, and I watched her stalking around the room, examining each painting. A memory washed over me.

"She got sold out of Sofia's last show, remember?" I asked.

"Well, I've got bad news for her," Bianca said. "While you two were off in the back, the gallery manager announced tonight's show was sold out too."

Ari was back a few minutes later, a scowl lightly holding her mouth not quite in place. "I seriously can't believe this happened again. Nina's going to hang on someone else's wall."

I elbowed Bianca, who elbowed Phoebe.

"I believe arrangements can be made regarding the Nina portrait," Phoebe said, and Ari leapt forward and tackled her and Bianca into a hug. I loved how hard she embraced people, literally and figuratively, and how well she fit into the family I'd already built.

We found CJ and Sofia so we could say goodbye, and congratulated Sofia over and over again. Outside we figured out the logistics of meeting at the restaurant in Echo Park, and finally decided we'd just take our own cars and deal with parking. I grabbed Ari by the hand and led her to the end of the block, where the Mustang gleamed.

"Nina Rice," she said, as her eyes widened. "What have you been up to?"

"I can't wait to tell you," I said, leaning over to unlock the car door for her. Nothing was automatic on this car either, but it was sexy on a Mustang. "Actually, hang on. Can I take a photo of you? Only like nine people follow me on Instagram."

"You can take as many photos of me as you want," she said, posing against the car with a casual lean. How did she do it, go from regular person to model, just like that? "Also I have a feeling more people will be following you now."

"I only care about my first follower," I said, posting the photo and tagging Lorna in the comments so she'd see Ari, the car, the future she'd wanted for me. The future I now realized I was allowed to want for myself.

"I have to fly back Sunday," Ari told me as I started the car and pulled out onto Second Street. "But what about you?"

"What *about* me?"

"Can you come with me?"

I started to say no, and then sorted out the week in my head. "Actually, yes. I need to be back by next week for my new job—don't get too excited, it's for Phoebe, and, no, I haven't finished my script yet—but, yeah, I can go for the week, if we can get me moved this weekend."

"We will get you *so moved*," Ari said, her arm around my shoulders. "*Fuck*, you're hot driving this car. I love a woman who can drive stick."

"Yeah, I bet you do," I said, instead of dwelling on that *love*. I had so, so much time to dwell on it later. There was no countdown clock, just Georgia and then the rest of our lives.

"Tell me everything," Ari said. "The job, the move, how you suckered your aunt out of this car at long last."

"There was no *suckering* involved, thank you, but I can't wait to tell you," I said. Our weeks apart flashed through my head, but so did the rest of it, Taylor and my exile, the life I thought I'd have and, now, the life I actually wanted. "Ari, I can't wait to tell you everything."

Epilogue
Six Months Later

"I know my therapist says not to automatically catastrophize, but I have bad news. Potentially party-ruining, friendship-ending bad news."

Ari hurried over to me from her makeshift spot tending bar for the houseful of guests. "If this is about the cake, don't worry, there's a backup cake in the garage."

I started to open my mouth to reply, but Ari grinned and held my lips in place with one finger.

"I love you very much, Nina Rice, but you've spent this entire week talking about how you'd never made a cake before, much less a giant one, but were still determined to make the perfect one for this party, you couldn't let anyone down, blah blah, and while I had great faith in you—"

"My cake-making abilities are untested at this point?"

"I was going to say, Bianca texted me with some concerns, none of which I was able to confidently address, so, backup cake. I'll go get it."

Ari pressed her lips against my cheek before hurrying off. I pulled off my apron and tossed it back into the kitchen, a room

I hoped to escape for the rest of the party. I might have gotten skilled enough to cook for Ari and myself on the nights we wanted to stay in, but it turned out that a large cake was another story entirely, a story I was not yet able to write.

Thank god for the backup cake. And, of course, for the people who knew me well enough to have it ready.

"Nina Louise," Lorna said, making her way over to me. She hadn't wanted to miss the party, so luckily Nat was up for driving her and Choon Hee down for the afternoon, as long as they were back in the suburbs before dark. For as much time as Lorna and I had spent together up there, it warmed my heart to see her in Los Angeles, here in my home.

"I gave up on the cake," I said. "But, don't worry, apparently there's a backup since mine is somehow both half overcooked and half goo."

"Oh, Nina, as if I've ever baked a cake that wasn't part goo. No, I wanted to check with you about something, since I'm aware you young people know a lot about gender that my generation didn't. I thought that Bianca and Phoebe's baby was a girl."

"She *is* a girl," I said. "Why are you asking?"

"That whole group of your friends over there kept shouting, 'let me hold him, let me hold him,'" she said, and I laughed, watching the loud, messy group of people in the living room.

"They're taking turns holding Ari's Oscar," I said, and Lorna laughed.

"Oh, well, I'll have to get into line for that too! Babies make me a little nervous, though I promise when you and Ari have yours I'll hold them plenty. An Oscar, though, that I think I can handle right now!"

"Lorna," I said, making eye contact with Ari as she reappeared with a huge box while hoping she hadn't heard that remark about *our babies*. It wasn't that we hadn't discussed kids—no topics were off-limits anymore, especially when friends were doing things like adopting babies and therefore making it a tough conversation to avoid—but it was far too early to treat them as some sort of decided thing. Getting a dog was the next thing on the list. We had plenty of time to figure out what was after that. Lorna just loved trouble.

"Ooh," I said, surveying the box as Ari made room for it on the dining room table. "Is that a grocery store sheet cake?"

"From Ralphs, the very best for our guests," she said with a wink. "This is what happens when Phoebe and Bianca let two former suburban kids plan their party."

Our friends, still exhausted and sleep-deprived, eventually gave in to the demands of their friends and colleagues who wanted a welcome party for Olivia Reyes-Suarez. Since Phoebe and Bianca didn't have the energy to hold the party themselves—nor the desire to have to kick everyone else out after an hour or two when Olivia needed to nap again—Ari and I had offered to host. I'd only officially moved in with her at the beginning of the year, but my things had been slowly accumulating for longer, so we were more than ready to throw a party. There was so much to celebrate.

Ari's house wasn't forever, we'd already decided, but it had been a busy year so far, and we wanted to make the next choice together. Now that the Oscars were behind us and Ari's next project was shooting locally—well, believe it or not, up near Hart Park—we'd have time to look.

I'd gotten really knowledgeable, after all, about real estate since selling Lorna's condo and realizing what I actually wanted to do with the largest sum of money I'd ever had in my possession. There was a life I'd started building with Ari, right here in LA, the little house and our friends and our careers. *Spend wisely, Nina Rice*, I'd thought, and then had made a baffled Ari murmur it into my ear. I'd worried Ari would find it hard to let me figure it out on my own, but she was better at letting me take my time, make choices at my own speed. But what was I even deciding between? Lorna hadn't stressed finances or long-term career goals. She'd asked what I wanted to run *to*, and my life in LA wasn't about running. This, I thought, I wanted to plant myself into, enjoy every moment. Where did I want to run *to*?

The doorbell rang, and it was CJ and Sofia, arms full of boxes from Porto's.

"More backup desserts?" I asked, and CJ cracked up.

"Bianca's been worried. Plus everyone loves these cheese rolls."

The house kept filling up, more and more, and I marveled that a year ago I'd probably spent my Sunday sitting alone in the condo, eating a bowl of tuna salad and waiting impatiently for the next day's crossword to post. Now my life was so crowded I didn't even know all of the people in my home right now. Though, of course, I'd probably pop away from the crowd for fifteen minutes once the crossword was up. My streak was still unbroken.

"Can we open the back door?" Chloe popped in from the kitchen, which had gone straight from baking disaster aftermath to party-overflow area. "It's getting a little hot."

"Open a window or turn on the AC," Ari called. "I don't want Steve to get out."

"Seriously?" called Cade from across the room. "How can an invisible cat get out?"

"Why would we go through the trouble of inventing an invisible cat?" Ari and I said at the exact same time and then burst into laughter. The day I'd officially moved in, USPS change forms submitted, utilities and cable bill coming to Ariane E. Fox and Nina L. Rice, a gray tabby cat had calmly walked out from under the living room sofa and hopped up on my lap, and that was that.

"You guys are disgusting," Chloe said with a laugh. "I love it."

"Hey, Chlo, can you help me with something?" Ari asked her.

She was up for it, of course, and before long, the rest of the Sunday brunch crew had been extracted from the party and was holed up in our bedroom with the door pulled to. Our numbers had grown: now it was Phoebe, Bianca, baby Olivia, CJ, Sofia-for-good, Chloe, Ari, and me.

"I have some news I want to share with you," I said, once everyone was sitting on the bed.

"Oh my god, you're engaged!" Bianca said.

"No, I—"

"Holy shit, your show's getting made!" Chloe said.

"If your show's getting made, you still need to give two weeks' notice," Phoebe said quickly. It turned out that I actually really liked working in marketing, thinking of the best ways to present information and learning what resonated with people. It wasn't my forever, I hoped. I'd already started to meet for monthly coffees with Peyton Butler, who I'd reached out to once I'd completed the revision class and had a sparkling finished copy of my script. (Ari? Not invited.) It was good I'd waited; everything Peyton loved most about my script had been added thanks to the class. But my day job was a place to spend each day with others who wanted to be smart and creative, a very good *right now.*

"We're going to be lost without you," Phoebe continued.

"What is *wrong* with all of you?" I asked.

"They love you and they're impatient," Ari said. "Get to it, babe."

"I am *trying.* So as you all know, Lorna gave me the money from the sale of her condo. What you don't know is that she'd told me to use it for the thing I wanted to run to. And, like, I kept thinking that I had that already. All of you and"—I made eye contact with Ari—"and *obviously*, yes, the woman I want to spend my life with, though please give us some breathing room on that timeline, you monsters. Anyway, you know where I kept thinking I wanted to run to?"

"Please don't tell me you're moving back to suburbia," Bianca said. "You're Olivia's favorite babysitter."

"No, I . . ." I got up and took the real estate printouts from my dresser drawer. I'd gotten one for everyone. "Do you know how cheap—I mean, cheap for Southern California—houses are in the desert? I bought a place in Palm Springs."

The group, collectively, shrieked in excitement, but calmed down quickly when the baby started to fuss. Still, it was clearly hard for everyone to remain calm, as they exclaimed quietly over the photos and the listing of features. It wasn't as big or as fancy as the Airbnbs we'd stayed in, and it was farther from the main strips, but it was enough. It was *mine*.

"Ari and I both like the idea of a place away, especially after all the attention she's had lately—"

"You're both GIFs now!" Chloe said in a loud whisper, and everyone but Ari and I exploded into silent laughter. It was true, though; a GIF of Ari kissing me after her name had been called at the Oscars had been making the rounds on social media, and it was going to take some getting used to, my face popping up to punctuate romantic or sexual Twitter thoughts.

"*Anyway*, my family isn't just Ari, my family is all of us. So now Phoebe doesn't have to spend time finding the best Airbnb. We filled it with Lorna's furniture from the condo, and she's helping us find everything else. I'll—Ari and I will host everyone now. You can go sometimes even when we're not there."

"Except you, Chloe, you're a security risk," Ari said, and everyone cracked up.

"That's fair," she said with a gleam in her eyes, though her expression warmed. "Nina, only you would take that pile of money and do this for all of us."

"No, any of you would," I said. "Well, no, probably some of you would have taken some of the money to pay down your student loan or invest in something for the future, but this is all the future I need. Also I plan to retire and die out in the desert a million years from now, not up in suburbia, so now that's settled."

Everyone congratulated me, while I heard Phoebe ask, *Nina, how much student loan debt do you have?* and then we were all laughing again, and even Olivia seemed to be cooing in harmony with us.

"We should get back to the party," I said. "Who knows what Lorna and her friends are up to in there."

Bianca held up her phone. "She's posted four times on Instagram with Ari's Oscar so far. But she's getting a lot of engagement so I get it."

Ari's publicist had actually contacted her a few months back to find out why the most candid photos of Ari were on an octogenarian's Instagram account. I'd repeated the story to Lorna but it really had just made her post more.

My friends trickled out and down the hallway, back to the party, but Sofia was slowly surveying the room's artwork.

"I don't often get to see where my work's hung." She nodded to the Nina portrait. Ari had already hung it in her bedroom before I moved in, before I'd had any say over what went into this room, and at first I felt strange seeing my own face on the wall every day. But I couldn't deny it; I loved what Sofia had seen in me and put on canvas to show everyone else too. I loved that my friends had wanted it, and I loved that my girlfriend had wanted it even more.

"It's the most important piece that I own," Ari said, walking up next to me and slipping her arm around me. "Well, that and the Hoff."

Ari gestured to the portrait, which we'd hung next to mine, once I'd moved in.

"Oh," Sofia said, her eyebrows drawn together in concern, and Ari and I burst into laughter. "I'm honestly not sure how I feel about that."

"Sofia, it's a long story, and it starts at a TGI Fridays with a girl I had an extra-large The Best Fridays™ Margarita–sized crush on," Ari said, holding my gaze with hers. "But I'm not the writer. I'll let Nina tell you the whole thing."

I grinned and tucked myself right against Ari, the place I belonged most of all, in any house, in any city, as we walked out of the quiet room and toward the joyous noise of the party.

"I can't wait to tell you the whole story. But first, let's make sure my aunt and her friends haven't stolen this year's Best Supporting Actress Academy Award."

Ari and I settled back into the crowd, together, our home packed with all the people we loved most. There was so much that I didn't know yet about my future, but the unknown had stopped scaring me. I liked them now, these possibilities piled up before us. With Ari at my side, and me at hers, I was ready for anything.

Acknowledgments

Thank you to my editor, Norma Perez-Hernandez, for your vibrant enthusiasm for this book. Working with you was truly such a fun, supportive experience, and I was thrilled you're as much of a champion for Nina and Ari as I am!

Thank you to my agent, Kate Testerman, who's been such a constant presence in my career and life, and supported me every step along the way in this journey to a new genre.

Thank you to the entire team that worked on this book, including Michelle Addo, Jane Nutter, and Kristin Dwyer. Thanks to Kristine Mills for the beautiful cover design that brought Nina and Ari to life. Thanks to, truly, everyone at Kensington! It meant a lot to release a queer book at a publisher that never made it feel like a token release.

Thank you to my early readers: Sarah Skilton, Kayla Cagan, Stephanie Strohm, Jessie Weinberg. Writing in a new genre was initially terrifying, and your enthusiasm made this whole thing feel possible.

Thank you to everyone who invented names of fictional things, shows, and films for this book, especially Christie Baugher, Josh A. Cagan, Akilah Brown, and Jessica Morgan. Thank you to Samantha Powell for guiding me through celebrity journalism choices.

Thank you to my entire writing community, in Los Angeles and beyond. Thank you to every rom-com writer who inspired me along the way! Thanks to every group chat where I whined about anything writing-related for the entirety of the time this book was written or on submission.

Thank you to my mother, Pat Spalding.

Thank you to all the powers that be (ABC, Shondaland, an ages-old curse?) that kept *Grey's Anatomy* on the air so that I could leave in every single reference, and also for providing me with many, many hours of entertainment. It's a beautiful day to save lives.

I finished writing *For Her Consideration* over a year before Ariana DeBose won her Academy Award (and Kristen Stewart was nominated and wore formal shorts to the ceremony!). The excitement over Ari Fox's representation in this world is not meant to diminish all of the accomplishments of the actual LGBTQ+ talent breaking ground, but to celebrate such achievements.

Lastly, I write these acknowledgments during terrifying times for the LGBTQ+ community, and I am full of anger, sadness, and frustration at the hateful behavior of those who elect to use their immense power to threaten often the very most vulnerable members of our community. I write about love and happy endings because I think joy can be a revolutionary act, but it's never far from my mind that there are so many battles still being fought. With this said, I want to thank all those who came before me, and all those doing the work now.